D0289564

Praise for Novels by

COURTNEY WALSH

IS IT ANY WONDER

"With her signature heart and charm, Courtney Walsh weaves a story of forgiveness, hope, and enduring ties that proves it's never too late for a second chance. An idyllic Nantucket backdrop, a deeply guarded secret, and an epic love story make *Is It Any Wonder* the perfect read for right now. Courtney Walsh once again shines as a master storyteller."

KRISTY WOODSON HARVEY, *USA TODAY* BESTSELLING AUTHOR OF *FEELS LIKE FALLING*

"Courtney Walsh's books always capture my heart! I love her poignant plotlines, quaint, small-town settings, and the romance she skillfully weaves through the pages."

BECKY WADE, AUTHOR OF *STAY WITH ME*

IF FOR ANY REASON

"Second chances and new discoveries abound in this lovely tale from Walsh, featuring a nostalgic romance set against the backdrop of Nantucket. . . . Readers of Irene Hannon will love this."

PUBLISHERS WEEKLY

"*If for Any Reason* is a 'double romance' novel, beautifully written, poignantly sad in parts, but full of hope throughout. It is altogether a lovely book, with a strong Christian message and a really good story, and I cannot recommend it highly enough."

CHRISTIAN NOVEL REVIEW

"Warm and inviting, *If for Any Reason* is a delightful read. I fell in love with these characters and with my time in Nantucket. Don't miss this one."

ROBIN LEE HATCHER, AWARD-WINNING AUTHOR OF
WHO I AM WITH YOU

"*If for Any Reason* took me and my romance-loving heart on a poignant journey of hurt, hope, and second chances. . . . From tender moments to family drama to plenty of sparks, this is a story to be savored. Plus, that Nantucket setting—I need to plan a trip pronto!"

MELISSA TAGG, AWARD-WINNING AUTHOR OF *NOW AND THEN AND ALWAYS*

JUST LET GO

"Walsh's charming narrative is an enjoyable blend of slice-of-life and small-town Americana that will please Christian readers looking for a sweet story of forgiveness."

PUBLISHERS WEEKLY

"Original, romantic, and emotional. Walsh doesn't just write the typical romance novel. . . . She makes you feel for all the characters, sometimes laughing and sometimes crying along with them."

ROMANTIC TIMES

"A charming story about discovering joy amid life's disappointments, *Just Let Go* is a delightful treat for Courtney Walsh's growing audience."

RACHEL HAUCK, *NEW YORK TIMES* BESTSELLING AUTHOR

"*Just Let Go* matches a winsome heroine with an unlikely hero in a romantic tale where opposites attract. . . . This is a page-turning, charming story about learning when to love and when to let go."

DENISE HUNTER, BESTSELLING AUTHOR OF
HONEYSUCKLE DREAMS

"Just the kind of story I love! Small town, hunky skier, a woman with a dream, and love that triumphs through hardship. A sweet story of reconciliation and romance by a talented writer."

SUSAN MAY WARREN, *USA TODAY* BESTSELLING AUTHOR

JUST LOOK UP

"[A] sweet, well-paced story. . . . Likable characters and the strong message of discovering what truly matters carry the story to a satisfying conclusion."

PUBLISHERS WEEKLY

"*Just Look Up* by Courtney Walsh is a compelling and consistently entertaining romance novel by a master of the genre."

MIDWEST BOOK REVIEW

"This novel features a deeply emotional journey, packaged in a sweet romance with a gentle faith thread that adds an organic richness to the story and its characters."

SERENA CHASE, *USA TODAY* HAPPY EVER AFTER BLOG

"In this beautiful story of disillusionment turned to healing, Walsh brings about a true transformation of restored friendships and love."

CHRISTIAN MARKET MAGAZINE

CHANGE OF HEART

"Walsh has penned another endearing novel set in Loves Park, Colo. The emotions are occasionally raw but always truly real."

ROMANTIC TIMES

"*Change of Heart* is a beautifully written, enlightening, and tragic story. . . . This novel is a must-read for lovers of contemporary romance."

RADIANT LIT

PAPER HEARTS

"Walsh pens a quaint, small-town love story . . . [with] enough plot twists to make this enjoyable to the end."
PUBLISHERS WEEKLY

"Be prepared to be swept away by this delightful romance about healing the heart, forgiveness, [and] following your dreams."
FRESH FICTION

"Courtney Walsh's . . . stories have never failed to delight me, with characters who become friends and charming settings that beckon as if you've lived there all your life."
DEBORAH RANEY, AUTHOR OF THE CHICORY INN NOVELS SERIES

"Delightfully romantic with a lovable cast of quirky characters, *Paper Hearts* will have readers smiling from ear to ear! Courtney Walsh has penned a winner!"
KATIE GANSHERT, AWARD-WINNING AUTHOR OF *A BROKEN KIND OF BEAUTIFUL*

"*Paper Hearts* is as much a treat as the delicious coffee the heroine serves in her bookshop. . . . A poignant, wry, sweet, and utterly charming read."
BECKY WADE, AUTHOR OF *MEANT TO BE MINE*

IS IT ANY WONDER

ALSO BY COURTNEY WALSH

Courtney Walsh

Is It Any Wonder

a Nantucket love story

Tyndale House Publishers
Carol Stream, Illinois

Visit Tyndale online at tyndale.com.

Visit Courtney Walsh's website at courtneywalshwrites.com.

TYNDALE and Tyndale's quill logo are registered trademarks of Tyndale House Ministries.

Is It Any Wonder

Copyright © 2020 by Courtney Walsh. All rights reserved.

Cover photograph of couple copyright © by Miodrag Ignjatovic/Getty Images. All rights reserved.

Author photo taken by Darge Photography, copyright © 2019. All rights reserved.

Designed by Lindsey Bergsma

Edited by Danika King

Published in association with the literary agency of Natasha Kern Literary Agency, Inc., P.O. Box 1069, White Salmon, WA 98672.

Is It Any Wonder is a work of fiction. Where real people, events, establishments, organizations, or locales appear, they are used fictitiously. All other elements of the novel are drawn from the author's imagination.

For information about special discounts for bulk purchases, please contact Tyndale House Publishers at csresponse@tyndale.com or call 1-800-323-9400.

Library of Congress Cataloging-in-Publication Data
Names: Walsh, Courtney, date- author.
Title: Is it any wonder : a Nantucket love story / Courtney Walsh.
Description: Carol Stream, Illinois : Tyndale House Publishers, [2021]
Identifiers: LCCN 2020017882 (print) | LCCN 2020017883 (ebook) | ISBN
   9781496434432 (trade paperback) | ISBN 9781496434449 (kindle edition) |
   ISBN 9781496434456 (epub) | ISBN 9781496434463 (epub)
Subjects: GSAFD: Love stories.
Classification: LCC PS3623.A4455 I8 2021 (print) | LCC PS3623.A4455
   (ebook) | DDC 813/.6--dc23
LC record available at https://lccn.loc.gov/2020017882
LC ebook record available at https://lccn.loc.gov/2020017883

Printed in the United States of America

26	25	24	23	22	21	20
7	6	5	4	3	2	1

For my readers,
many of whom have become my friends.
I am so thankful for you.

PROLOGUE

Dear Mr. Boggs,

It's been five years since you died, and I've thought about you every single day since. If I close my eyes, I can imagine I'm ten years old and you're down at the beach building sandcastles with me and Cody.

None of the other parents ever wanted to play with us, but you were always more than willing. I mean, you couldn't have actually liked being buried to your neck in sand . . . but you let us do it. You even smiled for pictures like that.

I can't help but think that what happened was my fault. At least indirectly. I mean, don't get me wrong, I hate it in movies when people seem so broken up with guilt over something that's clearly not their fault—but what happened to you kind of was my fault, wasn't it?

Is it any wonder that I wish I could take it back? I wish I could say I'm sorry. I wish I could rewind and change everything about that night. I hurt you. I hurt Cody. I hurt Mrs. Boggs and Marley. I even hurt my own parents because the moment they told us you were gone, everything changed. It was like we'd been plummeted into a jar of molasses, like we were moving in slow motion, swimming through a thick cloud of sorrow.

Will the cloud ever go away? Will it always hang here, a sad reminder that the choice of a foolish girl could impact so many lives, destroy so many friendships?

I don't know. And I don't know why I'm writing. I know you'll never read these words. It helps, though, at least a little bit. It makes me feel better putting it out there into the world, the fact that I'm so horribly sorry for what I've done.

I pray one day you can forgive me. I pray one day you will all forgive me.

Love,
Louisa

CHAPTER ONE

SEVEN YEARS LATER

This wasn't supposed to happen.

Not that there was time to think about it now. Not with the waves growing and the wind blowing and her paddle floating away, pulled out to sea by a storm she hadn't seen coming.

Louisa Chambers inhaled a sharp breath as the water swelled and a wave crashed over her head. Her legs kicked against the water of Nantucket Sound as she heaved her body up onto the paddleboard.

So much for a quiet morning out on the water.

She sighed. Her father would be so angry with her if she died paddleboarding.

"How many times have I told you to wear a life vest?" he'd say. "You don't challenge death, kitten."

He still called her kitten. She might actually miss that if she died.

She knew all too well the realities of death—she didn't need reminding. But maybe death needed to know she wasn't scared of it.

I'm not scared. I'm strong. I'm stronger than I look.

Again she willed herself to stay calm. Her paddle was officially gone.

She wasn't far from Madaket Beach—she'd hang on to her board and kick her way back. It was early, just after sunrise, but someone would be up soon. Mr. Dallas with his golden retriever, maybe. Or one of the McGuires.

But the wind intensified and pushed her in the wrong direction, sending her into deeper, choppier waters. The shoreline stretched on forever, and the water kept moving her farther and farther away from it.

Her hand slipped off the paddleboard, and she gasped as a wave smacked her in the face.

How many times have I told you to wear a life vest?

Her dad's voice echoed in her ear—louder this time—and rightfully so. She should've listened. She should've—*whack*. Another wave, this one bringing with it a mouthful of water. She spit it out and struggled back to her board, barely latching on to it as the current kicked up again.

She coughed, white-knuckling the paddleboard and scanning the shore, the horizon, the open sea.

Nothing.

That was when she began to realize she might actually be in danger. That was when she thought, *I could die out here.*

Who would handle the Timmons anniversary party if she died? How would she ever show Eric she was completely over him—even though, in reality, she wasn't sure she was? Who would water that stupid houseplant her mother had sent over from Valero and Sons "because you need practice keeping something alive if you're ever going to have children"?

She wanted to have children, so she needed to make sure that plant lived.

She draped her torso over the paddleboard and tried not to think about sharks. She tried to think about something happier.

Beaches on Nantucket Close after at Least a Dozen Shark Sightings.

It was the headline of an article she'd stumbled across online only two weeks prior. Were the sharks gone? Were they circling her at that exact moment?

And then, all of a sudden, the image of a smiling Daniel Boggs flittered through her mind.

Is this how you felt, Mr. Boggs?

That image had no business haunting her, not now when she'd been doing so well. But a wave tossed her forward, and she barely managed to hold on to the board, so she closed her eyes and prayed.

Because right about now, she needed a miracle.

Mr. Boggs had probably prayed for the same thing and look how that had turned out.

Maybe this was what she deserved. Maybe this was payback for what she'd done. Maybe this was God's way of reminding her that actions had consequences.

Actions like not wearing a life vest. Or breaking someone's heart.

She'd been working how many years to try to make amends for her mistakes? Would it ever be enough? Would forgiveness ever come?

It occurred to her that on normal days she was excellent at pushing these thoughts away. In fact, most days she didn't even have to work at it.

Apparently being faced with the end of one's life resulted in this. A deep dive into all the things she'd been successfully avoiding. As if there weren't more important things to be thinking about. Like staying alive.

If only she had a single clue how to do that.

"God, I'm pretty sure I don't deserve to be rescued, and I'm not in the habit of asking for help, which I'm sure you know. But it would be super awesome if you could maybe shift the wind and give me a push toward the shore."

The waves just kept pulling her deeper and farther away.

She supposed miracles were in high demand these days. And maybe it simply wasn't her turn. She clung to the board as fear welled up inside her. Panic buzzed somewhere down deep, and she tried to keep it from overtaking her.

She'd make a list like she always did to help sort out her anxiety.

A wave swelled, and she let out a scream (and she really was not the screaming type, so it surprised even her), but the water settled her back down, and somehow she still had hold of the board.

A list. Okay . . . what to list? *Things to do* seemed a bit pointless given her current situation.

Another swell, and she swallowed a mouthful of water. She coughed—hard—then drew in a clean breath.

Things I wish I'd done in my life. A bucket list made moments before my impending death.
- *I wish I'd worn a life vest.*
- *I wish I'd checked the weather forecast.*
- *I wish I had put on waterproof mascara (because when they find my body, it would be nice not to look so dead).*
- *I wish I hadn't wasted so much time on Eric Anderson.*
- *I wish I'd said I was sorry.*
- *I wish I'd mailed the letters.*
- *I wish I'd made it to my golden birthday.*

After all, she'd spent twelve years wondering if he'd show. Or maybe that pact had been long forgotten, sucked down to the depths like dirt down a drain.

The next wave enveloped Louisa completely, heaving her under for so many seconds she was certain she'd lost the way back up and into the air. But no, another toss and there it was again—glorious oxygen.

She inhaled a sharp breath and coughed.

I wish I'd fallen in love.

She looked up at the sky, which had turned gray and dark. She hadn't realized she had so many regrets. Her teeth chattered and she started to tire. These waves were kicking her butt. She'd practically resigned herself to dying when she spotted a headlight—a boat out in the sound.

She tried to lift her arm, but it was so heavy. She tried hauling herself onto the board, but she didn't have the strength. Maybe she wasn't doing as well as she thought. Maybe she'd already half died. She looked for a white light in the sky but saw nothing.

Maybe white lights were only for people who weren't responsible for someone else's death.

She'd never get over that as long as she lived, though it seemed that might not be much longer. Unless someone in that boat was the answer to her prayer.

She had to stay awake. She had to hold on. They had to see her. *Please see me.*

The boat cut through the water, tossing in the wind, and again Louisa tried to wave.

I wish I'd fallen in love.

⁓

It was supposed to be routine. Summer on Nantucket hadn't even started yet, but when Cody Boggs spotted the yellow paddle floating in the water, his gut wrenched.

They'd gotten a call from someone on the beach only moments ago—possible swimmer in the water.

"It's hard to make out," the caller had said. "But I felt like I should call. If it's a person, they're in danger."

Cody was already out on the water, his first time on the boat with the crew, so they sped toward the reported sighting. They were about to give up when Cody saw it. A paddle, but no kayak. No paddleboard. No canoe. No person.

Odd.

"Slow down," he told the ship's coxswain. He glanced at one of the petty officers. "Do you see that?"

A tight line creased the other man's brow. "The paddle? Yeah."

"I'm going to take a look." Cody pushed through the door and out onto the deck of the lifeboat, where two other men stood.

"See something, sir?"

"Not sure." Cody scanned the water through his binoculars, looking for any sign, pausing on the shoreline of Nantucket.

The one place he swore he'd never be stationed. The one place they needed him.

The paddle bobbed in the water. The wind had kicked up, one of those instances where the weather changed without notice.

Anyone could've thought it was going to be a decent day on the water. He would've thought so too at first blush, but he knew not to ever trust the ocean.

The coxswain turned the boat and sped parallel to the island, passing Madaket Beach. No sign of anyone in distress. But none of the men on that boat wanted to head back to the station without the absolute certainty they'd done all they could to ensure there was no one out in that water.

Cody shifted his gaze from the beach to the sea, scanning the vast ocean, looking for any sign of life.

Nothing.

His gut didn't usually steer him wrong. He was always ready for the tide to turn—on the water and in his life.

The coxswain opened the cabin door. "Head back to the station?"

"Go out a little further," Cody called back.

The man did as his XPO ordered, and Cody whispered a prayer. Same prayer he always whispered in these kinds of situations. "Lord, if I can save one soul, lead me to them now."

They cruised through the water, the wind tossing the forty-seven-foot boat around like a rag doll. They sped away from the shore, and Cody put the binoculars down, relying on his eyes to lead him to anyone who might be in danger.

His eyes, his gut, and the good Lord above. Those had always been his most trusted allies.

And maybe there was no one. Maybe this time his gut *had* steered him wrong.

"Nobody's out here, sir," a seaman named Jessup called out. "Wind's getting nasty. We should head back."

Cody planted his feet on the deck of the boat as water poured over the side. Nasty for them, yes, but deadly for someone in the water without a paddle.

Or maybe the paddle had floated away from somebody's dock. Or maybe someone had already perished and they were too late.

As the next swell jolted the boat, the men at his side lost their balance, both reaching for the railing to steady themselves. Cody didn't move an inch.

As the water lowered the boat back down, he spotted the faintest shock of red in the water up ahead. He lifted a hand, then turned to face the coxswain, who'd caught the same glimpse and now sped toward the object.

Could be nothing. But what if it wasn't?

The red object had disappeared, and Cody took out the binoculars again and scanned the water. The white-capped waves dispersed, and there it was, only this time, Cody had the object in his sights. This time, it was clear that this was no piece of discarded plastic—it was a paddleboard, and there was a woman clinging to it.

The person on the beach had been right. There was someone in the water.

The coxswain maneuvered the boat closer to the woman, slowly— and Cody locked his gaze on her. When they were close enough, one of the men threw a flotation device. The woman reached for it, but a wave pushed the ring out of her reach.

"She looks tired," Cody said, mostly to himself. How long had she been out here?

His heart kicked up a notch. He was trained for this, and yet there would always be a part of him that had to steady his own thoughts when it came to the ocean.

But then there would also always be a part of him that was filled with rage when it came to these watery depths. A part that refused to let them win.

The seaman at his side tugged the flotation device in and tried again, but the brutal waves poured over the woman's head, and the weight of the water pulled her under. Her hand slipped off the paddleboard, and she struggled to hold on.

The woman went under again, and after another wave, only her paddleboard surfaced.

Cody hadn't been promoted to executive petty officer because he was impulsive. Quite the opposite. He was levelheaded. Calm in the face of danger. He prided himself on it.

Maybe it was Nantucket that had cast a spell on him, stealing away all the work he'd done these twelve years to overcome what the ocean had stolen from him. What other explanation could there be for his grabbing a pair of goggles and diving into the angry water, determined not to let this woman drown?

Determined not to let this ocean win.

He glided through the water, the strength of the storm doing little to slow him down. He'd trained for this. He lived for this. To keep the sea from stealing souls—that was the goal. And he didn't like to lose.

The water wasn't going to get this woman, no matter how remiss she'd been to go out without checking the forecast. *Not today, ocean. If you want her, you're gonna have to go through me.*

He grabbed the floater that was attached to the ship as the woman bobbed up out of the water a few yards away—possibly thrown out by an angry wave. She didn't appear to be swimming anymore. Cody barreled toward her, catching her under the arms as a wave pounded into both their bodies.

He held on to the life preserver as two seamen pulled them in. They reached the boat, and the men on the deck helped get them on board.

Quickly they sprang into action. Cody tore the goggles off his face and checked to see if she was breathing. Her body had gone limp and her pulse was faint.

"Let me help, sir," one of the men said, and only then did Cody realize he was doing the job of the entire crew—something he'd likely have to answer for later.

He didn't care. Maybe he had something to prove. Maybe it was *this* ocean and *this* island that needed to be reminded that it couldn't beat him anymore.

One-two-three, he counted in his head as he administered rescue breaths. No response.

Not a great way to start out his sentence on Nantucket. Back after all these years only to lose one his first day out? That couldn't happen.

He closed his mouth over hers again. *One-two-three.*

"We were too late," one of the seamen said.

Cody shook his head, and just then the woman's eyes opened, she coughed up a bucket of water, and he turned her over.

Another rescue boat pulled alongside theirs, and Cody's entire body sighed in relief. *Thank you, God.*

The woman coughed again, then tried to sit up. She wasn't small or frail—she was muscular and athletic, the kind of person who made activity a part of her daily life. Would she be ticked off to find out she'd required saving? Lots of women were these days.

But as she shifted and brought her intense blue eyes to his, it wasn't anger or irritation he found there. It was recognition.

"Cody?"

He leaned back on his heels and studied her face—freckles that trailed across the bridge of her nose, hair darkened by the sea, and familiar eyes as bright as the sky.

"Louisa?" Her name escaped his lips, almost a whisper.

"You two know each other?" Jessup knelt beside him.

She hadn't looked away since she'd said his name.

Was their entire history flashing through her mind too? Was she wondering where he'd been? Whom he'd loved? Why he was back? Why he never called? Did she want to know how he and his family had survived after they left the island? Or maybe, just maybe, she was thinking of that stupid pact they'd made all those years ago. Back when things were simple and it seemed like there would never be a day they wouldn't be in each other's lives.

Of course, it was possible she was thinking none of those things. Maybe she was simply thinking that he was a jerk for saying the things he did.

She'd be right.

But there was a whole world she didn't understand, and he wasn't about to explain it to her. He stood.

Her eyes followed.

He didn't like it. He didn't like being watched. Being seen. Not by Louisa Chambers, anyway.

The crew of the other boat boarded their vessel and got to work. Soon Louisa would be headed for the hospital.

Once she was gone, Cody might be able to breathe again.

CHAPTER TWO

LOUISA SAT IN A WARM HOSPITAL BED, wondering if she could patent a new design for a hospital gown that was slightly more flattering than the tent they currently had her wrapped in.

Not that her attire mattered exactly, because, let's face it, the real objective here was restoring her health. But truly—would it be too much to ask for a girl to get something with even a hint of shape to it? With her long hair a tangled mess of salt water and her face still pale from nearly dying, she could use all the help she could get.

These thoughts, she realized, were wholly unlike her. And she blamed them on the almost-drowning thing. Or more accurately, on Cody Boggs. The man who'd saved her life.

She'd been assessed upon arrival at the hospital, and her condition had been declared "fair." As a result, she now found herself awaiting her discharge from the emergency room by way of a twelve-year-old Doogie Howser who'd told her he wanted to observe her for a few more hours before signing off and sending her home.

"We just want to be sure you're okay," he'd said when they first put her in this room.

She'd wondered if she should give him a lollipop because children typically liked those.

When had she gotten so old? Or maybe she wasn't old. Maybe she only felt old because she was quickly approaching thirty and she was still as single as the day she was born. With hardly any more clothes on at the moment.

A nurse entered her room, and Louisa could see a small crowd in the hallway.

"The news heard about the daring rescue," the nurse said with a sigh. Her name tag said *Kiki*, and she had short hair and a big, bright smile. "That is one hunky Coastie. You sure are a lucky girl." She wrapped a sleeve around Louisa's arm and started taking her blood pressure.

"Right. Lucky."

Kiki's eyebrows shot up. "Have you seen that man without all his gear on? I think you were pulled out of the water by a Greek god."

Through the small window in the door, Louisa caught and held Cody's gaze. His eyes practically drilled into her, leaving her with about as much oxygen as she'd had when she was underwater.

He looked away, a serious expression knitting his brow.

Cody hadn't always been serious. She supposed she had something to do with that. Or maybe she didn't. (How arrogant of her to think so!) Maybe he'd simply grown up and nothing she'd done made a bit of difference to him anymore.

But she knew that wasn't true, didn't she? She knew it because she still felt those deep pangs of guilt. She knew it because she was the one who had ruined everything.

Kiki rambled on and on about Cody's muscles (which were, in all honesty, impressive) and his dark hair and even darker eyes. "He's got this sort of mysterious thing going on. Do you want me to bring him in here? I mean, he did save your life."

"No," Louisa said quickly.

Kiki stopped what she was doing (what *was* she doing?) and stared at Louisa. Louisa quickly shifted. "Thanks, but I'll talk to him in a little while."

Kiki shrugged. "Suit yourself. If it were me, though, I'd be looking for every possible chance to talk to that man. And maybe slip him my phone number." She laughed. "I mean, if I was single. I'm not. I'm happily married. But you don't have a ring, so I think you should go for it."

Louisa closed her eyes. Of all the people to show up as an answer to her prayers. Was God trying to play a mean joke on her or something? *Are you just throwing this all back in my face or what?* She groaned.

"You okay?" Kiki again. Hadn't she left yet?

"Sorry, yes. How long until I can go home?"

"Oh, I couldn't say, but I'll go find the doctor for you."

Louisa let her head fall back on the pillow. Her family wasn't on the island yet, and she wasn't looking forward to calling them to let them know she'd nearly died that morning. Her mother would be sick with worry. Louisa could practically see her fanning herself with all the drama of a Southern beauty queen.

"Louisa Elizabeth Chambers, I cannot believe you were so reckless," she'd say. "Are you trying to drive me to an early grave?"

"Yes, Mother," Louisa would reply. "Because I secretly want your figurine collection and custody of Teddy."

Louisa had spent the whole of her childhood begging for a puppy, so when her mother announced she'd gotten a Bernese mountain dog to keep her company now that Louisa had moved away, she'd tried her best not to get angry. Daddy tried his best too, though sometimes Louisa wondered if her parents would one day have to cite "giant teddy bear dog" as the reason for their divorce.

So far they were holding it together, but for how long, Louisa didn't know. Maybe love wasn't really meant to last.

Why she was thinking about that, she had no idea. Same way she had no idea why her end-of-life bucket list had taken such a dramatic turn there at the end.

I wish I'd fallen in love? Who was she? Noni Rose, the famous Nantucket matchmaker who drank in love and romance like it was more important than air—something Louisa knew firsthand was quite far from the truth?

She rubbed her face with her hands. Maybe she shouldn't call her parents after all.

Her mother would view this near-death accident as a personal affront, as if Louisa had decided it might be fun to almost drown just to upset her mother's equilibrium. In recent years, JoEllen Chambers had taken up yoga, feng shui'd her entire house, and declared on more than one occasion that her only daughter could certainly benefit from a more minimalist lifestyle.

"You overcomplicate things," she'd told Louisa on their last visit to the island.

Louisa had rolled her eyes, but she knew her mother had a point. Mothers always had a point. Like when her mom told her all those years ago not to go on that date with Cody Boggs.

"There's too much at stake here, Lou," she'd said. "Danny and Marissa are our very best friends. If you break their son's heart, there will be messy feelings."

Louisa had ignored the advice, of course, because what did her mother know, and had she seen how gorgeous Cody had gotten this past year? He had muscles and that swift summer tan, not to mention eyes as deep and rich as chocolate cake and hair to match.

What if she had listened? What if she'd heeded her mother's advice? She wondered that often, unfortunately. Because if she'd been wiser, there was a good chance Mr. Boggs would still be alive and their two families never would've fallen out.

Conversely, however, her mother had been charmed by Eric Anderson, Louisa's only real grown-up boyfriend. (It didn't escape her that those two things seemed to contradict each other. After all, the very idea of a "boyfriend" didn't sound very grown-up.)

Everyone was charmed by Eric—he *was* charming. None of them ever saw him for who he really was. Last time she'd talked to her mom, the older woman had asked if there was any chance of reconciling with "that dashing Eric from the hotel." As if all her hopes and dreams were pinned on that relationship. As if their breakup had simply been another one of Louisa's silly mistakes.

So perhaps mothers didn't know everything.

Yes, maybe she wouldn't tell her parents. Maybe they'd never find out their daughter would be dead right now if it weren't for the strong, firm, muscular arms of their old pal Cody Boggs.

Yeah, and maybe pigs would fly.

"Should I come back?"

Her eyes shot open and instantly drank in the sight of a fully grown and eternally handsome Cody Boggs. This was terribly unfair, she thought, that he emerged from this morning's fiasco looking like he'd just stepped off a photo shoot for the "World's Most Eligible Bachelor" and she looked like she'd decided to try out life as a drowned sewer rat. With red hair, no less.

Thank goodness nobody had given her a mirror. Although right about now she was wishing she'd at least done a quick pass over the curls.

"Louisa?"

"Sorry," she said. She ran a hand over her hair and felt the frizz, stifled a groan. "No, it's fine."

"Just came to see how you're feeling," he said. "And to tell you how stupid you were to be out there without a life vest."

"You don't have to be ugly about it," she said. "I didn't mean to get out that far."

She'd been careful to stay within the designated swim zone—was it really her fault the current had picked her up and dragged her so far out? Maybe the empty beach should've been a clue. Everyone else knew better. She wanted to hide—it *was* her fault!

"Lou—" But he quickly caught himself. Probably realizing they weren't friends anymore and calling her by any nickname was a little too familiar for two people who'd split twelve years prior and had never spoken again.

He appeared to take a deep cleansing breath. "I'm sorry," he said—much more levelheaded this time. "Are you okay?"

"I'm fine," she said.

"You do know you could've died."

She stilled. "I know."

He was staring at her. She wasn't looking at him, but she could feel him studying her. Her face flushed with heat.

"Thanks for saving my life, I guess."

"You guess?"

She forced herself to look at him then. "Thanks for saving my life. I would've hated to have to tell my parents that I drowned. Especially since I wasn't wearing a life vest. My father would've killed me."

He kept his eyes trained on her for several seconds, then looked away. "This isn't funny, you know."

"I know," she said. "I'm sorry."

Then he was looking at her again, and as soon as she realized it, her toes tingled. *Traitors!* "It was pretty scary."

He wore that serious expression again, like an angry principal who'd just found out she was the one who'd vandalized the girls' locker room.

What was she supposed to say? That she'd been terrified out there? That she was panicked and counting the minutes before a big wave hit and took her under for good? That she wasn't so sure she deserved to be saved and, oh, wasn't it ironic he'd been the one to pull her from the water when her actions had inadvertently led to his father's death?

Did he wish he could throw her back?

"So you're in the Coast Guard now," she said dumbly.

He pressed his lips together as if trying to decide whether or not to respond to her statement of obviousness. In the end, he didn't get the chance because the door opened and Doogie walked back in.

"How are we feeling?" He gave his boyish smile, and Louisa glanced at Cody, who showed no sign of emotion. Did they teach them that in Coast Guard school? *Good afternoon, men. Today we're*

*going to learn how to affix a permanent scowl to your face and double
as a robot.*

"Just ready to go home, Doc," she said.

"I'm told we have you to thank for saving this one." Doogie
turned to Cody, who shifted uncomfortably but gave a firm nod.

At least he wasn't denying he was the one who'd done the saving.
That was something, she supposed.

"We sure are grateful, aren't we, Louisa?"

Eyes back to Cody. "Yes, *we* are."

She wouldn't dare say so, but she thought she might've seen just
the slightest twinge of a smile right there at the corner of his glorious
mouth, but robot training had paid off and he quickly returned to
his factory settings.

"Well, I don't have to tell you how lucky you were today, Miss
Chambers," the doctor said.

"No, you don't." Hadn't Cody already done that?

"But I'm going to anyway. If this man hadn't spotted you, you
would surely have drowned out there."

She stared at her folded hands in her sheet-covered lap. "I'm
aware."

And whoever it was that had called the Coast Guard—that was
someone she should send a box of chocolates to.

"Great," he said. "Your tests have all come back normal, but do
you have someone at home who can keep an eye on you?"

"I'll be fine," she said.

"That's not what he asked," Cody said, glaring.

She glanced at him, wishing she had *someone* to claim as her own
so she'd seem less pathetic.

"Yes, I have someone to keep an eye on me."

The doctor did a surprisingly good stink eye for someone so
young.

"I'll be fine," she repeated, this time more slowly.

"We do want to watch out for any odd or unusual behavior."

"You mean odder and more unusual than my normal behavior?"

He stared at her for a few seconds before clearing his throat, evidently unsure how to respond to her—which wasn't all that uncommon, now that she thought of it.

"Who will take care of you? Is there someone we can call?"

"A family friend. Maggie Fisher? You probably know her."

The doctor went quiet. "I do. I was sorry to hear about—"

"She'll make sure I don't die in my sleep," she cut in, avoiding Cody's curious expression.

"Very good," the doctor said. "I've signed your discharge papers. I've heard you're quite the workaholic, young lady. Best you head home and put your feet up for the rest of the day. Let your body recover from your morning. And I'll personally make sure Maggie knows how serious this is."

"Please don't."

"Give me your word you'll take a few days off and get in touch with Maggie immediately."

She nodded compliantly, knowing full well she would do no such thing. She had the Timmons anniversary party that weekend, and there was no way she was flaking out on them. She had a reputation to protect. A business to run. An ex-boyfriend to impress. And bills to pay.

She tried not to groan at the thought of all the medical bills.

The doctor shook Cody's hand, gave Louisa one last smile, and walked out the door.

"You're going to do what he says?" Cody asked sternly, though it sounded more like an order.

"You should try to look less mean when you talk," she said pointedly.

He might've actually snarled then, and the words *You're on thin ice* popped into her head—a sort of warning, she supposed, though she didn't make a habit of listening to the commonsensical parts of herself.

She swung her legs over the side of the bed and tried to push her hand through her hair but found the tangles problematic.

"You gonna answer me?"

"Oh, that wasn't a rhetorical question?"

"Louisa."

"I'll make sure to rest," she said, doing nothing to hide her exasperation.

"Why don't I believe you?"

"Because I'm lying?" She stood on unsteady legs, trying to ground herself, but her head was light and the room spun. She might've taken a step—she wasn't sure—and yep, she was going down.

In a flash, Cody's arms were around her, and though she was barely conscious, she was coherent enough to notice he smelled really, really good, but not coherent enough to keep that thought to herself.

Next thing she knew, she was back on the bed and the room went dark.

CHAPTER THREE

MAGGIE FISHER DIDN'T HAVE ANY KIDS OF HER OWN, but she'd become a sort of wacky aunt to both Louisa and Cody when they were kids, and these days Louisa was much closer to Maggie than to any of her actual family members.

Even if her parents had been in Nantucket year-round, Louisa wondered if Maggie would still feel like the only family she had. Things hadn't been right in the Chambers house for a very long time. The best thing Louisa had done for her parents was to move away. Never mind they'd replaced her with a dog.

None of that mattered, though. What mattered was that the local news had caught the story of her little mishap on the ocean, and while her parents might not learn about it from the news, Maggie definitely would. In fact, she was a little surprised Maggie hadn't shown up at the hospital.

After her brief dizzy spell, Cody got bossy and told her to lie back down. She ignored him, of course, and might've told him he didn't have any right to tell her what to do, *thank you very much.*

Did it matter that she sort of liked that he seemed to care? As if they had any chance of being friends again.

Now Louisa lay on her couch while Maggie fussed around the cottage, mumbling to herself. Louisa tried to ignore her, but Maggie seemed to emphasize certain words as she puttered.

Life jacket.

Weather radar.

Common sense.

She'd made her point.

Leaving the hospital, Louisa had had no intention of lying around the rest of the day, but as promised, the adolescent doctor had called Maggie and told her what happened. *Another traitor.*

Maggie brought her a cup of hot tea. Louisa didn't like tea, but she took it anyway for fear that her wacky sort-of aunt would add the word *ungrateful* to her mumbling.

"Thanks," she said without looking up.

Maggie plopped down in the chair Louisa had found at the Ryersons' yard sale two summers ago. It was white wicker and most likely meant for outdoor use, but the Ryersons had expensive taste, and this beauty was the perfect complement to Louisa's shabby-chic living space.

Louisa took a sip of tea (mostly to appease Maggie), then set the mug on the coffee table.

The cottage had been a labor of love for Louisa. Purchasing it three years ago had been a bit impulsive. Maggie said it was nostalgia, but Louisa genuinely wanted to take the house and transform it into something beautiful. It had been neglected for so many years.

She hadn't counted on Cody returning to the island, however. At some point he was going to find out she'd bought this cottage, right? Just like at some point Maggie was going to learn it was Cody who'd pulled her from the water.

Her mind took her straight back to the moment she'd been plunged into the depths by a wave so strong and merciless Louisa was certain its sole purpose was to end her life.

Her chest closed as her imagination made her relive the whole ordeal in vivid detail as if she needed the reminder. As if she could ever forget.

"I suppose I should ask if you're okay," Maggie said.

Louisa's eyes fluttered open, and she forced a smile. "Of course I am, Mags. It wasn't really that big of a deal."

Maggie's expression made it clear she didn't believe Louisa. And rightfully so. The old woman had always had a knack for seeing straight through her.

"I'm fine," Louisa protested. "And I have a lot of work to do."

"I called Alyssa," Maggie said. "She's handling everything."

Alyssa Martin was perfectly competent. Her best friend and business partner could handle most of what needed to be done for the upcoming anniversary party, but it would be missing Louisa's special touch.

That couldn't be bottled or duplicated. It was the *magic* she strived to create for every single client. It was what people always told her after an event: *"You have such a way of making everything so magical."*

It was probably a point of pride, but it mattered to Louisa. "I need to be there," she groaned.

"You can take a day."

"I own the business," Louisa said. "It's my responsibility."

"You have a very good partner who is eager to help, given the fact that you nearly drowned this morning." Maggie did nothing to hide her irritation.

Louisa had started her private concierge business a year ago, after spending five years as the concierge at one of Nantucket's prestigious boutique hotels. That job had given her connections, and one day Louisa realized she didn't want to spend her time simply catering to rich people. She wanted to make the island—and all it had to offer—accessible to everyone.

She wanted to create magic for as many people as possible.

That's when The Good Life was born.

The idea had come to her the way all ideas did—fast and furious.

She'd spent the night scribbling feverishly in her notebook, trying to keep up with the flow of possibilities. She'd gone to work the next morning exhausted but energized—and ready to hand in her resignation.

Of course, Eric was the first person she told. He wasn't only the hotel manager; he was her boyfriend, her best friend—she'd thought. And while he'd miss having her at the hotel, mostly he'd be thrilled for her because, naturally, he'd realize he hadn't seen her this excited about something before.

Louisa had stood in the doorway of his office, wearing a grin like the Cheshire cat, but Eric barely seemed to notice she was there.

Finally, after she cleared her throat twice, he looked up. "You're late this morning."

She waved him off. "I need to talk to you."

He frowned. "Louisa, are you having one of your big-idea days?"

She hated when he did that—made her feel small for being excited. He sometimes told her she wasn't acting professionally or like an adult should act. Usually in the moments when she was feeling spontaneous or adventurous. Eric was neither of those things.

Most of the time she'd done a good job of holding back that side of herself, but at the moment, it was hard to pretend she wasn't excited about her new plan. She was ecstatic! She was about to do something brave and amazing!

"I do have an idea," she said, trying not to let his attitude curb her enthusiasm. She sat across from him, on the opposite side of his desk, noticing it was neat and well-ordered. Everything in its place. By contrast, her desk was more what she referred to as "organized chaos."

It made her wonder what it would be like to live in a house with Eric. He'd probably be horrified at the sports bras hanging from her closet doorknob.

"I've got a meeting in five minutes—can this wait?"

She must've looked sad because he reached across the desk and took her hand.

"I'm sorry," he said. "I've just got a lot on my mind. What's your idea?"

"You sure?"

He focused his attention completely on her now. "Yes. I'm positive."

She smiled, then explained her plan for The Good Life. She even had a rough sketch of a logo. She laid out a mess of loose papers, all the ideas that had poured out of her the night before, as if a creative dam had broken inside her.

It had been ages since she'd had that kind of creative burst. Everything about it felt right. But afterward, everything about working for the hotel felt wrong.

"I think I need to give you my two weeks' notice."

Eric leaned back in his chair and looked her over for a brief moment. "Don't you think that's a little rash?"

"No," she said matter-of-factly.

"Louisa, you can't quit your job to start a business. What about your mortgage? You just bought that house."

"I know," she said. "I'll figure it out. I don't want a safety net. I want to make this work. And we'll still work together. I'll still refer people here."

His laugh bore an edge of condescension.

"What?"

He shook his head. "No, nothing."

"Eric."

"It's just another one of your ideas," he said. "I don't think starting a business is something you just jump into."

"Well, it's not like I don't know what I'm doing," she said. "I've been doing this job here for the last five years."

"Right," he said. "You're really good at it. But numbers and marketing and finding clients and paying taxes—how are you going to keep up with all that?"

Her heart sank. She hadn't thought of that.

"Maybe just work on it in your free time, and when you have a solid business plan, you can move forward. You know, once you know you're not going to fall flat on your face."

She felt like a kite that had just lost its lift. "Right," she whispered. Her eyes had filled with tears at the reminder of who she was—a woman people didn't take seriously. *Oh, that's Louisa. She's quirky.*

And she was. She knew it. But that didn't mean she was incompetent.

Eric obviously disagreed.

"It's a good idea, Lou," he said. "Let's talk about it more later. Maybe I can help with your business plan."

But all she heard was *You can't do this—or anything else—without me.*

She'd left his office in a daze, the wind stolen from her sails. She hadn't fallen apart, which was major progress, but the idea had lost its luster.

It still hurt to think about it now, the way he'd dismissed her so flippantly. Somehow she'd found the courage to move forward with her idea. It took a couple more weeks of realizing The Good Life wouldn't leave her alone. Then a conversation or two with Ally and a very pointed kick in the pants from Maggie, but she eventually started to believe in herself.

When she gave her notice at the hotel, she told Eric they were over. "I can't be with someone who doesn't believe in me."

He'd protested, of course, because he never wanted to look like the bad guy, but she knew it was the right thing.

She needed to find someone who supported her dreams, who thought her adventures were fun and intriguing, who didn't find the flaws in every single idea she had. That person might not exist, so for the time being, romance was not a priority. It hurt too much to realize someone wasn't who you thought they were. Besides, she was doing just fine on her own.

Mostly. She was doing mostly just fine on her own.

Her business was all-consuming, and she was determined to make it a success—not just to prove Eric wrong, but to prove to herself she had it in her. She worked hard, harder than she ever had when she was punching the hotel clock, but she wouldn't trade it for anything.

She'd been right—creating experiences for her clients, the kind they would never forget, the kind that would rank as the best of their lives, was fulfilling in a way her work hadn't been before.

Who cared if there was no man to celebrate her? She was a legitimate businesswoman. She was almost even a success. But she still had something to prove, and she knew it.

So the anniversary party was important. Fifty years was a long time for a couple to be married, especially nowadays. The Timmons family was counting on her—surely Maggie would understand that.

But one glance at the old woman's face told her that she was officially on lockdown.

"You want to talk about it?" Maggie asked.

"No." Louisa looked down so she wouldn't have to see Maggie's disapproval.

"Are you going to call your parents?"

"No."

"They might find out. Your dad still reads Nantucket news, and you know it'll show up online."

Louisa groaned again.

"Should I make you something to eat?"

"I had enough seawater to keep me full for the rest of the day, but thanks." Louisa glanced at her unwelcome guest.

"You keep cracking your jokes, but you know this isn't funny."

"I know." And if she forgot, there would surely be someone else to remind her. She didn't know how to respond to all these people who seemed to actually care about her well-being. She didn't like *feelings*. Admitting there was a trove of buried emotions underneath her happy-go-lucky exterior simply wasn't good for her.

"If I'd lost you, well, that just wouldn't do, now would it?"

Maggie's gray hair was cut short, and she wasn't fancy or elegant. She was down-to-earth and real. Maybe that was why Louisa liked her so much, why she'd been so drawn to her when she moved back.

"Real" was hard to find these days. The older woman had always prided herself on speaking her mind.

Some of that had rubbed off on Louisa, and she was glad it had. It came in handy sometimes to be able to say exactly what she was thinking. Though it occurred to her she could never put into words what she was thinking about this morning's events. Still too many *feelings*.

"Want to talk about your birthday party?" Louisa would love to talk about anything but her near-death experience.

Maggie grew quiet.

In the silence, Louisa heard the words the other woman didn't say. This would likely be her last birthday, and to that end, Louisa had proposed a big bash—a fish fry down on the beach, maybe, or a clambake. A party to end all parties—a celebration of the life of Maggie Fisher.

"I haven't thought much about it," Maggie said. "And I don't think now is the time for working. You need to rest, and that means turning off your brain."

Louisa sighed. Sometimes she feared that if she turned off her brain, she wouldn't get it to come back on.

There was a knock at the door, but nobody who visited her ever waited to be let in. Seconds later, Alyssa was standing in the living room.

"Is it true?" Louisa's friend asked breathlessly.

"That she almost died today? Yes, it's true." Maggie harrumphed in the wicker chair, and it occurred to Louisa that she should get new cushions just to freshen up the room a little. It had been at least two years since she'd done any redecorating.

Ally waved the old woman off, pushed Louisa's feet over, and sat down on the end of the couch, dropping her neat black purse onto the white wood-plank floor.

"Was it *him*?"

Louisa's eyes widened in an effort to communicate to her friend to *please shut up right now*, but Ally wasn't so great with nonverbal cues. Or shutting up.

"Was what who?" Maggie asked.

Alyssa picked up her bag and rummaged around. Ally was notoriously well organized—it was what made their business partnership so perfect. That was the reason Louisa had called Ally before she turned in her resignation at the hotel and pitched the idea of The Good Life to her college friend. As soon as Eric listed off everything Louisa wasn't thinking about, she knew she couldn't do it alone—but she wasn't about to ask him to help.

Alyssa was a much better choice. While Louisa loved all things creative, Ally thrived on order. She was a numbers girl, an everything-in-its-place girl.

Knowing this didn't stop Louisa from uttering a silent prayer, a last-ditch effort, that her friend's purse had eaten whatever it was she was about to pull out—which would, no doubt, tell Maggie more than Louisa was ready to share about her accident and the man who saved her.

She and God must not have been on the same page, though, because seconds later Ally took a sheet of paper from her bag.

"'Brant Point Coast Guard officer saves local woman during this morning's brutal storm,'" Alyssa read aloud.

Louisa tried to snatch the paper away, but Maggie beat her to it. For someone so old, the woman had crazy-fast reflexes.

"It's him, isn't it?" Alyssa asked matter-of-factly. Ally wasn't a romantic, but Louisa could've sworn her friend's question had been punctuated with a swoony sort of sigh, the kind reserved for older women who'd lost all their self-respect.

Louisa recognized the sigh because it was the same one that silently accompanied every thought she had regarding being rescued by Cody Boggs and his ridiculously strong arms.

"He still looks the same as he does in those pictures you keep hidden in the desk drawer." Alyssa looked at Maggie. "She thinks no one knows they're there."

Maggie only frowned.

"You know me, Lou—I'm a pragmatist—but even I can admit

this is romantic. The same guy you made that pact with all those years ago. Arguably your first love. The one that got away. Now back only a couple of months before the golden birthday, and not only is he *here*, he's a *hero*." Ally made these statements like a newscaster, listing off facts.

These were not facts. There was nothing romantic about throwing up salt water onto the lap of the aforementioned man.

Louisa stood, picked up her tea, and walked into the kitchen, aware that Maggie was reading whatever blog post Ally had printed out. Also aware that overzealous bloggers typically included critical details like names of heroic Coasties who rescued drowning women from the ocean.

Sigh.

"Louisa Elizabeth Chambers?"

Louisa grimaced. "Mary Margaret Fisher?"

But Maggie wasn't in a joking mood. She now stood in the doorway, and Louisa resisted the urge to remind the older woman that she was there to take care of her—not threaten her life.

"I *knew* it was him." Alyssa appeared at Maggie's side. "And back just months before your thirtieth birthday."

"You mentioned that already." Louisa glared at her friend.

"It was worth repeating." Ally remained unwilling to read Louisa's nonverbal cues.

"Haven't you done enough?" Louisa asked.

Ally's perfectly shaped eyebrows knit together in a straight line as if she was genuinely confused by Louisa's reaction.

Maggie hadn't moved. "Are you going to explain?"

Louisa felt like a caged animal with both of them blocking the doorway. "What is there to say? I should've worn a life vest. I didn't. I won't do it again."

"You're leaving out important details," Maggie said.

"Like this." Alyssa grabbed the sheet of paper and held it up facing Louisa. "Lou, this is Cody Boggs. I've heard you talk about him enough—I know his name."

Louisa didn't talk about Cody *that* much. And never to Maggie. Her eyes fell to the page where Cody's profile jumped out at her. Man, he was a beautiful human being.

"That *is* the guy," Maggie said. "You should've told me he was back and that *he* was the one who saved you from your own stupidity this morning."

"Have you ever thought about a career in motivational speaking?" Louisa asked dryly.

Maggie didn't flinch.

Louisa turned away, unfolded and refolded a kitchen towel. "I doubt he even remembers the pact. I hardly remember." What a liar. After all, thoughts of the pact had flittered through her mind as she'd made her near-death bucket list while flopping around in the water that morning.

Also on that list was *I wish I'd said I was sorry. I wish I'd mailed the letters.* Was this God's way of getting her attention? She considered pointing out to God he could've been a bit less terrifying in his approach.

"But what if he does remember?" Ally asked. "Do you think it's just coincidence that he showed up here *now*? Do you think it's a coincidence that he was your knight in a shining scuba suit?"

Louisa didn't bother correcting her. Cody hadn't been wearing a scuba suit. He'd been wearing an orange Coast Guard uniform, and while she couldn't be sure, she thought he might've had a bright-white halo hovering over his head.

"Were you ever going to tell me Cody was back on the island?" Maggie asked.

There was only one place for Louisa to go—out. She turned toward the back door and pushed it open, walking onto the porch, which had a great view of Brant Point, the very place where Cody was stationed—at least, she assumed he was stationed there.

Dare she say she *hoped* he was stationed there?

If he had to look at Brant Point lighthouse every day, there was no way he could *not* think about that pact they'd made when they were kids. They'd talked about it every year on their shared birthday, after all.

What if the accident really had been God's way of reminding her of what she wanted—a chance to make things right? What if this was her chance to say she was sorry and unload the years of guilt she'd been carrying?

It still angered her that one childish mistake had ruined so many relationships and maybe even so many lives.

She didn't know about that last part because she'd lost touch with the Boggs family, and it was too painful to go hunting them down. She was certain her mother still hadn't forgiven her, which meant Marissa Boggs hadn't forgiven her, which meant Cody also hadn't forgiven her.

"Did you know he was stationed here?" she asked Maggie without looking at her.

"Honey, I know we don't talk about Cody Boggs, but that boy doesn't keep in touch with me," Maggie said. "I'm guessing Nantucket is a part of his life he'd just as soon forget."

"Then what's he doing back here?"

"Seems like maybe he was sent back just in time," Ally chimed in. "Another Coastie might not have spotted you out there." Ally was doing everything she could not to sound pragmatic at the moment, and Louisa didn't appreciate it. She counted on her friend to keep her head out of the clouds.

Louisa shook her head. "If he'd known it was me, he probably would've left me to drown."

"Lou, you can't change the past," Maggie said. "All's you can do is learn from your mistakes and move on."

"I know," she said. "That's what I've done."

"That's what you think you've done," Maggie said.

"But you still have pictures of him in your desk drawer," Ally said.

"Lots of people keep old photos," Louisa protested, but even she knew the truth. She cracked her knuckles—she did that sometimes when she was nervous. "I just want to make it right."

Where had that come from? She didn't want to make anything right. She wanted to make it all go away.

"Maybe this one is best left alone," Maggie said.

"Why?" Louisa asked, not really wanting an answer.

"You don't like for anyone to be upset with you. You're a people pleaser. But Cody lost someone very important to him. You're going to have to let him feel however he feels—about you and about the past."

"Or maybe you could wear him down with your charm," Alyssa offered.

"What charm?" Maggie gave a laugh.

Louisa didn't want to think about it. She didn't want to admit that Maggie was right—that she absolutely could not stand it when anyone was upset with her. That she would fall all over herself to make sure nobody had a negative thing to say about her, or that Cody had a right to be angry.

"It's been a long time," Louisa said. "Maybe he's moved on."

"I'm sure he has," Maggie said, and Louisa felt a little stung at the thought. "But that doesn't mean he wants to be your friend."

"Ouch, Mags," Ally said.

"She's right," Louisa said. "But maybe I can win him over?"

"Let it be." Maggie was obviously not interested in keeping her opinion to herself.

"What about your birthday?" Louisa asked.

"What about it?" Maggie's brow furrowed.

"You deserve to have everyone back together."

"Why, because I'm a sick, dying old woman?"

"Don't say that," Louisa said.

"Don't tell the truth?" Maggie scoffed. "You know it and I know it. Otherwise we wouldn't be talking about a big birthday party that's more like a see-ya-on-the-other-side party."

Ally looked confused. "I thought it was a big birthday because you're a new decade or something?"

"Oh yeah?" Maggie looked at Alyssa. "What decade did you think it was?"

Ally glanced at Louisa, who only shrugged. Truth was, she had no idea how old Maggie was. The woman had more energy than most people Louisa's age, but her hair was gray and there were deep wrinkles around her mouth and eyes. It was impossible to zero in on a number.

"Don't answer that," Maggie said.

Without Louisa's permission, an idea took hold, and as was usually the case, she knew it wasn't going to leave her alone—not until she saw it through.

"Maggie, what if I invite my parents and Cody's family to your party? When they see each other, they'll realize how stupid they've been, and things will go back to the way they were."

Maggie stared at her, an incredulous look on her face. "Just like that?"

"You know Daniel and Marissa were like another set of parents to me. My mom and dad loved them like family. This not-talking thing has really gotten out of hand, don't you think? It's been long enough."

"Are you forgetting what happened, Lou?"

Louisa went quiet. "Of course not."

"There's a lot of history there. You can't wish it all away."

"I'm not. I just want to try and make it right."

Maggie frowned. "You're being naive. I know how you are, and I don't want you to get your hopes up."

There was a slight lull, and then Alyssa clapped her hands together. "I say we do it. What have you got to lose? Maggie, your birthday is before Louisa's, so if this works, we can still make the Brant Point pact thing reality."

"That's not going to happen, Ally," Louisa said. "And I'm okay with that. I just want the chance to say I'm sorry."

"But then you want your happily ever after," Maggie said.

"No, I want a fish fry down on the beach, just like old times." Those were some of her very best memories. She'd purposely not thought of them for years. "We'll invite everyone who loves you."

"Short list," Maggie quipped.

"Stop it. You know that's not true." Louisa felt suddenly weary, in spite of the adrenaline rush of a new idea.

"I know I'm not going to be able to change your mind," Maggie said. "But like I said, don't get your hopes up."

She shrugged. "Like *Ally* said, what have you got to lose?"

But even as she uttered the words, she thought of at least ten things that could go wrong. Knowing she was the reason for all of them made her stomach somersault like an Olympic gymnast with a killer floor routine, and that left her feeling woozy.

CHAPTER FOUR

JULY 30, TWELVE YEARS EARLIER

Louisa didn't remember a birthday without Cody. In fact, she was fairly certain she'd never had one. But this one felt different. They were eighteen. They were legal adults. They could get married if they wanted to.

They didn't, of course, because that would be ridiculous, and Louisa was headed to Boston University that fall on a substantial academic scholarship, whereas Cody still hadn't decided what he was going to do now that high school was over.

Maybe to the rest of the world, they were mismatched, but now, finally alone together after a day at the beach, Louisa looked at him, and she couldn't imagine spending a single day without him.

"What are you thinking about?" he asked her, his voice quiet.

She was rarely quiet, so when she was, he noticed. She forced herself to smile, in spite of the fact that she left for school in two weeks and her head had turned into a pile of mush. What-if questions raced through her mind, accompanied by the overwhelming need to cling to him, to protect what they had.

"You and me," she finally said.

"How great we are together?" His words nearly stole her breath away.

How would she survive without this—without him? How would she concentrate on school when her mind and heart were so wholly rooted wherever he happened to be?

He frowned. "What's wrong?"

A tear escaped, and she instantly wiped it away.

He wrapped an arm around her. He didn't need to ask her why she was crying. He knew. It was as if a shadow had followed them around all summer, and now here they were, nearing the end—it was all too real.

"I don't want to hold you back, Lou," he said. "You're going to meet a lot of people out there."

She pulled away. "What are you talking about?"

"Don't freak out—I'm just saying. I don't want you sitting in your dorm room thinking about me instead of making new friends and going out and having fun."

She relaxed a little. "But I want you sitting in a room thinking about me."

He laughed. "Louisa, we're always going to have this—us, Nantucket. We're always going to share a birthday and have endless stories of growing up together. And I hope we make it—I really do."

"But?"

"But I don't want to stand in your way. You've got huge plans, and I don't even know where I'll be in two weeks."

She did have big plans. At the moment, she hated that she did. She'd always respected the fact that Cody wasn't in a hurry to figure things out. When he told her he'd be taking a gap year, she hardly even protested—she didn't want him to think she didn't approve. She was his girlfriend, after all, not his mom.

But secretly it bothered her. Didn't he have any ambition? Wasn't there something he was passionate about? Was this going to be the thing that finally broke them up?

"What if next summer we come here and everything is different?" she asked after a pensive pause.

He turned toward her and took her hands. "We'll figure it out. And we've still got a couple of weeks, right?"

She nodded, sniffed, and wiped another tear all at the same time.

"How about this." He opened the picnic basket they'd brought to the beach and took out an unused napkin. "Do you have a pen?"

She reached in her purse and found a pen, then handed it to him, watching closely as he scribbled on the uncooperative napkin.

"What are you doing?"

He shushed her gently and went back to writing. "I have a proposal for you," he finally said.

"Cody."

"Not that kind of proposal." He handed her the napkin, and she read his words to herself.

We, Cody Boggs and Louisa Chambers, do solemnly promise that no matter where life takes us, we will return to Brant Point on the day of our golden birthday.

He'd drawn two straight black lines where they were meant to sign the agreement—which obviously wasn't legal or binding, but which charmed her just the same.

"This way, we know that no matter what, we're always coming home to each other," he said.

"But that's twelve years from now," she said.

"Do you think we're going to lose track of each other?"

She shrugged.

"Not if I have anything to say about it."

"Then why sign this?" she asked, blinking back new tears.

He reached out and touched her cheek. "It'll give us something to celebrate."

She knew it wasn't only that. She knew he worried they would lose touch, the same way she worried. She knew that while he hadn't said so, there was a part of him that thought she might meet someone new or they might outgrow each other. They'd argued about it off and on since the beginning of the summer. He was convinced she'd leave him for someone more serious, more put-together.

Still, she liked the idea of having something to hold on to—an assurance that no matter where life took them, along the same path or in completely opposite directions, they promised to connect one more time.

Right here, on their thirtieth birthday.

"I'll sign your crazy pact," she said. "But you have to promise me we're going to try to make this work."

He leaned over and kissed her. "I wouldn't have it any other way."

CHAPTER FIVE

"PHONE'S BEEN RINGING OFF THE HOOK."

Cody sat in the chair opposite Master Chief Duncan McGreery, staring out the window where the American flag hung proudly on the side of the black-and-white lighthouse. Brant Point was the backdrop for so many of his childhood memories. But he still never thought he'd be back here.

"When I told you to drum up good press for the Coast Guard, I had no idea you'd work so fast." The phone on the master chief's desk rang, and Cody winced at the sound. Peace and quiet would go a long way right now.

His superior took the call, and Cody only listened long enough for the sound bite.

"Yes, we do think XPO Boggs did an excellent job this morning. We don't like to use the word *hero*, but I'd wager that's exactly how Miss Chambers is feeling."

Don't bet on it.

The image of Louisa's lifeless body would haunt his dreams, same way the others did. But Louisa had survived. He'd saved her. That should ease some of his guilt, shouldn't it? He did a quick gut check. Nope. Still there. Would it ever be enough?

"Boggs."

Cody could tell by the other man's tone that he'd said his name more than once.

"Master Chief?"

"You okay?"

"Never better."

"Do we need to have a conversation about why you went in the water after that girl?"

"She was in distress," he said.

"But that wasn't your job," the master chief said. "Not to mention you broke protocol."

Cody could've guessed this would come up. He cleared his throat. "Just wanted to lead by example. You said the men needed that."

"Right, by example. You showed them how to break protocol."

Cody didn't respond.

Duncan wasn't only his superior officer; he was Cody's friend— one of the few he had. But being Duncan's friend had proven to be problematic the second the master chief had called about the opening at Brant Point station.

"I need some help building morale up here," Duncan had told him. "I need someone who can help me lead."

"Must be a hundred other guys who could do that," Cody remembered saying.

"Not like you," Duncan said. "It's a young crew, Boggs. They've had a rough go of it. Could really benefit from your kind of leadership."

Cody understood. The men at Brant Point needed to be led, mentored, and brought up by someone who didn't care about being their friend. That was Cody. It was what he was known for. Maybe this was always where he was meant to be. He'd done well for himself, despite the early setback. After all, he seemed born to lead, and just because it wasn't his original plan didn't mean he wasn't fulfilling what he'd set out to do—save people from the ocean.

He loved his job. He liked moving up through the ranks. He liked the responsibility of being in charge. He liked doing his part to save lives, to serve whatever community he was a part of—it changed every few years.

When he was promoted to executive petty officer, he'd been proud, but when he got his most recent assignment, that feeling quickly disintegrated.

Duncan was thrilled they'd been stationed together. In fact, he hadn't said so, but Cody had to wonder if the master chief wasn't responsible for making that happen.

Cody wanted to fight it. He wanted to tell Duncan that this was a bad idea, that it would stir up memories and he liked to keep those neatly folded and tucked in a trunk stored at the back of his closet.

But that wasn't how things worked. And Duncan needed him. Cody had a hard time walking away when he was needed.

So here he was. Sitting in an office at the Brant Point station. How surreal. He glanced out the window and saw the exact spot where he and Louisa had spent every childhood birthday he could remember.

Oh, the irony.

"Why don't you go home? Take the day?"

"No," Cody said—a little too quickly.

"It's not a problem, Boggs. You just got in—and that was a heck-uva first day."

Was it enough of a morale boost for the duty station that Cody could pack his bags and take the ferry back to the mainland?

"I'm fine, Chief."

"Boggs, I know Nantucket wasn't on your dream sheet."

Kodiak. Clearwater. Wailuku. Cape May. Honolulu. Juneau.

Nope. No sign of Nantucket on his dream sheet. Not that the dream sheet always mattered. Obviously not. Otherwise he'd be sipping a hot cup of coffee in Alaska right now.

"What've you got against Nantucket?" Duncan asked. "Most guys have the island at the top of their list."

Cody shrugged. "Just never been a fan."

Okay, so when he'd thought of Duncan as a friend, maybe he'd exaggerated a little. They were friends, but his master chief didn't know the whole truth. Why he'd joined the Coast Guard. Why he didn't want to be here. Why seeing Louisa was like seeing a ghost. Why it wrecked him to think—even for a second—how differently today could've gone.

If Duncan had known any of that, Cody had to believe he never would've allowed him to come here in the first place.

"Just let me get back to work, Master Chief," Cody said.

Duncan eyed him as if deciding whether or not he wanted to issue a directive and force Cody to go home.

"Fine," he finally said. He leaned back in his chair. "I need someone I can trust in my corner. Guys don't always respond well to new leadership, and these guys need to function as a team. You know that."

Cody forced himself to listen. It was important to hear the master chief's vision, important the two of them were on the same page.

But the image of Louisa—pale-faced with blue lips and that striking red hair, limp on the deck of the rescue boat—assaulted his memory yet again.

What was she doing out there alone at that hour—without a life vest, no less? If she were here, he'd tell her exactly what he thought of her extracurricular activities. After all, they'd never been the kind of friends who beat around the bush. Whatever the opposite of passive-aggressive was, that was Louisa. She had never hesitated to speak her mind, but she did it in a way that made everyone fall in love with her.

He'd never met anyone who didn't like Louisa Chambers. She was witty and smart and adorable. At least she had been. She'd gotten a little surly at the hospital. Maybe he simply had that effect on women.

He and Louisa had never actually "met." They'd just always known each other. There were pictures of them in diapers together.

Their parents had met in college ages ago, and since not a single one of them had a sibling, they all sort of adopted each other, became each other's family.

Sometimes Cody wondered if their mothers had intentionally gone into labor on the same day, as if they could've planned for such a thing.

Cody and Louisa were both born on July 30. Their mothers were certain it was a sign. Of what, they never explained, but their births cemented a friendship that was meant to last a lifetime.

They'd all been coming to Nantucket since college. Daniel and Warren worked as caddies at the golf course while JoEllen put Marissa up in her family's cottage. The girls waited tables for extra money, but even Cody knew work wasn't why any of them chose the island as their summer destination. It was an escape—a vacation. And it became the place all four of them returned to even after they were grown.

It was clear that both of these families were destined to live and breathe and play on Nantucket. It was in their blood.

But that was before, of course. Before everything—everything—went wrong.

"Boggs, you're distracted," the chief said. "I'm sending you home. I'm sure you've got unpacking to do."

Cody couldn't deny he was distracted, not without lying anyway. But the thought of going home to bare walls and unpacked boxes sucked the life right out of him.

"I'm fine, Master Chief."

"Why don't you go check on Miss Chambers?"

"What?" The man had his full attention now.

"Listen, I'm not going to get into it all now, Boggs, but the Coast Guard could use a win or two. I'm going to let it slide that you left the deck of your ship to go in after that woman, but only because it's already helping build morale around here and because it's got the community talking. Let's keep the momentum of this going. I want the people on this island to know us, to love us, to respect us. Then maybe they'll wear life vests when they're out paddleboarding."

Cody eyed the other man. "What aren't you telling me, Master Chief?"

"I want to make our presence on this island known," he said. "That's all."

"But that's not all," Cody said. "Why do these boys need a morale boost, and why are we working so hard to look good in this community?"

"That's not an uncommon goal," Duncan said. "We'll go over everything else later, when you're actually listening. Now go check in with Miss Chambers. It's the right thing to do."

Cody didn't try hard enough to stifle a groan.

Duncan's eyebrow quirked and the man shifted in his seat. "Problem?"

"I don't know that Lou—Miss Chambers will welcome a visit from me."

Duncan didn't move, but his eyes asked the question he didn't say. It was at that precise moment that Cody realized he didn't want to get into the details with his master chief or anyone else. What was he going to say anyway? *We used to be friends until she took my heart and sliced it in two like a slab of beef on the butcher block*?

He'd gotten over this a long time ago. Why would he even think of bringing it back up now?

But it was more than that, wasn't it? It was more than their silly teenage romance gone wrong. It was everything else that had happened between them and how it changed both of their families forever. That was a little more difficult to get over.

The chief scribbled something on a scrap of paper and handed it to him. "This is her address."

"You have it memorized?"

"I looked it up while you were daydreaming," Duncan said. "Get some rest, and I'll see you tomorrow."

Cody didn't bother protesting. He walked out of the man's office and down the hall, aware of the quiet murmurs that followed him as he went. It was as if nobody had ever saved a person from the ocean before. He knew that wasn't the case. But he supposed it would never get old to hear a story of how one person put their life on the line to save another person.

Maybe the world needed those stories to combat the stories where people purposely hurt each other every day. He should be proud to be a part of the good—why did it make him feel self-conscious?

Outside, Cody got in his Jeep and started the engine. Would Duncan ever find out if he skipped a visit to Louisa? He unfolded the piece of paper and read the address his chief had scrawled on it.

12 North Road.

Cody's eyes focused, then unfocused as he stared at the handwritten address. Surely it was a mistake.

His mind whirled back years. Decades. And somehow, if he really concentrated, it felt like yesterday.

It was the summer he would turn ten. They'd been vacationing in Nantucket since he was a baby, and Dad's investments were paying off, thanks to Mr. Chambers, who'd taught Cody's father how things in the financial world worked.

That summer when they arrived on the island, Cody expected to join Louisa and her family at their big cottage on the water, the one her family had inherited from her grandparents. That's the way it had always been. Their family took one side of the cottage, and Louisa's family occupied the other side. The house was big enough, and nobody ever got in anyone else's way.

It was the perfect setup. At least, he'd always thought so.

He and Louisa liked sneaking out of their rooms at night. They'd trudge out back and swing in the hammock strung between two trees, looking up at the stars and working like mad to keep their eyes open. He loved those nights. He loved their days on the beach. Their afternoon bike rides. The board game tournaments he and Louisa always seemed to win.

This year, though, Dad had the taxi turn down North Road

and drop them in front of a small gray-shingled cottage with giant bluish-purple hydrangeas out front and a sign above the door that said *Seaside*. He got out of the cab and stood in the treeless yard on the quiet street, no other people anywhere in sight.

His little sister tore off toward the house, shouting and giggling as she ran around the yard.

"What are we doing here, Dad?" Cody asked, aware of the quick glance between his parents.

"What do you think, sport?" Dad asked.

"Are we going to Lou's or . . . ?" The letters they exchanged from September to May were great, but it wasn't the same as hearing her laugh.

Louisa's family lived in Boston, but Cody and his family lived in his dad's hometown—Chicago. They often spent holidays together since they considered each other family, but would everything change if they didn't share the big cottage on Nantucket?

He didn't want anything to change. He liked things the way they were. Mom always said they had something special, something rare. Theirs was a safe cocoon of friends who'd been brought together as if they were always meant to be in each other's lives.

Dad smiled, faint wrinkles fanning around his eyes. "What would you think about staying here this summer?"

"Here?"

His mother's smile faltered.

"Is Lou going to stay here?" Cody asked.

His dad clapped a hand on his shoulder. "No, but we will spend every day with Louisa and her family, same as always."

Not the same as always. How would they sneak into the kitchen and steal the leftover lemon bars if they weren't even in the same house?

Cody frowned. "But why can't we stay there? They have the ocean right in the backyard."

"We're just a stone's throw from the ocean," Dad said. "See, out that way? 'Sconset Beach."

Cody could see the water wasn't too far, and while it wasn't as great as having the ocean in your backyard, it was still pretty great.

His father knelt down in front of him. "We've loved staying with Louisa and her family, kiddo, but we wanted a place that was all our own."

His eyes traveled left toward the small cottage on North Road. "So this is ours?"

Dad nodded. "All ours."

"I have my own room?"

"Yep."

"Cool!"

Dad laughed. "Cool!"

Seaside quickly became their safe haven. For several years, it was the place they'd escape to not just for summers but whenever Dad needed a break from work or when their family needed to "recalibrate," as Mom said. The little cottage got a lot of good use in those days.

But then everything changed. Everything good turned to dust right there in that cottage on North Road.

And now his master chief wanted him to go back to that exact place and check in with the woman responsible for all of it.

CHAPTER SIX

MAGGIE LEFT FOR THE STOP & SHOP AROUND TWO to pick up everything she would need to make dinner for them that night. Louisa had insisted that Alyssa go along, mostly because she needed a solid thirty minutes without someone fussing over her.

And to collect her thoughts after her near-death experience.

"The doctor said I was lucky," she'd said absently, only half-realizing Maggie was listening.

The old woman scoffed as she gathered up her shopping bags. "You tell that doctor luck had nothing to do with it. We don't believe in luck any more than we believe in pots of gold at the end of Nantucket rainbows."

"I believe in pots of gold," Ally quipped, but Maggie only stared at Louisa.

Lou got the point, and she couldn't argue. It sure did seem like God had heard her prayer for a miracle and answered. In a very masculine way.

Had she even said thank you? She'd gotten out of the habit of praying. She was too busy working to make sure God was proud of her. She'd made so many mistakes—she figured she still had a few years of work left before she and God could have a proper conversation.

Now, lying on the couch under a worn-out old quilt she'd picked up at a yard sale during one of her trips to the Cape, Louisa closed her eyes and let her mind wander.

What if she hadn't prayed? Would God still have sent Cody? Why Cody? Did that mean something? What if Cody hadn't spotted her out there? Surely she wouldn't have lasted much longer. What if she'd drowned? How long would it have taken someone to realize she was gone? What if . . . ?

A knock on the door shut off her unproductive line of thinking, though one last question popped into her head as she slipped her legs out from under the quilt and stood.

What if I never recover from this?

She knew she'd almost died. She wouldn't take that lightly. But it made her wonder why God had chosen to send her a hero when so many other people likely prayed that same prayer and he stayed silent.

People like Daniel Boggs.

She expected the door to open any second and for Maggie or Alyssa to walk back in, but whoever had knocked wasn't making a move for the doorknob.

She reached the door and opened it, unable to stop the gasp that escaped when she saw Cody Boggs standing on her porch wearing navy-blue pants, a short-sleeved blue button-down, and a hat that cast a shadow over his beautiful face.

He took the hat off and tucked it under his arm, then trained his gaze on her. "Should you be answering the door?"

"Should you be knocking on it?"

"I thought maybe someone else would be here."

She leaned against the door, partly because her knees had gone weak, and gazed up at him. She easily remembered the first time he'd kissed her. All she could think was *I'd do a better job kissing back now that I'm older.*

"Nope. Just me." She couldn't be sure, but she thought he might've glanced down at her left hand. Did she dare hope he cared whether or not she was still single?

Eric's face popped into her mind. He'd been handsome in a pretty, preppy way. She hoped Cody never found out about Eric. She'd been such a fool. He'd think so much less of her if he knew how she'd changed herself to become the woman she thought Eric wanted her to be.

"Did you want to come in?" she asked.

He shifted, an uncomfortable expression behind his eyes, and only then did she remember where they were standing.

"Oh, wow, Cody, I'm sorry—"

He held up a hand. "I'll come in for a minute."

Her house on North Road—her sweet, adorable, charming cottage—had once belonged to Daniel and Marissa. She hadn't forgotten, of course—it was why she'd bought the place. That was why she'd named it Seaside again and had a new quarter board made so everyone else knew it too. It just hadn't occurred to her in that moment, given her weak knees and shortness of breath.

As stifling and difficult as her memories of this morning were, she'd relive them a thousand times over if it meant Cody could go without reliving the memory of the night his dad drowned.

Should she tell him so?

He'd stepped into the entryway, and she closed the door behind him. Now what? Did she give him the tour? Did she tell him she'd made his old room hers and turned the master into a guest room—*because I like sleeping in the same place you used to sleep and because I couldn't bear to take your parents' bedroom?*

"Do you want something to drink?" she asked.

"I want you to lie down." He motioned toward the couch.

"I really am fine."

"Yeah, I know, but your body went through a trauma. When

all that adrenaline gets out of your system, you're going to crash. Someone needs to be here with you. You said Maggie was going to look after you."

"She is," Louisa said.

"Where is she?" Their eyes met for a split second, and he squeezed the cap a little tighter. She could tell because his knuckles turned white. In a flash, she wanted to know everything he was thinking, even though she was certain it would sting a little.

Unless he was thinking, *Oh, Louisa, you really are the love of my life. Let's put the past behind us and start again.* That certainly would not sting.

Odds of that? Slim to zero. No, never mind. She didn't want to know what he was thinking.

The memory of water holding her under like a bully at a child's pool party invaded her mind, and she forced herself to take a deep breath.

You're safe now.

She looked at Cody. She was safe because of him. An inexplicable knot formed at the back of her throat, and she turned away as her eyes clouded over. She would not cry in front of him. Not today. Not ever again.

She sat down and closed her eyes, willing away the tears, and when she opened them, he was standing beside the couch, holding the old quilt.

She felt the skin of her forehead crease in confusion as he gently laid the blanket over her lap, then sat across from her. His kindness stunned her. Shamed her. She didn't deserve it. Yet it sent a tingle through her body like a shock wave.

"What are you doing here?" The words came out as an accusation, which was not her intent. "I mean, I didn't expect to see you here."

He cleared his throat. Probably biting back an angry retort. "I didn't expect to see you here either."

She took his meaning. The cottage. *His* cottage. North Road.

He'd been so proud of this place that first summer when his family moved in. She'd overheard bits and pieces of their parents' conversations, enough to know that Daniel Boggs had learned to play the stock market thanks to her father, and he'd had a knack for it. He had, as her dad said, "a brilliant financial mind."

The best part, Louisa thought, was that Daniel had a kind heart. Cody's dad hadn't been raised with money, and having it never seemed to change him. He didn't hold on to it too tightly.

By contrast, Louisa's dad's life seemed to revolve around the stock market. His world was all numbers all the time. And though nobody said so, she had a feeling Warren wasn't "a brilliant financial mind."

He'd simply continued in the family business. Done what he was trained to do. But what if her father should've been an art teacher or a plumber? What if he'd gotten it wrong all those years ago, and that was why he always seemed to be hurried and neurotic in those days?

"Louisa?"

She glanced up and found Cody watching her, a look of concern lacing his brow.

"You zoned out for a minute."

"Sorry," she said. "That's not because of the accident. That's just how I am."

He sat so straight in the chair, she thought he might have a board attached to his back. Stick straight and stock-still, the man seemed unable, or unwilling, to move.

"Did you answer my question?" she asked because she genuinely couldn't remember.

He shook his head.

"Are you going to?"

"I don't have a lot of choice where they send me, Louisa."

Her name on his lips sounded wrong. Cody almost always called her Lou. Hearing him use her full name was like being scolded by a teacher in elementary school.

"So you're stationed here?"

"That's usually how it works."

She glared at him. "You don't have to be rude. I did almost die today."

"Whose fault was that?" She didn't think it was possible, but he turned even more rigid.

She looked away. "I'm sorry. I wanted to try paddleboarding before recommending it to my clients."

"Did you check the weather before you went? You know better, Louisa." A pause. "You should, anyway."

She stilled. She did know better. She knew because of what she'd seen. She knew because of what she'd lived through. Even so, there she was, pushing envelopes and chasing death. Was there something wrong with her? Did she think she deserved a watery grave just like Daniel Boggs's?

"I'm sorry you had to save me," she said.

He sighed—a heavy one to let her know he was genuinely annoyed with her.

Why *was* he here?

"That's my job," he said. "Don't apologize for that. But you have to use your head. You can't be out there alone in that weather. You know the ocean—it's not your friend."

"I know." It felt like he was on a personal crusade, what with the serious tone and all. She softened. She understood. The ocean had stolen everything from Cody. After a moment, she found his eyes. "So why are you here?"

"I just told—"

"No, here, in my living room."

He turned the cap around in his hands and stared at the ground.

"Someone made you come?"

"It was *suggested*, yes."

"Do you always do what you're told?" she asked.

"It's my job to follow orders." He didn't look at her.

"So you're checking in with the woman you saved because some superior officer made you."

He gave a soft shrug.

Of course. She'd been stupid to hope that he'd come on his own, that he was genuinely interested in her well-being, that he *cared*. He didn't care about her—he'd put her out of his mind (and his life) ages ago.

Because she'd been foolish. She'd run him out. That was the truth of it. She might as well have pushed him off a cliff and straight into another dimension. And to think there had been a time she was certain they'd know each other forever.

Funny thing, that. The silly notions of a teenage girl.

The front door opened, and she saw his expression change. There was no sign of the easygoing kid Cody had been. Instead, there was a man who seemed neat and orderly and controlled and without any personality whatsoever. But she also saw a man who did not want to come face-to-face with the past. And she and Maggie represented the past.

"We're having lobster rolls, and I don't want to hear another—" Maggie stopped short at the sight of Cody, who now stood (at attention?) in the living room.

Louisa couldn't help but admire him in that uniform. He made that thing look *good*. He'd always been a good-looking kid, but this adult version was a whole other level of handsome.

Never mind the tight line that seemed permanently etched in his forehead.

"Oh, my." Ally practically sighed the words as she drank in the sight of the man in Louisa's living room. "You're even more beautiful than Louisa said."

Louisa shot her a *Shut up!* look, but Ally seemed not to notice. Her friend was on a roll today.

Cody also seemed unfazed by the comment. Not a great sign, though she supposed he couldn't break character when he'd committed so fully to playing the angry military man.

Maggie stood a full foot shorter than him, but somehow her presence almost seemed larger. She took him in—all six feet, two inches of him, if Louisa had to guess—then shook her head. "Well, look who it is."

He gave her a stern nod. "Maggie."

Louisa knew that just would not do. Not for Maggie.

"You decided to come back to Nantucket, and you didn't even look me up? How am I supposed to not be offended by that?"

He shifted.

"No hug for your favorite aunt?" Maggie set her grocery bags on the floor.

Cody looked like a sturdy wall that someone was pulling apart, brick by brick.

And that someone was Maggie Fisher.

She stepped toward him, arms open, and he rigidly allowed her to hug him. It was almost painful to watch because the levels of affection seemed to be so mismatched.

Louisa and Alyssa exchanged a quick glance, and Louisa wondered if her friend was hoping for a turn in Cody's arms.

"You're staying to eat," Maggie announced as she slipped out of Cody's awkward embrace.

"Oh, Mags, that's not a good idea—" Louisa said at the same time Cody said, "I'm sorry. I don't think I can."

Maggie harrumphed. "I know you Coasties. You don't get a lot of home-cooked meals. And you're here, so you're obviously off duty."

"No, Maggie, he was ordered to be here."

Maggie frowned, and Louisa thought it would be a good idea to convince the old woman to tweeze her eyebrows. If she wasn't careful, they'd start to look like two fuzzy caterpillars.

"Are you still on duty?"

Cody paused. "No, ma'am."

"Ma'am?" Maggie laughed. "You can stop that right now." She picked up her bags and toddled off to the kitchen.

Alyssa stepped forward as if presenting herself to Cody. "I'm Alyssa."

He extended a hand, which she dutifully shook, and Louisa willed her friend not to say anything else that would embarrass her.

"Most people call me Ally."

Cody nodded, then looked down at their hands. Alyssa seemed to have no intention of letting go.

"I'm Lou's friend. We met in college. I tutored her in economics. She's told me about you. Not just about today, but before today—"

"Ally," Louisa cut her off. "Don't you need to go help Maggie?"

Ally looked stunned for a quick second, then finally let go of Cody's hand and walked into the kitchen.

"Sorry about that," Louisa said.

"I really can't stay," Cody said.

"Good luck telling Maggie."

A conflicted expression washed over his face.

"Sit down, Cody." Maggie was back, this time carrying a glass of iced tea. "I had to get good tea while I was out because Louisa never remembers to buy it. And you can't have a well-stocked kitchen without good tea."

He reached out and took the glass, then did as he was told.

It was strange to see, really. Cody had never been much for rules or taking orders. Why would someone like that choose a career in the Coast Guard? And why wasn't he the guy in charge by now?

"I suppose you're here to do some damage control," Maggie called out as she walked back to the kitchen.

"Ma'am?"

She popped her head out and shook a spatula in his general direction. "If you call me *ma'am* one more time, I will swat your backside with this and don't think I won't."

Cody almost smiled at that. Almost.

It was enough of a teaser to convince Louisa that the only thing in the world she needed to see to die happy was a genuine smile from Cody Boggs, though she had a feeling that would be hard to come by.

He was still every bit as icy toward her as she expected him to be.

Dumb mistakes. Can I just get a do-over?

"I'm wondering if they brought you in to do damage control since that boy almost drowned."

Cody faltered, clearly unaware of what Maggie was talking about.

Was it triggering to work around people who drowned or nearly drowned? Did it bring back all the unwanted memories she'd been working so hard to bury all these years?

If I could just get him to forgive me, maybe then I could move on.

Maggie was in the doorway again. "Kid's name is Jackson Wirth. He's seventeen or so." She paused. "They didn't tell you about this when you got here?"

"I've only been here two days," he said. "They haven't had a chance to tell me much of anything."

Maggie straightened. "Were you even on duty when you found our girl out there in the water?"

Cody pressed his lips together. "No. The guys were showing me the rescue boat. We were doing an equipment test when someone called it in."

"Someone spotted her out there?" Maggie asked.

"Someone spotted something," he said. "They weren't sure what it was."

"It was me," Louisa groaned miserably.

"Yeah, we got that." Maggie sounded annoyed. "Good thing you saw her."

"We almost didn't," he said. "We were just about to turn around when I—"

Louisa remembered her prayer. She needed a miracle. God had brought her Cody. Maggie was right—luck had nothing to do with it.

"When you what?" Ally asked.

"When we noticed something red in the water."

"See, Lou?" Ally said. "It *is* a good thing you have red hair after all. Aren't you glad you didn't dye it?"

"Not my hair, Ally," Louisa said dryly. "My paddleboard."

"Oh." She disappeared into the kitchen.

Maggie laughed. "An equipment test. Isn't that just like Jesus?"

Cody's eyes found Louisa's, but she couldn't hold his gaze. Suddenly the magnitude of what he'd done weighed heavily on her. *I could've died.* If he'd turned back one second earlier. If he'd given up on seeing anyone out there in the water. If he'd been less attentive or meticulous—she wouldn't be alive today.

Her heart sank.

"Food's ready," Ally called.

"All right," Maggie said. "Let's eat at the table like civilized humans, shall we?" She got up and returned to the kitchen.

Cody stood. Louisa knew she should follow suit, but the heaviness of the realization had pinned her in place.

"You okay?" The concern in his voice unnerved her.

Quickly she shook the thick cloud away and forced a smile. "'Course." She didn't need anyone else fussing over her. Hadn't she caused enough drama for one day? She'd sort through the mess of emotions later, when she was alone and there was nobody to bother.

Or not. She could just as easily sweep them away under a mental rug somewhere with all the other pesky emotions she'd prefer not to entertain.

Louisa swung her legs around to the side of the sofa and put her feet on the ground. "You ready for this?"

He seemed to not want to speak to her, but that would be rude, and she knew he hadn't been raised to be rude.

"I'll be fine." He stopped beside the couch and reached out a hand in her direction.

She stared at it like it was a foreign object, then realized he meant to help her up. He was still thinking of her as an invalid, as a person who'd nearly drowned.

Little did he know that if her legs were wobbly and her heart gave out, it would have nothing to do with her accident that morning and everything to do with him. She'd keep that to herself.

She slipped her hand in his and allowed him to help her up. It didn't escape her, the way it felt to touch his skin, to feel the warmth of him so close to her.

But once she'd found her footing, he took a step away, to let her go in front of him. It was politeness that caused him to offer her his hand—of course it was.

Yet the simplicity of it made her wish it had been something more.

That was something she had no right to feel, and she knew it.

CHAPTER SEVEN

CODY DIDN'T WANT TO SIT across the table from Louisa and smile and eat lobster rolls and pretend everything was fine.

But here he was.

Maggie bustled around the table the same way he always remembered her doing. It seemed impossible for the woman to sit still. She poured drinks. She fetched extra napkins. She piled freshly made potato chips onto their plates even though nobody was asking for seconds. She mothered. It was what she did.

Maybe that's why his insides had twisted into a tight knot. He didn't want to be mothered. Not by his own mother and certainly not by Maggie. Cody had become the one who took care of things. That was his role. He didn't need anyone else looking after him.

Louisa's hair had darkened to a deep auburn, a color you didn't see often and one that only made her blue eyes look bluer. If he sat here too long, he'd get lost in them and convince himself everything really could go back to the way it used to be, back when he was young and foolish and impulsive.

He'd been so stupid.

Maggie prattled on about who knows what and Cody choked down what ended up being the best lobster roll he'd ever eaten, not that he could enjoy it. Halfway through the meal, he realized the three women were staring at him, and once again he'd missed whatever question had been tossed his way.

"Jackson Wirth?" Maggie swallowed a bite, still focused on him. "You really didn't hear the story?"

Cody took his napkin from his lap and pressed it against his mouth, mostly because he needed something to do with his hands. "No, ma'am. I think I was supposed to be briefed this morning, but then—" He glanced at Louisa, whose eyes widened for a split second and then found her hands in her lap. "If it's important, I'm sure they'll fill me in tomorrow."

"They brought in a new master chief, right?" Maggie asked.

The old woman knew everything that went on around the island—she always had. People told her things. She heard things. She observed things. Regardless of how she came upon her information, if there was anything happening in Nantucket, Maggie Fisher knew about it.

"Duncan McGreery," Cody said. "He's a good guy."

"He's got a big job ahead of him," Maggie said. "Though I'm guessing your heroics today will make things a little easier."

Cody wished women would just say what they meant. They had this way of skirting an issue, forcing a person to ask questions, like leaving a trail of bread crumbs. It was exhausting. He preferred straightforward, which was how he remembered Maggie. Maybe she was determined to entice him into a conversation, and this was her tactic.

Louisa had always been straightforward. He wondered if she still was. Did her mouth still get her in trouble? Did she still say whatever popped into her head? He glanced at her. She looked tired, drained. What was on her mind right now? Was she okay?

"I'm not sure I follow," Cody said, aware that he wasn't going to get the whole story if he didn't engage.

This was how gossip worked, he supposed. He really wanted no part of the island rumor mill. He preferred to get his information from the source. But Maggie's insider information could prove to be useful, especially since Duncan had hinted that the crew needed a morale boost but had failed to elaborate.

"Maggie's trying to tell you that the Coast Guard got a bad reputation around here last year," Louisa said.

"It got blown out of proportion," Ally said.

Louisa frowned. "Not really."

"Aaron wasn't wrong," Ally said.

"He shouldn't have said what he said." Louisa again.

Maggie set her fork down with a clang. "Ladies, let's bicker about this later. We have a guest."

"A very confused guest," Cody said. He looked at his plate. His food was gone, so he picked up his iced tea and took a drink.

"Jackson Wirth and a few of the other boys were out surfing one night last fall," Maggie said.

"In the dark," Ally added.

"Yes, Alyssa, 'one night' implies that it was dark out." The exasperated look on Maggie's face made Cody smile inwardly. Her tone dripped with sarcasm.

Cody had to admit he still loved the old bird. Maggie's no-nonsense approach to everything had always been refreshing.

"The boys got caught in some pretty choppy waves, something our girl here can relate to."

Louisa rolled her eyes.

"The current carried them out pretty far, and Jackson wasn't strong enough to swim against it."

In a flash, Cody was eighteen again, in the water not far off the shore of Nantucket. He was lost, disoriented, destined for death—all because he'd been foolish and impulsive. He wouldn't have survived if it weren't for his father, who appeared as the waves pulled Cody under.

His dad hauled Cody toward the shore, close enough to ensure his son's safety. But the waves were fierce, and seconds later, the current captured his dad.

His father had said not to get in. "The winds are strong tonight," he'd said. "Stay out of the water."

But Cody was stubborn. And angry. And he had something to prove.

He'd proven nothing except that he was a stupid kid, same as every other cocky kid who couldn't handle the sea.

"The Coast Guard was there in a flash," Maggie said. "They tried to save Jackson, but he couldn't grab on to the ring, so they had to move on to the next survivor."

Cody winced. Nobody ever wanted to have to make the decision of whom to save first, but that was protocol.

"By the time they got Jackson out, he was unconscious. They aren't sure how long he went without oxygen."

"He's in a coma," Louisa said. "Has been ever since that day."

"Sounds like an accident," Cody said, aware that a lot of accidents could've been prevented. So many accidents were the result of one foolish decision.

"The winds are strong tonight. Stay out of the water."

"It was, but Jackson's parents were devastated, of course. They were angry he was the last one to be pulled from the water, especially because the other boys were all stronger swimmers," Maggie said. "They fired off a few accusatory remarks aimed at the Coast Guard."

"And the guardsman who'd saved Jackson fired back," Louisa said.

Cody frowned. Didn't sound like any of the Coasties he knew. They were trained to handle themselves. They were trained to rise above the criticism doled out by grieving loved ones.

"Who was the guardsman?"

"Aaron Jessup," Alyssa said.

"I know Jessup," Cody said. He'd been on the boat with them that morning. Cody was a little surprised they hadn't transferred him out of Nantucket. "What did he say?"

"All he said was it was really dumb for those kids to be out swimming at night and even dumber for them to be drinking," Alyssa said. "He wasn't wrong."

"It was insensitive," Louisa said.

"But it was true," Alyssa said. "You don't go swimming in the ocean in the dark when the water is that choppy. You're just asking to get killed."

The words hung there, and Cody tried to swat them away, but he couldn't. They were the smack across the face he didn't want or need. After all, the reminder of his own poor judgment was as fresh as an open wound thanks to his present company and location.

Louisa's jaw went slack as if she wanted to say something but couldn't find the words.

Cody cleared his throat and pushed his chair away from the table. "I should go."

"So soon?" Maggie stood.

Cody glanced at Louisa, aware that his abrupt departure would say something about himself to her. It would say, *I'm not over this yet. I haven't forgiven myself yet. I haven't forgiven you, either.* Even so, he couldn't sit at that table for another second.

"I just came to make sure Louisa was okay," Cody said. "But I have work to do." He nodded at Louisa, then at Ally. "Thanks for the meal."

Maggie shuffled behind him as he strode away, making quick work of the distance between the kitchen and the front door, as if he couldn't get out of there fast enough. Because he couldn't.

She was talking, but he wasn't listening. Something about a bonfire or a party—and then she added, "I expect you to come visit me now that you're on the island."

He gave her a wave and walked out the door, practically racing down the stairs of the little cottage and out to his Jeep. He started the engine and drove around the block, aware that Maggie stood on the front porch, watching him go. He didn't need to be watched. He needed to be alone.

It was everything. This island. Seaside. The story of this kid. Louisa nearly drowning.

Coming here had been a mistake. And he needed to figure out a way to undo it.

~

Dear Dad,

I'm sitting in the backyard of our house in Chicago. I'm wearing that black suit Mom picked out for my last homecoming dance—you remember, the one that I can't stand? I didn't want to wear it today, either, but they said it was important to dress appropriately for a funeral.

They asked if I wanted to say a few words about you or share a story or a memory, but I said no. I hope that's okay. I guess maybe I just didn't feel like sharing. Maybe I wanted to keep my memories for myself.

Or maybe I feel so guilty over what I did that the thought of standing up there made me feel like a phony.

Mom doesn't look the same. It's like someone sucked all the life right out of her. She's pale and sad all the time, but she's also angry. I don't know if she's mad at me or you or Lou or Lou's parents or everyone. Maybe it's everyone.

Everything's changed. We're moving. We sold Seaside. I'm looking for a job to help out where I can, but nothing is the same anymore.

I know you did what you did because you love me, but I wonder if you realized how hard it would be to live with the guilt of what happened.

Maybe it would've been better if I had been the one who drowned.

Maybe then none of this would hurt so bad.

Can you ever forgive me?

Cody

CHAPTER EIGHT

"YOU SHOULD'VE TOLD ME," CODY SAID. "It would've been nice to know what we were up against."

It was the day after his impromptu dinner at Louisa's, and Duncan sat behind his desk. "Let me remind you which one of us is in charge. Before you forget yourself."

Cody straightened. He was dangerously close to being out of line, and he knew it. His master chief might give him more leeway than most ranking officers would, but even Duncan had a breaking point.

Cody drew in a deep breath. "Apologies, Master Chief."

Duncan motioned toward the seat opposite his desk. "I intended to fill you in on everything I knew, but you had a pretty eventful day yesterday."

That was fair. It had been quite a day. And Cody hadn't exactly been mentally present for their conversation.

"Can you fill me in now?"

"I'm assuming you heard about the kid in a coma."

"Yes."

"And about Jessup's remarks?"

"Yes."

"Then you already know everything."

"Is this why they brought you in?" Cody asked.

"No, but this is the mess I inherited when the guy before me retired. We've got an image problem."

Cody sighed. "Great."

It was hard sometimes to get communities to listen to their instructions as it was, but if they had an image problem, it would be even more difficult. They needed people to listen; otherwise they would end up with more tragedies like Jackson Wirth.

"I know you're not much of a people person, but I'm going to need your help on this," Duncan said.

Cody's hands inadvertently fisted around the arms of the chair. "Yeah, you said that. But what am I supposed to do?"

"We need to fix the way the community sees us. I need *you* to fix it."

Cody stifled a groan. "This is not my area."

"Well, it is now," Duncan said. "There's a company here we can hire to help with the logistics, but we need to get out in front of this thing."

"Isn't it a little late for that? The kid has been in a coma for months."

Duncan leaned forward in his chair. "I think we've got an opportunity here."

"Meaning?"

"The community loves a good story, and yesterday you gave them a good story."

"I did my job."

"Shall we split hairs on whose job you actually did?" He stared at Cody with an arched brow.

Point taken. Cody should've been written up for his actions on the boat yesterday. A Coastie does what he can to save a swimmer in distress without entering the water. Had they exhausted all possibilities before he went in after Louisa? Probably not.

"To the rest of the world, you're a hero. They don't know that as the XPO, you really shouldn't have been the one in the water. To them, you went above and beyond, and that's what people need to know about us. We'll do whatever it takes to save a life. Even risk our own."

"That's the job."

"Right, but the general public doesn't always think that. Thanks to Seaman Jessup, they have a totally different opinion of us."

Cody frowned. "I have to believe most people are smarter than that. They're not all sheep—they can make up their own minds."

"Regardless, we need to get out in the community. We need to become more of a presence, maybe even hold an event or two where we mingle with the islanders. If they get to know us, they'll respect us. If they respect us, they'll listen to us. They'll die less."

"Sounds like you should've hired a community events coordinator," Cody said. "You know I wouldn't have applied for that job."

"I got a better idea," Duncan said. "We marry the Coast Guard with the community. We work together on a few events to get our name out there, but we work with people in the community. I thought about putting someone else on this, but after yesterday, after the way people are responding to you saving that girl, I knew it had to be you."

"I'm not so sure about that," Cody said, though he was absolutely sure this was a terrible idea. What he needed was to be transferred off the island. Not to cozy up with the locals and weasel his way into their community. He preferred to keep people at a distance.

"I'm sure," the master chief said. "Now, you can head out today and run a few drills with the guys." He slid a light-blue business card across the desk. "Be here tomorrow at 0900. We'll meet with them, and they'll help us get a game plan."

He picked up the card. *The Good Life.* "What is this?"

"Event planners. People who are better at this stuff than we are."

"That could be anyone," Cody said. "Because everyone is better at this than I am."

"You're going to be just fine," Duncan said. "Do you need to talk to someone about what happened?"

Cody stilled. "Why?"

Duncan shrugged. "It's important to process these things so they don't pile up on you. Sometimes a guy needs to unload."

"I'm fine," Cody said. A lie if he'd ever told one, but Duncan didn't need to know that. Cody didn't want to talk to a therapist or Duncan or anyone else. He wanted to stop thinking about Louisa's cold body, about the initials and hash marks tattooed on the inside of his arm. About the hovering memories that followed him wherever he went on this island.

Not thinking was the only way he'd survive being stationed here—but he wasn't sure how to make that happen.

~

Louisa woke up with a bad headache and an achy body. She should probably stay in bed another day, but she was too restless. Two days at home with Maggie had been more than enough.

The old woman had returned with a coffee cake and now bustled around the house, pretending to be busy.

Louisa glanced at the clock. Ally had scheduled a meeting at nine thirty, and she needed to prepare. She didn't even know who the client was.

"I could stay around and help out this morning," Maggie said as Louisa not-so-subtly moved her toward the front door.

"I'll be fine," Louisa said.

"You shouldn't be working so soon." Maggie stopped at the front door—*so close*—and stood unmoving, like a boulder lodged down deep in a crack in the earth.

"You know I can't afford to turn anything down right now."

"Well, you can't afford to die either," Maggie said.

Louisa wasn't so sure. If she died, she wouldn't have to face all the feelings she'd been having the past couple days.

"Really, Mags," Louisa said. "I'm fine. Now go. I have a meeting."

She stared at Louisa in that pointed way she sometimes did when she wanted to make it clear she saw straight through her. "Are you okay, Lou?"

Louisa waved her off. "I told you. I'm fine."

"You said that when Eric broke up with you too," Maggie said. "And we both know that was a lie."

Well, that hurt.

"I broke up with Eric," she said lamely.

"Tomato, tom-ah-to. You're not the greatest at dealing with your emotions," Maggie continued, as if she had a personal mission to unravel Louisa's sense of calm, which was barely intact in the first place.

"I'm fine," Louisa repeated for the third time. "But I won't be if you don't leave."

Maggie studied her, no doubt trying to decide whether she was going to cooperate. Finally she said, "Promise me you'll take lots of breaks."

"Go home, Mags." Louisa pushed open the screen door.

Maggie started to walk out, then turned and faced her. "You'll call if you need anything."

"Sure."

"That wasn't a question, you'll notice," Maggie said.

"You go home and rest," Louisa said. "You need to take care of yourself, too."

Maggie waved her off. "I'm sturdy, and I'm already dying. You've got a few years left in you."

"I wish you wouldn't talk like that," Louisa said.

Maggie laughed. "You don't like the truth, do ya?"

"It's not the truth," Louisa said. "Don't you believe in miracles?"

Maggie stepped forward and clasped her hands around Louisa's. "'Course I do. It was a miracle the handsome Mr. Boggs found you out there—that I'm sure of."

"Then it can be a miracle that saves you too."

Maggie squeezed, then patted Louisa's hands. "I'll call you later."

With Maggie gone and Alyssa in Cape Cod picking up supplies for the Timmons anniversary party, Louisa had time to tidy the office and prepare for her meeting. She knew nothing about the prospective client, and her conversations yesterday had been about everything except work. Maggie had practically forbidden anything that might bring on stress.

But now she felt unprepared.

Alyssa had texted her that morning. Do you want me to reschedule this meeting?

No, I'll be fine.

They needed every possible client they could get. The Good Life was still relatively new, still building a strong client base. Failure was not an option.

It was as if Louisa needed to be successful on behalf of all women who weren't being taken seriously in the professional world. Women who were deemed too funny or cute or quirky or whimsical. Women with their heads in the clouds, who loved adventure. Women with boyfriends who didn't believe in them.

Turning down a job would be unwise. The paycheck wasn't a sure thing anymore, so she needed to be smart. Her accident had come at a terrible time. Why couldn't she have almost died at the end of the season, when she'd already stockpiled enough cash to last a few months? Then maybe she could've afforded a few days off.

The Good Life did a ton of business online—it was where most of her leads came from—but when she had meetings, she held them in her home office. The office had a separate entrance, and she'd decorated it carefully in the same cottage style as the rest of the home, but with a slightly more upscale feel. For instance, none of the furniture had been purchased from anyone's yard.

There was a desk positioned in front of two large windows, built-in shelves on either side.

She'd chosen summery colors for the space—teal, salmon, sea green—filling the room with Nantucket-inspired artwork, like a framed watercolor map that hung on the wall next to her diploma from Boston University and an old photo of Louisa and her parents on the dock only a short distance from the cottage's backyard.

Come to think of it, Daniel Boggs had snapped that photo.

She walked around to the other side of the desk and sat down, shaking the mouse of her computer until the old Mac sprang to life.

She tried not to think about the fact that the computer was probably in its last year and that soon she'd have to find a way to buy a new one, and instead clicked over to her email.

She'd deleted several junk emails without reading them when her eyes fell on one from McKenzie Palmer, a local woman who wrote a blog on all things "ACK." If McKenzie wanted to hire The Good Life to plan an event, it could mean huge things for a somewhat-new private concierge business.

She clicked on the email.

Dear Miss Chambers,

I heard about your brush with death and the Coast Guardsman who saved your life. I've been wanting to branch out a little and feature local stories of heroism on my blog, and I wondered if you might be willing to share your story with me? It could be great exposure for you and your little business.

Time is of the essence. If we're going to do this, we should get something out before people lose interest and the next swimmer nearly drowns.

Sincerely,
McKenzie Palmer

Louisa's eyes darted back to the words *little business*, and she tried not to let them irritate her. Maybe it wouldn't be as bothersome if she hadn't heard it before.

If McKenzie wanted to feature her business, that would be one thing, but telling the world she'd stupidly gone out into the choppy and unsafe waters without a life vest? No thank you.

She clicked Reply and started typing:

Dear Miss Palmer,

Thank you so much for reaching out. While I appreciate your interest in my story, I think I would prefer to keep this one to myself. If you'd like to discuss The Good Life or any other aspect of Nantucket, however, I would be excited to connect.

Have a wonderful day,
Louisa Chambers

The knock on the door reminded her of the work she should've been doing. Thankfully, she wasn't nervous. She found these initial conversations easy to navigate. She told prospective clients about her business, she listened to what they needed, gave them some ideas on how she could help, and then she usually followed up with an estimated breakdown of services and costs.

It was based off of the work she'd done at the hotel—work she'd been very good at. She only hoped the nearly dying thing didn't cramp her style today. Would she even be able to concentrate?

She walked to the door and smoothed her blue sundress, straightening her white jean jacket and noticing her toenails needed to be repainted already.

As was customary, she whispered a silent *Help me nail this one, Lord,* and opened the door, surprised to find two men in blue uniforms on the other side.

Cody Boggs and a man she didn't recognize.

"What are you doing here?" she asked without thinking.

A surprised expression washed over the other man's face, and Louisa quickly pivoted.

"I mean, if you're here to check up on me again, I really am fine.

I have nothing but high praise for the Coast Guard in the wake of my accident."

"Louisa—"

"I know you guys have an image problem on the island, but you won't hear a negative word from me. In fact, you won't hear anything from me. I just got a request to talk with a very popular blogger here on the island, and I turned her down." *Why am I still talking?* "I don't need to share the gory details of my stupid mistake, but if you need me to help make you guys look better, I can try to figure out a way to do that without tanking my own reputation. Or telling my father what happened."

Both men were frowning now.

"Louisa, this is Master Chief Duncan McGreery."

"You brought the master chief? Was that really necessary?"

"We aren't here to talk about the accident," the master chief said. "May we come in?"

"I have a meeting; I'm sorry."

"I set up the meeting with your assistant. Or your business partner?" The man smiled warmly. "Alyssa Martin?"

Louisa pulled out her phone and opened the calendar, realizing she really should've made that—and not McKenzie Palmer's email—her priority for the morning. "You're my nine o'clock?"

The master chief's smile held tight. Meanwhile, Cody's expression could only be described as terse.

"I'm sorry. I misunderstood." No matter how many times she made a fool of herself, it never got any easier.

"May we come in?" the master chief asked again.

"Of course." She stepped out of the doorway to allow them to pass, first Duncan and then Cody, who leaned toward her and said, "You talk too much," so quietly she was certain his superior didn't hear.

She closed the door behind them and willed herself to stop acting like an idiot.

I am a professional. I am good at my job. I just want to tell him how sorry I am.

That last thought slipped in without her permission. She swatted it away.

"How can I help you gentlemen?" Now she'd switched to full-on formal. It was a wonder she didn't spin in a circle and emerge dressed in a designer business suit fit for a sixty-year-old woman.

Judging by Cody's stance, he wanted to be here as much as she wanted him here. Following orders again, she assumed.

"Please, have a seat."

Her palms were sweating. She remembered her plan to invite his family to Maggie's birthday party. His family and her family and him and her. Suddenly it all felt like one giant ridiculous idea. She couldn't even sit in the same room with him without sweating.

But it was for Maggie. It would make Maggie happy, whether the old woman knew it or not. And Louisa needed the closure. She needed to at least try to make it right.

How can I make this right, Lord?

Her so-called prayers were feeling frantic these days, but she hoped God could sort through her neuroses and send her answers.

Anytime, Lord.

"I'll get right to it, Miss Chambers," the master chief said.

"First things first," Louisa interrupted. "Can you tell me what to call you? Because in my mind I'm calling you 'the master chief,' which is a long title that takes up quite a bit of space, but I want to be respectful."

"Call him Master Chief McGreery," Cody said, clearly annoyed.

"Oh, even longer," Louisa said.

"You can call me Duncan," he said. "I'm not much into titles."

"Isn't that disrespectful?" she asked.

"Not at all." Duncan smiled.

"Yes, it is," Cody said. "At the very least call him Chief."

Louisa glanced at Cody, then back at the other man. "I think I'll call him Duncan." She thought of a list of things she'd like to call Cody, too, but she kept those to herself.

"What should I call you?" Duncan asked.

"Louisa," she said. "Or Lou. Most of my friends call me Lou."

"It suits you," Duncan said.

Her eyes drifted back to Cody, who apparently didn't share his master chief's kind demeanor.

"I'll get to the point, Lou," Duncan said.

Cody stiffened.

"As you mentioned, we have an image problem."

"Sorry for the rambling," she said.

He held up a hand and smiled again. This guy was the perfect person to handle their image problem. He was handsome, kind, and he had a lovely set of very white teeth. At his side, Cody looked miserable and grumpy like a man auditioning to play Scrooge in a community theatre production of *A Christmas Carol*.

Any director would cast him, too.

"We would like to improve our reputation here and our relationship with the community."

Louisa forced herself to listen as the master chief explained his hopes for the Coast Guard as it related to the people of Nantucket. Of course the Coast Guard had been a presence on the island for years, but the goal was to integrate more with the locals, the idea being that if they won the respect of the people, the people would be more willing to listen and therefore obey the advice of the Coast Guard.

Advice like "Wear a life vest."

"You know about Jackson Wirth and our issues there," he said. "We've come under fire, and his family isn't about to let it go, not as long as their son is in a coma."

"Would you, sir?"

Duncan paused, a thoughtful expression on his face. "You don't beat around the bush, do you?"

Cody's eyes were full on her—she could feel it—and she didn't like the effect it had on her. Louisa was confident in this space. She knew her business, and she knew what she was good at.

If only that confidence carried over into her personal life, where she was something of a disaster. Sometimes she felt like two people occupying the same body. One, smart and self-assured. The other, full of doubt.

"I don't like to, no," she said.

"That's refreshing," he said. "Too many people tend to hold back what they're thinking."

She dared a glance at the neatly dressed Coastie at Duncan's side. Cody held back everything he was thinking, didn't he? Whom did he tell his secrets to?

"You think the Wirth family is justified in their criticism of the Coast Guard?" Duncan asked.

"I think they're hurting—grieving—and people sometimes say and do things they don't mean under those circumstances," Louisa said.

Her mind wandered back to the day after Daniel Boggs drowned.

"This is your fault, Lou!" Cody had shouted at her, face red and splotchy from crying. "You're the reason my dad is dead."

Those words still haunted her sometimes. Not only because they stung, but because she believed them. She absolutely believed it was her fault, and she'd spent her whole life trying to make amends for that.

It's why she had to repair what was broken. She had to bring their two families back together. She couldn't bring Daniel back, but at least she could try to put the people he loved back together.

Or maybe Daniel wouldn't want that. Maybe he'd want his wife and kids to walk away from the Chambers family and never speak to them again.

She'd never know.

"So how do we fix it?" Duncan asked. "We'd like your help improving our community relations, restoring our reputation. We want to do good on the island."

"You do," she said. "The haunted house at Halloween. The Valentine's Day dance."

"You're right, we do, but I'd like to go above and beyond. Is there something more we can do to increase visibility, connect with people on a personal level?"

Louisa sometimes felt like an idea machine. While she didn't always know how to go about implementing things, she never wanted for good ideas. She'd always considered that her one true talent.

"What if you did a fundraiser for the Wirth family?" she suggested.

"A fundraiser?" Duncan looked intrigued.

"Sure," she said. "Someone organized a clambake for them when the accident first happened, but it's been months of medical bills, and I'm sure they could use the extra support."

"What kind of fundraiser?"

Louisa didn't often organize fundraisers. Her business was more about arranging Nantucket dream vacations—fishing excursions and delightful accommodations—or finding the perfect chef to cater a party, those kinds of things. People hired The Good Life for any number of tasks—Alyssa coordinated many of the daily errands they were contracted to do. One client had hired them to arrange his move off the island to South Carolina. Another one hired them to oversee the design aspects of her home renovation.

"Let me give it some thought," she said. "I'll talk with my team—" the "team" consisted of her and Alyssa, but they didn't need to know that "and get back to you in the next day or so?"

Duncan nodded. "You can send your ideas to Cody. Or maybe you two could just get together again in a few days? I've put him in charge of this project, so he'll be your contact."

She glanced at Cody, who looked like he'd rather be having his wisdom teeth extracted. Handsome, friendly, jovial Master Chief Duncan McGreery had made crotchety, crusty Cody Boggs the face of the United States Coast Guard on Nantucket? Should she tell him it was a mistake?

Louisa and Ally prided themselves on being able to handle just about anything that came their way—and they dealt with a lot of difficult personalities. Still, she'd bet money that working alongside Cody would be her biggest challenge yet.

She considered turning the job down, but that was impractical. She desperately needed the work. She wasn't at a point where she could be picky, especially not with a reason as lame as "I don't want to have to deal with this man or the way I feel when I'm around him." For pete's sake, she was an adult, whether Eric believed it or not.

Cody would have to get over it. Why did he insist on being so crabby toward her anyway? Everybody liked Louisa. She was utterly likable. He was the one with a less-than-personable demeanor.

"It'll be great press for the two of you to be working on this project together, given your history," Duncan said.

Louisa frowned, while the crease in Cody's forehead deepened. "Our history?" she asked.

Duncan looked confused. "You almost drowning, him saving your life."

Her heart steadied, but only slightly. "Right," she said.

"Okay, we'll leave you to the brainstorming, unless you think you might benefit from our help?" Duncan shifted forward on his chair.

"No, that's okay," she said. What she meant was *There's no way I can think with Cody staring at me.* "I do my best thinking when I'm alone." She stood. "I can work a few ideas up and get them to you by Friday."

She ignored the red flag waving at the back of her mind.

She had the Timmons anniversary party Friday night. She was overpromising. She might've even been overselling her abilities a little because she wanted to look good in front of the first boy she'd ever loved.

Great. She was officially a ninny. That's what Maggie called girls who made senseless decisions because of boys. Ninnies. She'd never thought of herself as a ninny before, but here she was, acting like one.

Seconds later, she was walking both men toward the door. They said their goodbyes (she was *very professional* if she did say so herself), but as soon as they were gone, she dropped into the nearby armchair and buried her face in her hands.

This summer was turning out to be a disaster, and it wasn't even June.

CHAPTER NINE

LATER THAT DAY, CODY STOOD IN THE KITCHEN of his small apartment, provided by the United States Coast Guard. He had unpacked his one duffel bag the day he arrived, but he'd yet to touch a single box or figure out a way to furnish the place. As it was, the only thing he'd had time to get was a bed, an armchair, and a small television.

It was quiet. Too quiet. And he hated it.

He called the base. Duncan answered. "Boggs, you're off duty. Don't you know how to relax?"

Cody didn't say so, but no, he really didn't.

"You live on an island. Go for a swim. Fish. Kayak. Go out with some of the guys. But you're done working today."

Cody couldn't be sure, but it seemed like his master chief was still concerned about his well-being. As if he'd never rescued someone from the water before.

He was fine. Never mind that saving a life always reminded him of the ones he'd lost. He turned his arm over and studied the tattoo on the inside of his bicep—hash marks underneath two simple letters, D. B.—a painful but important reminder of why he chose this life in the first place.

Duncan hung up, and Cody plopped down in the lone armchair and sighed. He didn't like sitting still. He needed to get out and do something. He changed into his running shorts and an old Nike T-shirt, tied his shoes, and headed out the door.

He'd run. That would clear his mind and give him a way to fill time for the next forty-five minutes or so. He'd figure out what to do with the rest of the day when he got back.

But ten minutes in, Cody realized running the streets of Nantucket didn't clear his head; it clouded it. So many memories inched their way into his mind, and soon he found himself jogging toward their beach.

Not Brant Point, not the space where he and Louisa had made that ridiculous pact to meet on the day of their golden birthday, but *their* beach. His family's beach. That's what he'd called it after they moved into Seaside, because that's how it had felt.

It had felt like he'd hit the jackpot. It was every kid's dream to spend their summer days like that—running through the sand, diving into the surf, eating hot dogs off the grill and ice cream from the Juice Bar.

When his dad died, it wasn't only that he lost his father—he lost everything. They lost everything. The cottage. The beach. The dream.

Everything changed that day. Because of him. Because Cody had been foolish and impulsive.

He ran toward the spot—the place where they'd pulled his father's lifeless body from the water. Cody could hear his own screams echoing in the air overhead, mixing with the sound of his footfalls on the pavement. He stepped off the road and into the sand. His calf muscles tightened at the extra resistance.

Off to the side, something glistened, right near the spot where his father had drowned. He slowed his pace, aware of his struggle to get a deep breath, but he wasn't sure if it was because he'd pushed his pace or because his heart simply couldn't function properly in that space, looking at that ocean, that spot, with those memories infiltrating his brain.

Still, he pressed on, moving toward whatever it was that glimmered in the sun. A cross. An expensive-looking stone cross with flecks that reflected the light had been planted in the ground like a gravestone. When he reached it, he discovered that at the base of it was a small brass marker with the words *In Loving Memory of Daniel Boggs. Husband. Father. Friend.*

His vision blurred the longer he stared, confusion rippling through him like a wave on its way to shore.

His father was buried back in their Chicago suburb, and his mother had only wanted to forget they'd ever been on Nantucket, so she certainly had nothing to do with this marker. Daniel had been well-liked—loved, even. He was that kind of guy. The kind of guy Cody could never be. One who enjoyed people, enjoyed talking, always eager to help. Cody hadn't inherited those qualities. He found people difficult to connect with, though sometimes he wondered if that was a result of his circumstances.

Who had he been before his father died? Was that the man he was supposed to have become?

This was all too much. Too much introspection for one day. The run was supposed to help him forget this kind of emotional garbage, but it wasn't working.

He knelt down and ran a hand over the cross. It was sturdy. How long had it been there? His hand brushed against something on the back of it. He leaned around and saw something affixed there, a small piece of paper. There were no flowers, no other markings to indicate anyone had been there recently—but whatever this was said otherwise.

He removed it from the cross, not caring if he was invading someone's privacy—this was meant to memorialize his father. Didn't he have a right to know what it was?

It was a small card, about the size of a business card. One side was blank, and the other had been written on with black marker.

It read: *Miss you, Danny. IOU.*

Cody frowned.

The white card appeared to be new, like it hadn't weathered a single rainstorm. Like it had been put there recently.

But it had been nearly twelve years since his dad died. Who on the island still remembered enough to come down to this mysterious memorial and leave a note? And where had this cross come from in the first place?

His stomach twisted. Did he want to know?

He reread the words. *Miss you, Danny.*

His mind rushed back years. He and Louisa were lying on giant beach towels and their parents were all lined up underneath one of those beach tents meant to keep out the sun.

Cody had never understood the point of those tents. The reason you went to the beach was to be in the sun, wasn't it? He and Louisa were tired and quiet, and they could overhear their parents' conversation, reminiscing about a summer years before when they'd all first met.

It wasn't uncommon for them to retell this story. They told it to Cody and Lou. They told it to each other. They loved to think about—and romanticize—the way they'd become "the Fab Four."

"You all have me to thank," Louisa's mom said, her Southern drawl so lazy he thought it might put him to sleep. "If I hadn't dumped Danny, none of us would be here."

Cody's dad let out a hearty laugh. "That's not how I remember it, Joey."

Louisa squinted at him. "Why does she call him Danny?"

"Why does he call her Joey?"

They both rolled their eyes then at the silliness of their parents, who were all good-natured about the way their friendship had begun.

Daniel and JoEllen met in a business class at Boston University. They were assigned to work together on a group project and hit it off right away.

"He was smitten with me," JoEllen said.

Cody didn't say so, but he thought it was rude of her to talk like that in front of his mom.

Louisa groaned. "She's so full of herself."

"Not too smitten, or he wouldn't have set you up with me." Warren laughed.

JoEllen swatted her husband on the shoulder, and Cody noticed his mom stayed quiet. She didn't like thinking or talking about Daniel and other women. His father must've sensed it because he wound his arm around his wife and squeezed.

"Everything worked out just as it was supposed to," he said, placing a tender kiss on Marissa's temple.

JoEllen smiled at Marissa. "I knew you two would be perfect together."

Daniel and JoEllen had apparently realized they were better off as friends, and they stayed that way for months. And then they set each other up with their now spouses, Warren and Marissa.

Marissa had been a roommate of JoEllen's, though she confided in Cody once that they were great roommates because they had so little in common. Warren and Daniel were fraternity brothers. The rest was, as they say, history.

They weren't the normal kind of family friends, however. They were so much closer. Cody was positive that Daniel would've jumped in the ocean to save every single one of them if they were being overpowered by the waves.

Why couldn't it have been someone else he'd been saving that night? Why did it have to be Cody?

He shook aside the memories, the sound of his father's laughter dancing on the waves, and turned his attention back to the cross in front of him, the note in his hand.

Lots of people loved his father, but only one person that he could think of called him Danny. JoEllen Chambers.

What if . . . ?

He shouldn't have come here. He didn't need anything messing with his memory of his father. In his mind, his father was the real hero. His father was the one who jumped in to save him in the middle of the choppiest waters they'd seen that summer. His father was the one who gave no thought to the fact that he'd warned Cody not to swim, no thought to the fact that Cody had disobeyed. He was the one who braved the waves and the rip currents and the darkness to save his son's life.

He was the one who died.

Cody stood, tucked the card in his pocket, and gave the cross one last, lingering look as if staring at it could provide answers. Whoever had been here had known his father enough to want to keep his memory alive. They missed him enough, even all these years later.

He turned toward the road and started running again, unsuccessfully willing the questions to stop. So much for clearing his mind. All this run had done was create more confusion.

Unfortunately, he could come up with only two people on the island who might be able to help him.

And he was in no hurry to dredge up the past with either of them.

CHAPTER TEN

"WHAT DID THE COASTIES WANT?" Alyssa had returned from the Cape and now stood in the office where Louisa had set up her Big Dream whiteboard.

The whiteboard had been with her for years—It was a staple in her creative process. Anything and everything she thought of could go up on the whiteboard. Even if an idea didn't make it past the board, it often cleared the way for an idea that did.

Currently the whiteboard was empty.

"You could've told me it was the Coast Guard I was meeting with," Louisa scolded.

Ally looked sheepish. "You might not have taken the meeting if I'd done that."

She wasn't wrong.

"So what did they want?" Ally stood in front of her, looking put together and proper, as she always did. Somehow she managed to put up with Louisa's tendencies toward the opposite, and Louisa was grateful. She knew The Good Life would really be floundering if it weren't for Ally's business sense.

Louisa filled her in on her meeting with Duncan and Cody, and when she finished, she drew Ally's attention to the blank white-board.

"I see you've made progress," Ally said.

Louisa sighed. "I think almost dying was bad for my creativity."

"You think?"

The door opened, and Maggie walked in. "You've been back here for hours. You need to take a break."

"I need to figure out a fundraiser idea for the Coast Guard," Louisa said.

Maggie furrowed her brow, and again, Louisa wondered what would be the least offensive way to buy the woman a pair of tweezers.

"What've you got so far?" Maggie plopped down as if she'd been invited to do so. Louisa wondered if the old woman ever planned on going back home.

Louisa glanced at the whiteboard.

"What are we raising money for?" Ally asked.

"Jackson Wirth's family," Louisa said.

Ally frowned. "That's a bad idea."

"Why?"

"Because the Wirth family has been very outspoken against the Coast Guard."

"Right, so we're taking the higher ground here," Louisa said. "It's good PR."

"Good PR would be doing that interview with McKenzie Palmer." Ally sat on the couch and crossed one leg over the other.

"How do you know about that?" Louisa moved to the other side of the desk and sat. She didn't like feeling cornered.

"She called me," Ally said. "Look, the Coast Guard needs to expand their reach in the community, but so do we, Lou."

"I agree, but not at my expense." Louisa's accident made her feel foolish—why would she want to plaster that all over the Internet?

"Well, we at least need to get it out there that you and Cody are working together on whatever this is."

"No, we don't." Louisa leaned forward, arms on the desk. "That's the last thing we need to do."

"Are you kidding? People will go crazy for the idea. You working on a project with the man who saved your life? People will eat it up. Everyone loves a good romance."

"This is not a romance," Louisa said. "This is business. Right now I need you to focus on ours."

"Fine, but you're missing out on a great opportunity."

"And a great guy," Maggie added.

Louisa disagreed. She needed to think. She needed to fill the whiteboard with ideas, the same way she had a million times before. "Can we focus, please?"

Both women hesitated, then finally relented.

"We could do a 'Men of the Coast Guard' calendar?" Alyssa suggested. "I'd buy that."

Maggie waggled her fur babies. "Me too."

Louisa rolled her eyes. All right, so she was on her own.

For whatever reason, that intimidated her for the first time she could remember.

~

On Friday morning, after hours of brainstorming, Louisa drove toward the Coast Guard office, eager to present the men with several options she'd finally come up with for potential fundraising ideas.

Every Valentine's Day, the Coast Guard held a community dance, and it was always a big hit—that was the kind of event they needed here. Something that would draw in the community, make the Coast Guard look good and effectively raise funds for a very worthwhile cause.

She had a handful of ideas, but one in particular that excited her.

The idea had been Maggie's. Apparently the old woman had been inspired by a rerun of *Gilmore Girls*.

"Did you ever watch that show, Lou?" Maggie had asked her as she shoveled a spoonful of coleslaw into her mouth.

"'Course I did," Louisa told her.

"Then you'll agree my idea is a winner."

In the end, Louisa did agree, but she wasn't about to say so. Instead, they spent another two hours brainstorming possibilities, and all she could think was *Cody isn't going to go for any of these.*

Now she parked her teal Vespa outside the Coast Guard station at Brant Point and inhaled a sharp breath. Before she could remove her helmet, she glanced up and saw McKenzie Palmer standing outside the building—and at her side, Cody Boggs.

Louisa wanted to run for cover, but it wasn't like her Vespa was easy to hide. Did these sweet little motorbikes come in camouflage?

She watched with a little too much curiosity for a long moment as McKenzie tossed her head back, flipping her perfectly styled long blonde waves and resting a hand on Cody's bicep.

Gross. How obvious could she be?

But even as she had the thought, it occurred to her that Cody was smiling. At McKenzie Palmer. And they looked really lovely together.

She got off the bike and pretended to be searching for something in her cross-body bag, purposely turned away from the scene playing out in front of her.

"Louisa Chambers, as I live and breathe."

McKenzie had a Southern accent. It was curious because as far as Louisa knew, the woman was from Iowa, but who was she to judge? Though she thought if a person was going to fake an accent, it would be smarter to pretend to be British. That accent was simply delightful. But this put-on drawl of McKenzie's? No thank you.

Yet the woman had influence in the community and especially online. Louisa couldn't afford to make an enemy of her. Not that Louisa had enemies.

She turned to face McKenzie.

"Did you come down to thank your hero in person?" McKenzie's smile spread across her face like cream cheese on a bagel.

Great, now I'm hungry.

"I've already thanked him," Louisa said.

"He sure is hunky," McKenzie said. "Single, too. I asked." She raised her eyebrows. Unlike Maggie, McKenzie Palmer *had* invested in a pair of tweezers. Her neatly coiffed brows matched her perfectly groomed everything else. She looked like she'd just stepped off a magazine shoot. And judging by her blog, she most likely had. Sometimes Louisa wondered if McKenzie had hired a photographer to follow her around all day, snapping photos of her posing on the cobblestone streets of Nantucket. Seriously, who took those photos?

"Have you thought any more about my story idea?" McKenzie asked. "This whole damsel-in-distress thing won't last forever."

"I'm not a damsel in distress," Louisa said. She was perfectly capable of taking care of herself. She didn't want to be reduced to one of those women who needed a man to swoop in and save the day.

But if Cody hadn't swooped, she would've died. The weight of that might never escape her.

"XPO Boggs said he'd talk to me." McKenzie's expression turned wry.

"Great. He's full of stories, I'm sure." She tried not to sound sarcastic. She didn't try hard enough.

"You really should be more grateful to him, Louisa," McKenzie said. "He's a hero. An *actual* hero, and you're not the only person he's saved."

Maybe not, but Louisa knew it likely mattered very little how many people Cody saved. He hadn't saved the one person who mattered most. That was probably what drove him in the first place.

"I have a meeting, McKenzie," Louisa said with a wave. "Nice to see you."

"You, too," she called out in her singsongy voice. Louisa couldn't be sure, but she thought two or three chirping sparrows circled around McKenzie's head as she walked away.

She turned back to the station and inhaled a sharp breath. *Here goes nothing.*

The melody of "My White Knight" from the Broadway musical *The Music Man* drifted through her mind as she strode toward the door. She groaned. She didn't need old-time love songs in her head right before she sat down with Cody Boggs.

She walked inside the station and instantly felt out of place. She shouldn't have agreed to meet here. She should've insisted he come back to her office so she could pitch her ideas.

"Hey, you're that woman." One of the guardsmen stood a few yards away. "The one we saved the other day."

Oh yeah, this would be fun.

"That's me," she said.

He grinned at her. "You got lucky."

Luck had nothing to do with it.

"I'm here to see XPO Boggs." She'd stolen his title from McKenzie. Truth was, she had no idea what Cody's rank was or what it meant, but nobody needed to know that.

"'Course you are," the man replied. "All the pretty ones want to talk to Boggs."

"Louisa?"

She turned and found Cody standing in the doorway of what she could only assume was an office.

"We can meet in here." He took a step into the nondescript room, furnished with a desk, two bookshelves, and a window that faced the ocean.

She stood awkwardly in the doorway. "I like what you've done with the place."

He eyed her for a split second, then motioned toward the chair on the opposite side of the desk. "Have a seat."

He clearly didn't have time for witty banter today, which was a shame because she felt especially witty at the moment.

She did as she was told and felt suddenly self-conscious about the plan she'd concocted for this fundraiser. Maybe she should scrap the whole thing and start over. Go home. Work on the final details of the Timmons anniversary party. Come back to this with a clear head.

"So?"

She found him watching her, which would be off-putting if it wasn't so nice.

"Louisa?"

She drew in a breath. "Sorry. It's odd, right? Being in the same room again?"

"It's just business," he said.

Right. Business. So why did it feel like something else entirely? Why did it feel like an audition to earn a spot back in his good graces? Or a reality show gone terribly wrong?

"I have another meeting in half an hour," he said.

"Are you this sweet to everyone, or did you save the sugar for me?" she asked without thinking. Sometimes she really wished she had better control over her mouth.

His eyebrows shot up.

"Sorry, forget I said that."

"Forgotten."

"Right." She took out the small folder she'd put together outlining her plans. "I have three ideas, but there's one that I think is the strongest."

"XPO Boggs" leaned back in the chair, and the expression on his face seemed to say, *Impress me.*

She wasn't sure anything she had to say at this point would impress him. Odds were, he was going to hate this idea. He was a guy, so he wouldn't understand it. And that made her job that much more difficult. She not only had to execute the fundraiser; she had to convince him to let her.

It would be easier if he wasn't staring at her *like that.*

She told herself to calm down. He was just a guy.

A guy who'd saved her life. A guy who'd stolen her heart a whole lot of years ago. A guy she couldn't stop thinking about, no matter how mean he was to her. A guy she desperately wanted to win over and also desperately wanted to kiss.

"You're zoning out."

She blinked three times, quickly, and tried to focus, aware that she'd never felt this strongly about Eric in the entire eighteen months they'd been together.

She set the papers on the desk and fixed her gaze on him. "I don't make a habit of going on the ocean without checking the weather," she said without thinking. "I'm usually very good about it, in fact. I try to do something active every day—it helps my business if I have firsthand experience of things to do on the island."

"That sort of backfired on you." Now he was just being smug.

"Obviously."

"I'm thankful we were there when we were," he said with the sort of finality meant to end the conversation.

"Yeah, me too," she said. "I wasn't too keen on the whole dying thing."

He looked like he was considering smiling but thought better of it. At least she could imagine he wanted to smile, even if he was still wearing that morose expression. What did this guy do for fun anyway?

"You should've worn a life vest."

"I know," she said. "But I wasn't going out far. I was in what is usually calm water, the same area where people swim."

"The ocean is pretty vicious when it wants to be," he said.

She stared at her folded hands in her lap. "You know when I was out there, certain I was about to drown, I thought about you."

She didn't dare look at him. He didn't say a word.

"I thought about your dad."

"Louisa, we should talk about this fundraiser."

She took his point. *Don't talk to me about my dad.*

"Right. Of course." She cleared her throat. "I think you're going to love what we've come up with."

CHAPTER ELEVEN

"I LOVE IT," DUNCAN DECLARED.

Duncan had told Cody this fundraiser project was his, but as soon as he saw Louisa sitting in the office, he pulled up a chair and listened to her pitch.

"Yeah?" Louisa beamed at the compliment.

Man, she was pretty. No wonder Cody had taken it so hard when she broke his heart. Losing her was like losing something precious— and he knew it, even when he was eighteen, even before that, if he was honest.

"It's brilliant. Make it happen." Duncan's smile was wider than necessary in Cody's opinion. Did he have a thing for Louisa?

The master chief was five years older, divorced, and he supposed, a good prospect for a single woman. But not Louisa. *Not his Louisa.*

"Good work, Miss Chambers." Duncan stood. "I knew we were right to come to you."

And now she was blushing. Did *she* have a thing for Duncan? Why did he feel like he should give them privacy?

Get it together, Boggs.

He cleared his throat. "We're really doing this?"

Louisa's smile faded. Somehow he'd become the wet blanket in the room.

"Go over the logistics and come up with a plan," Duncan said. "This is gonna be good." He took out his phone and typed something as he walked out—a tweet, no doubt. One of McGreery's other brilliant plans had been to start a Twitter account for their station.

Never mind that it was working. People were paying attention to the videos and tweets, and his master chief was increasing their visibility on the island. It was one of his strengths. It was not one of Cody's.

"So how do we do this?" Cody asked.

Louisa shuffled some papers around, and a white envelope fell from the folder in her hand. It slipped across the desk, and he saw his mom's name written in a frilly script. Louisa quickly stuffed it back inside the folder.

"What was that?"

"Nothing," she said.

"Louisa?"

"You know the whole time we were growing up, I don't think you ever called me Louisa except . . ." Her voice trailed off.

He remembered.

It was the night of their first kiss. Their sixteenth birthday. Their parents had thrown them a party, and they'd snuck two extra pieces of cake and were eating them on the dock out back, their first moment alone.

They had a ritual of spending the last moments of each birthday together, eating cake and exchanging their birthday wishes. The wishes had to be written down—one of Louisa's rules. Her other rule? They each got up to five wishes. He told her that was greedy. She said it wasn't too much to ask since it had to last a whole twelve months.

She handed him a slip of pink paper, and he set down his slice of lemon cake with almond cream cheese frosting (Louisa's favorite), then handed her his small piece of paper. She set down her slice of strawberry cake with homemade strawberry frosting (Cody's favorite), and then she smiled at him.

That smile—it did him in. He had no doubt it could light up the midnight sky. He also had no doubt he was a goner. His little crush had become so much more, but telling her? It had been a dumb idea—misguided and foolish.

But it was too late, and he knew it. No way she was going to give his paper back to him now.

"Ready?" she asked.

He thought about all the previous years when they'd done this. His wishes had ranged from "Drive a dump truck" to "Visit Greece." Hers had ranged from "See Justin Timberlake in concert" to "Live in Nantucket year-round."

Every single one of her wishes was in a box in his closet, and he was pretty sure his were in that big old hope chest in her bedroom. And since they were always on Nantucket for their birthday, the wishes stayed here. As if that was where they belonged. It was their thing.

What if the words he'd written this year ruined that?

"Can I make one change to mine?" he asked.

"No way, Boggs," she said. "Once it's handed over, it's a done deal."

Louisa was his best friend. Was he making a terrible mistake?

"Here we go," she said. "On the count of three."

He nodded. She counted. On "three," they both opened their papers. Cody's was scrawled on a sheet of scratch paper he'd found by the phone in the entryway. Louisa's was neatly typed and printed from the computer in her father's office.

Louisa's said:

Lou's Wishes on the Day She Turns Sixteen

1. See the Rockettes at Christmastime
2. Convince my parents to get a dog
3. Buy a car
4. Tour Italy
5. Tell Cody how I really feel about him

Cody's paper read:

Cody's Big Dreams on the Day He Turns Sixteen

1. Get a car
2. Learn to play the guitar
3. Qualify for state in two swimming events
4. Take the sailing trip with my dad
5. Get up the nerve to kiss Lou

He reread her last wish. *Tell Cody how I really feel about him.* How did she feel about him? Slowly their eyes met. Something inside him shifted. Her baby blues were trained on him, and in that moment, everything changed.

"Louisa." He'd whispered her name—not because he thought it was sexy, but because he was so nervous, his voice didn't come out.

She smiled shyly, which wasn't like her. It made his head spin.

"You don't have to get up the nerve," she said. "I'd love it if you kissed me."

His heart flip-flopped. He'd only ever kissed one other girl, Sydney Markham, on a dare. It hadn't been pleasant. He was pretty sure he was bad at it, and she was definitely bad at it. But that didn't stop him from wanting to try again.

He leaned across the dock until their faces were nearly touching and she smiled. "Finally."

Their lips met, and he drank her in. She smelled fruity and tasted like strawberry frosting. If it hadn't been his favorite before, it sure was now. His lips searched hers for several seconds until he pulled away. "Finally?"

She grinned. "I've got a crush on you, Cody Boggs."

From that day on, they weren't just friends. They were so much more.

How stupid he'd been to think it would last forever. Nobody found love just following them around on the beach. It didn't work that way.

He was older now—he knew better. He'd dated plenty of women to confirm his suspicions on the subject—love, the real thing, was fleeting and hard to find. In fact, there was a reason he was still looking for it, though he wasn't looking very hard. He'd practically made up his mind he was better off alone.

It's not like he was good company.

Now, sitting across from Louisa, a world between them, he forced himself not to romanticize old times. He'd be smart to think about how everything ended—and why he hadn't spoken to Louisa Chambers since.

But it was hard to think about those things under her watchful gaze, with a million questions begging for answers.

"Why do you have an envelope with my mom's name on it?"

She hugged the folder to her chest. "Can we just talk about the fundraiser? Please?"

"Louisa."

"Maggie's dying, Cody."

The words were like a swift punch to the gut.

"She's dying, and it's almost her birthday, so I'm planning a big party for her." She paused. "Your family should be there."

"She's dying?"

Louisa nodded slowly. "Congestive heart failure."

Maggie had always been there, for Louisa especially, who had a tortured relationship with her own mother. Maggie was a Nantucket mainstay. She'd been born and raised on the island, and according to his parents (and Louisa's), she used to "take in strays"—that's what she called people who had no one else on the island. People like their parents when they were younger. People like Louisa now.

It was Daniel who'd first brought the old bird into their lives, and once she was there, she refused to walk out. She was intent on taking care of them, and in a way, they took care of her too. After all, Maggie never had kids of her own.

If what Louisa said was true, they were all about to suffer a great loss.

He let out a heavy sigh. "This isn't a good idea."

"Look, whatever happened, it didn't involve Maggie. She was important to all of us. She's still important to me. And if there's any way I can make this happen for her, I'm going to."

"My mom's finally in a good place, Lou."

Her eyes shot to his at the sound of her nickname on his lips. *Old habits.*

"Maybe leave her out of this."

She shifted. "Let's talk about the fundraiser."

He knew in that moment she wasn't going to let it rest. Louisa Chambers didn't let things rest. It was against her very nature to give in. She'd gotten an idea in her head, and there was no way to convince her it was a bad one.

"So the Inaugural Jackson Wirth Coast Guard Regatta," she said.

"That title could use some work."

Her forehead crinkled. "Be quiet. It's a great idea. Your master chief even said so."

"Good luck getting the rest of the guys on board."

Her face fell. A chink in her confident armor, and he'd been the one to put it there. Nice.

"What is your business again, exactly?" He tried to keep his tone from sounding irritated.

Louisa snapped her jaw shut and looked at him. "The Good Life," she said.

"But what do you do?"

"It's a private concierge business."

"Does that include planning fundraisers?"

"Not usually, no."

He squared off with her. "Then why are you doing this?"

She tucked the paper with her typed-up notes about the fundraiser back inside the folder. "It's a good job."

"And what, you need the money?"

"Of course I do," she said. "I just started my business a year ago."

"But you had enough money to buy Seaside?"

She shifted. "My grandpa passed away."

"I'm sorry to hear that."

"He left me some money."

"So you bought our old cottage?" Why was he pressing the issue? He didn't care. It was great for her to live there—it was all in the past. But then maybe it wasn't. Maybe knowing she was living in the last place he'd seen his father alive had burrowed its way under his skin.

"I'm sorry, Cody."

"Just tell me why, Louisa."

She didn't respond. Really, what could she say? No reason would be good enough, and she probably knew it. She should've left the cottage in someone else's hands and she should leave his family out of the plans for Maggie's party.

He'd call his mom and tell her about Maggie's health. She and his sister could say goodbye their own way. Louisa had no idea what they'd all been through. How long it had taken them to find a new normal. And he wasn't about to tell her because it was none of her business.

"I should go." Louisa stood. "I have a big anniversary party on a yacht tonight."

He stood too.

"I'll be in touch." She started for the door, but before she walked through, she stopped, reached into her bag, drew something out, and turned back toward him.

"It would mean a lot to Maggie if you came." She handed him a white envelope. On it, in the same frilly handwriting, was his name.

She didn't make eye contact before she turned and left the room. But once she was gone, a part of him wanted to call her back in. Because as angry as he still was, there was something about Louisa that made him feel at peace.

And he hadn't been at peace since the day his father died.

CHAPTER TWELVE

THE TIMMONS ANNIVERSARY PARTY went off without a hitch. The older couple couldn't have been more complimentary to Louisa and Ally.

"We nailed it," Ally said, halfway through the party.

Louisa murmured a reply, but mostly she couldn't stop watching the beautiful couple of honor. They were surrounded by friends and family. Children and grandchildren and siblings and people they'd known their whole lives.

Four members of their wedding party shared memories of that happy day fifty years prior, and Mr. and Mrs. Timmons beamed.

Louisa had hosted parties before, many of them celebrating a wedding anniversary. Sometimes the couples seemed to be putting on airs. Throwing a party to make themselves look good in front of their friends. Once, she caught a husband upstairs in a compromising position with his daughter's college roommate while his wife accepted congratulations from a house full of guests.

But the Timmons family was different. They were the kind of family Louisa wished she had. Genuine and honest and loving.

Around eight that evening, as the sun hung low in the sky, sending light like shimmering diamonds across the ocean, all the boats in the harbor began honking, and the people on board clapped and cheered in celebration of the sweet old couple who'd loved each other for over fifty years.

It was a little surprise Louisa had planned for them, and they were both equally delighted when they realized the honking and clapping were for them.

The captain had brought their yacht to the exact location Louisa had asked him to, and seconds later, fireworks started in the sky above the island. More cheers from the Timmons family rose into the night air, filling the sky—and Louisa's heart. *This* was why she loved her job.

She slipped away toward the stern, honking and shouting mixing with the crackle of fireworks overhead. Arthur and Tawny Morris waved as their sailboat passed. Louisa lifted a hand, waving back her thanks for their participation.

Another crack overhead drew her eyes, and as the firework disintegrated into nothing, her gaze fell, catching on the Coast Guard rescue boat cruising slowly by. A rhythmic, overzealous pounding reverberated in her chest as her eyes scanned the men on the boat. The captain sounded the horn in celebration, and the Coasties cheered.

As the boat made its pass, her eyes locked on to Cody's and didn't let go. He stood still as a statue, near the back of the boat, watching her. Another honk. Another round of applause. Another firework.

And then the rescue boat grew smaller on the horizon until finally he was gone.

～

It had been over a week since Louisa had almost drowned, and she'd yet to sleep through the night.

The dreams that woke her were less like nightmares and more

like reliving her worst fears. Every time she closed her eyes, the waves forced her under again. Twice she'd woken up gasping for air.

Was this normal? Should she talk to somebody about it?

She attributed her stress to the fact that she had to give a presentation to the men stationed at Brant Point later that day. Her stomach turned at the thought.

She'd given dozens of presentations over the years. Pitch meetings with clients and business owners. In her previous job, she'd sold the hotel and all it had to offer along with her brilliant ideas for a perfect vacation or party to countless visitors and potential visitors.

But ever since she'd started The Good Life, ever since it had become her own business she was selling, a knot of worry had formed in her belly, and it tightened with every presentation or meeting. Today the knot had doubled because not only was she presenting her idea, she was presenting to the Coast Guard. She was presenting to Cody.

She'd spent the better part of the week floating from Maggie's birthday party to day-to-day errands for a client named Josephine Rebeck to dreaming about the Coast Guard fundraiser. She'd given Cody and Duncan the basics. She already knew Duncan liked the idea. Why was she so nervous?

She forced herself out of bed, showered, and dressed in a casual yet professional blue wrap dress and a pair of sandals with straps that twined around her ankles. She might've chosen the dress because every time she wore it, people complimented her bright-blue eyes, and she might've wanted Cody to notice them too.

Maybe.

She fastened the buckle on her sandal and gathered her notes. As she picked up the stack of folders on her desk, a white envelope fell out and landed on the floor.

She'd mailed all the invitations to Maggie's party except this one.

Something about the way Cody had asked her to leave his family out of the festivities had given her pause. Normally she would've ignored him and done what she wanted anyway, but he'd been so earnest.

She wondered—not for the first time—what their life had been like after Daniel had died. Cody had obviously channeled his pain into something good and become an expert swimmer who saved the lives of foolish people like her.

But what had become of Marissa and Marley? All Louisa knew was that after Daniel died, Marissa sold Seaside and moved the family back to Illinois.

Now wasn't the time to think of any of these things. She should be practicing her pitch. But she couldn't help it. Cody's return to the island had her mind reeling. Their families had been so close once upon a time. And their circle had always included Maggie. Cody's mom would want to know if the old woman was dying.

Wouldn't she regret it if she didn't get to say good-bye? Surely she, more than most, knew the value of a life.

But maybe Marissa was remarried with a new family now. Maybe she'd moved beyond all the sorrow and had found a way to exist without the love of her life.

Louisa's heart lurched at the thought. It seemed impossible. Their love had been so true. And it seemed wrong that Marissa not only lost her husband, but her best friends too.

She turned the invitation over in her hand. She'd found an address for Cody's mom through an online search. All the envelope needed was a stamp. This party was the perfect excuse to get them all together again. To clear the air. To say how sorry she was.

This was her chance to make things right.

She walked over to her desk, opened the top drawer, and found her book of stamps. She peeled one off and stuck it to the corner of the envelope. As she walked out, and before she changed her mind, she left the envelope in the mailbox with the flag up, made her way to her Vespa, tucked away the items she needed for her presentation, and headed off in the direction of Brant Point.

There was only the slightest niggle of concern that she'd made a mistake, but that wasn't too hard to ignore since her choice was easy to justify.

She pulled up in front of the station at the same time Ally arrived, thankfully double-fisting disposable cups from Island Coffee.

"You're my hero," Louisa said, taking one of the cups.

"Coconut milk latte, one packet of stevia." Alyssa's smile faded. "You look like you could use it."

"Thanks for the vote of confidence."

"Are you sleeping?"

"Not well." They walked toward the door, Louisa's nerves dancing a jig in her belly. "Not at all."

"Lou." Ally put a hand on Louisa's arm to stop her.

"I'm fine," she lied. "I've just been restless."

"You almost died, Louisa," Ally said. "You might need help processing some of that."

Louisa didn't want to think about it. She wasn't about to tell Ally that the accident was only part of what kept her up at night.

The door opened and Cody stood at the top of the stairs. *There* was the other part.

Cody hadn't opened the door because he saw them standing out there—that was obvious by the look on his face—but now here they were, staring at each other.

At her side, Alyssa let out a barely audible sigh.

"Hey." Cody wore his uniform today, and for a split second Louisa thought perhaps they should've gone with Ally's calendar idea.

Ally gave her arm a shove.

"Hi," Louisa said.

They moved toward the door. Cody stepped out of the way to let them through, and as she passed, she inhaled the unfamiliar scent of him. Manly, clean, woodsy. She liked it. When she'd known him all those years ago, he mostly smelled like sunblock, summer, and the ocean.

She'd liked that too.

But it also set her nerves on edge. *He* set her nerves on edge.

How was she supposed to be professional with him staring at her? And he would stare—that's what he did. He watched with such dark intensity she couldn't help but wonder what he was thinking.

Not that she really wanted to know. But oh, how she wanted to know.

"We've got you all set up in here," he said without even a hint of expression.

By contrast, Master Chief Duncan McGreery walked into the room with that wide smile that made Cody look like a grumpy old man.

"Good to see you again, Miss Chambers." Duncan shook her hand. "You look like you've fully recovered from your brush with death."

"Please just call me Louisa," she said. "And I'm doing well, thank you."

"Good to hear."

She looked down and saw he was still holding her hand. Cody's jaw twitched, and for a split second she wondered if he'd noticed it too.

"I'm Alyssa Martin." Ally leaned in toward Duncan. "But you can call me Ally."

Duncan squeezed Louisa's hand before reaching out and shaking Ally's. "Good to meet you. We're excited to hear where you've landed with your ideas. Cody, would you mind showing them in?"

Cody practically groaned. Okay, so he didn't groan, but Louisa imagined him groaning because the look on his face was like a visual groan that said, *I don't want to be here.*

Louisa would pour on a little extra charm, just for him. She smiled at Duncan, then followed Cody into the room where the other guardsmen were gathering.

According to what she'd read, there were twenty-five men stationed at Brant Point. While there had been women in the past, there were currently none. So she had to sell twenty-five men on an idea that would play much better with women. And she had to do it in front of Cody Boggs.

No problem.

She took her place at the front of the room while he made his way to the back wall, where he stood and stared with all the expression of a stone-faced statue. Well, this wasn't unnerving at all.

"I don't know if I can do this," she whispered to Ally.

Ally stopped shuffling the folders she was sorting and faced Louisa. "Yes, you can."

"Not with him standing back there watching me." She shook her head. "Don't look!"

She'd caught Alyssa mid–head turn, but it was too late. Her friend jerked her eyes back to Louisa's. "I don't think he saw me."

Louisa sighed. He'd definitely seen her. Ally was brilliant, but she was kind of a ditz.

"He's just a guy, Lou."

No. He was not "just a guy," and that was the problem. He was Cody. She'd broken his heart, and he'd saved her life.

But not just that. He'd done it so well. He'd done it in a way that had left her daydreaming about him. She never thought she was the type to want to be saved, but now that she had been, she wondered what other dangerous situation she could put herself in just so they could do it again.

"Are we ready, ladies?" Duncan stood beside them.

Ally glanced at Louisa as if to ask for an answer to the man's question.

Ally was right. She could do this. She'd done this so many times before. It's what she did. And she was great at it. She straightened her shoulders and smoothed her dress. "Of course."

Duncan got the attention of the other men in the room, and the murmurs quieted, all faces turned toward the two women standing at the front. All faces except Cody's. He seemed intent on staring out the window.

"If you've been around Nantucket, you might've heard of Louisa Chambers. She's a private concierge here on the island, and she and Alyssa Martin are here to help us improve our image in the community."

In the back, a man with dark eyes shifted in his seat. Louisa recognized his face. Aaron Jessup. His photo had been on all the blogs and in the newspaper after Jackson Wirth's accident. He'd done his job well. But then he'd screwed up.

She knew how that felt.

Nobody asked why they needed to improve their image. It was as if everyone knew, and the tension in the room rose because of it. Charming this crowd definitely wouldn't be a piece of cake.

"Louisa?" Duncan turned to her as if to hand over an imaginary baton. "You're up."

She forced herself to smile, though the nerves pulsing inside her made it very difficult to concentrate. "Good morning, gentlemen."

Was her voice as shaky as it felt?

Alyssa was passing around the beautiful handout Louisa had made the night before, outlining their ideas for the fundraiser. She stopped and looked at Louisa, a telltale sign that Louisa was not off to a strong start.

Ally gave her a look as if to say, *Get it together,* and Louisa forced herself to obey.

She closed her eyes for a quick second, drew in a tight breath—a mental reset of sorts—then started in on the pitch she'd practiced.

Within a few minutes, she had the skeptical guardsmen smiling, laughing, and yes, maybe even eating out of the palm of her hand. She was good at this, regardless of whatever XPO Grumpy thought of her. She had a self-deprecating way about her that people appreciated, and given the fact that this crew had saved her life only a week ago, it was easy to make fun of herself.

No matter how much the whole event still haunted her dreams.

"The goal is to increase your visibility in the community," Louisa said. "To get people to pay attention when you tell them to wear a life vest." She paused for a ripple of ironic laughter and made a face that let the men know she was their first offender, then continued. "Or to stay off the water. Our plan will foster goodwill on the island, and it will shine a light on the excellent and important work you all do."

Louisa picked up her iPad and opened it to her presentation notes, then outlined her plan for a Coast Guard–sponsored regatta. A full day on and around the water. The thought of it turned her stomach. Would she ever want to go back in the ocean again? She'd been reminded how brutal and angry it could be.

"The goal is to stack the whole day with activities people will want to participate in. There will be a number of races for serious sailors, as well as a few geared toward young sailors. The entire day will be an opportunity to get you in front of people. We can teach them about water safety, show them what to do if they find themselves in a precarious situation at sea, give tours of the base, that sort of thing."

"How is that going to make money?" a very young-looking guardsman asked.

"Well, that's the fun part," she replied. "There will be an entry fee for anyone who wants to sail, of course, and we'll have business sponsorships, but what we're most excited about—and what we think will be the biggest draw—is our 'Race with a Coastie' event."

A mix of reactions from the men in the room.

"Race with a Coastie?" someone asked.

"We're going to do an auction night," Louisa said, her confidence dwindling, but doing a decent job of faking excitement.

"So you're going to auction us off?" a guy in the front row asked.

"Basically, yes," she said.

"Cool," the guy said with a grin.

"People in the community will get the chance to bid on you, for lack of a better word," she said. "The highest bidder wins a chance to race with you on the day of the regatta. The auction will be a completely separate affair. Once the teams are formed, you'll need to have a couple of practices with your teammate, and then the day of the race, it's every team for themselves."

The men began chattering, and Louisa's nerves started to settle. Then she glanced at Cody and wondered if he was being paid to stand guard at the back of the room. He looked like a bouncer outside a bar, for crying out loud.

The other guardsmen seemed to like the idea, so Louisa let them talk for a minute while she drew in a deep breath and tried to avoid Cody's gaze. He was watching her now—she could feel it—and it sent electric impulses to every nerve ending in her body. She turned away and took a drink of water.

"What's the money going to go for?" someone asked.

Louisa set her water bottle down and turned around. Her eyes shot to Cody's—he likely knew this was a touchy subject for the men in that room. Still, his expression remained unchanged.

"We did a lot of thinking on that, too," Louisa said, feigning confidence. "We decided the best cause was the family of Jackson Wirth."

The previously noisy room quieted.

Then a chorus of "You're kidding" and "What did she just say?" and "Jackson Wirth, the kid in the coma?" echoed throughout the room.

"I know his family has been critical of the Coast Guard," Louisa said.

"They annihilated us," one of the guys said. "And all we did was our job."

In the back, Aaron Jessup crossed his arms over his chest. Okay, she knew this part would be hard. But she believed in her idea.

"Look," she said. "I understand what it's like to be criticized and have your name dragged through the mud."

"Do you, princess?" Aaron said. "Really?"

"Seaman Jessup." Cody's tone warned.

Jessup stood. "She doesn't have any idea what she's talking about."

"Sit down, Seaman," Cody said.

Louisa tried to tell herself he wasn't defending her—he was doing his job as an officer in the Coast Guard—but it didn't work. It felt like he was defending her. And that feeling was altogether too warm and fuzzy. A tingle shot up her spine.

He does care.

Jessup did as he was told, but he'd locked his glare onto Louisa so tightly she thought she might snap.

"Louisa?" Cody gestured as if to encourage her to continue.

"I understand this is a difficult subject," she said. "But I really do think it would go a long way in repairing the damage between the Coast Guard and the community."

"Seems like we're saying we've got something to be sorry for," Jessup said. "Like we did something wrong so we have to pay them off to try and make it right."

"But we didn't do anything wrong," the guy next to Jessup said.

Louisa didn't bother to point out that it was Jessup's thoughtless commentary that had caused them trouble in the first place. If he'd just kept his opinions to himself, none of this would've happened. One could argue that they did have at least their insensitivity to be sorry for.

"You saved those boys," Louisa said. "I know there were comments made during a heightened emotional state, but this is where we are now, with a community that needs to understand that what you do is important. They need to know you're here for them when they get into trouble and you're the resource to help them prevent an accident." She glanced at Cody. "With the recent heroism displayed by Officer Boggs, the timing couldn't be better."

"People really do love you guys," Ally said.

"The fundraiser is going to be a really fun, lighthearted way to get you guys out there," Louisa said. "You can let me handle the messaging regarding Jackson Wirth. I'll make sure it's clear why we're doing this."

The pause felt long and stubborn, and then—thankfully—a big guy in the back said, "Are we going to take bets on which one of us will bring in the most at the auction?"

The chatter started again. They sounded positive, excited even.

"We'll keep you posted on all the details," she said above the din. Aaron Jessup was still glaring at her. He broke eye contact, then stood and walked out.

"That guy hates us," Louisa said to Ally.

"I've always felt bad for him."

Louisa narrowed her gaze on her friend. "He dug himself into this hole."

"But I can understand why he said what he did. I mean, Jackson's parents were pretty critical. And ungrateful."

"He is going to make our job a lot harder."

Ally quieted and looked away.

"Good work, ladies." Duncan was beside them now. "XPO Boggs is your point person on this, but keep me in the loop and let me know if you need anything."

"We will." Louisa glanced at Cody, still standing against the wall at the back. "Thank you."

Duncan smiled at her. "You've done good work here. We're really looking forward to it. Why don't you send me some dates and we'll get going?"

"Sounds good."

He walked away, and Louisa turned toward Ally, but her friend was no longer in the room. She gathered her things together, stuck her iPad back in her bag, and said a silent prayer of thanks that she'd survived.

A tall guardsman approached her. "Great job today, Miss Chambers." He was probably a year or two younger than Louisa and handsome, with nice eyes. "Can I call you Louisa?"

"That is my name," she said politely.

"I'm Charlie," he said. "Charlie Pope."

"Good to meet you, Charlie."

She glanced back to where Cody had been standing, but the spot against the wall was empty. She felt her insides tense at not knowing where he was.

"Will you be bidding at the auction?" He leaned a little closer to her, his face warming, and *oh*, he was hitting on her.

She inched back slightly. "I don't think so. Feels like that might be a conflict of interest."

"It's for a good cause, though, right?" His eyes were full on her in a way that suddenly made her uncomfortable. She could charm anyone, but when it came to actual relationships with men, she was something of a failure. Her mother said she talked too much. She called it "nervous brain dump," and Louisa couldn't argue. She did seem to suffer from this very specific affliction.

"It's a great cause," she said. "I should go find Alyssa." She started past him, but he grabbed her arm to stop her. She looked at him, then at her arm.

"Sorry," he said, letting her go. "Just wanted you to know I'm hoping you bid on me." Another grin.

"Louisa, I'll walk you out." The voice from behind her was like a sound from heaven, as once again Cody Boggs swooped in to save her. She didn't even have to turn around to know it was him, strong and protective, like a guardian angel.

Normally her independent nature would've bucked at the idea of a man protecting her, but she couldn't help it—it made her insides tingle. Had he been watching out for her this whole time?

"Nice to meet you, Charlie," she said.

Charlie winked at her.

Louisa turned and found Cody standing there, waiting for her to pass but glaring at Charlie. She walked past him, and he followed her out of the room.

"For the record, winking at a woman is not cute. It's creepy." She laughed.

Cody didn't.

They were outside now, and Louisa realized she still didn't know where Alyssa had gotten off to.

"Do you want to tell me how great I did on my presentation?" She smiled.

He raised an eyebrow.

"Come on, don't pretend you don't think this is all going to be awesome."

"It was fine, Louisa. I'll see you later."

"Would it kill you to smile once in a while?"

"Have a good day." He turned then as if to end the conversation and disappear all at once.

"Okay, bye," she said with only a slight edge of sarcasm playing in her tone.

Ally came out of the station, passing him as he went back in. "What was that about?"

Louisa slung her bag across her body. "Cody being Cody, I guess."

"Cody being hot?" Ally waggled her eyebrows.

Louisa hopped on her Vespa and strapped the helmet on. "Cody being grumpy."

"Like I said."

Louisa groaned. "He can't stand me. He'll never forgive me, and having to work with him on this project is pretty much my worst nightmare."

Ally squeezed her arm. "Give him some time."

"It's been twelve years."

"Right, but you haven't been in each other's lives since then. Give him some time now to figure out how he feels."

"Oh, I know how he feels. That's the problem."

"Okay, so we could quit," she said.

"I never quit," Louisa said.

"Then figure out how to deal with him." Ally pulled her hand away. "I'll see you back at the office a little later."

"Fine," she murmured.

She started the Vespa, checked that her bag was secure, and sighed. *"Figure out how to deal with him."*

It seemed like it should be easy, but she knew better. Ever since he saved her life, the man had turned her insides out, and she wasn't sure how to right herself.

CHAPTER THIRTEEN

CODY DIDN'T NEED OR WANT A LOT OF TIME OFF. Time off in Nantucket meant time to think, and thinking was about the last thing he wanted to do.

But his schedule was two days on, two days off, with every other weekend free. Suddenly that felt like a lot of time to keep his mind occupied.

Now he stood in line at a new coffee shop on Washington Street. He figured if he only visited places that weren't here twelve years ago, he was safe. He didn't need his memories accosting him in public.

The place was busy. Maybe he should get out of the Coast Guard and open a coffee shop. Maybe the civilian life was the way to go.

But no. He'd joined to save people. To *do* something. And every day there was more to do. Every day, more people to save.

Five people lost. Six if he counted his dad. He always counted his dad. Six he couldn't save. How did he make amends for those?

"Hey, you're that guy." A woman sitting at a nearby table spoke loudly and, to Cody's horror, pointed at him.

He glanced around as if to indicate he didn't know what guy she was referring to.

She stood. "You're the guy who rescued that woman from drowning the other day."

Oh, so he *was* that guy. Heat rushed up the back of his neck and he wished he could turn invisible.

"You're a hero," she said with a wide grin.

"No, ma'am. Just doing my job."

A young boy with blond curls at the back of his neck clung to the woman's leg, arms wrapped around her waist. She knelt down and put an arm around him. "See that man, Carson? That man is a hero. He saved a woman's life."

The boy's eyes widened, and for a brief moment Cody felt like Captain America. But then the onlookers in the little coffee shop began to look at him, and that feeling got awkward in a hurry.

He tried not to notice the chorus of "That was you?" and "Wow! A real-life hero!" but within seconds, everyone in the coffee shop stood and began applauding him.

Cody did his best to wave them off, reminding himself that these people were simply being kind and appreciative. Never mind that his "act of heroism" had done nothing to fill the void he'd been working so hard to fill since that awful night twelve years ago.

The young woman behind the counter flashed a grin. It was his turn to order, but all he wanted to do was walk out. He reminded himself of the reason he was on Nantucket—to make the Coast Guard look good. How would it look if he bolted in the middle of his impromptu appreciation applause?

He turned to the crowd, lifted a hand, and said, "Thank you," though he doubted anyone could hear him above the ovation. Finally the clapping stopped. The talking continued, however, and Cody heard snippets of conversation—as the story of Louisa's rescue reverberated throughout the small coffee shop.

"What would you like?" the woman asked.

He ordered a large black coffee and a blueberry muffin to go.

She poured the coffee, put the muffin in a bag, and handed them both to him in record time. "On the house for the hero."

"That's not necessary," he said.

"Neither is saving lives, but you still do it." The woman shook the bag in his direction, the paper making that crinkling noise.

He took it, along with the hot cup of coffee, and thanked her, then started toward the door. If he'd been wearing a hat, he would've tipped it at the other patrons, but instead, he kept his eyes on the exit in hopes of a clean getaway, trying to ignore the constant chatter.

He'd almost made it to the door when someone said his name.

Cody turned in the direction of the man's voice and stopped moving. There, just inside the door to the Handlebar Café, was Warren Chambers, Louisa's father and Cody's dad's best friend.

So much for not being reminded of all he'd lost.

Warren had aged. He was grayer now, with thinner hair, and there were deep wrinkles around his eyes. But mostly he looked the same. And here he stood, staring at Cody, looking a little like he'd seen a ghost. Cody likely wore the same expression.

He shifted the bag to his left hand and extended his right hand toward the older man. "Mr. Chambers. Good to see you."

There was a tangible tension in the air—a reminder that things were broken between their two families—the kind only covered with the politeness of good manners. Cody didn't know much about the rift between Louisa's parents and his mom, but he knew his mom wanted nothing to do with them anymore.

At first he'd thought it was her grief reacting to Warren and JoEllen, like being with them was too painful, too great a reminder of what she'd lost. He'd assumed she would eventually come around—hoped for it, even. But all these years later, Marissa Boggs still seemed to have a chip on her shoulder where the Chambers family was concerned. This was why he hoped Louisa had the good sense not to invite her or his sister to Maggie's party.

Whatever had happened between the Boggs and Chambers families, it wasn't something any of them needed to relive anytime soon. And it wasn't something a fish fry on the beach could cure—no matter how much Louisa wished it could.

"That happen everywhere you go?" Warren's grip was firm as he shook Cody's hand.

"I can honestly say that's a first, sir."

The man released Cody's hand and straightened. "I gather you saved someone's life here recently?"

Cody felt the confusion spread across his face. "Yeah, that's right." It had been over a week and Louisa still hadn't told her parents what happened? That was so Louisa.

"A boater or . . . ?"

"Paddleboarder," Cody said, feeling like he was lying simply by omitting the details.

"Life vest?"

Cody shook his head.

"When will people learn?" Warren crossed his arms over his chest. "Someone said you're in the Coast Guard?"

"That's right. Since I graduated."

"Impressive. You're stationed here?"

"Yes, sir," he said. "Brant Point."

Warren nodded. "Can't think of a better place to live."

Cody could think of a hundred better places to live, starting with Siberia.

"Good to see you, son."

The word, a simple identifier, stopped Cody cold. Nobody called him *son*. Not anymore.

Warren clapped a hand on Cody's shoulder and walked toward the line at the counter.

And Cody tried hard to swallow the lump at the back of his throat.

～

Louisa wouldn't say that Maggie was a hoarder—at least not to her face—but the woman had crammed so much stuff into her cottage, it was a miracle she ever found her way to the front door.

Louisa had promised to help her sort through her things, and though neither of them said so, she knew it was because Maggie wanted to get her affairs in order before she became too sick to do so.

They could both see the end on the horizon. Louisa kept wishing that horizon further and further away.

"You hear back from anyone about my birthday?" Maggie asked, sorting through a box of *National Geographic* magazines that dated back to the seventies.

Louisa glanced down and noticed that so far, all the older woman had done was move the magazines from the box to a stack on the floor.

"Is that your giveaway pile?"

Maggie held up a magazine with a cowboy on the cover. "I can't give these away."

Louisa only stared.

"These could be worth something, Lou."

"To who?"

"To a collector. Let's list them on eBay."

Louisa groaned. She didn't have time to list this stuff on eBay, but how did she tell Maggie her house was full of junk?

"Maybe I should've had you wait till I was dead to go through all this stuff," Maggie said. "Then you could've just tossed it and I'd be none the wiser."

Louisa had had the same thought as soon as she showed up that morning and saw that everything normally stuffed in the two extra bedrooms of Maggie's cottage had been carted out into the living and dining rooms.

Why had she offered to help Maggie get things in order? Surely that had been a momentary lapse in mental clarity.

She looked up at the older woman and saw the sadness behind the grin she'd fixed to her face. Maggie didn't want to die, no matter how brave her face was. And it was important to Louisa to make sure the old woman knew her wishes were going to be carried out.

"I don't want a sad funeral," Maggie said as she picked up the stack of magazines and put them back in the box. She took out a Sharpie and wrote *eBay* on the side of it. Louisa sighed, but she had to admit, she was amused by the whole scene.

Maggie was unlike anyone else she knew, and she always had been. Louisa's father described the old woman as "feisty," and it fit her. She was knit into the fabric of Louisa's life the same way she was knit into the fabric of Nantucket. She'd simply always been there. Before she retired, Maggie was a postal clerk living in a house she'd inherited with almost no expenses. She never had kids, so she poured all her time and effort into other people's, including Louisa and Cody.

There were many families who loved Maggie, but none quite as much as the Chambers and Boggs families. Louisa had always appreciated the woman's no-nonsense outlook on life, her honest advice, and her unexpected kindness. While she wouldn't dwell on it now, Louisa knew she'd miss her terribly when she was gone.

"So, what, we should celebrate?"

"Yes," Maggie said. "I'll be with Jesus and you suckers still have to endure winter in Nantucket." Maggie's laugh turned into a cackle and then disintegrated into a cough.

A brutal reminder of the road ahead.

The cough worsened, and Louisa stood. "I'll get you some water." She stepped over the boxes and made her way to the kitchen, but a knock on the door interrupted her. She pulled it open, then stopped breathing at the sight of Cody, standing on the front stoop wearing workout clothes, his gray T-shirt darkened by his sweat.

Her breath returned and she let out a sharp exhale, the sound of Maggie's hacking an unwelcome reminder that she couldn't linger on his masculinity for another second.

"Come in. Sorry. I'll be right back." She hurried off to the kitchen, filled a glass with water, then rushed back through, motioning for him to follow her. She handed Maggie the glass, and the old woman paused long enough to drink.

More coughing. Another drink.

"Is she okay?" Cody asked, moving closer, his training obviously telling him he needed to do something.

"She will be," Louisa said, though the untruth of that statement didn't escape her. Today she probably would be. Tomorrow—who knew? She seemed to be getting worse.

Finally the cough subsided.

"Okay?" Louisa asked.

Maggie nodded and wiped her cheeks dry, handing Louisa the water glass. "That's what I get for cracking myself up."

"Why don't you get up off the floor?" Louisa set the glass on the table and knelt down beside Maggie, bracing her underneath her arm.

Maggie shifted, and Cody knelt at her other side. Together, he and Louisa helped Maggie up onto the love seat.

"We aren't done," Maggie said.

"We can take a break." Louisa perched on the sofa beside the old woman. "I'm tired of looking through all this junk anyway."

Maggie cackled again.

The old woman wasn't sentimental, so in spite of her own sadness, Louisa purposed to stay upbeat. She could cry later. And she knew she would.

Louisa glanced at Cody, who stood awkwardly, staring at them. She'd told him Maggie was dying, but seeing it firsthand was something else altogether. Concern had spread across his face, and Louisa's stomach ached at the sight of it.

He'd always been so good. So caring. So kind. Never mind that he now treated her like a pariah—at this moment, he reminded her of the boy she'd known all those years ago. The size of her heart doubled just thinking about that boy.

"Cody, can I talk to you in the kitchen for a minute?" Louisa asked.

He nodded, but before they could leave, Maggie grabbed both of their hands. "She's going to tell you that I'm dying."

"No, I wasn't," Louisa said. She was simply going to give him an out—a way to avoid having to watch any of this.

Cody looked from Maggie to Louisa and back again.

"I'm an old lady," Maggie said. "This is what happens when you get old."

"You're not that old," Cody said.

"Do you know that for sure?" Maggie winked at him. "I might be 102."

"Are you?"

"Feels like it today," she said.

"She might've mentioned something already," Cody said. "What do you mean, though, by 'dying'?"

Maggie let their hands go and tossed him an incredulous look. "Dying. Dead. Going to walk through the pearly gates. Do I really have to explain this to you?"

Cody sat in the chair next to the love seat, that line of concern still knit across his brow. He glanced at Louisa again, and she sank back down onto the sofa. The pause doubled in length, and Louisa shifted where she sat. Maggie draped a blanket over her lap and sighed.

"You really think they're going to let you into heaven?" Cody asked dryly.

Maggie and Louisa both glanced at him, and then the old woman let out a loud burst of laughter.

Cody's smile looked forced, and Louisa imagined his heart had broken a little too, lightening the tone and dealing with Maggie's reality the way she would want him to. She kind of loved him for that.

"We're sure this is a done deal?" Cody asked.

"Death?" Maggie said. "Yeah, it's pretty final."

"I mean, there's nothing they can do for you?"

"Nothing I'm willing to do."

Louisa had had a similar conversation with Maggie when she first learned about her illness.

"It's no use," Louisa said. "She won't be reasoned with."

Maggie clapped a hand over Cody's. "If I get to choose, I'm going out on my own terms, though it is a little disappointing since I never did start my charity."

Ah, the charity. Maggie hadn't spoken of it in ages, but it had always been her dream to found an organization to help under-privileged children. Maggie wanted to share Nantucket with every-body she could, and the charity would make that possible. When had she given up on that idea?

He gave her a firm nod; then Maggie leaned back on the love seat. "What brings you by today?"

Louisa had been wondering that herself. Was he here to talk about the fundraiser? Maggie's party? To tell Louisa he forgave her and wanted to rekindle all the love they once had?

What a stupid idea. She didn't need a man to be happy. Eric had taught her that. Eric, the crusher of dreams. She was far better off on her own.

Remember that, Louisa.

"I see you dressed your best to come calling." Maggie chuckled.

"I was out for a run."

The image of him running alongside the ocean, like a model in a commercial for men's aftershave, sprang to Louisa's mind.

"Why?" Maggie asked. "You only get a handful of years on this planet. Running seems like such a torturous way to spend them."

He smiled. A real smile. It was lovely. And it made Louisa's toes tingle. For the briefest moment she wondered what the stubble on his chin would feel like underneath her fingertips.

We are not believers in love, Lou, the sensible part of her brain reminded her.

She shoved thoughts of his skin aside while simultaneously won-dering how his face smelled after he shaved.

"You look like you have something on your mind," Maggie said, focused on Cody.

Did he? Louisa studied him for a moment while he was looking at Maggie—tough job, but someone had to do it.

He leaned forward, elbows on his knees, and stared at the ground.

Oh. Maggie was right. He *did* look like he had something on his mind. Maggie always had a sixth sense about the people she loved. She supposed Cody still fell into that category even though he'd been gone a long time.

It had to be difficult being back here after all these years. As far as Louisa knew, this was his first time back since his dad died.

How sad.

All at once his crabbiness seemed less about her and more about something much bigger. Her heart softened toward him. Was it wrong that she wanted to take him in her arms and hug that look right off his face? Or kiss him. Maybe she really just wanted to kiss him.

She shook the thought away and tried to stay in the room instead of daydreaming about something that was never going to happen.

"Out with it," Maggie said.

He shifted, then reached inside the pocket of his gym shorts (gym shorts had pockets?) and pulled out a small white business card.

Probably McKenzie Palmer's phone number and a request for him to call her.

He handed it to Maggie, and Louisa tried not to peek. But then she got so curious, she scooted closer and read the handwritten message, scrawled in black marker.

Miss you, Danny. IOU.

Louisa took the card and turned it over. Blank on the other side except for the spots where the marker had bled through. She scanned the card again. "Where'd you find this?"

Cody looked tense and out of sorts. Maybe he should request a transfer. This couldn't be good for him.

"Do either of you know anything about a memorial down at the spot where my dad died?"

"The cross?" Louisa asked, and when he nodded, she said, "Not really. It kind of just showed up at the end of one summer."

"When?"

Louisa's mind ran through the years. It had been odd when that cross went up because it wasn't something that happened immediately after Daniel's death. "It was about two years ago."

"So ten years after he died."

"Right." How had she not put that together? The cross went up around the tenth anniversary of Daniel's death. Nobody knew who put it there.

"Was it you?" Cody asked, eyes trained on Maggie.

Maggie stilled. "I wish it had been. I wish I'd thought to do that for your father. He deserves to be remembered."

He turned to Louisa. "You?"

She shook her head, longing for answers to soften that line of worry across his forehead.

It was strange. Daniel had known everyone on the island. He was charming and friendly and kind. He helped people whenever he could. But to see a memorial go up in the spot where he'd died without a single word—it had struck her as odd. She'd called her parents to tell them about it, and bringing it up seemed to upset her father. He and Daniel had been so close back in the day—Louisa thought maybe none of them had recovered from what they'd all lost.

But there was something else too, something about how quickly her dad changed the subject, as if talking about it was still too painful.

Shouldn't they be able to discuss Daniel's death by now? She and Cody weren't kids anymore, and her parents had had years to process it. But it remained the elephant in every room. The wall of tension that kept them all frozen in time, paralyzed by a past that had once been full of joy. How was it that joy could be so haunting?

She'd always wondered what she and Cody didn't know about the story because it certainly seemed like there was more to it than she'd been told. Why had her parents never reached out to Marissa in all this time? Why hadn't they reconciled? What was it that still kept them apart?

She could see Cody trying to sort out the possibilities—where would his questions lead him?

"Your parents?" Cody asked, sounding hopeful.

"I asked them," Louisa said. "They said no, and honestly that summer they didn't make it to the island until late in the season. I remember because they asked me to go down there with them. We left flowers at the cross."

"Do you think we could go talk to them about it?"

"They're still in Boston."

Cody looked at her, brow laced with confusion. "I just saw your dad at a coffee shop."

Louisa's heart sank. She wasn't sure if she was embarrassed to admit she wasn't close enough with her parents for them to tell her when they were back on the island or if she was simply hurt they hadn't told her they were here.

"You didn't know?" Cody's gaze was too intent.

"I must've forgotten," she said. A lie he'd surely see right through. "I can ask them again, I suppose, but I think they would've told me if they'd discovered anything." She realized the irony of that statement given the fact that they hadn't even told her they'd returned to Nantucket.

Did that mean they knew about her accident? Surely not—they would've shown up at the door the second they got wind of that. But she should probably tell them before someone else did. The thought made her groan. More proof that Louisa was a giant screwup.

After a long moment, he finally looked away. "Can you think of anyone who would've had that memorial made? Or anyone who might've left this note? It had to be recent—it looks brand-new."

Maggie drew in a deep breath. "A lot of people loved your dad."

"Right," Cody said. "But twelve years later?"

"It has been a long time." Maggie coughed again. "I really can't think of anyone in particular."

He sat unmoving for what felt like an eternity, then took the card back and stood. He tucked it into his pocket. "If you think of anyone or anything—let me know."

"You don't have to run off," Maggie said.

"I still need to unpack," he said.

She nodded. Cody glanced at Louisa, and she willed him to be okay, but he quickly broke her gaze and started toward the door.

"I'll see you out." She stood and moved toward him as if he needed an escort. As if he'd want it to be her.

He didn't, obviously, because he didn't even acknowledge her, but again, grace rushed through her as she reminded herself of all he'd been through.

He opened the door and hurried out, and she had to jog to catch up. "Cody."

He stopped but didn't turn, and for a brief moment, she admired the strength radiating from him. Muscles shredded by hours of training, arms that had saved numerous lives, including her own. And yet, mixing clearly with that strength was a vulnerability he was trying to conceal.

She walked around to stand in front of him, but he stared over her head, refusing her eyes.

"What are you not saying?"

His jaw twitched. Was he grinding his teeth?

"Nothing."

"I can tell something is bothering you."

He looked away. "I'll handle it on my own."

"You think your father had something to hide?"

Now he looked at her. "We all have secrets, Lou."

The words felt like an accusation. A decade-old wound reopened and exposed.

Cody took a step as if to walk around Louisa, but she moved at the same time and blocked his way. Once she'd blocked him, though, she realized she wasn't sure why or what she planned to say.

"Maybe I can help?"

His jaw twitched again. A sign he was either annoyed or uncomfortable—or both. She didn't care. He'd stopped trying to escape and she had his attention, and now that she was standing this close to him, her head felt dizzy and that fantasy of kissing him had come back.

Because his lips were full and they were *right there*. If she stood on her tiptoes, she was sure she could reach them . . .

"How?"

His gruff question was like a smack across the face, which she desperately needed given how ridiculous that rabbit trail had been.

"Well, I know everyone," she said. "I mean, that's my job."

"But you have Maggie's party. And the regatta. You don't need to try and track down some mystery person for me."

"Well, I won't do it by myself. You'd have to help me." She crossed her arms over her chest and waited for him to respond.

"Maybe it's better we leave it alone," he said. Another smack.

She took a step back, desperately needing space between them. "Okay." Something inside her called out, *Forgive me, please. I'm so sorry.* But the words didn't come.

"What would we do?" He seemed to be simultaneously loathing and considering this idea.

"Start asking questions, I guess. Dig around for answers. See who's still here that knew your dad."

"What would I do?"

"Grunt work," she said. "Get me coffee. Make me sandwiches. That sort of thing."

She couldn't be sure, but she thought for the faintest moment a smile played at the corner of his gorgeous mouth. And then it was gone.

"Fine," he said.

"Yeah?"

"I guess."

"Okay, when do we start?"

"Tonight?"

She frowned. "Really?"

He shrugged.

"Okay. I can come to you or we can meet somewhere."

"I have one chair," he said. "Can we meet at your place?"

"One chair?"

"I'm just one guy," he said.

In a flash, sadness washed over her at the thought of how lonely his life must be. How did a single guy make any temporary housing feel like a home?

"Louisa?"

She looked up at him, embarrassed by her sudden and overwhelming emotion, and righted herself. "Tonight then. My place. I'll even feed you."

"No, I'll bring dinner. Can you write up an estimate for your fee?"

"Cody, this isn't work. I would never charge you."

"It is work, Louisa. I'm paying or we don't have a deal."

She tried not to read into that, but all she could think was that this man didn't want anything between them to be confused. Business dealings only.

"So?"

She stammered something even she didn't recognize, but she must've been nodding because he said, "Great, see you tonight then," and began to walk away.

Helping him with the Coast Guard was great and all, but helping him with something personal—that was actual penance. A way to make things right. A way to make up for her mistakes.

Will you forgive me now?

"Cody," she said to his back.

He turned.

"We might find something you don't like."

His expression didn't change. "We might find something we both don't like."

"What do you mean?"

He looked away. "Forget it."

As if she could. "You're sure you want to start digging around in the past?"

"Yep."

He didn't wait for her to say anything else, and honestly, what would she have said? She watched him walk away, and once she got over the initial shock of their conversation, she took a moment to admire the man who used to be the boy who'd won her heart all those years ago.

She said a silent prayer that maybe one day she'd actually do something to earn his forgiveness once and for all.

CHAPTER FOURTEEN

LOUISA STOOD IN FRONT OF HER FULL-LENGTH MIRROR and surveyed her outfit. Was a blue cotton romper appropriate for a meeting that wasn't work but that she might get paid for with a man who wasn't nice but who was inherently kind?

She slid her polished toes into her gold sandals and buckled them around her ankles, then ran her hands through her long auburn waves. Maybe she was trying too hard.

There was a knock at the door.

Oh, well, not much she could do about it at this point.

She made her way downstairs and saw the outline of Cody's sturdy frame through the frosted window of her front door. He stared out across the yard, giving her just a moment to admire him.

He'd showered and now wore khaki shorts and a faded light-blue T-shirt with some sort of logo on it. They practically matched and obviously should take a photo tonight to prove how good they looked together, which was an absurd thought if she'd ever had one, given that the man could hardly stand to be in the same room with her.

But the blues were so perfect, it was like they'd planned it.

Would their children have blue eyes too?

Knock it off, Lou.

She opened the door and forced a smile in spite of the nerves wriggling around in her belly. "Hey."

Did she sound like she was trying to be sexy? Because she absolutely was not, but the accidental huskiness in her own voice startled her. She cleared her throat.

He held up a brown paper bag. "Dinner."

She opened it and inhaled. "Jetty burgers?" She glanced up and found him looking at her, same way he had all those years ago—with a twinkle of something special in his eye.

He remembered.

She'd forgotten how much she'd loved him once upon a time. Convinced herself first love never amounted to anything anyway. Except when it did.

How was it possible to have the same feelings hanging around so many years later? Nostalgia. That's all this was. Nostalgia and a desperate need to be forgiven. She had to get her thoughts under control. Her mind had a way of getting her in trouble. It was, after all, her mind that had convinced her Eric loved her.

But when you love someone, you are their biggest cheerleader, a champion of their dreams.

Eric had shown his true colors the second she told him about The Good Life. Then she went back and thought of the many little ways he'd made her feel small. Twice he'd asked her to "put on something more professional" when heading out to a work event. Once he told her not to laugh so much because it made her seem much younger than she was. And then there was the time he'd belittled her in front of a hotel guest because she was "incessantly chatty." "Mrs. Sandstone isn't your friend, Louisa. She simply wants her theatre tickets."

Louisa hated the way he made her feel. She was determined to never let anyone else treat her that way.

The thought twisted something inside her. She could never go through that again. She would follow Cody's lead and focus only on business.

She'd pretend it didn't even faze her that he'd gotten Jetty burgers. Her favorite. She liked them loaded with ketchup, pickles, onions, lettuce, and—she drew in another breath—"Did you get bacon?"

He appeared to be stifling a smile.

Louisa knew she had a long way to go at winning him over, but a stifled smile was a start. She couldn't let herself love him, but maybe they could at least be friends?

She moved out of the doorway and motioned for him to come in. He stood awkwardly in the entryway. They should've met somewhere public, somewhere with no memories attached to it.

"I thought we could eat out back," she said. Right, because there were no memories out there. She hadn't thought this through. "Or maybe in the kitchen?"

Years ago, when they were all together, they only ate indoors if it rained. Her mind spun back to one bright afternoon when she and Cody were about twelve. Her parents brought sides and dessert, but Cody's dad was always in charge of the main course. He called himself "the Grillmaster," and Louisa believed it. One year her family arrived on the island with a set of barbecue tools and a long apron they'd had printed with that title right on it.

Wonder what happened to that apron . . .

After a full day on the beach, Louisa's freckles had popped, her milky-white skin had burned, and she was ravenously hungry. Cody's shoulders were the color of darkened toast, and his hair had lightened in the bright summer sun.

They were out back when the storm started, and while everyone else ran for cover, Daniel stayed on the deck, flipping burgers and "saving dinner." Cody, Marley, and Louisa stood on the dry side of the glass door with her parents and his mom, motioning for Mr. Boggs to come inside.

"We'll make something else, Daniel! The storm is too bad!" Marissa called out, struggling to be heard over the fierce downpour.

Cody's dad waved her off as a crack of thunder shook the house. He raced around the cottage and into the garage, returning moments later with the biggest golf umbrella Louisa had ever seen. He balanced his spatula in one hand and the umbrella in the other, carefully flipping the burgers so no water touched them, but as soon as he closed the lid to the grill, he folded the umbrella, spun back to face them and grinned, letting the water soak him straight through.

Marissa opened the door a crack, and the water, which seemed to be coming down sideways, pelted the door. "Daniel!"

"Why are you all hiding inside?" he called out. "It's a beautiful day!"

He laughed that infectious, jovial laugh, and Louisa giggled. Her feet were bare, her pink toenail polish chipping at the edges. She wore her swimsuit and shorts and her hair was still damp from their long day at the beach.

She opened the door and raced out on the deck as Mr. Boggs hopped onto the grass, kicking up water from a puddle that had formed.

"LuLu!" he called out. "Are you the only other soul brave enough for a wild adventure?"

She let out a scream as she followed him into the yard and ran around, the rain soaking her, and then all of a sudden, he stopped and looked up at the sky, arms stretched out wide. "Feel that, Louisa?" he hollered over the sound of the rain. "That's God making everything new. No matter what, he can always make things new."

Ever since that day, when it rained, the words drifted through her mind, a quiet comfort, even on the days that felt overwhelming. *"That's God making everything new. No matter what, he can always make things new."*

How many times in her life had she relied on those new and fresh days? How many times had she been grateful for a second chance? She glanced at Cody, standing in the doorway of her kitchen, and thought maybe this was one of those times. A second chance. An opportunity to do better.

She glanced down and saw he was holding an unmarked box under his right arm. "What's that?"

"Some of my dad's stuff," he said.

The box appeared to be taped shut. "What's in it?"

"Not sure. I've never opened it before."

In a flash, she heard his screams, echoing through the past. She'd been there as they pulled Daniel's body from the ocean. She remembered the heartbreak on Cody's face, in his sobs.

"I'm so sorry, Dad. I'm so sorry."

The words sliced through her like an arrow, and all the sorrow of that moment returned in a beat. Cody didn't look at her as he set the box on her kitchen table. How many times had he moved over the years? And how many times had he packed this unopened box, hauling it from place to place?

The silence hung between them, thick like a cloud of sadness.

When he finally looked at her, she forced any expression of pity from her face. "Hungry?"

"Yep."

She got two plates from the cupboard as he took the burgers wrapped in white paper from the bag.

"You're not seriously going to use a plate, are you?"

Their eyes met, and she saw the memories playing out in front of them like a movie on a screen. When they were kids, they never bothered with plates. They pulled their Jetty burgers straight from the bag, leaving them partly wrapped as they ate. They dumped two orders of fries out into the bag and generously showered them with salt, sliding them through a shared blob of ketchup. It was a ritual, really.

She'd frozen in place, clutching the plates. Was she allowed to do things the way they'd always done them? She'd assumed it would annoy him.

But he sat down and set the burgers on the table, then dumped all the fries into the bag as if it were no big deal. And honestly, shared fries *were* no big deal. She should stop mentally making them into a big deal because he was clearly unmoved. This was just dinner between two people who used to know each other.

Two people who used to kiss each other.

"You okay?" He was looking at her now, and the realization threw her off-kilter for a second.

She forced a nod, then set the plates down and handed him the saltshaker, which he used liberally to make the fries even more delicious.

She then folded the bag and shook it up, coating every single french fry with as much salt as possible, rolled the top of the bag down, and set it between them. She glanced up and realized she was smiling. He quickly looked away.

She turned toward the fridge for the ketchup and swallowed the pesky sadness that had crept in uninvited.

It's not like old times, she reminded herself. No matter how familiar parts of this ritual were.

She sat across from him and unwrapped her burger, inhaling the greasy goodness and trying not to calculate how much extra time she'd have to work out tomorrow in order to account for all these calories.

She took a bite. The calories were worth it.

They ate in silence for several seconds, and then finally Louisa couldn't take it anymore. "It's probably weird being back here, huh?"

Not what she'd intended to say, but at least it filled the space.

He swallowed the food in his mouth and reached into the bag, pulled out a wad of fries, and shrugged.

"You're eating all the fries," she said.

"Better step up your game then."

Her eyes locked on to his, and for a fleeting moment they were friends again.

"Probably weird living in my old house," he countered.

Her turn to take a handful of fries. She shrugged.

So far this conversation was the equivalent of driving around a cul-de-sac.

"I always liked this house," she said.

He took a swig from the bottle of water she'd set out before he arrived but said nothing.

"It had started to fall apart a little," she said. "I guess it was important to me to fix it."

"Why?" He'd stopped chewing. What had she done to earn his full attention? She wanted to know so she didn't do it again.

Should she tell him the truth? That she'd made such a mess of things that she felt like she owed it to his family somehow to protect the space that had been theirs? That she'd spent the majority of her life trying to make up for foolish mistakes that felt so petty and ridiculous now but that had such a harmful effect on so many people?

"Are we going to talk about this every time we see each other?" she asked instead.

He didn't answer.

"I liked the house," she said. "I wanted to keep it from becoming an eyesore. That's all."

"That's all?"

She paused. "There was a lot of happiness here once. Maybe I was trying to hold on to a sliver of that too."

"Did you?"

"Sure," she lied. "Nothing but happy times since I moved in."

He popped the last bite of his burger into his mouth and rolled the paper into a tight ball. "Should we get started?"

She glanced down at her half-eaten burger and set it aside. "Uh, sure."

He pulled the box onto the table in front of him and ripped the tape off as if it were a package he'd ordered from Amazon.

But as soon as he took the lid off, she could tell by the look on his face that he hadn't expected the sucker punch of emotion that washed over him. She hadn't expected it either, but her eyes had filled with tears.

He glanced up at her and put the lid back on the box. "I just remembered I've got to get down to the station and check on some stuff for Duncan."

She frowned. "Cody."

He stood, picked up the box, and walked toward the front door. She followed him but said nothing, aware that this was a battle he would have to fight on his own. And fearing with almost 100 percent certainty her presence only made things worse.

As much as she wanted a chance to make things right, the best thing she could give Cody right now was space. Because what he needed was very different from what she wanted.

Knowing that almost broke her heart.

CHAPTER FIFTEEN

THIS WAS A BAD IDEA.

Cody stormed out of Louisa's house, which still felt a lot like his house, and drove the Jeep back to his place, trying not to think about the box on his front seat.

They'd left Nantucket in a rush after his father died, but once they got home, they had to leave that house behind too. There was no money.

Cody could still remember hearing his mom on the phone with someone he could only assume was a money guy.

"There's nothing left?" she'd asked, a waver in her voice. "But where did it all go? Daniel was a fanatic about saving."

Cody found out later that while his father was a financial genius, in the weeks leading up to his death, he'd withdrawn large sums of cash, leaving their personal accounts drained. He had no life insurance policy—an oversight to be sure.

Where had their nest egg gone? How could his father have been so stupid as to drain everything? And worse, where did that money go?

Sure, he had investments—some they couldn't take out right away, some that would sustain them for a time—but their lifestyle had to change. Their security was gone.

The questions were too big, too heavy, and he wasn't sure he wanted to know the answers. Besides, the seething cocktail of his mother's anger and grief was enough to keep him from digging around. He decided that his dad must have had a plan for it. His father always had a plan.

Right?

It didn't matter. At least that was what he told himself. Wherever it was, his dad's nest egg was gone. None of it was left for Cody, Marley, or their mom. The pain of that sliced through their family like a newly sharpened knife through a ripe cantaloupe.

His father's death turned his mother into a different person. She went from joyful and engaged to nearly catatonic, and the only thing Cody wanted to do was take her pain away.

When it came time to pack up the house, she haphazardly filled boxes, and Cody and Marley went behind her to try to make sense of the disorganized mess. Their last night in the house, Cody realized his father's office door was still closed, and as far as he knew, nobody had packed anything from inside.

He pushed open the door and inhaled—the scent of his dad's aftershave still lingered in the air. Nagging guilt nearly overtook him. How was it possible that his dad was really gone? Weren't fathers invincible? Cody had always thought so.

The room was tragically frozen in time, photos on the wall, books filling the shelves. His father was a voracious reader, and as Cody ran a hand over his collection of crime novels and history books, he tried to take a mental snapshot so he'd never forget this room.

"What are you doing in here?"

He spun around and found a haggard, tired version of his mother standing in the doorway.

"We should pack up Dad's office."

"No," she said. "Everything stays here."

Cody didn't understand. His father's office was full of things they would want. Memories, sure, but paperwork, too. What if there was something important they needed down the road?

"Let me handle it, Mom," Cody said. He refrained from adding, *You're not thinking clearly.*

"What could we possibly need? Everything is gone." She moved away from the door and motioned for him to pass through, which he did, grudgingly. "Don't go in there again."

But he did go in. That night, when his mother was in a prescription pill–induced slumber, he went in and packed everything he could into a box that would pass for one of his own. He didn't look through the contents of the desk; he just silently moved them from the drawer to the box, put the lid on it, taped it up, and wrote his name on the side.

And that was how it had stayed all these years. Until tonight when he stupidly opened it like a kid on Christmas. Like there was joy to be found inside.

Right on top was a sheet of paper with his father's handwriting on it, and the sight of it had nearly knocked him out cold.

After the tidal wave of emotions crashed through his body, he was certain this was not a path worth investigating. The past needed to stay in the past. End of story.

He cut the engine, grabbed the box, and walked inside. What was he so afraid of? Bank statements and tax documents? Like he'd always said, his dad must've had a plan—they couldn't possibly know what he'd been thinking in the weeks leading up to his death. But Cody had chosen to believe there was a reason for what seemed like major financial mismanagement.

A memorial at the place where he died changed nothing about that. An IOU note from someone who missed his dad didn't change anything either. Cody knew who his father was.

He set the box on the empty kitchen counter and stared at it.

He knew who his father was.

Except what if there was more to his father than the man he knew?

Men had secrets, even fathers. What if his dad had a whole life Cody knew nothing about?

After several long seconds, he brought the box into the living room, dropping it on the floor in front of his solo recliner. He continued staring at it as if he could open it by telekinesis. As if that would make it hurt less. If he were smart, he would've left it with Louisa, paid her a nice sum to go through it, and asked her to track down whoever it was that had left the note behind.

But Louisa wasn't a detective, and frankly, the less she knew about his personal life the better. He'd been foolish to accept her help in the first place. She had this infectious enthusiasm that he couldn't help but find amusing—even now, when he wanted nothing to do with her, he found himself wondering when he'd see her again.

He'd also made the mistake of noticing she smelled like vanilla cupcakes, and the scent of her lingered in spite of the distance he'd purposely put between them.

Without thinking, he tore the tape off the box again and stared at it, questions forming at the back of his mind. Or maybe the questions had always been there and he'd simply been too stubborn to admit it.

His father was a hero. He'd died saving Cody. Nothing inside this box would change that.

Cody opened the lid and the twelve-year-old stack of papers and photographs stared back at him. He didn't have to dig far to find a picture of the two of them, snapped when Cody was around ten years old. His dad had taken him fishing—their first ever guys-only camping trip. Cody was proudly holding a largemouth bass that was nearly as big as he was. He remembered that moment. He remembered pulling the fish from the lake, something he never could've done without his dad's help.

He studied the faces in the photo and noticed his father's grin was wider than his own. Perhaps he was even prouder of their catch than Cody had been. A pang of sadness rose up within him, and he said a silent prayer of thanks that he hadn't gone through the box in front of Louisa.

He could feel her wanting to fix things. He could feel her trying too hard. The last thing he needed was for her to feel validated in her obvious concern for him. He was fine. He'd be fine. He just had a lot to process.

He started scanning through the pages—mostly work papers, mostly unhelpful, and he tried not to let his mind wander back to that night.

He'd wished he could undo it so many times. If only he'd listened.

If only Louisa hadn't been making out with the pizza delivery guy behind the dumpster of the restaurant where she was working. If only he hadn't decided to surprise her, showing up early and catching some guy pressed against her—an image he'd tried without success to scrub from his mind for months after.

He'd waited until the guy—Nate—went back inside, using every bit of his willpower not to deck the idiot. Cody was bigger and stronger, never mind that Nate was two years older, already in college.

"Just friends, huh?" he spat as a look of sheer panic washed over Louisa's face.

"Cody, I'm so sorry—it's not what you think."

He rolled his eyes. "I told you that guy was flirting with you, Lou. I asked you to shut it down."

"And I did," she said. "I thought I did." She pushed her hands over her hair, smoothing out her ponytail. "I'm so, so sorry."

"Do you like this guy?" His mind spun with the same phrase, over and over—*Please say no.*

But she didn't say no. She didn't say anything. She hesitated just long enough to give him his answer. He turned to go, and she grabbed his arm.

"I don't know, Cody. I don't know how I feel. It's confusing, and he's older, and he knows what he wants—"

"I bet he does." Cody scoffed.

"I'm so sorry. I'm just—freaked out about leaving, about being apart. Nate understands and—"

"And I don't." He faced her then, looked her square in the eye. "I know how I feel. I've always known."

Tears slid down her cheeks. "I'm so sorry."

"You know that guy is just using you, right?" He could feel the anger in his words, fueled by his own pain at a betrayal he hadn't seen coming.

"Cody, please—can we talk about this?"

"I don't want to talk to you right now." He'd been so dense. He really believed when they made that pact only a couple of weeks before that they'd survive her going off to college. They'd already done long-distance; they'd proven they could make it work.

Louisa was leaving in a matter of days—and instead of focusing on the two of them, she was "confused about her feelings" and kissing someone else?

He left then, raced home and slammed the door behind him. He stomped upstairs and turned a circle in his room like a rat in a cage. He wanted to punch something—or someone. He needed to blow off some steam.

A knock on the door interrupted his thoughts, and his dad poked his head in. "Hey, champ."

Cody turned away. He didn't want his dad to see him like this. He didn't want anyone to see him like this—losing it over a girl. How idiotic.

But Louisa wasn't just any girl. He'd loved her for as long as he could remember.

"What's going on?"

Cody's sigh was heavy. His heart felt like a brick stuck in the center of his chest. He unloaded the whole story, and of course, his father responded calmly, the way he always did.

Some guys had parents who took up their offenses for them. Cody wasn't one of them. Instead, Daniel Boggs put on his practical cap and tried to talk Cody off the ledge.

"You and Louisa are young," he said. "Maybe a little time apart would be good for you. Maybe she needs to figure out how she feels, and maybe you need to give yourself a little space too."

"Space for what, Dad?"

He shrugged. "Lots of fish in the ocean."

"That's so dumb. You know how I feel about her."

His father stilled. "You're right. I'm sorry. I don't know why she did this, and I know it hurts. I have a feeling she's hurting pretty good right now too."

"Are you kidding? She deserves to feel hurt. *She* did this to us."

"Stop shouting," his father said, still calm.

Cody spun around. "I need to get out of here."

"Where are you going?" His dad followed him into the hallway.

"For a walk."

"The winds are strong tonight," Dad called down the stairs. "Stay out of the water."

Now Cody blinked back tears as he tossed aside a stack of printed emails and pages of documents with numbers on them. It would take some time to sort through everything, but he'd give it a shot. He didn't have anything better to do.

Three hours later, after combing through many pieces of paper that made very little sense, he found a bank statement dated three weeks before his father died. It looked like all the other bank statements he'd already sifted through, but this one showed something out of the ordinary—three large cash withdrawals from his parents' joint savings account, all within a few days. Oddly, these withdrawals were for uneven amounts. Instead of $50,000, he'd withdrawn $52,675. Instead of an even $25,000, Daniel had taken out $25,382.

His father was used to dealing in large sums of money, but it was strange, Cody realized, that he'd made the withdrawals from the personal account, leaving it nearly empty. Worse, there was no paper trail to indicate where the money went. Only withdrawals for cash.

Cody picked up the card he'd found affixed to the cross and turned it over in his hand.

Miss you, Danny. IOU.

Was JoEllen Chambers somehow connected to these cash withdrawals? Was she the one who'd left this note? Warren was on the island, which meant his wife likely was too. And this crisp white card looked brand-new.

He set the card down next to the bank statement and wondered if opening up that box was another mistake. Because if what he was thinking had even a shred of truth to it, this secret wouldn't only devastate his mom; it would devastate Louisa.

No matter how angry he'd once been with her, he never, ever wanted to hurt her.

~

Letter in Louisa's mailbox the morning after the dinner of disaster:

> *Louisa,*
> *The master chief informed me of your hourly rate. Enclosed is a check to cover the cost of last night's meeting. I apologize for wasting your time. In giving it more thought, I've decided some things are better left buried in the past.*
>
> *Cody*

CHAPTER SIXTEEN

CODY STOOD ON THE DECK OF THE LARGE CUTTER, overseeing the main-tenance of the ship. Most of the guys understood that maintaining their equipment was part of the job, and as such, these kinds of workdays could draw the crew closer together.

So far, the only one complaining was Seaman Aaron Jessup.

This guy might be the perfect person to take his frustration out on. After yesterday, Cody needed to blow off some steam.

He was just about to make a strong point to the seaman when someone called his name from behind. He turned around and saw a young seaman recruit named Carlos standing on the dock with a gorgeous redhead who looked seriously out of place.

"Someone here to see you, sir," Carlos called out.

The other guys whistled, and Cody ignored them. "Take a break."

"I got a feeling our break isn't gonna be as good as your break," one of the guys hollered.

Cody shot the guy a look that shut him right up, then met Louisa on the dock, dismissed Carlos, and did his best not to meet her eyes.

She saw straight through him, and right now, he wanted to keep his thoughts to himself.

He especially didn't want her to know that he'd had a dream about her last night. He'd pulled her from the water, and the moment she recognized him, she wound her arms around his neck and he'd kissed her without a single moment's hesitation. The kiss had been enough to wake him—breathless and disappointed when he realized it wasn't real.

Those weren't feelings he could allow.

He made a point of looking over her head.

"Sorry to bug you at work." She leaned around him and waved to the guys, who were undoubtedly staring at them.

"Do you need something?" It was painful to be so short with her, but it had to be this way. He couldn't risk letting her in.

"I came to clear the air."

He raised a brow. He'd forgotten this about her. She had this overwhelming need to say every thought that popped into her head, regardless of the consequences.

It was seriously cute.

She shifted. She might pride herself on speaking her mind, but it made her nervous. Funny she hadn't outgrown that. "You saved my life, and you might wish you could take it back, but there it is, you're a hero. And I did something really awful to you a lot of years ago, and I wish I could take it back, but there it is, I'm a jerkshovel."

"A what?"

"A jerkshovel. It's like a really big jerk."

"It's nice to know you're still making up words."

"I can't stand how weird things are between us," she blurted. "I know we aren't friends anymore, and that's my fault. I know that on July 30, you're not going to be standing at Brant Point lighthouse or sharing your golden birthday wish list with me. I know you blame me for your father's death. And I'll never be able to explain how much I regret that night. I was young and immature, and Nate was older and he paid a lot of attention to me, and he said you and I weren't a good match because I was more mature than you, and I think I let him get in my head. Then I got swept up in—"

"Louisa—" He cut her off. It all sounded so juvenile now, but the consequences had been disastrous.

"I'm really, really sorry, Cody. Tell me what to do to make it up to you."

He kept his gaze steadily above her head. He could feel her words drawing him in—winding themselves around his core. It had been a long time since he'd let anyone get close to him. Actually she'd been the last person he'd let get close to him, and it hadn't worked out so well. He'd be smart to remember that.

He straightened. "I don't know what you're talking about."

"Don't pretend," she said. "You've been awkward and standoffish with me since you got back."

"I'm fine, Louisa."

"Then why did you leave that note in my mailbox? Why did you give me this?" She reached into her bag and took out the check he'd written her.

What was he supposed to say—that he'd left it because he didn't want to owe her anything? He didn't want to owe anyone anything.

She shoved the check into his chest. "I told you I didn't want your money."

He took the check and looked away, just in time to meet the eyes of the men on the boat, none of whom were minding their own business. They all hurried back to work.

"I told you I wasn't trying to help you as part of my job," she said. "I want to be your friend again."

He looked at her then. "I don't really have friends."

Her shoulders slumped so slightly he almost didn't catch it. She searched his face, getting too close to the places he kept hidden, the places he didn't want her to see.

"On purpose?"

He didn't answer. It was too complicated to explain. "I just decided not to start digging around. It's nothing personal."

"Feels personal."

"It's not."

"I know you're not dropping this." She'd always known which of his buttons to push, and she made a point of pushing them. "I know this is bugging you as much as it's bugging me."

"Why is it bugging you?"

She fidgeted. "Because I want to help."

"Louisa, what I said back then—"

Her upheld hand silenced him. "Forget it."

But she obviously hadn't forgotten it or she wouldn't have brought it up.

He'd yelled at her—he'd been so angry with her the day after his dad died. She'd come over that morning with her parents, and even his mom treated her badly. It was obvious she blamed Louisa. After all, if Louisa hadn't upset him, Cody wouldn't have been in the water. He would've been out somewhere with Lou. He would've come home, gotten into bed, and gone to sleep. He would've woken up the next day with two parents and one less tragedy.

But that wasn't the way things went. So he blamed Louisa. It was easier than blaming himself. Not that he'd ever stopped doing that.

"I'm dropping it," he said. "I decided it's not important who put that cross up."

She squinted up at him. "What did you find?"

He chewed the inside of his cheek. There she was—reading him like a book. Sometimes that charmed him. Sometimes it didn't. Guess which it was today.

"I didn't find anything," he lied.

There was the smallest quirk of her eyebrow, and he knew she didn't buy it.

"It's nothing, Lou."

She crossed her arms over her chest. "You know I'm not going to let this go until you tell me the truth."

That was a fact. He glanced back at the ship and found several of the guys still watching him from the deck. Vanishing into thin air sounded really good right about now.

"What is it?" she pressed.

"Louisa, just let it go," he said through gritted teeth.

"You know I can't do that."

"You can," he said. "And I didn't find anything, so nothing I tell you here is going to ease your guilty conscience."

Her face took the words like a slap. She clung to the strap of her bag across her chest and took a step back.

"Sorry," he said.

"I'll see ya." She turned and walked away so quickly he couldn't have caught her without jogging.

He raked a hand through his hair and heaved a sigh.

That was one way to get Louisa and her questions and these memories out of his life. Just not the way he intended.

Way to go, you idiot. Way to go.

CHAPTER SEVENTEEN

TOPPER'S RESTAURANT AT THE WAUWINET was fine dining at its very best, which was why Louisa's mother loved it so much.

JoEllen Chambers loved all things *fine*, so when Louisa called her that morning to confirm that she and Louisa's father were indeed on the island, her mother instantly insisted on lunch at Topper's.

Louisa had begrudgingly agreed and now sat as straight as a board at a table near a window, trying not to replay Cody's comments about her guilty conscience—proof that he still thought about their undoing.

No. It wasn't proof of anything. It only meant that he still hadn't forgiven her, and she was foolish to try to repair what was broken between them.

She was scrolling through her phone mindlessly, waiting for her perpetually late parents, when a man's voice interrupted her.

"Hi, Louisa."

She glanced up and found Eric standing beside her table. He wore a black suit, white shirt, and red tie. He looked like a politician. A smug one. "Eric?"

He smiled at her.

"What are you doing here?"

"You didn't hear? I took a job managing the Wauwinet."

Louisa was bad at pretending, but she tried to muster a smile. "Really?"

The Wauwinet was a beautiful hotel. This was a step up for Eric—a big one.

"Yes," he said.

"Wow, congratulations."

"I'm surprised your mom didn't tell you. She and your dad were in here last night." He chuckled. "She seems convinced we're getting back together."

Louisa let out a nervous laugh. "Funny. She didn't mention it."

Eric sat down across from her. "I told her I'd be open to it."

Louisa waited for the flutters of butterflies. She counted to five and felt nothing. "I think things are just as they're supposed to be."

Eric leaned in closer, his hands on the table, dangerously close to hers. Still, she felt nothing. "I've been watching your business closely."

She raised her eyebrows as if to say, *Oh?*

"I think I could help you take it to the next level," he said. "Or you could do the really smart thing and come here. Work for me. It'll be like old times."

Louisa moved her hands from the table and folded them in her lap. "My business is doing quite well, actually."

He leaned back and studied her. "I heard about your auction idea," he said. "It's . . . interesting."

"It's brilliant," she said in a tone she hoped radiated more confidence than she felt. "I bet you wish you'd thought of it."

"I don't plan fundraisers, Louisa." He smiled coyly as if he hadn't just zinged her.

She let the barb roll off her back and checked her phone. *Where* were her parents? "I'm meeting someone, so if you don't mind . . ."

"What happened to us, Louisa?" Eric asked. "I thought we were really great together."

Why did he want to talk about their relationship now? Weren't they past analyzing it?

Louisa watched the entrance of the restaurant with intensity, as if she could will her parents into existence. "We were great together until I realized you didn't believe in me."

He frowned. "That's insane. I was your biggest fan. I still am."

She shook her head slightly. "I'm going to go call my parents. They're late."

Eric lifted a hand to stop her from standing. "I'll go. I just miss you, is all."

Not even the hint of a flutter.

At that precise moment, Warren and JoEllen Chambers appeared in the doorway of the restaurant and rushed over to greet them.

"Oh, Eric, you're here again." Louisa's mom swooned. "Do you ever stop working?" Then to Louisa: "He is such a hard worker, Louisa. Don't you think?"

Louisa didn't respond. Instead, she watched as her parents embraced Eric like he was their long-lost son. Did they remember she was sitting there and they'd yet to see her since they returned to the island? Some daughters might expect a hug. She knew better.

Her mom finally (finally!) sat down next to Louisa, but her dad still stood next to Eric as if they were old friends. They were talking about golf or some such nonsense, and Louisa was itching to run straight back home.

Why had she agreed to this lunch?

"Louisa, Eric has some great ideas on how to make your business legitimate," her father said.

"I'm sorry?"

"A business manager might not be a bad idea."

"He's a hotel manager. Not a business manager." Louisa's stomach churned. Could she leave without appearing *too* rude? "And I think Alyssa and I are doing pretty well for ourselves."

"Of course," her dad said. "It's just a thought."

"I'll leave you to your meal," Eric said. He turned to Louisa. "Maybe we can get coffee sometime? Catch up?"

Louisa mumbled a response and Eric walked away.

"Such a nice young man, Louisa," her mother said. "I still don't understand why you ended things with him."

"No, I don't suppose you would," Louisa said.

"I beg your pardon?"

Louisa inhaled. She didn't need to have an argument with her mother. While she wished her parents—and Eric, for that matter—would view her as an adult, an intelligent adult who was perfectly capable of running her own business, they didn't. The only way to change that was to act like an adult. And that meant not throwing a tantrum or lugging around her childish *feelings*.

"It was good to hear from you," her mom said. "I wasn't sure when we would get to see you—you're always so busy."

"You didn't tell me you were back."

Her mother draped her cloth napkin on her lap, then glanced up at Louisa. "Of course we did."

"You actually didn't."

Her mother's eyes moved upward as if she were searching a mental memory bank. "Hm. I could've sworn I told you." She waved her perfectly manicured hand in the air. "Oh, well. How are things? How is your little business doing?"

"It's not a little business, Mother."

Her dad laughed. "Louisa, when are you going to come to your senses and go back to work at the hotel? Or here? Eric said he'd hire you back in a heartbeat."

"You asked Eric if he'd give me a job?"

"It came up in conversation. Nobody understands what it is you have against him. Sounded like he'd be willing to give you another chance on the romance front too." Dad smiled as if he'd just issued the best news ever.

Should she try to explain herself? Should she tell her parents that she didn't want to be with someone who made her feel like her ideas were silly and frivolous? Should she tell them she didn't like it that they sometimes made her feel that way too?

"Should we order?" Louisa asked.

They picked up their menus and looked them over in silence.

"I heard you ran into Cody." Louisa didn't look up from her menu.

Neither did her father. Her mother, on the other hand, slapped hers down on the table. "Cody Boggs?"

"Oh yeah," her father said. "I saw him at a coffee shop. They were giving him a standing ovation for saving someone's life."

Cody hadn't mentioned that part.

"He saved someone's life?" Mom asked.

"Someone who wasn't wearing a life jacket." He punctuated his sentence with a knowing *What have I always said?* look.

Louisa lifted the menu a little higher. Cody had refrained from ratting her out. That made her heart squeeze a little. Gosh, she loved that man.

She closed her eyes behind her menu and finally blurted out, "It was me."

She had their attention.

"What was you?" her mom asked, the lilt of her accent slightly more pronounced.

"The person who forgot the life vest."

"Oh, Louisa, what have we always told you?" her mother said. "You could've died out there."

"I know, Mom," she said.

"Are you okay?" her father asked.

"Sure, I'm fine. The wind took a turn and the current took me out farther than I expected it to. But I learned my lesson."

Her mother shook her head. "Really, Lou. Sometimes I think you should move back in with us. You simply cannot be trusted to make wise decisions."

Louisa's eyes dipped back to her menu. There was nothing worse than proving her parents right—and she seemed to have a knack for getting herself into situations that did just that.

No wonder nobody took her seriously.

Eric reappeared in the restaurant, caught her gaze, and held it. Still no butterflies—only the horribly uncertain feeling that she'd left a trail of mistakes behind her. And she didn't know how to clean it up.

CHAPTER EIGHTEEN

THE FOLLOWING DAY, CODY MET WITH LOUISA at the station for an update about the Coastie auction. He gave her a list of men prepared to participate, along with the details he'd collected about each one.

She flipped through them hurriedly, scanning the facts. Today she was all business. He knew he'd hurt her feelings. He should apologize.

"Is that what you needed?"

She tucked the pages inside her padded notebook. "Yep."

"Louisa—"

"Just make sure that everyone is there on time Friday." She pulled another sheet of paper from the notebook and handed it to him. "Dressed in uniform and looking sharp, please."

He took the page. "I will."

"We've sold a decent number of tickets, but anything you can do to help spread the word would be great too."

He nodded in agreement.

She steeled her jaw. "The next hurdle is a big one."

"How can I help?"

Louisa straightened and pushed her hair behind her shoulder. The simple move drove him crazy. He wanted to run his fingers through those long red waves, which was ludicrous considering what a stellar job he'd done ticking her off yesterday.

"We need to go see Jackson Wirth's parents."

Cody frowned. "Why?"

"We can't do a fundraiser for them without their permission," she said. "It just feels wrong."

"Giving someone money feels wrong?"

She looked at him then, and he felt like he'd just been zapped by an electric current.

"It's about more than that," she said. "We're dragging him back into the limelight. Mr. and Mrs. Wirth might not appreciate that."

"And if they say no?"

Louisa drew in a breath. "There are lots of great causes out there."

"When do we go?"

"I'm going tomorrow," she said. "Alyssa set up a meeting, but she didn't give them any details."

"I can make that work."

"We have to take the ferry," Louisa said. "He's in a hospital on the Cape."

A twinge of excitement coupled with a wave of nausea raced through him at the idea that he would be spending the better part of the day with her.

"I'll be there."

A pause hung between them, and finally she tucked her notebook inside her bag. "Great. I think that's everything. I'll see myself out."

With that, she was gone, leaving a trail of ice in her wake.

What did he expect? Did he think he could throw her mistake back in her face seconds after telling her it was forgiven and not face consequences? Besides, wasn't this what he wanted—to be rid of her prying eyes? The distance would be good for him—give him space to sort out his own feelings.

Why, then, did her cold shoulder make him feel like—to quote Louisa—a jerkshovel?

He sighed and went back to work, wishing for the millionth time that things were different.

~

The ferry left Nantucket at 7:40 a.m. and would arrive in Hyannis about an hour later. That meant one full hour of ignoring every single thing about Cody Boggs. It meant pretending that the way he looked in his uniform had no effect on her. It meant sitting next to him on too-close-for-comfort seats and acting as if she hardly noticed. And it especially meant not drawing in deep, long breaths just to memorize the way he smelled after a shower and a shave.

So far she was doing a terrible job.

"Are you going to do that the entire ride?" he asked with a nod toward her knee, which she only just that moment realized was bouncing like it had a motor hidden somewhere inside it.

She stopped and focused her attention out the window.

When she was a kid, these ferry rides to and from the island were filled with emotion—excitement on the way to the island and sorrow on the way back. Today the ride was also filled with emotion—namely a mix of dread and nervousness. And she was doing her best to hold on to her anger so she didn't go and fall in love with the man sitting next to her.

"Do you want some coffee?"

She glanced at him and found him sitting so still he looked like a statue.

"Do you drink coffee?"

Why was he being nice to her? It was confusing. If he'd just treat her like a jerk all the time, it would be a lot easier on her heart.

"Lou?" He said her name like they were friends.

They were not friends.

"I do drink coffee," she said.

"You look like you might need some."

She frowned.

"You've yawned three times in the last five minutes," he said. "Have you been sleeping?"

She wanted to tell him she was just fine and needed nothing from him, but she really could use the caffeine. And no, she wasn't sleeping, not that she'd tell Cody that.

"I'll go get you some." He stood.

"I'm fine."

"I'm getting a cup for myself anyway." He walked away and she noticed two women, probably a few years younger than she was, staring at him.

One of them glanced at Louisa and caught her eye. "You're a very lucky girl." She grinned while the other woman raised her eyebrows in agreement.

Louisa went back to staring out the window. She'd always made a habit of scanning the ocean, looking for any sign of life in the watery depths. Sometimes she'd catch the tail of a dolphin or the blowhole of a whale coming up for air. It was in those moments she felt like a little girl again.

She clung to that feeling—life before she learned how cruel life could be.

"Here you go."

Cody's voice shook her from her thoughts. She turned and found a cup of coffee offered in his outstretched hand.

She took it. "Thanks."

He sat back down, and the two women came into view again. One of them smiled and shook her head, as if to say, *That man is fine.* For a brief moment, Louisa imagined that he was hers, that they were headed off island for a fun weekend in the city, that there wasn't a mountain of hurt between them, that all the broken things had been repaired.

The thought of it brought tears to her eyes.

"You okay?"

She nodded quickly and took a sip of coffee, purposefully forcing all of this emotion out of her head where it belonged.

CHAPTER NINETEEN

CODY MIGHT HAVE LOST HIS FATHER, but at least Daniel hadn't died a slow, languishing death in a hospital bed.

He'd gone quickly, without warning, snapped off the earth like a precious jewel in the hands of a crafty thief.

Now, walking the halls of the hospital where Jackson Wirth had been since his accident, Cody was almost grateful for that. Yet he hadn't gotten to say good-bye. That, he would never be grateful for.

"Room 403," Louisa said. "This is it."

"Maybe we should've met them somewhere else," Cody said quietly.

"They won't leave his side," Louisa told him. "One or both of them is always here."

The weight of their burden felt heavy on his shoulders.

"Ready?" Her expression softened toward him for the first time since they boarded the ferry.

He nodded as Louisa knocked on the door.

"Come in," a woman's voice said from inside the room.

Louisa drew in a breath, then pushed the door open. Cody

followed her into the room, where a boy lay in the hospital bed, covered in a lightweight white blanket. Tubes extended from his arms and mouth, hooked to a machine that hummed in a steady rhythm. Artificial breath keeping him alive.

Next to the bed sat a tired-looking woman with a sullen face, and a middle-aged man stood behind her chair. Both of them took one look at Cody, dressed in uniform, and frowned.

"What's he doing here?" the woman asked.

"Mrs. Wirth, my name is Louisa Chambers, and this is Cody Boggs of the United States Coast Guard," Louisa said.

"I don't care what his name is," the woman said. "I don't want him here."

"I can wait outside." Cody started to turn, but Louisa's hand on his arm stopped him. He forced himself not to think about how soft her skin was or the delicious vanilla smell of her. He met her eyes, and she quickly turned back to Jackson's parents.

"We're so sorry for what you're going through," Louisa said.

The woman's lips drew into a tight, thin line, but the man's face relaxed.

"Thank you for that," he said. "It's been hard."

"We check in on Jackson's progress often," Louisa said.

The woman scoffed. "What progress?" Her eyes flashed, and Cody could see her anger was only a cover for the deep sadness and fear she was feeling. Anger, he often found, could keep a person safe. How many years had he worn that same cloak so he wouldn't have to feel anything?

He'd been doing so well too, right up until he moved back to the island.

"The doctors aren't hopeful." Jackson's father put his hands on his wife's shoulders.

"I'm so sorry," Louisa whispered.

"Why are you here?" the woman asked.

Louisa cleared her throat. "Deborah, we'd like to do something for your family, and we wanted to make sure it was okay with you."

Jackson's mother didn't respond.

"What did you have in mind?" Mr. Wirth asked.

Louisa glanced at the chair on the opposite side of Jackson's bed. "Do you mind if I sit down?"

"Please," Mr. Wirth said.

Deborah kept her gaze tightly on her son.

Louisa stilled at Jackson's side. Cody watched as she studied the boy. "I read that he liked old cars?"

Deborah looked up at Louisa, then back to Jackson. She leaned in closer to the boy. "Yes. They've always been his favorite thing. Ever since he was little."

Louisa gave a soft nod.

"He dreamed of owning a garage full of old Mustangs," Jackson's dad said with a smile. "One from every decade."

Silence hung in the room, and Cody wished he could bolt. Louisa sure was taking her time here. He glanced at Jackson's mom. Wiry and thin with wispy hair on the brink of changing color, like oak trees in autumn.

Louisa leaned forward, gaze still on Jackson. "He sure is a handsome kid." She smiled then and looked at Mrs. Wirth.

Louisa had always been good with people. She was so natural and easygoing. She was friendly and charming and not the least bit shy. But this—it was more than that. She was genuine. He never once got the impression that she was trying to sell anyone on anything. She had a job to do, sure, but she made certain that job was beneficial to someone who needed a little light in their life right now.

Maybe his family shouldn't have pushed her away in their own hour of need.

"We're hosting a regatta," Louisa said quietly. "A whole day of bringing awareness to water safety and to raising money for a worthy cause."

"What cause?" Deborah asked.

Louisa looked up and straight into the woman's eyes. "Your family."

"We're not a charity case," Deborah said.

"Honey, let her talk," Mr. Wirth said. He glanced at Louisa. "Our insurance covers some of Jackson's expenses, but we've taken a second mortgage on our house to try and cover part of what's left."

Louisa nodded. "Medical bills can be so hard. We just want to help ease the burden if we can."

"Who's 'we'?" Deborah's shoulders had gone stiff, as if she knew there was something about this idea Louisa wasn't telling her, something she wouldn't like.

"The event is hosted by the Coast Guard station at Brant Point," Louisa said firmly, and once again Cody admired that she didn't try to sugarcoat the truth.

"No way," Deborah said.

"Deb," her husband said quietly.

"Mr. and Mrs. Wirth," Louisa said kindly, "we know you're in a lot of pain right now."

The woman's lower lip quivered. "You don't know anything about our pain."

Louisa inched back in her chair. "You're right. I don't understand this kind of pain."

Deborah swiped a tear that slid down her cheek.

"But I might." Cody hadn't meant to say the words out loud. He felt Louisa's eyes on him.

Jackson's parents looked at him too, confusion on their faces.

"I don't know exactly what you're going through, but my father drowned when I was eighteen," he said.

Deborah's face softened, but only slightly, and the man stilled.

"It's the worst thing that's ever happened to me."

Deborah wiped her cheek again. "You want to use Jackson to ease your guilty conscience." The anger was back. It flashed in her eyes, hot and cold at the same time.

"No. We only want to help," Cody said, and he meant it. It was the first time he wondered if the pain he'd endured might actually be able to help someone else.

Maybe he should've kept his mouth shut. It wasn't like he'd figured out anything about grief or loss.

"That Coast Guardsman should've done more. He should've gotten Jackson out first. Instead, he waited too long, and our son may never wake up." With that, her voice cracked. "I don't know much, but I know he is not supposed to be in this bed right now."

He wouldn't remind her that Jessup had tried to save Jackson right away. He wouldn't say that it was an accident because that might negate her feelings, and she was certainly entitled to them. Besides, they weren't here to convince her she was wrong.

They were only here to offer help.

"If you don't want us to name the regatta after Jackson," Louisa said, "we won't. But the community would love to do something to support your family right now. We'd love to have the chance to honor your son."

Deborah turned away and didn't say another word.

Louisa slowly stood. She rummaged through her bag and withdrew a blue business card, just like the one Duncan had given him before his first meeting with her.

"Think it over." She held the card out to Mr. Wirth. "Let us know."

He took the card with a quiet nod. "We will."

"It was good to meet you both," Louisa said.

Deborah remained still, refusing to look at either of them, but Louisa seemed unfazed.

"Thank you," Mr. Wirth said. "We really appreciate it."

Louisa shook his hand, radiating warmth as only she could do. "We would love to help."

He was certain Mrs. Wirth was likely biting back angry words, but she said nothing as the two of them escaped into the hallway.

"Well, that could've gone better," Louisa said. "But I suppose it's what I expected."

Cody tucked his hat under his arm and drew in a tight breath. "Do you think she'll come around?"

Louisa shrugged. "I'm not sure. I don't want to push her, so I'll start looking at alternatives, but I really would love to do something to help their family if we can."

He studied her for a long moment, thinking that her authenticity inspired him. He didn't meet many truly genuine people—or maybe he simply didn't stick around long enough to find out if they *were* genuine.

With Louisa, there was no question.

"You okay?" She studied him now, her big eyes fixed on him.

"Yep. Good." He started toward the elevator. "I hope they come around."

~

Email to Louisa two days after her visit to Mr. and Mrs. Wirth:

Dear Miss Chambers,

We appreciate your visit to Jackson earlier this week. I apologize if we seemed ungrateful in any way. As you can imagine, there is a lot of emotion to sort through. The truth is, the day before your visit, the doctors told us we were only prolonging the inevitable. Our Jackson is gone. Deborah knows it. I know it. But neither of us is ready to let him go.

I know our anger seems misplaced, and maybe it is. Maybe we are simply looking for someone to blame. Because believing it was human error and not something God allowed to happen to our son is easier.

Because if God simply turned his face in Jackson's hour of need, where does that leave us?

Anyway, we would be honored for you to name the regatta after our boy. He was so joyful and full of life once upon a time. I think he'd get a kick out of something so cool being held in his honor.

Thank you for your kindness.

Sincerely,
Manny Wirth

CHAPTER TWENTY

IF THERE WAS ONE THING LOUISA KNEW AROUT NANTUCKET, it was that the people on the island loved a good party. And if there was one thing she knew about herself, it was that she loved to throw one.

Her time at the hotel had helped connect her with the island's top philanthropists, and that was proving to be very helpful.

As soon as she got the go-ahead from Mr. Wirth, she began to spread the word, and as she suspected, people were eager to help. Crisis and tragedy bonded people together, and while what happened to Jackson was horrible, it seemed the community was willing to unite around his cause.

Now Louisa stood at the back of the yacht club, supervising the decorating for the Coastie auction, part one of her grand plan. They'd sold tickets to the event that night, and thanks to the buzz she'd created around it, they were already in a good place.

She watched white lights being strung over a pergola on the beach and whispered a quick prayer that everything would go off without a hitch. Not only because she truly wanted to do something meaningful for the Wirth family, but also because Eric was going to be there.

Ally had broken the news to her the day before, and after her initial shock, she remembered that she was a confident, almost-successful business owner. If Eric wanted to show up and watch her be amazing, let him.

At least that was what she'd told Ally. The truth was, it had knotted her insides, knowing she might run into him. She'd mostly learned how to avoid him, though it wasn't always easy. Tonight it would be impossible.

But tonight wasn't about her. And it *really* wasn't about Eric. It was about a family who could use some hope. She would focus on them, and she'd be fine.

"Louisa!"

She turned and found McKenzie Palmer standing on the deck overlooking the private beach Louisa and her team had just finished decorating.

"Wow, what an amazing job you've done here."

Louisa forced a smile. She hadn't wanted to invite McKenzie, but Ally talked her into it because "if McKenzie blogs about The Good Life, that will book us for the rest of the summer."

Leave it to Ally to make perfect business sense.

She tried to remember that now. "Hi, McKenzie."

"I was so excited to hear y'all were doing this for poor Jackson Wirth. Cody said you two saw him this week? How is he?" Her eyelashes fluttered.

Cody said? "You talked to Cody?"

Stop it, Louisa. Your jealousy is showing.

"Oh, darling, I'll talk to that man every chance I get." She flashed a smile.

Shameless.

"Didn't you two grow up together? Do you have any pointers for me? Anything I should know?"

Louisa's heart raced and her palms turned cold. The image of

Cody and McKenzie cozied up in his one chair invaded her mind even though she had no idea what that one chair looked like. She was not going to discuss him with this *blogger*.

If McKenzie wanted Cody, she'd have to find her own way over the giant wall he'd built around himself. Louisa certainly wasn't going to draw her a map. Not that Louisa would know where to begin, sadly.

"Will you be coming to the auction tonight?" Louisa turned her attention to the flowers at the center of the nearest table.

McKenzie's smile widened into a wry grin. "Are you kidding me? All those Coasties decked out in uniform? I wouldn't miss this for the world."

"Great." Louisa was fairly certain her tone communicated a lack of enthusiasm, but then she never had been able to fake much of anything.

"See you later." McKenzie sauntered off, leaving Louisa feeling frumpy and a little less excited than she'd been feeling ten minutes ago. She'd rather gouge her eyeballs out with a fork than watch McKenzie flirt with Cody all night.

She shoved the thought aside and walked across the deck and through the restaurant, waved to the manager, who'd been a godsend in ironing out the details, then headed out front toward her Vespa.

She'd almost made a clean break when she heard laughter coming from the parking lot. She turned just in time to see McKenzie's epic hair flip. The woman was parked right next to Louisa's scooter and at her side was (of course) Cody Boggs. He'd said he might stop by, but she'd expected him an hour ago.

Louisa wished she could turn and run the other way, but that might be a little too obvious, even for her. What did she care if McKenzie had a thing for Cody? It wasn't like she had any claim to the man.

Unfortunately.

She swatted that thought away and soldiered on.

McKenzie perked right up when she spotted Louisa. "Oh, Louisa. We were just talking about you."

Cody looked away.

She resisted the urge to ask what exactly they were saying about her, slung her bag across her body, and gave them both a nod.

"Do you need help with anything?" Cody took half a step away from McKenzie, who still wore that precious smile Louisa couldn't stand.

Her inner monologue chastised her. *Be nice, Louisa. This is not good behavior.*

"I think we're good," Louisa said sharply. "Just finished up."

"I got caught out on the cutter," Cody said as if he were apologizing.

McKenzie practically purred. "Did you save someone else's life?"

Cody's eyes were still fixed on Louisa, who thought she might collapse under the weight of his gaze. "Just routine. Mechanical issues. All good now."

"Oh, thank goodness," McKenzie said. "We sure wouldn't want you to miss the auction tonight. Would we, Louisa?"

Louisa clenched her teeth together so tightly she thought they might crack. "We sure wouldn't, McKenzie. I'll see you guys later."

She would've loved for Cody to dismiss McKenzie and tell her he'd like to talk to Louisa for a moment and say he'd been thinking about it and she was right to clear the air, and he was wrong to make her feel bad for a mistake she'd made so many years ago, and he'd given it a good thinking over and he'd forgiven her after all. *And oh, by the way, could we try that whole relationship all over again from the beginning? Clean slate and everything?*

But he didn't dismiss anyone except Louisa, with a slight wave goodbye and a complete removal of attention. And he didn't say a single one of those things. Instead, he glanced at McKenzie, who asked if he'd like to go see where the auction would be held, and then followed her off toward the restaurant like a stray dog in desperate need of a warm bath and a cuddle.

Louisa swung her leg over the Vespa and gave her bag a tug. While she absolutely refused to glance in Cody and McKenzie's direction, she did note out of her peripheral vision that he tossed a quick look back at her.

Well, how do you like that?

She steeled her jaw—something she was incredibly good at—started the engine, and drove away, trying her best not to imagine a conversation that would draw him closer to a woman with whom he had no past, no baggage, and no cross words.

She wondered if maybe it was all better this way.

CHAPTER TWENTY-ONE

LOUISA KNEW TONIGHT WASN'T ABOUT HER. She knew that, and yet she'd stood in front of the full-length mirror in the room that used to be Cody's for a solid thirty-five minutes fussing over which dress to wear, then which shoes, then hair up or hair down.

Truthfully the whole scene made her entirely disgusted with herself.

She was not that girl. She was the girl who could pick up and leave at a moment's notice. Low maintenance. Hair in a ponytail, makeup-free—that was Louisa.

As her heels clicked up the sidewalk toward the restaurant, she caught a glimpse of her long teal gown in the window. This was *not* Louisa.

She stopped and surveyed herself for a long moment, then heard a whistle behind her. She turned toward the offender, ready with a pointed comment about catcalling, when she saw Alyssa grinning at her from the parking lot.

Louisa laughed. "Don't draw any more attention to me than necessary. I feel ridiculous."

"You look amazing." Ally moved toward her. She was wearing an equally formal gown, though hers was black and a little less flashy. Somehow Ally still looked like an accountant. The glasses maybe? Louisa should've gone with black. Would it be easier to blend in if she had?

"*You* look amazing." Better to turn the attention back on Alyssa, who was much more classically beautiful and always more put-together than Louisa. Louisa could maybe pull off "girl next-door," but "beautiful" and "elegant" were out of her reach. She'd accepted this a long time ago, but every once in a while—when McKenzie Palmer was around, for instance—she wished it weren't the case.

They walked toward the entrance of the restaurant, certain they were the first ones to arrive. Louisa needed to make sure everything was as she left it. Next, she would check in with the chef and the serving staff. She had a whole list in her purse because everything had to be perfect.

As they approached, the door swung open and two men in uniform appeared on the other side.

"Don't you both look beautiful?" Master Chief Duncan McGreery greeted them warmly, looking perfectly handsome in his uniform. Handsome but not in a spine-tingling, knee-buckling way. Not handsome like Cody Boggs, who stood beside the master chief, back straight as a stick, no expression on his face.

She caught and held Cody's gaze, unmoving for several long seconds.

"I bet you're glad you saved her life now," Ally said. "Otherwise you never would've gotten to see her in that dress."

Louisa elbowed Ally as heat rushed up the back of her neck. How pink were her cheeks? Embarrassment had never looked good on her.

"Everything looks wonderful out back," Duncan said. "Louisa, you've outdone yourself. And I hear the Wirth family came around thanks to you."

"Not only me." She tossed one quick look at Cody.

"Come on in. Let's run through the evening's program." Duncan ushered her past Cody (who smelled like an evergreen forest in heaven) and outside to the beach, where the tables had been set up next to a small stage.

"Couldn't have asked for better weather," Duncan said.

"No, we sure couldn't."

The man took a quick look around. Tall circular tables had been covered with cloths the same dusty lavender as the many hydrangeas that were starting to blossom around the island. They'd been arranged for optimal viewing of the small stage and decorated with center-pieces of white and blue hydrangeas in low glass vases.

White lights had been strung around the outdoor space, and a buffet table featuring large galvanized-metal containers and three tiers of appetizers would later be perfectly arranged to encourage grazing.

There was also a bar neatly positioned inside an old wooden boat Louisa had brought in from her shed of "treasures waiting to be dis-covered." Sometimes it was good to be a collector—not quite to the same degree as Maggie, but enough to have cool focal-point pieces like this one.

They would set up several glasses and self-serve drinks in the boat, which had a beautiful, colorful floral centerpiece in the middle of it. Louisa's vision had come to life. The men of the Coast Guard might never fully appreciate all the detail that had gone into it, but hope-fully the potential bidders would.

And even Eric wouldn't be able to deny she'd created something truly special.

"Run me through the evening," Duncan said.

Right. She was working. *Focus.* She found it terribly hard to concentrate with Cody standing *just over there* and *looking like that,* but she stuttered her way through an explanation of the plan as she glanced around the space. Appetizers and cocktails, straight into a quick run-down of the regatta, the fundraiser, and what they were actually bidding on.

"Then, of course, the auction itself."

When she finished, she looked at Duncan, who appeared wholly unimpressed with her explanation. "I promise I won't stutter so much tonight."

"You do seem distracted," he said.

Her eyes were inadvertently drawn to Cody, who was not looking back, then quickly back to Duncan.

His eyes crinkled at the corners. "Your own real-life hero, eh?"

Louisa shook her head, pretending not to understand what the man was talking about, but she had little energy for pretending, and frankly, Duncan didn't seem all that interested. In fact, he'd already walked away and here she was, alone.

Typically Louisa was perfectly comfortable being alone. She wasn't the type of person who wouldn't go to a movie or sit in a restaurant by herself. But somehow, right now, she felt out of place, like she needed something familiar to cling to.

A teddy bear or hard-bodied Coast Guardsman would suffice.

She forced her feet to move toward Ally, who was running through the menu again with the servers. She also forced herself not to pay attention to the pair of eyes that followed her from the stage to the deck.

Eyes the color of chocolate pudding that made her heart do a backflip.

"What is wrong with you?" Ally took Louisa by the shoulders and turned her away from the rest of them. They walked a few steps toward the water.

"I'm afraid everyone will find out I have no idea what I'm doing. And when they find out, I'll be wearing the equivalent of a grown-up prom dress."

"You have every idea what you're doing," Ally said.

Why did Louisa sometimes need this reminder?

"People are starting to show up," Ally said. "So pull yourself together."

And that's exactly what she did. She pulled herself together. She greeted guests, made snide yet funny remarks about getting their checkbooks ready, kept the staff on task, and managed to avoid running into Cody even once.

It wasn't hard, after all. He seemed intent on taking up the same square of space off to the side, away from everyone else, and yet she (hardly) noticed that he was rarely alone back there. Between the other guardsmen and a steady stream of bubbly, beautiful women, Cody had plenty of company.

She was still angry, but at the moment she couldn't remember why. She couldn't deny there was a part of her that wanted to walk right up to him and act like nothing was wrong. How would it feel to joke with him about the fact that Mrs. Drummond had brought a tiny dog in her purse or that Martine Gullenbacher's false eyelashes were flicking up at the edges like spiders at a hoedown?

But the part of her that wanted that laid-back, easygoing friendship with him was quickly put in its place by the part that finally did recall Cody's harsh words toward her. If he thought she was trying to ease her guilty conscience, then he didn't know her at all.

Or maybe he knew her too well, and that was really what had upset her.

A ball of angst wound itself up and curled into a comfy position inside her stomach like a kitten in front of a fireplace. If he was never going to forgive her, she wished he'd just leave. It would be easier to move on if she didn't have to see him every day.

"You ready?" Ally was standing beside her, and she held a stack of cards. "These are all the fun facts about each Coastie. Some of them are cheesy—I'm not going to lie—but they're cute, and I think the crowd will get a kick out of them."

Louisa knew this was part of her job. She'd even practiced some of what she would say in the midst of agonizing over her dress, her shoes, her hair. She was ready.

She scanned the beach and landed on Cody. And beside Cody—McKenzie Palmer. And just behind the two of them—Eric, standing with her parents, who'd made a late entrance.

Okay, maybe she wasn't ready.

Was there a single person there who didn't think she was a total disaster?

McKenzie threw back her head in a laugh so loud Louisa wondered if she was going for the world record in guffawing. Was she laughing at something Cody said (unlikely) or at her own joke? Louisa groaned. It didn't matter. She had a job to do. She couldn't get caught up in any of this. They were expecting large bids tonight, and it was up to her to get them. She was a professional. A business owner. A grown-up. It was what she'd been trying to prove all along. Here was her chance.

She made her way to the stage, drew in a deep breath, and looked out over the crowd. Some of the people quieted at the sight of her, but the low hum of chatter still filled the air.

From the back, Ally gave her a quick thumbs-up. Ally believed in her. That was enough, right?

Then she looked at Cody, which was a grave mistake because Cody was one of the people who'd quieted at the sight of her, and he was steadily focused in her direction.

She locked on to his gaze, trying to ignore the fact that at his side, McKenzie Palmer was still rambling. He seemed not to notice. He seemed only concerned with throwing her equilibrium off with his intense stare.

How was it possible that Louisa felt that stare all the way down to her toes?

"Are we ready?" Duncan had emerged from the crowd and stood on the stage beside her, drawing her attention.

When she looked back at Cody, his eyes were no longer on her.

Drat.

Louisa gave Duncan a nod, then took the microphone, welcomed everyone, thanked them all for coming, and explained who they were raising money for. She described the details of the regatta and did her very best to make the whole event sound like the kind of thing they would all want to be a part of. Because it would be, she was sure of it. Once she figured out the details.

Then it came time to open the bidding.

Most of the guardsmen were no longer out in the audience. As she'd instructed, they'd headed to the backstage area to prepare for their debuts. Apparently the whole event had created a healthy competition in these boys, and they were about to see who brought in the biggest payday.

"We'll start the bidding with—" Louisa glanced down at the card in her hand—"Carlos Delgado."

The good-looking Coastie came up onto the stage and grinned at her. Then he turned to the audience and flexed his biceps, showing off well-defined muscles and eliciting a chorus of *ooh*s and *aah*s from the crowd.

Louisa waited for Carlos to return his attention to her, then smiled. "As you can see, ladies and gentlemen, Carlos is very shy."

Laughter rippled through the audience.

"Carlos is twenty-four years old and has competed in the CrossFit Games twice, finishing in the top ten both times."

Another flex from the young guardsman.

"Carlos loves animals and has been a member of the US Coast Guard for three years."

He turned to her. "You forgot the best part."

She reread the card in her hand, then looked up at him, confused.

He turned to the crowd. "You forgot to tell them I'm the Coastie with the Mostie." This time he flexed both biceps and gave the audience a cocky nod.

Laughter filtered through the crowd again, and Louisa shook her head. She tossed a look toward the spot where Cody had been standing before the auction started, but he was gone.

It unnerved her, not knowing where he was.

"Ladies and gentlemen, let's start the bidding."

One by one, Louisa introduced the guardsmen, and one by one, the good people of Nantucket pledged large sums of money for the chance to enter the regatta with a genuine sailor. The bidders were as different as the men they were bidding on.

One guy bid on James Conley, an "Alfred Haynes Junior Yachtsman of the Year and all-around likable guy" for his thirteen-year-old son, who, he said, was very interested in sailing (but who, Louisa noticed, seemed much more interested in his iPhone). Another guardsman was bid on and paid for by an older woman named Dorothea Quinn, who was convinced that she had what it took to win that regatta if she just had the right partner.

It went on like that until finally Louisa only had three cards left.

"Okay, big spenders," she said into the microphone. "Only a few chances left to win the Coastie of your dreams. We are down to our final three men. Shall we see if we've saved the best for last?"

She glanced into the wings and spotted Cody standing there. It was difficult not to notice he looked like he'd rather be having a root canal.

Slowly he brought his gaze to hers, then tugged at the collar of his shirt. She did a quick sweep of the audience and saw McKenzie Palmer standing at the back, poised and ready to bid.

Louisa's heart sank.

She glanced down at the card with all of Cody's details written on it and chastised herself for not thinking this through. Surely she had to expect that Cody would participate. This was why he'd been brought to Nantucket in the first place. He was here to make the Coast Guard look good.

She turned toward him again. He *definitely* made the Coast Guard look good.

The crowd had stilled. Even Eric and her parents had stopped chatting and were staring in her direction.

Ally caught her attention, gave her a pointed look, as if to say, *Hurry up*, and Louisa did her best to get it together.

"Please welcome to the stage Executive Chief Petty Officer, and real-life hero, Cody Boggs."

Excited applause tore through the crowd as Cody took the stage. Eric stiffened. Her parents exchanged a concerned glance.

Louisa loved looking at Cody. She always had. How many days had she sat on the beach admiring him as he tore through the waves or worked on his surfing skills? She thought she'd fallen in love with him the summer before her junior year of high school, but looking at him now, she realized she'd never *not* been in love with him.

Somehow that realization hurt a little more than she thought it should.

The image of his face the moment she woke up on the deck of the cutter ship invaded her mind. Fear. Concern. Worry. Followed by the realization that he'd just saved the life of the woman whose actions had led to his father's death.

And yet he'd still pressed on. Still took his time with her. Still came to the hospital and made sure she was okay.

"Louisa?"

She found him staring at her, probably anxious to get this over with already, and here she was, mentally waxing poetic about the person he used to be. About the couple they used to be.

"You okay?"

She quickly righted herself with a stern mental talking-to and forced herself to smile, turning her attention to the words on the card Ally had given her. Thank goodness for that card or Louisa might stand here dumbly for the rest of the evening.

"Well, ladies and gentlemen, standing in front of you is my personal knight in shining scuba suit—" She looked up from the card and found Ally smirking wryly. Louisa would deal with her later. "Cody is new to Brant Point station, but he's already making waves. A three-time state champion swimmer, honors graduate of the Coast Guard Academy, and decorated officer, Cody guarantees that with the right partner he will take home the top prize at the Jackson Wirth Coast Guard Regatta."

She allowed a brief amount of trash talk from his fellow guardsmen. A brief moment to pull herself together and reread the card and the details he'd chosen to share. Some of which she hadn't been aware of until that moment.

She realized how much she missed being the first to know everything about Cody Boggs.

"Sounds like fighting words to me," she said into the mic.

Cody gave a playful shrug, but his cocky grin looked like a put-on. She didn't even know he was capable of pretending. His smile quickly faded. Ah, that was more like the Cody she knew.

"Let's see, shall we start the bidding at—"

"Five thousand dollars."

Everyone turned toward the voice in the back, a smattering of whistles and chatter filling the space, but Louisa didn't need confirmation of the identity of their first bidder.

McKenzie Palmer stood with her hand raised, a smug expression on her face. She'd started the bidding high on purpose. She'd sent the message that she was willing to pay for what she wanted.

After a long pause, Louisa remembered she was the one running this event. "Five thousand dollars. Our first bid on Cody Boggs. Do I hear fifty-two hundred?"

Louisa said a silent prayer that someone—anyone else, but preferably one of Dorothea Quinn's lifelong friends—would pop their hand up, but no one did.

"Five thousand going once?" McKenzie called.

Louisa's head spun with images of McKenzie and Cody that started with her first sailing lesson and ended with a white dress and a walk down the aisle. Her palms turned clammy, and the microphone slid lower in her hand.

Louisa cleared her throat. "I know this is unorthodox, but I'd like to bid." Her voice echoed through the speakers.

The crowd murmured excitedly, and Louisa caught a few phrases that told her that at least the front row approved. The girl and her hero. Of course they should be together.

She imagined her face had turned redder than her hair, and she could feel Cody's eyes on her, not to mention Eric's and her parents'. What was she thinking?

"Well, what's your bid?" McKenzie asked from where she stood.

"What?" Louisa looked away. "Oh, right."

She'd taken on this fundraiser in large part because she needed the money. Was she really going to give away her earnings in an attempt to keep another woman's hands off of Cody, who might actually enjoy her hands on him?

"Well?" McKenzie was getting impatient.

"Fifty-two hundred."

"Fifty-three." McKenzie waited exactly point-two seconds before firing off her next bid, as if there was nothing but money in her purse.

Louisa glanced at Cody, who shook his head at her, probably aware that she could not afford to continue down this path. Or perhaps he simply didn't want her to win. Perhaps he wanted to spend his limited days off with McKenzie. She was, after all, petite, well-built, blonde, and beautiful. Not to mention uncomplicated and apparently wealthy.

Who knew bloggers made actual money?

"Fifty-four," Louisa said.

"Fifty-five." McKenzie squared her shoulders and stared at Louisa, practically daring her to go higher.

Louisa glanced at Ally, whose expression said, *What in the world are you doing?* After all, Ally managed their business account. She knew Louisa couldn't afford this.

Still, Louisa heard herself say, "Fifty-six."

And then she saw a shift in McKenzie's posture. Her shoulders slumped ever so slightly, and a look of defeat fell on her face.

That was when Louisa began to panic because reality set in. A reality she hadn't considered. She didn't have $5,600 just lying around. She silently prayed that McKenzie had one more bid in her, but the woman shook her head to indicate she was out.

Louisa did a slow turn toward Cody, who looked less than pleased.

"Do I hear fifty-seven?" she squawked into the mic, but the crowd responded in silence.

Finally a guy at the back shouted, "Looks like you won him fair and square!"

Then a lady hollered out, "Maybe he'll do mouth-to-mouth again."

The crowd laughed and Louisa's heart wrenched. What had she done? She was jealous and impulsive and it was going to cost her precious, hard-earned money. Stupid. Stupid. Stupid.

"Sold?" Cody asked.

Louisa raised the microphone. "Sold."

Was there a return policy on Coasties?

CHAPTER TWENTY-TWO

"COME ON, DUNCAN. SURELY YOU CAN MAKE AN EXCEPTION."

"I'm sorry, Miss Chambers, but you of all people should know the rules. You made them. No refunds. No returns." The master chief winked at her—he seemed to be enjoying this.

"Right."

Cody watched as Louisa's brow knit into a tight line, and he could see the worry behind her eyes.

Most days since returning to Nantucket, Cody had been able to keep his feelings for Louisa squarely locked up in a box marked *Do Not Open* and shoved to the back of his mental closet. Most days he would describe Louisa as cute. She had a cute personality and a cute little nose that turned up at the end. She had a cute laugh and made cute, quirky comments.

But today, in that dress, *cute* was the last word he would've used to describe her. He could feel the box moving out of that closet at the back of his mind, begging to be opened.

Louisa turned heads. She didn't even realize it, but with her deep-red hair and that killer blue dress, everything about her stood out. She wasn't skinny or waifish—she curved in all the right places—and standing back against the wall watching her try to make a return on her most recent impulsive purchase, Cody didn't know whether to be offended or amused.

He cleared his throat and she spun around, a hand-in-the-cookie-jar expression on her face.

"Unhappy with your purchase already?" He could have some fun with this. He shouldn't, but he could.

She stammered for a few seconds before he raised a hand to let her off the hook.

"I know you can't afford it," he said.

Her shoulders sank in a deep exhale. "I really can't."

He watched her fidget, clearly uncomfortable. "So what were you thinking?"

A sheepish look came across her face. "I was just trying to drive up the bid."

He only stared.

She looked away, refusing to explain further.

"I'll split it with you," he offered.

"No," she said. "This was my mistake. I'll figure it out."

"A mistake, huh?" He crossed his arms over his chest and looked at her. "Ouch."

She met his eyes for only the briefest moment. She stepped out of her heels and picked them up, tucking them under her arm. "We both know that you and I trying to sail together is a giant mistake."

"Oh, I don't know, Lou," he said. "We made a pretty good team once upon a time."

Now he had her attention. But he wasn't sure he wanted it. What was he doing? He was flirting, that's what. And he should stop. He was walking a tightrope, and he knew one wrong move and he'd fall—hard.

"That was a long time ago," she said.

He watched her tuck a long strand of hair behind her ear, eyes lingering on her pink cheeks, her full lips.

The tightrope underneath him wobbled.

He hadn't returned to Nantucket thinking he'd reconnect with Louisa. He didn't even know she lived on the island. While there were a lot of old feelings that had been stirred like soup in a pot, the thing that struck him most was that what drew him to her most were things he didn't know about her back then.

She was smart and fearless, yes, but she had such a kindness about her—it was rare to find someone who was so genuine in their concern for other people. Most people really only cared about themselves.

She was different. She would never intentionally hurt him, right?

Yet she *had* hurt him. And that mistake had unraveled so much of his life. He wasn't sure how to reconcile the Louisa who'd broken his heart with the woman standing in front of him.

She scoffed quietly. "You can't do this."

Whoa. What had he done?

"*I* can't do this." She stormed past him as if she couldn't get out of there fast enough.

"Do what?" He followed her. "Louisa?"

She spun around and looked at him, and for a split second he thought maybe there were tears in her eyes.

"You can't tell me I'm only being nice to try and ease my guilty conscience and push me away like you did just to pull me straight back in by flirting with me." She looked up at the ceiling, blinking quickly. Same thing she'd always done to keep from crying.

He thought she looked equal parts beautiful and adorable when she did.

What was wrong with him? He shouldn't be thinking about her like this. She was at most a friend, nothing more. She could never be anything more.

"I'm sorry," he said. And he meant it. She was right—it was unfair of him.

Never mind that he liked being around her, liked the way he felt when he was with her. He wanted to know all of her three million quirks, and he wanted to hear her say his name over and over.

Get a hold of yourself, Boggs. You could leave here with McKenzie. Wouldn't that be easier? Less messy?

"I tried to clear the air with you and you pushed me away," she said, a little angrier now. "You were right."

"I was?"

"Yes. Distance is good. Because this—" she waved her hands back and forth in the space between them—"is no good for anyone."

A man dressed in a suit, with pants that almost reached his ankles, strode over. If it weren't for the fact that he stopped next to Louisa (and the fact that he wasn't wearing socks with his loafers), Cody might not have noticed him.

"Buyer's remorse?" He smiled at Louisa, who glanced at Cody and stiffened.

"Not now, Eric."

"Do you need a loan?" He'd leaned toward her, but he hadn't lowered his voice.

"I'm fine," she said.

But she wasn't fine. Obviously she had history with this guy. Cody took a step toward her.

Eric extended a hand toward Cody. "Eric Anderson. Louisa and I used to date."

"He doesn't care about that," Louisa said. "Would you just go?"

Eric withdrew his hand and glanced at Louisa. He didn't say a word, but the way he watched her made Cody want to deck the guy.

Finally Eric walked off.

Louisa was right. This was no good.

He looked away. "Maybe you and McKenzie can trade or something."

"You want me to train with Charlie Pope?" She glared at him.

"Yep."

McKenzie had bid on—and won—Charlie, the last guardsman of the evening. He wanted Louisa spending time with Charlie almost as much as he wanted someone to yank out his toenails, but no way he was telling her that.

She nodded blankly. "That would probably be better for everyone."

He forced her gaze. "Yep."

But he didn't mean it. He wanted to explain himself. If only he knew how to put into words what he was thinking.

This was easier. This was smarter. Distance between them was necessary and good. Teaching her to sail and spending any additional time with her was not.

"I'll go find McKenzie," she said.

He watched her walk away and found himself praying McKenzie had already left. Because while his head knew distance was smarter, his heart wanted nothing more than to curl right up next to Louisa and stay awhile.

Cody hadn't intended to spend the day after the auction sitting on Maggie Fisher's sofa, surrounded by boxes of old newspapers, but here he was.

Maggie was in the kitchen making him tea, though he'd told her twice he didn't much care for tea. Her response? "Nonsense. Everyone likes tea."

So in a few minutes, he would drink tea because that's what you did when you were with Maggie Fisher.

After what seemed like a lot longer than it should've taken to make tea, Maggie returned to the living room carrying a tray. He quickly stood and took it from her.

"I'm not an invalid," she said with a snap.

He ignored her and set the tray down on the coffee table, then poured her a cup.

"You're *my* guest," she said. "Just because I'm dying doesn't mean I can't pour a cup of tea."

"Oh, I know," he said. "But now you don't have to."

She sat across from him with a defeated shrug. "You're just like your dad."

The words played at the corners of an old wound, threatening to uncover pain he'd put in its place a long time ago.

Maggie laughed. "Your dad was a charmer. You got his good looks."

He really didn't want to talk about his dad. Yet wasn't that why he was here?

"Thanks," he said lamely.

She eyed him over her teacup. "What brings you by? I'm sure you've got better things to do than hang out with the likes of me."

He leaned forward on his knees. "You're really sick, huh?"

"A little bit, kiddo."

He didn't want her to die, he realized in that moment. He didn't like that the people he loved had gotten older, himself included. Time was cruel, the way it marched on without permission.

But then he supposed it didn't march on for everyone, did it?

"I wanted to ask you about the note I found on that cross."

"I already told you it wasn't me." Her cup clinked on the saucer, and a bit of tea sloshed over the side. "I wish it was."

"No, I know." How did he put this? More importantly, did he really want to poke around in the past? He'd tried to drop it, but the questions about the memorial and the note nagged at him.

That's why he found himself here. Maybe Maggie could help.

"I was thinking about how the person who wrote that note called my dad Danny," he said.

Maggie looked at him, her face blank. "So?"

"Nobody called him Danny," he said.

Maggie set her cup down on the table. She leaned back in her chair and rested her hands on her stomach, eyeing him thoughtfully. "Sure they did."

"They really didn't."

"I remember hearing people call him Danny," she said.

"Who?"

Maggie frowned as she struggled to locate a bank of memories she likely hadn't considered in years. "I'm not sure. Joey?"

Joey. JoEllen. Cody tried to keep his face from giving away what he was thinking.

He failed. Maggie straightened and narrowed her gaze. "You got your father's poker face too."

"What do you mean?"

"I mean you don't have one."

Cody sighed. "I'm not trying to point any fingers or anything. It's just that I don't know anyone else who ever called him Danny."

The old lady's brows pulled into a straight, bushy line. "Warren called him Danny sometimes. Even I called him that once in a while."

It sounded like she was reaching.

"Look, Maggie, do you think there might've been something going on between my dad and Lou's mom?"

"What?"

Cody spun in the direction of Louisa's voice and found her standing in the doorway holding a grocery bag, a horrified look on her face.

"Louisa?" Cody stood.

"What are you talking about?"

Great. This was exactly what he was trying to avoid. He rubbed his temples.

"I knew you weren't dropping this." She stormed into the room and set the bag on the coffee table with a thud. "You said you were going to drop it, but I knew you wouldn't. You just didn't want my help."

"Well, can you blame me, Lou?" His words came out a little louder than he wanted them to, but this woman was maddening. Didn't she realize he was trying to spare her from whatever he might find?

"I'm a big girl, Cody. I can handle it."

He stuck his hands on his hips and studied her. For several minutes they stood there, engaged in a standoff he knew he would lose. Louisa might've changed over the years, but she was still as stubborn as ever.

"Stop it, you two," Maggie said. "Cody, I think you're barking up the wrong tree."

"I'll say." Louisa huffed and crossed her arms over her chest.

Cody turned a circle, wishing he *had* dropped it.

"Why would you even ask a question like that?" Louisa asked.

"It doesn't matter," Cody said.

"Obviously it does." She glared at him.

He drew in a breath. No way he was getting out of here without telling her what thought kept troubling him. Might as well get it over with. Might as well pour salt in the wound.

"Your mom is the only person I know of who ever called my dad Danny."

"Your mom called him that," Louisa said.

He shook his head. "She didn't. I know because every once in a while, she'd say something under her breath that made me think she didn't love that JoEllen had a nickname for my dad. I think that's why she refused to use it. That was what your mom called him when they dated, so my mom never called him anything other than Daniel."

Slowly Louisa sat down in the armchair next to Maggie.

Cody sat across from her. "We don't know anything, Lou."

"But you think they were fooling around."

Cody shrugged. "I have no idea."

"They weren't fooling around," Maggie said. "They would never."

"People do dumb things sometimes," Cody said.

Louisa didn't respond.

"No, Daniel loved your mom." Maggie turned to Louisa. "And your mom loves Warren."

"Cody's right," Lou said. "You can love someone and still do stupid things." She met his eyes for a split second.

His pulse raced.

"I need a nap." Maggie stood and toddled out of the room, disappearing as if it were perfectly normal to do so. She'd left Cody and Louisa alone, and he wasn't sure whether to thank her or call for her to hurry up and come back.

Louisa found his eyes. "If I could do it over, I would."

He shook his head. He didn't want to talk about this.

"I mean it, Cody. If I hadn't upset you, you never would've gotten in the water that night, and your dad never would've drowned."

It was what he'd said to her after the accident—that it was her fault. Of course she still believed it was. If only she knew; if only he could take it back.

He stilled. He could go on blaming Louisa, but at night, when the lights were out and the demons were tormenting, it wasn't her he was angry at.

"It was my fault," he finally said, though he wondered if he'd spoken loudly enough for her to hear. He stared at his shoes, the rug underneath them, anything except Louisa's eyes, which he could feel were focused on him.

"He told me not to go in. Did you know that?" He nearly choked on the words. He drew in a breath and glanced at her.

She shook her head quietly.

"He told me the water was choppy. The last thing he said to me was the very thing I disobeyed." This all felt brand-new. How did he stop the pain?

She inched forward as if she wanted to touch him but wasn't sure if she should. "It wasn't your fault."

But she didn't know. She didn't know that his father's words had nearly kept him out of the water, but he'd made a purposefully rebellious decision, one he would change a thousand times over if he could.

He stood. "I should go."

"No." She stood and faced him. For a few long beats, neither of them spoke. It was as if, in that space of time, there were no words—not a single thought forming in his mind.

The past drifted away, and all that was left was Louisa. Her soft skin. Her red hair. Her barely noticeable freckles that would surely pop once she got more sun.

The air sizzled between them, and the only thing he could think of was her lips, full and pink, and the way they might taste.

"It wasn't your fault," she whispered again. "And I know your dad would do the same thing again if given the choice."

He didn't want to think about that right now. He'd been trying not to think about it for days.

"I have to go." He didn't like the way she made him feel, unsteady on his own two feet. Like he could fall at any moment, like she might even be there to catch him. He didn't wait for her to respond. He walked around her toward the door, aware that she followed close behind.

Of course she did. This was Louisa. They'd almost shared a moment—she was going to see it through.

"Do you really think my mom and your dad were having an affair?" she said to his back.

"Forget it, Lou. Pretend you never heard me say that." He'd almost reached his Jeep when she grabbed his arm. He forced himself not to think about how it felt to be touched. In recent years, he'd rarely allowed that from anyone other than the people he was rescuing. When they clung to him, it was out of sheer terror. What would it feel like to have someone cling to him simply because they wanted him?

"You know I can't forget it," she said.

He faced her then, and he wished he hadn't. He wanted to kiss her. He remembered the way her kisses made him feel—invincible.

Was she remembering too?

"Tell me what you're thinking," she said.

He glanced down at her hand on his arm, and she quickly pulled it away. He instantly noticed the absence of her soft skin on his. He wrestled with the desire to take her in his arms right there and show her just how much he'd missed her.

"Cody?" Her eyes pleaded with him. Who was he kidding? He never could say no to Louisa.

"I don't even know, Lou." He paused. "Maybe it's nothing, but your mom called him Danny. She was the only person I ever heard call him that."

"I'm sure other people called him Danny. It's not an uncommon nickname."

"But not often, not like your mom."

She looked away.

Cody shifted. "I know it's a long shot, but could your mom have left this note?"

"Even if she did, does that mean they were sleeping together?"

Of course not. Why would he jump to that conclusion? It was a pretty big leap. "There's something else."

Her brow furrowed. He tried to ignore how cute that made her look.

"After my dad died, we found out he'd basically drained his savings account. He had some money tied up in investments, but not enough to live on. Not enough to keep Seaside. It was so shortsighted for someone so smart."

Louisa didn't respond, but he could practically see her trying to make sense of it.

He went on. "And I discovered this week that the amounts he withdrew were strange. Why would someone take out three different large sums of money in odd amounts? Why $52,675 and not $53,000? Why $25,382 and not $25,000?" He'd memorized the sums. Sometimes he'd think of the numbers out of the blue, repeating them over and over as if doing so would force them to make sense.

Again, Louisa frowned. "That doesn't sound like him."

No, it didn't. Daniel Boggs was nothing if not perpetually prepared. He was a planner. He was a thinker. He was smart and responsible. Leaving his family with so little was the most out-of-character thing he could've done. Which was likely why his mother had gotten so angry, so bitter over the whole thing. She'd clearly created a scenario as to what had happened to that money.

Had that story involved JoEllen Chambers? Was that really why their families had fallen out?

"There must've been a reason," Louisa said. "Did your mom ever say anything?"

"No. If she knew anything, she didn't tell us. But she was angry about something."

Louisa found his eyes. "She thought he was cheating?"

He shrugged. "I don't know, but she didn't even want to pack up his office. She wanted to leave him in the past. And you know how much she loved my dad."

Louisa's face fell. "She didn't pack up his office?"

"No. That box I brought over the other day was all I was able to save."

"I'm sorry, Cody," Louisa said, "that things turned upside down for you."

He swatted the apology away as if it didn't matter. "It's fine. I joined the Coast Guard. I was a good swimmer, and I—" He stopped short of saying he wanted to save lives. He wouldn't tell Louisa that he'd joined so he could prevent the ocean from beating him ever again. And he definitely wouldn't tell her the academy wasn't his first choice. "I sent all the money I made back to my mom. It wasn't much, but it helped. She got a job. Marley got a job. We made it work."

"But I'm sure it was different than you were used to."

He let himself look at her for a split second, then realized she'd done it. She'd found a way in. Somehow she'd gotten him to open up about the one topic he'd had no intention of discussing. "I need to go."

"Maybe I can help?"

He stopped, hand on the door handle of his Jeep. "You can't."

"I can talk to my mom. I'll know if she's lying. She's never been very good at that."

"Just drop it, Lou," he said. "You don't need to deal with this."

But he could tell by the look on her face that asking her to drop anything was an exercise in futility.

"Just let it go," he said.

She shrugged.

"Louisa." His tone sounded stern, like a warning, but Louisa wasn't afraid of him.

She turned and started for Maggie's house. "I'll let you know if I find anything out." She gave him a quick wave and went back inside.

Cody couldn't help but feel a twinge of relief that for the first time in a long time at least he wasn't alone.

~

Today 9:35 PM

Louisa: When is our first sailing lesson?

Cody: I thought you traded me?

Louisa: I tried. The fundraiser has a no-return, no-exchange policy. All sales are final.

Cody: Who made up that rule?

Louisa: Well . . .

Cody: Bet you're wishing you weren't such a stickler right about now, eh?

Louisa: Tomorrow?

Cody: I'll meet you at the marina at dawn.

Louisa: What time is dawn?

Cody: Look it up, sailor. You're in my world now.

CHAPTER TWENTY-THREE

LOUISA HADN'T SLEPT WELL. The nightmare was back, and this time Cody pulled her from the water and then threw her back in. She awoke sweaty and gasping for air.

If this continued, she really might have to get professional help.

The regatta was less than two weeks away, and now, because of her impulsiveness, she not only had to plan all the details; she also had to train for the race. She knew she wouldn't be much of a partner, but she didn't want to embarrass herself.

She'd done that enough already for one summer.

She arrived at the marina at exactly 5:07 a.m., just in time for a truly spectacular sunrise. As she trudged up the dock toward the water, she spotted Cody in a small sailboat, borrowed from a client of Louisa's. He noticed her and waved.

At least that was something.

The knowledge that their birthday was quickly approaching bounced around in her mind, as if there were a clock ticking and the alarm would go off on that exact day. For so many years she'd built up their pact, and only now did she realize it was because a part of her hoped—even with so many years of silence between them—that on their birthday he'd keep the promise they made.

It was a foolish hope; even she knew that. But without it, she had to admit defeat, and now—especially now that she'd seen him again—she wasn't ready to do that.

"Morning," she said.

She wouldn't tell him how she'd stopped by her parents' cottage last night, full of rage. She wouldn't tell him they weren't there, but she'd left three messages and two texts for her mother to call her back. And she especially wouldn't tell him that so far, in spite of the emergent tone of said messages, she'd received nothing but silence from JoEllen Chambers. Because then he would know exactly where she stood with her own mother—somewhere in the far-off distance. And that was a tiny bit too personal for 5 a.m.

"I brought you some coffee." She held up a thermos as she reached the edge of the dock.

He held up a disposable cup. "I brought *you* some coffee."

She smiled. She couldn't help it. He had to think of her to buy her coffee. That was progress, right?

"Then we should be set for the whole morning."

She stared at the boat, the sound of the water lapping against it echoing in her ear. She stared at it until the noise of the ocean spiked her heart rate and she struggled to find a breath.

"Here, let me help you in."

Cody had saved her. He was safe. He knew what he was doing. She was being ridiculous—a baby, really. She wasn't afraid of water. She never had been. Even after Daniel's accident, she'd still gone swimming in the ocean. Sometimes without a life vest.

One little brush with death wouldn't change that. Was there such a thing as a "little" brush with death?

She glanced down at his outstretched hand. He must've mistaken her hesitation for an unwillingness to touch him because he moved it away.

"Sorry," she said, reaching toward him.

He took her by the elbow and helped her in. Under her feet, the boat shifted, and she struggled to steady herself. She fell forward into his thick, hard chest, noticing he didn't even move.

"You okay?"

She looked up at him and nodded. Were her cheeks flushed? She sure felt like they were. She stepped back and cleared her throat.

"I'm sure you've done this before," he said.

"Yeah." She moved gingerly toward the center of the boat. "I mean, usually my dad or Eric handled most of the hard work."

He didn't respond.

Why did she say that? It wasn't even exactly true. Eric had always found ways to avoid being the one to man the sails.

Cody cleared his throat. "But you at least know the parts of the boat," he said. "I mean, if I tell you to go to the stern, you know where to go, right?"

"To the back." Her stomach turned. Could a person get seasick while still tied to the dock?

"Great." He untied the boat, and they started moving away from the marina.

Louisa watched as the other boats grew smaller and smaller, saying nothing, trying her very best to keep her nausea in check.

After a few minutes, Cody glanced at her. "Everything all right?"

"Mmm-hmm." She nodded, perhaps too enthusiastically. It rattled the insides of her head around, and a pain started throbbing at her temples.

"You're quiet," he said. "That's not like you."

"Are you saying I talk too much?"

"Yes." He stared at her.

She would've smiled if she didn't feel so sick.

"You look a little green."

"I'm fine."

He turned away, focused on the water. "Should we review the parts of the sailboat?"

"Sure," she squeaked, knowing full well that whatever information he tried to give her in that moment would fall on deaf (and nauseated) ears.

He started with the rudder. "It's attached to the tiller, here." He had one hand on it. "Think of the tiller like your boat's steering wheel."

That was all she heard before her mind was caught somewhere between the middle of her nightmare and the memory of the angry ocean stealing her breath, turning her over like a child somersaulting down a hill.

She tried to focus on her breathing, but she couldn't hear herself inhale. Was she still breathing? She reached up around her throat. Why was it so hard to breathe? Her heart raced, and her vision clouded over. She dipped her head down, and the waves were above her. She braced herself for impact, certain she was about to be thrown into the surf, certain there was no way out of it.

"Louisa?"

Through the depths, she heard his voice. It was muffled, though, as if she were listening from underwater.

"Hey, focus on my voice." A little clearer now but still muffled.

The sound of the waves grew distant.

"Breathe, Lou." Cody drew in a slow, deep breath, and Louisa mimicked him. *Slow, deep breath.*

"Count to ten with me," he said. "Look at me." He forced her gaze. "Count to ten."

Slowly he started her off. She did as she was told. She closed her eyes and inhaled, then exhaled, until the pounding in her head began to subside.

Her eyes fluttered open, and she found Cody staring at her. They were close, only a few inches apart, and he was holding her hands.

She was still unsteady, though she was fairly certain her breathing had returned to normal.

"Feel better?"

He'd saved her again. On her own, she certainly would've died just now. Okay, maybe not actual death, but she could've at least passed out.

"I'm sorry," she said, inching back. "I don't know what's wrong with me." One glance at the water, and the oxygen disappeared again.

Cody took her face in his hands. "Focus on me."

Well, if you insist.

"Have you ever had a panic attack before?"

Louisa shook her head.

"Okay, you're not dying. You're fine. I'm going to get us back to the marina."

He started to turn, but she clung to his arms, unable—or unwilling—to let him go.

He faced her again, kindness in his expression. "This was a bad idea. You should've said something."

"I didn't know." Her eyes were wet with fearful tears, and she could only imagine what a disaster she seemed like to him. Her heart had kicked up again.

"Okay," he said. "This is what we're going to do. Tell me something you can touch."

His T-shirt underneath her fingers was soft and worn. "Your shirt."

"Great. Something else?"

She reached up and touched his chin. "Your skin." It was smooth, like he'd just shaved that morning.

"Tell me something you hear."

"Birds." Her breath began to steady, her pulse to slow. "Seagulls." She closed her eyes. "An airplane." It was faint, but it was there.

"What can you smell?"

"Your aftershave." She opened her eyes and scanned his face, which seemed neither embarrassed nor flattered that it was him she was latching on to in that moment.

"Good. Anything else?"

"Your shampoo."

"And what do you taste?"

Her eyes fell to his lips, and she wondered if she could tell him what she *wanted* to taste. "Nothing."

"Nothing?"

She shook her head. Her pulse and breathing had returned to normal. "I'm sorry."

"Don't apologize," he said.

"No." She looked up. "I'm sorry, Cody."

It might've been the panic of the moment that heightened every single emotion she was having. Every nerve ending in her body seemed on high alert, and there was a good chance Louisa might burst into a ball of flames simply from sitting this close to Cody. Or it might've been that she still, after all this time, could easily fall in love with the man who'd stolen her heart all those years ago.

He was different, of course. He was older, more jaded. He wasn't friendly and seemed impossible to know. But that didn't stop her from wanting to know him. She wanted to know him more than anything.

Her breath seemed short all over again, but this time for very different reasons. She glanced down and found his hands still wrapped around hers.

He shifted. Was he uncomfortable? Was this awkward?

The wind tugged strands of her hair from the elastic she'd used to tie it into a ponytail, and it caught at the corners of her mouth. He reached over and pushed it away, smoothing it back with such kindness it overwhelmed her.

Eric had never been this kind or attentive. He'd always been in a hurry.

"Are you having nightmares?" Cody asked.

She nodded, willing away the knot at the back of her throat, which seemed to only tie itself tighter.

"How long?"

"Since the day you saved my life."

He nodded. "Me too."

"Nightmares?"

"Since the day my dad saved my life."

Her heart lurched. How was it possible that he continued to go in the water? Continued to war with this vicious ocean and keep these taunting dreams at bay?

He picked up her hands and pressed them to his mouth. His eyes were closed, and he inhaled a breath deeper than any of the ones she'd just taken. "You should've told me." Her hands were at his forehead, and he seemed to be working very hard to keep his distance.

Something inside her called out to him, begging him to draw her closer, to give in to this—whatever this was. They were meant to be together. Surely he felt that now? It was undeniable. It was obvious. The fish in the ocean below them could probably feel the electric currents radiating from their boat.

And then, as if his senses had been knocked back into him, he backed away and gently let go of her hands.

"Listen, we need to head back in," he said. "So I want you to sit here and stare at your shoes. Don't look up. Don't even look at me, even though I know how much you like to stare."

She started to protest, and he smiled.

"I'm kidding, Lou."

Once again, she did as she was told. "I'm so embarrassed."

"Don't be. It happens."

"Obviously not to you. You're in this water every day. You even get in without a boat. You pull people out of it."

"Well, it's been a few years," he said.

"What do you mean?"

He steadied his gaze ahead of him as if looking at her would hurt too much. "I tried to become a rescue swimmer," he said. "Right after . . ."

Her head turned woozy. "You . . . ?"

"I always swam, you know. I was good at it. But after that night—something changed." This felt important, like a genuine connection, and she wasn't about to interrupt. What if he thought better of it and closed back up?

"A lot of guys don't make it," he said. "I wasn't going to be one of them. I was going to be the best." He shifted. "I did awesome in the pool, but when we got into open water, I froze. I panicked. Forgot all my training. The only thing I could remember was that night. I failed."

Louisa gazed back down at her shoes. "But you figured it out, right? I mean, look at you now."

"It took some time, but yeah. I figured it out. I realized I didn't have to be a rescue swimmer to be a part of the Coast Guard. That's when I applied to the academy. There really wasn't another option for me."

She dared a glance up. "But why?"

He didn't look at her. He seemed to be deciding whether or not to answer her question. "Because I was tired of the ocean winning."

Louisa didn't have to look at him to know his jaw was locked in a tense square. As she suspected, he saved lives to prove a point. He saved lives because he was trying to make up for the one who'd died to save his.

"How many people have you saved?" she asked.

He didn't answer—not right away.

"Cody?"

"I don't know." He rolled up his sleeve and revealed six hash marks and a set of initials—his father's—tattooed on the inside of his bicep. "But I know how many I've lost."

She started to say something, but no words seemed appropriate.

"We're back."

She glanced up and saw they were at the marina, and something inside her shifted. She could swim from here to the dock if their boat capsized and went under. She'd be fine. She was safe. Because of him.

"You can probably petition for another partner," she said as they reached the slip and he began to tie up the boat.

"Rules are rules, Chambers." He half smiled at her, and her heart stuttered at the sight of it. "I'm stuck with you."

"I think we can make an exception."

"I've never been one to back away from a challenge." He gave the rope a final tug. "And you just might be my biggest challenge yet."

The words wound their way around her heart like warm hot chocolate weaving its way to an empty stomach. Maybe she shouldn't allow them to give her hope, but she did. They did. They filled her right up, and for a moment, she even forgot what a fool she'd made of herself.

He stepped out of the boat and onto the dock, then reached both hands in her direction.

"Some challenges are more trouble than they're worth." She took his hands and stepped out, thankful to be on land again.

"Not you, though," he said. "You've always been worth every bit of trouble."

She tried not to read into his comment, which could clearly be taken as flirtation. This time, though, that didn't upset her.

"I'll take you home," he said after he'd gathered their things.

"I'm fine," she protested, but deep down, she wanted him to take her home. Maybe get reacquainted for a while. Maybe reacquaint herself with his lips?

"Louisa?"

"Hmm?"

"You're zoning out again." His brow was a deeply set line of worry.

"Sorry."

"You do that a lot."

"Sorry. I'll pay better attention." She slung her bag over her shoulder and fell into step beside him, and it occurred to her that in that moment, there was nowhere else in the world she'd rather be.

~

Louisa had received twenty-seven RSVPs to Maggie's birthday party, including one from her own parents, one from the Meyers family who'd left the island six years ago and hadn't returned due to their ailing health, and one from Freddy Santino, the man

Maggie claimed was her first love. They'd gone to elementary school together, and the old lady swore he wouldn't remember her in a million years.

But here he was, agreeing to come to the fish fry at the beginning of July.

Marissa Boggs had not responded.

CHAPTER TWENTY-FOUR

LOUISA STOOD ON THE PORCH OF HER PARENTS' COTTAGE and inhaled a deep breath. It hadn't been a great day. After her panic episode in the sailboat, Cody had driven her home, then told her if she needed a ride to get her Vespa later on, he could come back.

She assured him that Alyssa could take her, of course, and she'd already been enough of a burden on him. But secretly she wanted to tell him that yes, she would very much like to see him when he finished work that evening, and could he please stop by, and—*oh, look, I just happened to make dinner for us and why, yes, it will be served by candlelight.*

But things had grown quiet between them again on the ride to the cottage that used to be his and was now hers because she'd foolishly purchased it thinking somehow it would keep them connected.

She had so many questions she wanted to ask him: Had he ever looked her up? Did he still think about her? Would he like to get married and live happily ever after? So much for her post-Eric plan of swearing off love forever.

Of course, even she knew to keep these thoughts to herself.

She stared at the front door of her parents' cottage. Was she doing the right thing? Should she do what Cody asked and butt out? Besides, if something *had* been going on between her mother and Daniel, did she even want to know?

It seemed counterproductive to keep digging when the only thing in the world she wanted was to put back together what she'd destroyed. Her family. Cody's family. Her and Cody.

How did she do that?

She looked down at her feet and prayed for wisdom, something she did sometimes, though she noticed God seemed to have doled out fair amounts to everyone else while Louisa still waited in the wings for her portion.

"Louisa?" Her father's voice spun her around. He stood in the yard wearing a fisherman's hat (he didn't fish) and carrying a bucket. Teddy lolled beside him.

"Teddy!" Louisa bounded over to the giant dog and rubbed his ears, speaking unrecognizable gibberish as was customary when addressing an adorable animal.

"Well, hello to you, too," her father said.

"Hey, Dad." She stood.

"Hey, kitten. It's good to see you."

He started walking around the house toward his precious hydrangea bushes. She and Teddy followed.

"So what brings you by?" He knelt down next to the flowers and removed a trowel from the bucket, which, she could see now, was filled with gardening tools. Teddy sniffed the tools for a handful of seconds, then harrumphed down onto the ground beside her father.

"I'm here to see Mom," Louisa said.

"Did you knock? I think she's inside."

"No, you snuck up on me before I could." She started off in the opposite direction, eager to talk with her mom while her dad was occupied.

"Don't be a stranger," he called out.

She walked in the back door and found her mother standing at the sink, filling a pitcher for sun tea and humming a song Louisa eventually recognized as "I Saw Her Standing There" by the Beatles.

The years had been kind to her mother. JoEllen's dark-red hair was neatly cut into a longish bob that reached to her shoulders and curled under. She took care of herself and always seemed polished and professional, though Louisa knew she'd barely worked a day in her life.

It baffled her, really, that her mom had a college degree she had no desire to use.

"Hey, Mom."

Her mother startled and hit the faucet on the sink. She spun toward Louisa and clutched her hand to her chest. "You scared me."

"Sorry."

Her mom waved her off. "It's fine. You look tired. Have you been getting enough rest?"

"I'm okay." *I nearly died again this morning, but I know you don't want to hear about that. You probably only want to talk about two things—yourself and when I'm going to reunite with Eric and give you grandchildren.*

Her mom walked toward her, and for a brief moment Louisa wondered if the older woman might actually hug her or show some other sign of affection.

Instead, JoEllen stopped right in front of Louisa, gave her a once-over, then inched back. "You need to have your brows done."

"It's good to see you, too, Mother."

"Of course it's good to see you, Louisa." Her mom walked back toward her pitcher of tea, screwed the lid on, then moved toward the front door. She set the pitcher on the porch and gave it a pat. "Do your thing, Mr. Sunshine."

Louisa refrained from rolling her eyes. It occurred to her in that moment that her family was weird.

Was she weird? Oh, gosh, she was, wasn't she?

"Louisa?"

"Hmm?"

"Still got your head in the clouds, I see." Mom had gone back into the kitchen and had probably asked Louisa a question, but Louisa had no idea what it was.

"What did you say?"

"Honestly, Louisa. I really hoped you'd outgrow this daydreaming."

"This daydreaming is the reason I'm now a successful business owner."

Her mom raised a brow. "Successful?"

Louisa shrank under the accusation. She *was* successful. She had her own business. She paid her bills. Never mind that her bank account was nearly empty and she had no idea how she would ever pay for her impulse buy of one handsome Coast Guardsman.

"I suppose you must be if you have over five thousand dollars to give away at a charity auction." Her raised brow seemed to accuse.

"It's for a good cause." Louisa sat on the tall stool at the kitchen island and plucked a grape from the bunch in the fruit bowl on the counter.

In the lull, Louisa wondered if part of the reason it had become so important to repair the relationship between her family and Cody's was because of this thinly veiled tension that always existed between her and her mother. Had it been there before Daniel had died? Did she really think that making things right between Marissa and her parents would fix her own relationship with them?

Louisa knew her mother blamed her for Daniel's death. She'd implied as much more than once.

The day Louisa had told her she'd decided to move to Nantucket full-time and work for the hotel, her mom said, "Are you sure that's a good idea? It will be a constant reminder that your actions have consequences."

Louisa hadn't bothered correcting her. She hadn't taken the time to explain that she'd already learned that lesson and was currently punishing herself for it on a daily, hourly, minute-ly basis.

Louisa had always believed her mother's passive-aggressive anger toward her was a result of the fact that she'd lost Marissa, her best friend in the world. But now, in light of what Cody suspected, she wondered if it was more than that.

The thought of it made Louisa's stomach roll.

"Are you here to ask for money?"

"What? No. I've been on my own for years, Mom."

Her mother took a Diet Coke from the refrigerator.

"Still drinking that, are you?"

She opened the bottle and poured it into a glass. "Leave me alone. I know all about how bad it is for me."

"You know aspartame is worse than real sugar."

"Why are you here, Louisa?"

"Can't a girl stop by and say hello to the parents who never text or call?"

"Oh, Louisa, you've always been so dramatic." Her mother took a drink. "So have you had a sailing lesson yet?"

In a flash, Louisa was back on that boat, touching Cody's T-shirt, inhaling the scent of his aftershave, hearing the sound of the birds, and wondering how it might taste if he brought his lips to hers.

"Just one," Louisa said.

"Just you and Cody?" Her mother's expression had turned troubled.

Louisa nodded.

"How is he?"

Beautiful. Kind. Muscular. Handsome. Strong. Gorgeous. Broken. "Fine, I guess."

"Is he speaking to you?"

"We're working on the regatta together, Mother," Louisa said, realizing they were veering wildly off course. "Hey, do you know anything about that memorial someone put up for Daniel?"

"The cross?"

"Yes."

"No."

Louisa eyed her mother.

"I mean, I know it exists."

"Do you know who put it there?"

Her mother shrugged. "How would I?"

"You and Dad were his closest friends."

"That was a long time ago. Maybe Marissa had it installed. Or Cody?"

"They didn't."

Her mother shifted. She looked uncomfortable. Did she have something to hide?

She opened the refrigerator and pulled out an apple, then found a cutting board and knife and started slicing. She'd eat it with sharp cheddar cheese, same way she had when Louisa was a girl. It was a JoEllen delicacy Louisa had never cared for.

She liked her cheese on crackers and her apples with peanut butter.

Or maybe she just didn't want to be anything like her mother.

"Cody found something on the back of the cross," she said cautiously, scrutinizing her mother's every move.

Mom glanced up mindlessly but continued cutting. "And?"

"It was a note for his dad."

Her mother stopped cutting.

"It was addressed to Danny."

"Danny?"

Louisa nodded. "Danny."

"Why are you looking at me like that?"

"Did you leave the note, Mom?"

"I did not," she said. "Other people on this island knew Daniel Boggs. Maggie, for instance."

"Maggie knows nothing about it," Louisa said. "And to my knowledge, she never called him Danny."

Mom set the knife down and gave Louisa her full attention. "What do you really want to ask me, Louisa?"

Louisa's palms had gone cold. Was she really about to accuse her mother of having an affair? "Were you sleeping with Cody's dad?"

Apparently yes, she was going to accuse her mom of having an affair.

Her mother gasped. "No, I was not."

Well, shoot, Louisa actually believed her.

"Daniel and I dated very casually before we met Marissa and Warren. I was the one who set them up, if you'll remember."

"I know the story," she said. "But nobody else called him Danny."

"Lots of people called him Danny," Mom said. "People he worked with. His boss. Your father. Maggie even called him that now and then."

"I never heard anyone but you call him that."

"How do you remember back that far, Louisa? It's been ages, and you were young." She found the cheddar in the fridge, took it out, and began hacking at it.

"Mom." Louisa waited until her mother finally—finally—looked up. "Was there something going on?"

"Something going on with what?" Her father walked in, and Louisa noticed he'd put on a few pounds.

"Louisa thinks I was fooling around with Daniel Boggs." Her mother rolled her eyes. Her father laughed that hearty laugh of his.

"I didn't say I thought that. I was just asking if it was a possibility."

Her dad started drinking a Diet Coke too.

"That will kill you," her mother said with an air of condescension directed at Louisa.

"Life is killing me, Joey," he said. "Why are you digging this up now, kitten?"

"Forget it," Louisa said, feeling suddenly sheepish and regretting coming here in the first place. It was clear that her birthday wish the day she turned nine—*I wish my parents would be like other kids' parents*—had not come true.

"Suit yourself," her father said. He took a swig of soda.

"Did you know that when Daniel died, he had no money in his bank account?"

Neither of her parents answered for a moment.

"I don't think we should be talking about this," her mom finally said. "It feels wrong."

"What feels wrong is that Mr. Boggs—Daniel—left his family with practically nothing. Doesn't that seem a bit strange?"

Her father stiffened, the smile fading from his face. More wrinkles than last year, she noticed. "The market ebbs and flows. I'm sure if Daniel was low that week, it would've picked back up in a month or so. That's the way it goes." He took off his hat and fidgeted with it, avoiding Louisa's eyes.

Louisa didn't buy it. That's not how it went when you had a family. You made sure there was enough money to at least see them through a few months of "low." Especially someone like Daniel, who was arguably the best father Louisa had ever known.

"Leave this alone, Louisa. No good can come from poking around graves." Her father's face had turned serious, enough to almost convince Louisa to obey.

Almost.

He held her gaze for several seconds as if to punctuate his sentence and finally looked away.

Louisa couldn't help but wonder what the man knew—because it sure felt like something.

CHAPTER TWENTY-FIVE

TWO DAYS AFTER THE BOTCHED ATTEMPT to take Louisa sailing, and Cody still couldn't shake the image of her on the boat, struggling to get a breath. It was almost as bad as the image of her lifeless body on the deck of the cutter. That one haunted him at night—no matter how many times he tried to replace it with the image of her in that teal dress, looking just about as beautiful as a person could look.

"How are the regatta plans coming along?" Duncan was at his door, interrupting his thoughts, and while he should thank his superior, truthfully he just wanted to cling to the image of Louisa in that dress for a few more minutes.

"Good," he said. "I mean, I think they're good. I'm meeting with Louisa later today for an update."

"How are you two?"

Cody frowned. "Sir?"

"Things seemed a little strained at the auction. Is there something going on there?" He paused for a beat, then held up his hands. "Never mind. That's not my business. But I think if you have half a shot with a girl like that, you better take it."

Duncan had no idea what he was talking about.

"She's beautiful. She's smart. She's successful."

"So why don't you ask her out?"

Duncan's eyes twinkled, and Cody swore if the man were a cartoon character, there'd be a bell dinging on cue with his smile. "I would if I didn't think she was hung up on my second-in-command."

"It's really not like that," Cody said.

"Enjoy the meeting. It's slow here, so don't come back when you're done."

"Chief?"

"You heard me, Boggs. You're done for the day. Go plan this regatta and make it a good one. The Coast Guard *and* the family of Jackson Wirth are counting on you."

~

Cody knocked on the door to Louisa's office and braced himself for the rush of oxygen that would inevitably leave his body the second he saw her.

She appeared in the doorway. And there it went—all the air in his lungs.

She motioned for him to come in but didn't say anything. It wasn't like Louisa to be quiet. He fought the urge to ask her what was wrong, but she quickly launched into the latest plans for the regatta. Food vendors. Spots for the Coast Guard to set up demonstrations. Various races with various prizes. She said nothing about the Race with a Coastie event and nothing about Jackson Wirth.

She ran through details so quickly, he was certain she wasn't even listening to herself, let alone expecting him to listen to her.

"What's wrong with you?" he interrupted when she was in the process of telling him about the kayaks she'd secured for the day of the event—another activity she'd added to the itinerary.

Her eyes drifted up toward his, but she didn't respond.

"Something's obviously bothering you."

"What makes you say that?" She dropped her pen onto her desk and pushed her iPad away.

He shrugged. "You don't seem like yourself."

She half laughed, but it was clear she wasn't amused. "How would you know? Maybe this *is* me being myself."

All business. Cold. Quick. No, this definitely wasn't Louisa.

"You haven't smiled once since I walked in here," he said.

"Maybe I don't feel like smiling when I'm around you."

He felt his eyes widen. "Ouch."

She covered her face with her hands. "I'm sorry. That was super mean. It came out wrong."

"What's the matter?"

She let out a heavy sigh and moved her hands away from her face, but her eyes were focused on the ceiling above her. "I went to see my parents. I think I'm still recovering."

"I'm sorry." He didn't pry. Not because he didn't want to, but because he wasn't sure how much she wanted to share. If he was really going to keep his distance, he'd have to do a good job of keeping her at arm's length.

Why was it so hard?

She waved him off. "It's fine. I'm used to it. Or at least I should be. My mom's never forgiven me for—" She looked away.

He could see the sadness on her face. He knew how it felt to carry the guilt of that night, and he wished he could carry it for her.

She pressed her palms into her eyes. "Plus, I accidentally bid on you and now you're stuck with a disaster of a partner for the race, and it's next weekend, and you know I'm not going to be over whatever this is by then."

"Oh, I don't know," he said. "Stranger things have happened."

She sighed. "I can't sleep. I keep waking up certain I'm dead. It's horrible to almost drown."

"I know," he said quietly.

She looked at him. Had she forgotten that his father died because Cody had nearly drowned? Did she not realize that he, too, had overwhelming nightmares and a strong, healthy fear of the water?

If she had forgotten, she remembered it now. He saw it in her eyes.

"It seems so easy for you," she said. "Being in the water."

He distinctly remembered the day he got back in the water. He didn't take it slow or easy. He plunged himself into the ocean, determined not to let it steal anything else from him, and it nearly killed him all over again.

It took some time, but eventually he overcame his fear. He'd dedicated his life to saving the people the sea wanted to steal.

"Cody?"

He'd shared too much that day on the boat—getting any deeper with Louisa was a bad idea.

"You've got this regatta stuff figured out, right?" he asked.

She looked confused at his abrupt subject change and started to scan the work on her desk. "Yes."

"Okay, I trust you." He stood.

"You're leaving?"

"No, *we're* leaving."

Her frown line deepened.

He looked at her outfit—a pink striped sundress with a pair of brown sandals. He could see her pink toenails. Was it strange that even her feet charmed him? "But you can't wear that. Go change."

"Where are we going?"

"Training."

"For what?"

"For the race," he said. "I don't know if you remember, but I'm a pretty competitive person. You might not have meant to bid on me, but you did—and I have no intention of losing."

Her face fell. "Cody, I don't think I can—"

"Louisa. Enough excuses. You can let this thing control you or you can take control of it. This is a mental battle."

"Well, I'm losing," she said.

"And I'm here to help. Go change."

Finally she relented. She left him standing in her office feeling out of place. This room used to be a cozy little family room where he and his parents and sister, along with Louisa and her parents, would spend their evenings playing board games or, if he was really lucky, video games. Their television had been hooked up to a DVD player and a gaming system but only got local channels with an antenna.

Maybe that's why he still preferred books to TV and quiet to noise. His parents had loved their simple life, so he supposed it made sense that he, too, would grow to love a simple life.

His phone buzzed in his pocket, and he took it out to reveal a text from his mom.

Call me when you have a minute.

He didn't talk to his mom often, but he knew without asking that she wouldn't love that he was spending time with Louisa. Why did he feel like he was betraying her simply by being here?

He shoved the phone into his pocket without responding and looked up in time to see Louisa walk back into the room.

She wore a pair of shorts and a tank top over her swimsuit, and she carried a towel. "Is this appropriate attire for whatever you have in mind?"

He forced himself not to smile at her, though he really, really wanted to. He wanted to pull the elastic out of her hair and let those long red waves fall down around her shoulders and then bury his face in them. Instead, he just nodded and pushed open the door, thankful for the fresh air that served as a dose of reality.

She jogged to catch up to him. "Where are we going?"

"You'll see."

"What if I refuse to get into your Jeep until I know where you're taking me?" She stopped and planted her feet. She really could be maddening when she wanted to be.

He faced her. "Then I guess you'll miss out." He was starting to learn when to call her bluff. Obviously a good choice because seconds later she was jogging to catch up to him again. He opened the passenger door and motioned for her to get in.

"I can open my own door, you know." She hopped up onto the seat.

"Right, but you know that's not how I was brought up."

Her eyes softened. "I know."

He started the engine. "Ready?"

"I'd be more ready if you told me where we were going."

He pulled out onto the road. "Where's the fun in that?"

She looked out the window. "I didn't realize we were having fun."

He glanced down and noticed her hand on her lap, and he pushed away the desire to reach over and pick it up. She wore rings on three of her four fingers. Only her ring finger was naked.

He'd given her a ring once, a plain silver band. He didn't have money for anything else, but he told her it was a promise ring. He promised he'd love her forever. And he would have too.

He'd dated other women, but his lifestyle didn't lend itself to a long-term relationship. He liked to keep things simple and uncomplicated. That way nobody got hurt.

That's what he should be thinking about right now, not the way the sun highlighted her skin or the way she was beautiful without trying.

Louisa had this quiet confidence he didn't see in most of the women he met. Maybe that's why he wanted to help her overcome this new fear of the water—because she seemed unafraid of everything, and he wanted her to stay that way.

He envied her that.

He drove down Polpis Road, drinking in the serene scene in front of them. He couldn't be sure, but as they passed underneath the trees that led into Quidnet, he might've heard her exhale for the first time since he arrived at her house.

Her body had gone from rigid to relaxed, and it occurred to him he was still waiting for that to happen to him. He'd been a ball of nerves from the second he arrived back on the island.

"I know where we're going," she said.

"Sesachacha Pond." He kept his eyes on the road.

Was she thinking about the time they rode their bikes out here and spent the day? They'd gone kayaking and swimming and eaten a picnic lunch and pretty much had the kind of day that made people fall in love with each other.

Gosh, things were simple then. He missed it.

"Thought we'd start off slow." He parked the Jeep and turned off the engine.

The pond was separated from the ocean, and the swimming was easy. No seaweed and no waves. If she'd been smart, she would've spent that morning paddleboarding here.

"I'm fine, you know." She got out of the Jeep, clinging to her phone as if her life depended on it.

He reached over and pried it from her hands. "You can leave that here."

She watched him as he opened the door of his vehicle and put the phone in the glove box.

"I thought about it, and we can go to the marina and go back out today," she said. "I really am fine."

He stood in front of her, loving that she was only a few inches shorter than he was. He liked that she was independent—and that it annoyed her to have this weakness.

"You know I'm an officer in the US Coast Guard, right?"

She shot him a look dripping with irritation.

"So you know I am trained and certified to save you should you get pulled under by a giant, man-eating fish."

"You think you're really funny, don't you?"

He let himself smile for a fleeting moment, then turned toward the water. "I want you to feel safe, is all."

She was at his side. Their arms brushed against each other as they walked. He didn't move away. Neither did she.

"I do feel safe," she said. "I'm with a three-time state-champion swimmer." She pushed her shoulder into his.

"Oh, I've got way more impressive credentials than that."

She stopped, eyes wide. "You do?"

He'd forgotten this about her. She was easy to get close to. You wanted to tell Louisa things—wanted her to know everything about you so she would tell you everything about her. And she always did. A true open book.

He noticed she was still standing in the spot where she'd stopped. He turned toward her and squinted into the sun. "You coming or what?"

"Spill it."

He groaned and started back toward the water.

"I'm not going in till you tell me," she called out.

"Forget I said anything," he called over his shoulder.

She crossed her arms over her chest—her way of digging in her heels.

"I was just blowing smoke, Lou. Forget I said anything."

She didn't move, and neither did a single muscle in her face. Not even the slightest twitch of an eyebrow. When it came to staring down an opponent, she was better than anyone he knew.

"I got a medal once. It's not a big deal."

"Obviously it is," she said. "Why didn't you put that on your Coastie auction facts and figures?"

"Would you have paid more for me if I had?" He tossed her a half grin, and for the briefest moment they were back to who they used to be—not an ounce of painful history between them.

"So, what, you saved someone from a burning ship or something like that?"

He shrugged. "Something like that."

She watched him for a long moment, and an unspeakable *something* passed between them.

"You're not going to give me the details, are you?"

"I'm a man of mystery."

She rolled her eyes. "Fine. What's your big plan, skipper?" She walked past him, toward the water.

"Skipper?" He followed her.

"Your new nickname. I think it suits you." She grinned at him over her shoulder, and he could see that she'd moved past whatever moment they'd almost shared.

Or maybe he'd only imagined there was a moment. Maybe he'd only imagined there was anything between them at all.

CHAPTER TWENTY-SIX

AGAINST HER BETTER JUDGMENT, Louisa trudged toward Sesachacha Pond. She remembered the first time she saw the name of the pond on the map—she butchered its pronunciation so badly, the other kids on the beach laughed at her for a solid five minutes. They called her the "Sesa-cha-cha girl" that entire summer.

"What's with them?" Cody had asked, and Louisa only shrugged. She didn't know what was with them. She didn't know why the name of this pond was funny or what she'd done to make it more so. She only knew that when they pointed and laughed at her, her cheeks flamed and her skin burned. She wanted to hide.

"What's your problem?" Cody had shouted in their general direction.

One girl, a summer resident named Autumn who wasn't a part of the mockers, quietly came over to them, as if she had something to say.

"It's pronounced 'Sack-a-juh,'" she said. "But I kind of like your way better." Autumn smiled then, and she became one of Louisa's best friends, second only to Cody Boggs.

Louisa had gone home that afternoon with a sunburn, feeling a little less like a social outcast thanks to Autumn and Cody.

Now, standing near the water, she wanted to turn and run, but her desire to leave had less to do with the water and more to do with the fact that Cody had her insides all tangled up. She stole a glimpse of his profile, highlighted by the shadows of the late-afternoon sun.

"What are we doing here?" she asked. "Where's the boat?"

"No boat," he said.

She looked at him full-on, doing nothing to hide her confusion. "What do you mean 'no boat'?"

"You trust me, right?" He held his hand out in her direction, and she stared at it for several seconds like she didn't know what it was.

When she didn't move, he dropped his hand. "Oh. So you don't trust me."

"No," she said. "I do."

"Then let me help you."

When he said it, he sounded so earnest, so intentional, she had no choice but to obey. It didn't matter that she was certain she was beyond help or that her dreams haunted her even when she was awake—in that moment, the only thing she needed was what he wanted to give: a small piece of himself.

His hand was back, an offering of hope, and she took it because it had been a long time since she'd felt hopeful, and she missed that feeling.

"We're going to go slow," he said.

"I bet you say that to all the girls," she said with a thoughtless laugh.

He looked at her, but she kept her eyes down, away—anywhere but locked on to his. She had no filter. Where was the nearest hole to fall into?

She willed herself to stop being so ridiculous and tried to act casual, like they were just two buddies hanging out on the beach and not two people who'd been more than friends once upon a time but who were not friends at all right now. She forced herself not to think about the way his hand wrapped around hers made her feel—like she could do anything.

Her foot slipped and splashed in the shallow water. His arm was around her waist in a flash, steadying her and keeping her from falling.

"You okay?"

"Sure," she squeaked.

"I don't, you know."

She righted herself and looked at him. "Don't what?"

"Say that to all the girls." He still had a hold of her hand.

"You don't go slow?" Her heart dropped. Why would he tell her that?

He laughed. "That's not what I meant. I meant there haven't been a lot of girls."

Oh. Well, that she hadn't expected. Was he telling the truth?

He pulled his shirt off and tossed it onto the dry sand a few feet away, then gave her a once-over. She still had shorts and a tank top over her swimsuit, and frankly that was just fine with her. Except then she'd be in wet clothes the rest of the day.

Why couldn't they be holding a dogsled race? Then her body could remain covered in layers and layers of clothes.

She removed her tank top and chucked it onto the shore. Her suit was hardly revealing—she'd gotten it for actual swimming, after all. Looking good on the beach had never been her concern.

She stepped out of the water, took her shorts off, and threw them on the pile. When she turned, she found him looking at her, and all at once her entire body blushed. "What?"

He looked away. "Nothing."

Was he . . . smiling?

She made her way back out to where he stood. "What now, skipper?"

"Now we swim."

A wave of panic rolled through her.

"Slowly." He stood in front of her and took both of her hands, then started walking backward. Each time the water rose enough to notice, he stopped and talked to her, usually about something unrelated to the water.

He asked what had happened to Muffin (her hamster), and she told him about Teddy and how one day she planned to dog-nap him simply on principle. After all, she was the one who'd wanted the dog in the first place.

Another step. "So you and that guy from the auction . . ."

Her eyes darted to his, then back down to the water. "Eric."

"Was it serious?"

"I guess. Kind of."

"Why aren't you together?" Another step.

"He didn't believe in me," she said matter-of-factly. There were many reasons she and Eric weren't together, but at the heart of it, this was the one that mattered most.

She could practically feel Cody's frown.

"I told him I wanted to start my own business. He gave me a list of reasons why I shouldn't. I guess I got tired of believing people who don't believe in me."

Another step.

"That's funny."

She frowned. "Funny?"

"No, I mean, because to me, you've always seemed kind of invincible. Confident, you know, like a person who could do anything."

Her cheeks grew hot. "Really?"

"Even end up waist-deep in the water."

She followed his gaze, and only then did she notice how far they'd traveled. "Well, look at that."

They stood still for a long moment; then he broke the silence. "You're still really close with Maggie."

He said it as a statement, not a question.

She glanced down. "You know I always wanted to live here year-round. Everyone said it was crazy, but Maggie said I should go for it.

She said the island was beautiful in the summer, but it was magic in the winter. She was right."

"You spend a lot of time with her?"

Another nod. "She's like the mother I never had." She looked up, certain her expression had turned sad, which was unintentional.

"And she's really dying?"

"She's really dying."

His eyes were on the water occupying the space between them.

"That's why I want to have this party for her," she said. "She needs to know that everyone loves her, that we're all okay."

"You don't think she knows that?"

She moved her gaze to his. "I think it makes her sad that none of us talk anymore."

The water lapped around her waist, but she didn't feel scared or nervous at all. Her hands were still locked inside his, and she thought she could stay like that forever.

"You and I are talking right now," he said.

"Only because we have to," Louisa said.

He frowned. "Or maybe because we want to."

She studied him for any hint of what he was thinking, but she came up empty. Cody Boggs had become difficult to read. He said these things that made her think maybe they could start over, that maybe he did forgive her—but then in the next breath, he'd say other things that made her positive he'd crafted a permanent parking space for the chip on his shoulder.

She braced herself for the flip side of his coin, but it never came. Instead, he gave her hands a tug and drew her a little farther into the water.

Seconds later, she realized the water was at her shoulders and she was still breathing normally.

"Okay, I'm taller than you," he said.

"Not by much."

"Yeah, I get it, you're tall." He smiled at her—a real smile. She felt it in her toes. "But I'm going to ask you to do something that requires you to trust me a little."

"Haven't I already proven that I trust you? Look where we are." She glanced back toward the spot where they'd left their clothes, and her pulse kicked up.

"No," he said firmly. "Look at me. Don't look back there."

She did as she was told.

"You're safe, okay? Remember—elite swimmer."

She inched back and looked into his deep-brown eyes. She had the feeling he was about to ask her to do something terrifying. So why wasn't she scared?

"I want you to lie back. Just float in the water."

"No way." If she could run in neck-deep water, she would—straight for the shore. He was crazy if he thought she was ready for that.

"Lou, how many times have you been in the ocean?"

She shrugged. "I don't know. Lots."

"Right. Lots. But this summer was the first time you've ever had a close call."

"Yes."

"And even you admit that could've been avoided if . . ."

"If?"

"If you'd been a little more careful."

She glared at him, but the innocent expression on his face told her he wasn't going to apologize for speaking the truth.

He put a hand on her back and sent a shiver straight down her spine. "I'm going to be here the whole time, and I'm not going to let go of you once."

Goose bumps crawled up her arms, but they had nothing to do with the temperature of the water.

"Okay?"

She nodded. Her hair was tied up in a bun on top of her head, and she knew that taking it down after it was wet would be painful, so she pulled the elastic out and wrapped it around her wrist, shaking out her long hair until the ends of it landed in the water.

She glanced up and found him watching her, turning her self-conscious, but she didn't look away.

His eyes dipped to her lips and hung there for several torturous seconds.

She'd tried to tell herself it was futile to fixate on this man, but when he looked at her like that, all reason went out the window.

"Ready?" His voice was husky, almost a whisper.

"I think so." Slowly, carefully, she leaned back. Water crawled up her neck and into her hair, which spilled out in waves around her. His hand steadied her, strong and firm under her back as her legs floated up in the water until she was lying there, at the mercy of the water.

She closed her eyes, and for a moment it was as if she were on a cloud, floating through the air, weightless. She was aware of his body next to her, strong and secure and easy to lean into.

Water covered, then uncovered her torso as she floated, and the sun warmed her face.

It was tranquil, pleasant even. She drew in a breath, then another one.

But then, out of nowhere, the image of the waves, angry and hungry, forced itself on her, and she was helpless to ignore it. Her breathing picked up, and she tried to return to the peace of the moment before, but the memory of the violent water that had dragged her down assaulted her. It was like trying to outrun a much stronger and faster enemy.

Cody's grip on her tightened, but only slightly as another memory penetrated the calm. She couldn't breathe. It was like someone had two tight hands wrapped around her neck. Her eyes shot open, and the concern on his face nearly jolted her back to the present.

She gasped for breath and struggled to pull herself up, flailing around like she forgot how to move, how to swim, how to walk. But she realized in a flash she didn't have to remember any of those things because he was remembering for her. He quickly swung a hand underneath her and picked her up, as if she weighed nothing (which she most certainly did not). He leaned closer, his lips brushing the side of her forehead, and whispered, "You're okay, Louisa," as he moved closer to the shore.

In the distance, she heard a dog bark, a child laugh, but soon the noise of the day was drowned out by the beating of her heart as her pulse began to slow and she told herself she was okay. She was fine. Cody was here.

When they'd reached shallower waters, he stood her upright, but instead of letting her go, he pulled her into him, wrapped his arms around her, and let her stand like that, head on his shoulder for so many minutes she wondered if she'd forgotten her own name.

Really, she was fine. But she couldn't bring herself to move away from him. Not when his skin smelled like pine trees and his heart beat so clearly in her ear. She could've stayed like that forever and been perfectly happy.

After what felt like hours, he slowly peeled her body away from his and brought his gaze to hers. "I'm sorry. I might've pushed you too quickly."

She shook her head. "I want to try again."

His brow knit into a tight line of worry. "No. We can try again another day. The regatta isn't that important."

She steeled her jaw. "Not for the regatta. For me."

He, more than anyone else, would surely understand that.

He thought about it for too many seconds, and while she didn't like asking anyone for permission, she knew she needed his. She wouldn't overcome this fear on her own, and he would keep her safe. It's what he did.

Finally he nodded. "Okay."

And he walked her back into the water and held her until the nightmare couldn't torment her anymore.

CHAPTER TWENTY-SEVEN

WHEN HE GOT HOME, Cody did the thing he'd been avoiding all day—
he called his mom. She answered on the first ring.

"I was starting to worry you were off on a supersecret mission,"
she said by way of greeting.

"Hey, Mom."

"How are things?"

"Good."

"You're taking care of yourself?"

"Yep. Everything is fine."

"Save any lives lately?"

The image of Louisa floating in the water pummeled him.

"I'm sure you have. You don't have to tell me about it."

It was like this with his mom sometimes. She thought everything
he did—even cleaning the boats or checking the engines or running
training drills—was top secret. But it was time to tell her the truth.
And she wasn't going to like it. Because while he'd been back in
Nantucket for weeks, he'd yet to break that news to his mother.

"I actually called to tell you something," she said before he could find the words.

"Oh?" His mind spun with possibilities. Maybe she'd finally started dating again. Wouldn't that be something?

"I got an invitation in the mail."

His heart dropped. *Louisa.* He'd asked her not to send it, but she'd sent it. Why was he not surprised?

"It's for a birthday party for Maggie Fisher. You remember Maggie, right?"

He grunted an affirmative response.

"Well, it's her birthday, and you know how big of a deal birthdays always were to us—I mean, of course you probably remember those big bashes we threw you kids—" She stopped.

"I remember."

"I've decided I'm going to go."

He must've been quiet for an unusual amount of time because his mom said his name as if she'd said it already and he hadn't responded. He shook away the shock and focused on her voice.

"I think it will be good for me," she said. "I think it might be good for you, too."

"Mom—"

"I know how you feel about everything, about your father, and I was angry for a long time—mad at God, mad at your dad . . ."

"Mad at me?"

She paused. "Honey, I was never mad at you."

He wanted to reach out and grab those words, to pull them close and let them wash over him, taking away all the guilt and shame he'd been dragging around behind him like a too-heavy backpack. Instead, he slapped them away. Because he knew better.

"It was an accident," she said quietly.

"But it was my fault."

If she were here, she'd likely hug him and he'd stiffen at her touch. Because she could say those words a hundred times over, but he wouldn't believe them even once.

"It was no one's fault," she said.

"Not even Louisa's?"

The line turned cold on the other end.

"It was an accident," she finally repeated.

It wasn't something she'd ever said before. He'd always assumed she blamed Louisa because it was too painful to blame her own son. And let's be honest, they all needed someone to blame.

"Are you sure you want to go to this party, Mom? You know the Chambers family will probably be there."

She sniffed and he worried she was crying, but she quickly found her voice. "I need to do this, honey. I don't expect you to understand."

He didn't expect her to understand what he was about to tell her either.

"Mom, I'm in Nantucket."

If a jaw going slack had a sound, he'd just heard it on the other end of the line. "You're what?"

"I got stationed here," he said. "It's not a top secret mission or anything—they moved me to help build morale, to bring about awareness for what we do here."

"Why didn't you say—?"

"Because I didn't want to upset you. You've been through enough already."

"I'm not a delicate flower, Cody. You can tell me these things."

"Not about this," he said. "Not about Dad."

She cleared her throat. "It's been years."

"Well, it's not like we've moved on." He wouldn't push, but it was true. She wasn't over the way Daniel left, as if it had been his choice. She wasn't over the fact that her life turned out nothing like it was supposed to.

He knew how that felt.

But the betrayal she must've felt when she saw those empty bank accounts—that, he didn't fully comprehend. And his suspicions about JoEllen Chambers were only going to make it worse.

Louisa, you shouldn't have sent that invitation.

"I think I've done a pretty good job bouncing back." There was defensiveness in her voice.

"You did, Mom," he said. "We're all doing just fine. But coming back here—it's not going to be easy. I'm afraid all it's going to do is set you back. A lot."

"Why would it?"

He sighed. *Because he's everywhere. His laugh, it catches on the wind and plays on a continuous loop over the ocean. Here, you can't push him out of your mind. You can't forget.* "It's just hard, is all."

"Well, you've always told me it would be good for me to move on, so maybe this is what I need. Closure. I'm glad you're there." She paused. "But you should've told me."

"Yeah."

"Have you . . . ?" She stopped as if trying to decide whether or not to probe him. He wasn't sure if her hesitation was because she was worried about upsetting him or herself.

"What?"

"Have you seen anyone we knew?"

It wasn't like she cared if he saw Brenda and Jonathan Singer, the people with the yippy dog who had lived next door. She didn't want to know if Dr. Smithton and Mary Beth Jeffries were back in town. She meant Louisa. She meant Warren and JoEllen.

"Yeah," he said after too many seconds of silence. He refrained from telling her he'd spent the afternoon holding Louisa in his arms. She wouldn't understand. "Why did they become the enemy, Mom? They didn't kill Dad."

Now she *was* crying. She thought she was going to come here and go to a party on the beach and have zero feelings about it? Was she crazy?

"You said it yourself—it was an accident."

"It was senseless," she said.

"It wasn't her fault." He realized he actually meant it. He didn't blame Louisa. He had for a long time, mostly because he needed to—but going in the water that night, it had been his choice. And it had been his father's choice to go in after him.

"We shouldn't talk about this," his mom said.

"You shouldn't come to the party," he said.

"I already sent in the RSVP."

"Mom, they're all here. And there's something else." He really didn't want to have this conversation. He wanted her to go back to her life in Chicago and let her imagine he was still in San Diego. But he couldn't escape it—and he knew she deserved to know.

"What?"

So he told her. About the memorial and the note on the back of it.

"A note?" she asked. "What did it say?"

He told her that, too.

She went quiet again.

"Mom, it could've been anyone," he lied. "Someone he worked with or—"

"Joey."

His heart dropped.

"I always thought she regretted giving your dad to me."

"What are you talking about?"

"Nothing," she said. "Never mind."

He dragged his hand over his forehead and wished he could travel back in time to try to figure out how to keep this conversation from happening in the first place.

"I don't think it was her."

"Either way," she said, "it doesn't really matter now."

He tried not to groan. Because it did matter, and being here made it matter more.

"Mom, the party is in a month," he said. "Don't book tickets. Don't come here."

Then his mother's voice shifted as if she'd found a new resolve. "Too late, honey. I already booked my ticket. I'll text you the details so you can meet me at the ferry. Or not—either way."

Unsent letter to Marissa Boggs:

Dear Mrs. Boggs,

It's been six months since Mr. Boggs died. I haven't been able to stop thinking about him or you or Cody. In fact, you're all I think about. I know you probably never want to talk to me again. I know you're probably mad at the way I treated your son, and hate me for the way he reacted to what I did.

I didn't mean to hurt him.

I guess that's the thing about mistakes. We never mean for them to happen.

My mom made me see a counselor, and he said I need to forgive myself. He said if I ask, God will forgive me, and I believe that.

But what about you and Cody and Marley? Will you forgive me? Can you ever forgive me?

I don't know if I'll ever move past this until you do. And that's not me trying to convince you to say something that isn't true—I just wanted you to know how deeply sorry I am for the mistake I made.

My mom misses you. Maybe, even if you can't forgive me, you can somehow still find a way to be friends with her? I know it would make things so much better.

Louisa

PS—I don't think Cody will ever talk to me again, but could you let him know that I'm going to spend the rest of my life trying to make up for what I've done?

xoxo

CHAPTER TWENTY-EIGHT

"MAGGIE, HAVE YOU EVER THROWN ANYTHING AWAY?" Louisa was standing in one of the spare bedrooms on the second level of Maggie's cottage while the old woman rested comfortably in an armchair downstairs. She'd hollered her question toward the hallway, but either Maggie hadn't heard her or she was ignoring her.

Odds were good it was the latter.

Louisa had come over to continue the daunting project of helping Maggie go through her possessions. She showed up with lobster rolls and potato salad from Bartlett's Farm. They ate dinner, and Maggie asked her twice if she'd seen Cody.

Both times, Louisa's mind drifted back to earlier in the day, when she let herself be held in a pond by the man who'd won her heart all over again. The care he'd taken with her, the patience he'd shown as she'd tried and failed and tried again to conquer her fear—it had astounded her. And she couldn't lie—feeling his hand on the small of her back, brushing up against his skin . . . it had made her positively euphoric.

She'd responded to Maggie's question with a perfectly benign reply, but Maggie was no fool. That was how Louisa had ended up knee-deep in bank records, certificates, receipts, tax returns, and whatever else the old lady hadn't thrown away.

She'd run from that arched, bushy eyebrow—the one that made it clear that Maggie knew there were a lot of *feelings* attached to Louisa's benign response.

Besides, what was she going to say? *Yes, I have seen that beautiful man. He helped me overcome my fear of water this afternoon by holding my weightless body in the pond, and yes, I might've taken a little longer to get over said fear because I really didn't want the moment to end, and yes, I did go home imagining what his lips taste like now that we are both adults, and I may have even wished that one day I would find out again for myself.*

No. Those were things to keep to herself.

She shoved the thoughts aside and tried to focus on the papers in her hands. She had three piles: *Keep. Pitch. Ask Maggie.* So far her *Ask Maggie* pile was the largest. There was just so much here—so much she didn't understand.

She started in on a box marked *Mail* and found piles of unopened letters. Her sigh could've been heard on the other side of the globe. But apparently not by someone sitting in a chair at the bottom of the stairs.

She opened the envelopes and removed the contents. Letters from Louisa's father's office. Statements going back years. A lot of years.

She knew Maggie had been a client of her father's. Oftentimes, when they were all together, Cody's and Louisa's fathers would end up around a table talking money with Maggie. Maggie wasn't overly wealthy, not like most people Warren dealt with, but Louisa knew Maggie trusted her dad to help her take what she did have and turn it into more. Judging by the number of envelopes in this box, they'd worked together for years. Did they still? Louisa didn't know.

She combed through the papers and put them in chronological order, and once she finished, she hoped to get a clear picture as to whether or not this could all be thrown away. Did people keep their bank statements?

But then, these weren't just bank statements—they were records of investments. Louisa wasn't a financial whiz like Daniel or even like her father, but she did understand at least some of what she was looking at. She sifted through page after page detailing Maggie's profits and losses. She'd done well for several months—make that years—and then she hit some pretty substantial losses. Then a gap in the statements. Several months missing or unaccounted for, but then they picked back up again with a deposit of $52,675.

Louisa frowned. $52,675? It might not have caught her attention, but hadn't Cody said his father's withdrawals had been oddly numbered?

She flipped back to the previous statement and realized that a few weeks before this deposit was made, a withdrawal in the same exact amount had been made.

But why?

She scanned the page for anything out of the ordinary but found nothing. It was on the same letterhead, had the same form letter attached to it. The only things that changed were the dates and the account balance.

Louisa flipped to the next page and saw that Maggie started making money again after that, following months of losses. Each month, another profit. And then the statements stopped.

Was the account closed, or had this box simply gotten too full? She pulled another box, also marked *Mail*, from underneath the guest bed. She yanked the tape off and opened it up. Full of letters exactly like the ones she'd just opened.

Another epic sigh. Not that she regretted helping Maggie—she didn't—but she did have a lot going on at the moment. The regatta. Maggie's party. Her plan to make Cody fall in love with her. It was a full plate.

She took the statements out and began opening them, discarding the envelopes and unfolding the papers, same as she'd done before.

As she did this mindless task, once again her imagination ran away from her. Back to the pond. Back to his strong arms. Back to that feeling of floating.

"Louisa?"

She spun around and found Cody standing in the doorway. She dropped some of the papers she'd been clutching. Was he real? Was she dreaming? Had he materialized out of thin air as a result of her foolish mental ramblings?

"Sorry; didn't mean to scare you."

Her face flushed and she tried to gather herself. "No, it's fine. I didn't hear the door." How had she not heard the door? And could he tell by the look on her face she'd just gotten to the part of the daydream where they were about to start kissing?

"I let myself in. I saw Maggie through the window—she's asleep in the chair." His eyes widened as they drifted down to the mess she'd made.

"It's organized chaos," she said, looking around. "What are you doing here?"

"I talked to my mom tonight."

She went still. "That's good." He probably heard the uncertainty in her voice.

He stood straight, like a man who'd been trained to do so. "Not good, actually."

"Is she okay?"

"She's coming for Maggie's party."

Louisa's heart nearly burst. "That's great." She stood up, setting aside the stack of unopened mail in her hand. "That's so great."

"No, Lou, it's really not great."

Her heart deflated. "It's not?"

"I asked you not to invite her." He seemed to be talking through gritted teeth and trying very hard not to lose his cool.

"And I decided to ignore you." She tried to sound sorry but avoided his eyes.

"I should've known."

Louisa folded her arms across her chest. "I know you're upset, but your mom has a right to be here. She has a right to say good-bye."

"But that's not why you invited her." He took a step closer, keeping his voice low, but his anger was easily detected.

"It is too."

"No, it's not," he said. "You told me as much. You're trying to fix this. You think that if everyone comes back together, they'll all be one happy family again."

She could feel a flame flicker inside her. "Well, what's so wrong with that? What's wrong with wanting the people I love to love each other again?"

"They're past that, Louisa."

She lifted her chin. "They are not."

He paused. "You know they are."

Why did she feel like they weren't talking about their parents? Why did she feel like this was his way of telling her that no matter how kind he'd been—no matter how gentle his touch or patient his demeanor—the two of them were beyond repair?

No birthday wish would ever bring them back together.

"You can't fix everything, Louisa. It's broken. Leave it alone." His tone had softened, but she heard the warning in his voice. What was he so afraid of?

"You know I can't do that." His face blurred behind the cloud of tears that filled her eyes.

"Yes, you can. You have to learn to leave things alone."

Normally she would've had a witty retort at the ready, but she simply didn't have the energy to be funny right now. She didn't want to know what "things" he was talking about, and she couldn't shake the idea that it wasn't "things" at all—it was people, namely him, that he wanted left alone.

"All right." She was aware of the stubbornness in her own voice. "If you want me to leave things alone, then I won't tell you what I just found."

He stuffed his hands in his pockets, looking like he was trying not to care.

She picked up the mail she'd sorted and pretended to sort more. She also pretended that it had no effect on her whatsoever that he was standing within a foot of her, so close she could inhale the scent of him—a scent that was starting to become familiar and one she was certain would always make her think of him.

"Fine." He said it like it was a complete sentence and not one he wanted to say.

She looked at him. "Fine what?"

"Don't do that, Louisa. Tell me what you found. Was it a dead chipmunk? Because I'm pretty sure there's got to be some sort of animal carcass in this mess."

She thumbed through the pages and found the one with the abnormal cash deposit. He took it, scanned it, then looked up at her, a lost expression on his face.

She pointed to the total—$52,675—and waited for the light bulb.

"That's the same amount as one of my father's withdrawals," he said.

"I thought it might be," she said.

"Was there another one for $25,382?"

"No. At least not that I've found yet. There's a lot more to go through."

"Did you ask Maggie about it?"

She shook her head. "To be honest, I don't think she has any idea what all is up here. These envelopes were still sealed. It was like she handed her money over to my dad and never thought about it again."

"But she still gets money from her investments?"

Louisa shrugged. "I suppose I could ask her that."

He surveyed the disaster in front of them. "Maybe there's another clue in here somewhere."

A line of tension stretched between them.

"I can help you look?"

Her heart flip-flopped at the idea, and in that moment Maggie's messy house felt like a gift from God. After all, without it, they'd be through her files in no time. As it was, this was likely to take days.

She summoned her most nonchalant voice and muttered a quiet "Okay."

"Where do we start?"

~

After two more hours of sorting, skimming, and filing, they hadn't turned up a deposit or withdrawal for $25,382, but they had discovered that Maggie Fisher did just fine for herself financially.

The deposit of $52,675 had resulted in a great return, and it was still making money for their old friend. She wasn't rich, but she was comfortable.

"I guess your dad knew what he was doing."

Louisa shrugged. "Who knew?"

Cody was looking at the paper that recorded the investment of $52,675, and his forehead creased with what she could only assume was confusion but very well might've been worry.

"Do you think this means that your mom and my dad weren't having an affair?" he asked absently.

"You didn't really believe that, did you?"

He met her eyes. "Didn't you?"

"Maybe for a second, but then—no. I asked her about it, and she was pretty convincing. Besides, your parents were perfect together."

"And your parents?"

Were her parents perfect for each other? She didn't think so. But maybe the accident had simply changed them. Maybe they had been perfect together once upon a time.

"My parents seem to tolerate each other," she said with an unamused laugh. "Maybe they should never have gotten married in the first place."

"Don't say that." He set the paper down and gave her attention she didn't want. "I'm really glad they did."

She stopped sorting and dared a look up, found his eyes full on her. Something inside her twisted. "I guess."

There was a charged pause between them then, a spark that was impossible to ignore. How was she supposed to function with him this close to her?

Louisa set the stack of pages on the floor in front of her, busying herself with anything to keep her mind off the fact that Cody was watching her, then took the page that marked the deposit and set it down too.

"What are you doing?"

"I don't know." She flicked through the papers, practically begging them to speak to her. But they stayed quiet. She split the stack in two and put pages that were sent before the deposit—including the big withdrawal—on one side and pages that were sent after the deposit on the other, then put the paper with the deposit details in the center. She stared at them.

"Is this a magic trick?"

She shot him a look. "Hilarious."

A lopsided grin lit his face. "Just checking."

She picked up the top page of each stack and compared as if trying to spot the differences in one of those magazine games. "Wait . . ."

"What?"

"Look." Each paper had a set of initials at the bottom: the person sending the letter and, she assumed, the person who typed it. The ones before the deposit were labeled *WC/dab*. The ones after the deposit were labeled differently: *TK/dab*.

Cody studied them. "I don't understand."

"Well, I'm assuming WC stands for Warren Chambers," she said. "And DAB?"

She frowned again. "Your dad didn't work at my dad's firm. What was your dad's middle name?"

"Joseph."

"Probably a secretary or something then. I think my dad had one named Dorothy? I bet it was her. TK is probably Ted Kauffmann. He works with my dad. They play golf together a lot."

"But does that mean your father isn't Maggie's financial adviser anymore?"

Louisa shrugged. "I'm not sure."

"We could ask Maggie," Cody said.

Louisa straightened the papers. "I don't want to bother her with any of this. Maybe it doesn't matter anyway."

But one look at him told her it did matter—at least to him.

She wanted to kiss him. She knew she shouldn't, but she really did. She wanted to take every question spinning around his head and answer it, to make sense of the things he not only wanted—but needed—to know.

If she helped him do that, would he forgive her then?

"Okay," she finally said. "Let's go wake the old girl up."

CHAPTER TWENTY-NINE

THEY TRIED FOR FIVE STRAIGHT MINUTES to wake Maggie, but she slept like the dead. A poor analogy, Cody realized as soon as it popped into his mind.

The woman not only talked in her sleep; she fought in her sleep, and twice Cody ducked out of her way only seconds before getting clobbered.

Louisa didn't even try to quiet her laugh.

"Go ahead and laugh," he hissed. "But if she swings at you, I'm not going to save you."

She covered her mouth with her hand, but another giggle escaped.

Maggie stirred again, this time flopping her head over to the opposite side. She let out a giant exhale right in Louisa's face.

Louisa drew back and grimaced. "Ew, I think she ate pickles."

Cody couldn't help it. He laughed. And as soon as he did, Louisa's entire face beamed. She prided herself on making people smile, and even he knew he was a particularly difficult case.

"I can ask her tomorrow," Louisa whispered. "About the statements."

He stood. "Okay. Are you leaving now?"

"Yeah. I should get home." She grabbed an afghan off the couch, unfolded it, and draped it over Maggie's lap.

She was kind in the simplest ways. It made him want to know her—not the person he thought she was or the person she had been, but who she'd become. Who was that girl? Would that girl like him? Would that girl want to go out for dinner?

They walked in silence toward the entryway, and Louisa switched the lights off. She lingered a moment by the door. Cody followed her gaze into the living room, where Maggie snored softly by the blue light of the television.

"I'm going to miss her," Louisa said quietly. She glanced at him and smiled, then turned toward the door.

He followed her outside into the warm June air. The sky was especially dark that night, the result of either a new moon or a thick fog, he wasn't sure which. A dog barked in the distance, but otherwise they were completely alone. Maggie lived near the water and not much else. Her closest neighbor was a short walk away.

"She's lucky to have you," Cody said, aware that his voice disturbed the silence like a rock thrown into a still pond.

Louisa slowed her pace. "I'm the lucky one." Her expression turned thoughtful. "Maggie's always filled in the gaps created by my mom."

Louisa and her mom were polar opposites. For starters, JoEllen seemed much more concerned with appearances than Louisa ever had been. Also, JoEllen was nice, but she wasn't kind. Not like Louisa.

"It bothers you, huh?" Cody asked. "That you guys aren't close."

Louisa shrugged. "A little, I guess. I think what bothers me most is that when I broke up with Eric, she called him and told him to wait until I came to my senses. She said my little business would fail, and I'd see he was right."

"Yikes," Cody said.

"She doesn't believe in me either."

"So how'd you become so fearless?" he asked.

Louisa stopped when they reached Cody's Jeep, parked next to her bike. "I don't feel that way at all."

"It seems like you've got something to prove," he said.

She stilled. "Maybe. I think I've always felt like I needed to do all the good I can—you know, to make up for my mistakes."

He studied her face. Her nose was just slightly crooked after being broken when she was in grade school. Most people probably didn't even notice that, but he did. She told him once she hated it—it was so imperfect. He told her that's what made her interesting to look at. And she was. He could look at her all night.

"Lesson tomorrow?" he asked.

A look of disappointment skittered across her face. He should've told her that her mistake was forgiven, that she could stop trying so hard. She had nothing more to prove. He just couldn't find the words.

She quickly regrouped. "You're going to make me get up before the sun, aren't you?"

"Best time of day," he said. "You don't want to miss the sunrise."

"It's so early," she groaned.

"You're the one who bid on me," he said. "You only have yourself to blame."

She rolled her eyes. "Yeah, yeah. I'll be there." After a pause, her voice became sincere. "I'm sorry I invited your mom."

"It's okay." He understood now—her strong need to put everyone back together. It came from a good place, even if it was misguided. Even if it would most likely end in disaster. Should he try to prepare her for that?

His mom had mentioned closure, but once she was faced with the haunting memories of the past, there was a chance she wouldn't react the way Louisa hoped she would. She had years of anger strapped to her back.

They stood there in the darkness for several long seconds, neither of them in a hurry to leave, and Cody felt something between them shift. The pretense and caution disappeared and left in their place a connection so deep he thought it might unravel him.

He didn't want to hate her anymore. He *didn't* hate her anymore.

But in place of that anger he'd carried with him was a feeling much more disturbing—affection. True, honest, genuine affection for her. He wanted to know everything about her. He wanted to spend all his free time with her. He wanted to go out with her and stay in with her, and man, if he didn't want to kiss her senseless right now.

"I should probably get going." Her voice was barely above a whisper. Did she feel it too?

Was it wrong to pray for rain, just to have a reason to drive her home, to prolong this goodbye? "Yeah, me too."

She smiled. A kind smile. A polite smile. An I-can't-tell-what-you're-thinking smile. It nearly did him in.

This was bad. Get-out-of-town bad. He needed to put some distance between them—fast. He took a step away from her before he did anything he'd regret, like scoop her into his arms and take her home with him.

"See you tomorrow."

He hurried into his Jeep and started the engine, then drove off without looking back. She'd always had the ability to cast a strange sort of spell over him—it made him act irrationally and led to terrible decisions. He needed to remember that this was why he didn't let himself get all brainless over women. Ever. It was also why he didn't drink alcohol or do drugs.

Cody had decided a long time ago never to lose his focus again—and love, as intoxicating as it was, led to a loss of focus. And that led to disaster.

He drove into town. He was hungry, and he needed to clear his head. He knew a lot of the guys hung out at the Rose & Crown, a bar downtown, and they probably had burgers, so he parked the Jeep and went inside.

Music blasted through mounted speakers, dampening the din of chatter. He looked around at the crowd and spotted a single face he recognized—McKenzie Palmer.

Cody wasn't stupid. He knew plenty of women like McKenzie,

and he could tell she was into him. Under different circumstances, he might've cared, but if he were honest with himself, the only person he spent any time thinking about was the redhead he'd just left standing alone in Maggie's yard.

McKenzie wasn't one for taking hints, though. In fact, it seemed his disinterest in her only made him more appealing. She spotted him and waved. She might've even squealed—it was too loud to tell for sure. She hopped off her barstool and sashayed toward him.

She was beautiful, he supposed. He'd overheard some of the guys talking about her, but until this moment, he hadn't really paid attention.

"Good evening, XPO Boggs. Fancy meeting you here." She was standing so close to him, he could smell her shampoo. Flowers. He liked the way Louisa smelled better.

"Just came in for a burger," he said dumbly.

She grabbed his hand and tugged. "Come sit with us. I've got a great spot." She pointed a finger toward the bar where she'd been sitting. "Plus, everyone is always trying to impress me, so I can get your food really fast." She laughed.

He allowed himself to be led over to the bar and then sat next to McKenzie and her friend, a dark-headed girl with teeth so white he wondered if they were painted.

"This is Giselle," McKenzie said. "She helps with my blog."

Cody extended a hand toward the other girl. She picked it up and studied it as if he'd just handed her a clay pot. "Nice hands." She grinned. "You're hot."

He put Giselle around age twenty-three. It was amazing how a few years could widen the gap between people.

"Derek, can you get my friend a burger with the works?" McKenzie fluttered her lashes and flashed a smile toward the bartender, who shot Cody a look.

"To go," Cody said.

The man disappeared through a door, and Cody turned to find McKenzie pouting. "You're not going to stay with us?"

"Sorry; I've got to get up early." *To see Louisa.*

"I never get up early," McKenzie said. "It's against my religion."

"You should try it," Cody said. "I never miss a sunrise if I can help it."

"No way." Giselle slammed her glass on the bar. "Mack and I are creatures of the night."

Both women laughed.

"I could come home with you," McKenzie offered. "Keep you company. You could show me what's so great about the sunrise."

Her hand was on Cody's leg.

He inched back. "Sorry to disappoint you, but I actually have to sleep."

"Sleep is overrated." Her eyes said what her mouth didn't. Her hand squeezed his leg.

"Not when you have a 5 a.m. training session."

"Training? Like, for the regatta?" McKenzie laughed. "Like you're ever going to get Louisa to do anything useful in that boat."

He looked away.

"You should've figured out a way to let me win you," she said. "I actually know what I'm doing. And I don't just mean on the boat."

Charlie Pope appeared beside them. "Hey, hey, what's up, guys? Hey, cap, how good of you to grace us with your presence this fine evening."

Charlie Pope was drunk.

"I take it you guys aren't training at 5 a.m.?" Cody asked McKenzie, who had won Charlie at the auction for a lot less money than she'd bid on Cody.

"No." McKenzie grinned. "We have a much looser philosophy about the race."

"Yeah, we don't care if we win." Charlie wrapped an arm around McKenzie's shoulder. "The real prize will be seeing you in a bathing suit."

McKenzie laughed. "In your dreams, buddy."

"Let's dance!" Giselle stood, and Cody caught sight of a butterfly tattoo on her back, just above her belt. Her eyes flashed as she looked at Charlie, who might as well have been a rabid dog. He followed her off, and McKenzie stood, then leaned in close to Cody.

"Do you really have to leave? Just stay for one dance."

Cody almost turned her down. But he couldn't keep himself locked away forever. Besides, there were no emotions attached to anyone in that bar. No risk of losing control or acting foolishly.

McKenzie picked up a bottle of beer and stuck it in Cody's hand. He set it back on the counter.

"Come on, you." She smiled and sauntered off toward the dance floor—and like an idiot, or like a man desperate to forget about life for a while, he followed.

CHAPTER THIRTY

LOUISA KNEW THE EARLY MORNING TRAINING SESSIONS WEREN'T DATES. She knew that, and yet she prepared for them as if they were.

Because the regatta was technically Coast Guard business, Duncan gave the guys a bit of leeway so they could spend time training with their sailing partners, which meant that Louisa was spending every morning with a very off-limits man who happened to be excellent at sailing and saving lives.

And probably kissing. She bet he was still excellent at kissing.

It had been about a week since they'd found the strange bank statements, and Maggie had been absolutely no help in clarifying anything. The day after they'd unsuccessfully tried to wake her, Louisa had shown the old woman what they'd found, but Maggie's face was as blank as the day she was born.

"I have people who handle all that for me, dear," she'd said.

"My father?"

"Used to be. Then he turned me over to some other guy."

Louisa showed her the first statement after the odd sum showed up in the account. "Around this time?"

Maggie shuffled across the kitchen. She was wearing polyester pants and white tennis shoes, along with a floral button-down top. She danced a little as she walked, which she did often—she said she was moving to the music in her mind.

Maggie hummed. "No idea when." Then she frowned. "Actually, it wasn't long after Daniel died. Or maybe before? I don't know; the details are foggy. I'm old."

"Why would my father give your portfolio to someone else?" Louisa asked as Maggie filled a bowl with Lucky Charms. "You know those are bad for you, right?"

"I'm so glad the food police have joined me for breakfast," Maggie quipped.

"I'm just saying," Louisa said innocently.

"Well, in case you were wondering, I've entered the I'll-eat-whatever-the-heck-I-want phase of my life," she said. "It's not like this is what's going to kill me." She laughed.

Louisa understood that this was Maggie's way of coping with her diagnosis, but sometimes the weight of it was too heavy for jokes. It wasn't lost on her that Maggie's death would be pretty devastating.

Maggie shook the box of cereal at Louisa. "If I remember right, these are your favorite?"

Louisa eyed the box. "They *were* my favorite. When I was ten."

Maggie scoffed. "If it were my dying wish to share a bowl of Lucky Charms with you, would you really turn me down?"

Louisa leaned against the doorjamb. "Is that your dying wish?"

Maggie shoveled a bite into her mouth. "One bowl won't kill ya."

Finally Louisa snatched the box, took a bowl from the cupboard, and poured the cereal in. She turned and found Maggie holding out the jug of milk.

Louisa poured it over the marshmallow-dotted cereal and took a bite, aware that Maggie watched her with a bit too much interest.

"Good, right?" She raised her runaway eyebrows.

"It *is* good." She'd forgotten how good. "Are you going to answer my question?"

"What question?" Another bite.

"Why would my dad give your portfolio to someone else?"

"Not just anyone. Ted Kauffmann."

"So? My dad knows you. It seems like he would want to handle your finances."

"All I know is he called me and said he thought Ted would do a better job with my type of investments. I don't really ask questions."

Clearly. She didn't even open her statements.

"Besides, Daniel agreed. He said this was what was best. I figured if anyone was going to look out for me, it was those two. So I didn't put up a fuss."

"Daniel?"

"Yes, and we all know how savvy he was."

Louisa knew. Everyone knew. Warren might've been groomed for this, but Daniel raised-by-a-mechanic Boggs was the natural. Louisa thought it was fabulous. She loved a self-made man. And she'd loved Daniel. Everyone did.

"How else was Daniel involved in this?" Louisa asked.

Maggie tipped her bowl back and drank her sugared milk. "He wasn't." She wiped her mouth with the sleeve of her shirt.

"But he had a withdrawal from his personal account that matches this number," Louisa said, pointing to the statement.

Maggie's brows turned into one straight line. "Coincidence?"

"It was two days before this deposit went into your account."

The old woman shrugged. "Ask your dad. He would remember better than me."

But Louisa knew that wasn't an option. Her father had told her not to go "poking around graves"—which in a way she'd obeyed because she wasn't poking; she was digging.

Now, as she trudged toward the marina, her heart kicked up a notch. She wasn't sure if it was because she and Cody had only practiced in the pond before this point or because she could see him up ahead, readying their boat.

This is not a date.

She could tell that to herself a million times over, but no part of her heart was buying it. Her mornings with Cody had become the thing she looked forward to most in her days. And she couldn't say for sure, but he seemed to enjoy them too.

He spotted her and waved.

She admired him as she grabbed on to the straps of her backpack and plodded toward him. Every day she wondered if this would be the day the buzzing sensation she felt down to her toes whenever she saw him would finally go away.

Her stomach somersaulted as if in reply to that question. Today was not that day.

"You ready for this?" He stood at the center of a small sailboat.

She clung to her backpack, which was filled with unnecessary items save the water bottle she'd filled that morning in case they got stranded in the middle of open water. Never mind that their plan for the day wouldn't take them more than a mile out, and Cody had promised to keep land in sight at all times.

She'd gotten better in the pond—but this, the ocean, was a whole different fear. Still, it struck her as she packed a raincoat, an umbrella, a tin of Altoids, and a hairbrush, that this new fear of water was beginning to define her. And she didn't like it.

"I'm ready," she said.

He offered his hand, and she told herself to stay cool. He'd helped her into the boat every morning that week. She'd yet to stay cool. Today would be her day.

She reached out and took a step, but she quickly lost her footing and started to fall. His other hand snapped to her waist, where he promptly steadied her and took her breath away at the same time.

So maybe tomorrow would be the day she stayed cool?

"Sorry," she said.

"You're clumsy."

Only when I'm with you.

"Yeah, aren't you glad I'm your sailing partner?"

He smirked in her general direction but didn't reply.

Her second attempt to get in the boat proved to be successful, and she sat down. While Cody rigged the boat, he quizzed Louisa on various sailing terms, none of which she knew before this week.

He pointed. "What's this?"

"Tiller."

"Connected to . . . ?"

"The rudder."

"And this?"

"Mainsail."

"And this?" He held up a life vest.

She shot him an unamused look, but secretly she was very amused. This past week during their not-dates, she'd purposed to wear him down, to make him like her again. His whole mood seemed different today, so maybe it was working.

She tugged the life vest over her head as they made their way out of the marina and into open water.

"I was thinking we should go talk to that Ted guy." He kept his eyes straight ahead, shaded only by the bill of his ball cap.

She was thankful he didn't look at her. She much preferred to study him without his knowledge. She leaned back, resting against the side of the boat, letting him do all the work because he was far better at it than she was. And she was far better at admiring his biceps. If they had any hope of not embarrassing themselves at the regatta, it was only because of Cody.

"What do you think?" He glanced at her.

"We can do that if you want." She didn't tell him the downside of that was Ted could possibly tell her father they'd paid him a visit, and she really didn't want him knowing about any of this.

"You could invite him to the regatta. He's probably got money to donate."

In the distance, she could see Brant Point lighthouse, and the memory of simpler times drifted through her mind. "Sure."

"You think it's a bad idea?"

"No, I think it's fine," she said.

She could feel him looking at her. "What is it then?"

"Do you remember all those birthday wishes we made?" She found his eyes, held them for as long as he would allow. "I kept yours in a jar and stashed them in my hope chest."

His jaw twitched.

"I think my funniest one was 'I want to raise chickens.'" Should she tell him how it broke her heart to think of the years they'd lost being angry with each other or that she couldn't help but wonder if his being here now was a chance to make things right?

"This is our big year," she said as if he didn't know. "Thirty on the thirtieth."

More jaw twitching.

"Do you ever think about it?"

He drew in a tight breath. "Not really."

Her heart dropped. "Yeah, me neither. I think I only remembered because of the wishes. And the contract I made you sign."

"You kept that, too?" He looked at her now with kindness, not disdain, making her feel a tiny bit less like jumping ship.

"I kept everything," she said. "I'm not as bad as Maggie, but . . ." Her voice trailed off under the weight of his gaze. "Maybe it was stupid. I mean, who makes a pact like that? Obviously I was worried you'd go off and do something amazing and forget all about me."

His forehead crinkled. "The pact wasn't your idea."

"Yes, it was."

He eyed her. "No, it wasn't."

"I was the control freak who drew up a contract."

He looked away, shaking his head. "I can't believe you don't remember."

Her mind raced back to that day on the beach. Had she remembered wrong?

He seemed to be on to a different topic—namely, sailing instruction. "Your turn."

She frowned. She didn't feel like learning anything about that boat. She wanted to figure out what she was forgetting about their pact. She wanted to remember it—in detail. Should she suggest a reenactment? She was pretty sure most of their conversations that summer ended with kissing—and she was a lot better at that now. Oh, how she wanted to show him.

Another boat approached from the opposite direction. Cody kept his eyes forward, and Louisa didn't move.

"You're slacking."

She stood.

"I'm going to teach you to change direction."

"I have full confidence that you can handle it."

"Louisa, you paid big money for my expertise."

She groaned. "Don't remind me." She still had half of her pledged money to pay. Maybe she should buy a lottery ticket.

"Morning, sailors!" Louisa looked up at the other boat and discovered her favorite person, McKenzie Palmer, was on board. Beside her, Charlie Pope, the Coastie Cody had warned her about.

"McKenzie?"

"You weren't kidding about the sunrise, Cody," McKenzie called across the water. "It was a beauty today. You might've turned me into a morning person."

He didn't respond.

"Still on for tonight?"

Cody did not look at Louisa, who once again begged herself to stay cool. "Uh, sure."

"Great!" McKenzie tossed her long, wavy, too-perfect-for-this-hour ponytail behind her shoulder, and Charlie sailed them off. "Queequeg's at six. Meet you there."

A rock of dread lodged itself in her gut, but Louisa kept her eyes forward. "She's friendly." She did a poor job of keeping the annoyance out of her tone.

"Yep," Cody said.

And that's all he said. That's it. No explanation of when he'd told McKenzie about the sunrise. Had it been that morning, before he left their mutual dwelling? He didn't say. He also didn't explain why he was meeting her later. A date?

"You wanna try this?" he asked, because in his mind, everything was just fine. Because they were just friends. Barely even friends.

Maybe it was time Louisa started remembering that.

CHAPTER THIRTY-ONE

"WHAT ARE WE DOING HERE?"

Ally was always so impatient. Louisa should've known she was a poor choice to bring along on her stakeout. Her business partner was meticulous, not only with the details of her business, but the minutes of her day.

"Just getting a good lay of the land," she said. "You know, for the regatta."

The regatta was two days away, and the land had already been surveyed. In fact, Ally had drawn a map and handed it over to Duncan so the guardsmen could set everything up. Louisa had arranged for local vendors to take part in the event, and she'd strategically assigned them each a spot next to another vendor that wasn't a direct competitor. The amount of thought that had gone into it was astonishing, and trying to pretend sitting in Ally's car staring out the window was necessary for work was truly one of the most ridiculous things Louisa had ever done.

"Ooh, I love this song." She turned up the radio and started singing: "'Time keeps on ticking, ticking, ticking . . . into the future.'"

"Those are not the words. And don't try to change the subject." Ally turned down the volume just as Cody emerged from Queequeg's with McKenzie at his side.

Queequeg's, the cozy restaurant Louisa had always loved, was the perfect spot for a date. With its gray shingled siding and the adorable deck with outdoor seating, it was charmingly Nantucket. She faintly recalled McKenzie had written a glowing review of the popular spot on her popular blog.

Must be nice to be popular.

"Oh," Ally said. "Now I get it. You're spying."

"Not spying."

"Stalking?"

"Not stalking."

"Louisa, this is textbook stalking. You need to get a grip."

She sighed. "What does he see in her?"

"Nice curves, great hair—" Ally shoved a french fry into her mouth—"hard to say."

Louisa groaned. "He never looks at me like that."

"Vaguely annoyed and ready to run? You're right, he doesn't."

"You think he's annoyed?"

Ally squinted. "No, I'm just trying to make you feel better."

Louisa sighed.

Ally reached over and took Louisa's hand. "I'm sorry, Lou. I know you like him a lot."

I love him a lot.

But she didn't say that out loud. She'd never say that out loud. Because of all the humiliating things she'd done, loving someone who didn't love her back ranked right up there at the top.

~

Louisa woke up on Saturday—regatta day. She had no reason to be nervous. She'd put in all the hours necessary to make this a great event. She'd contacted vendors and organized booths. She'd spoken with Manny and Deborah Wirth the day before, and they planned to be there, though Deborah was definitely struggling now that the day had arrived.

Louisa assured them it would be an uplifting day—a great way to honor their son and bring awareness to water-safety issues that could help save lives in the future. The day would be about the details—something she was very good at.

So why was her stomach churning the second her eyes opened that morning?

Her phone buzzed on the table beside her bed.

Are you ready to kick some serious butt?

She smiled despite herself. Cody was thinking of her. Sure, it was only because of the race, but still. She was on his mind. Her—not McKenzie Palmer.

She quickly texted back: You know I am!

But that exclamation point was a little bit misleading. After all, she'd missed their scheduled practice session yesterday—she claimed she had too much to do, but the truth was, she couldn't shake the image of Cody with McKenzie. As if that one day of not seeing him could've convinced her to give up this misguided fantasy that she and Cody had some sort of magical connection. She was an adult—it was time to start acting like one. And that meant no flirting or joking around with Cody. No daydreaming about what it might feel like to step into his arms and let herself be held.

Today she would be the crew to his skipper. She would handle the jib and keep an eye on the compass while he maneuvered their boat like a chess piece across a board, dealing with the big-picture tactics he claimed would help them win.

Truthfully, she hadn't picked up much skill in the way of sailing. She'd found herself far too distracted by her instructor to remember much of what he said. The only thing she'd really paid attention to was how good he looked when he said it.

As she trudged out to her Vespa, it occurred to her that her lack of concentration could pose a legitimate issue now that they were heading out on the water. But she was ready. She'd made her peace with the ocean—and besides, Cody would be there. If she were somehow thrown into the watery depths, he'd get her out again.

Would it be wrong to engineer such a scene?

She made her way toward the yacht club where the regatta would take place, pulling into the first parking spot she saw—right next to Cody's Jeep. Her stomach turned over when she spotted him down by the water. He was helping with the setup—how early had he gotten here?

She slung her bag over her shoulder and walked toward him, trying to ignore the memory of McKenzie on his arm exiting the restaurant the other night. She'd tried to deny it, but they really did look lovely together. McKenzie was shorter than Louisa and much, much smaller. Maybe Cody should have someone like that instead of someone like her—tall and sturdy with unattractive red hair and freckles.

She forced the thoughts away with a silent groan. This wasn't helpful for anyone.

"There you are," he said as she walked up. He took his ACK ball cap off, repositioned it back on his head, then squinted at her. "Feeling good?"

She nodded. She wore a lightweight white sundress with her strappy gold sandals and carried a change of clothes for the race in her bag. She'd oversee the regatta's preliminary events, then hand everything off to Ally when it came time for the race.

All the details had been handled, though at the moment, she wished she'd left something undone so she could busy herself.

"You're probably well-rested since you bailed on me yesterday." He started walking toward the water. "We're going to tie the cutter ship up right over there. Give people tours, and then right next to it, we'll have water-safety information. I told the guys to make sure it wasn't boring."

She'd followed him but only half listened. "I didn't *bail* on you."

"I was just joking."

She crossed her arms, aware that she was being overly sensitive but somehow helpless to stop herself. *Ninny.* "Well, maybe I just thought you needed more sleep after your busy night out."

Shut up, Louisa.

He frowned at her. "What are you talking about?"

"Nothing, forget it." She sounded like a jealous girlfriend when she knew she had no right to sound that way. She turned to go—she would check on the food stations and see if anyone needed anything—but he grabbed her arm.

"Louisa."

She could feel her cheeks were flushed. Heat crawled up the back of her neck. She plucked her sunglasses off the top of her head and stuck them on her face as if they could conceal her emotions.

"Sorry; I think Ally might need me." She raced off, leaving him standing there, probably wondering when she'd lost her marbles—and she would happily tell him she'd lost them the day he rescued her from the angry ocean and maybe he should've simply left her there. Maybe if she'd floated off in the sea, she would've landed on another island, one that wasn't inhabited by haunting memories or men she desperately wanted and couldn't have.

"Morning!" Ally had arrived and now approached Louisa, clipboard in hand. She rattled off her list of to-dos, not pausing for breath until she reached the end. "I think we're in really good shape."

Louisa forced herself to sound normal. "Good. Maybe you could touch base with the food vendors as they arrive and I'll go check on the silent auction. I'll bring the items out and line them up on the tables."

Ally's eyes drifted over Louisa's head. "He's here early."

She didn't have to turn around to know who her friend was talking about. "Yep."

Ally's eyebrows traveled toward her forehead. "Yep?"

"Yes, he's here early."

"Oh, and look," Ally said. "So is she."

Louisa turned and saw McKenzie and a dark-headed girl (not a woman because Louisa wasn't sure she was even out of college) running toward Cody, who was tying the cutter to the dock and talking with some of the other guardsmen.

She quickly looked away. "I'll be inside."

People started showing up for the regatta around nine in the morning, when the festivities began. Louisa had hauled all the silent-auction baskets out to the tables they'd set up near the food booths, and she did a perfectly stellar job of pretending Cody Boggs wasn't there at all.

He was busy with the water-safety protocols and giving tours to little kids, which he did with such charm and kindness Louisa couldn't help but notice it made her heart double in size. For a fleeting moment, she pictured him with kids of his own, a little boy maybe, with dark curls and a carbon copy of his brown eyes. She could see Cody carrying him on his shoulders, making him laugh, protecting him from the monsters under his bed. He'd be a good dad.

"Is this where you want the trophies?"

Louisa turned toward a man carrying the box of awards she'd had engraved for the race winners. The kids' race started in twenty minutes—this guy was cutting it really close.

"Sorry they're late. We found a mistake on the way out the door. Thought it was better to get it right. I think my boss emailed you?"

Well, she couldn't fault him for that. "Thanks. You can set them here."

She led him to the table they'd reserved for the bling, right next to the podium where the announcer would give the play-by-play for each race.

Louisa was helping the man unload the trophies and medals when she accidentally glanced over toward the Coast Guard setup and accidentally noticed that Cody was no longer there.

She scanned the crowd and braced herself for the impact of seeing him with McKenzie (again)—would it ever get easier? But it wasn't McKenzie he was talking to. It was Louisa's dad.

Oh no. Would Cody ask him about Maggie's accounts? She hadn't been clear enough that she had a strategy when it came to broaching the subject with her father. Namely, *Don't broach the subject with my father.* But Cody was curious, so he'd likely broach away.

"I think the medals are upside down."

"Huh?"

Louisa turned and found the trophy deliveryman pointing to the medals she'd just laid out on the table. They were, in fact, upside down.

She glanced up just in time to see Cody walk off with her dad and shake hands with someone else. Her stomach roiled.

Could this day get any worse?

CHAPTER THIRTY-TWO

WHEN WARREN CHAMBERS SHOWED UP next to the cutter, Cody shook his hand, all the while wondering if he had the answers to the questions that kept Cody up at night.

So many questions about his dad, about Maggie's money, about the memorial on the beach and all the things he didn't know about his parents.

His eyes drifted over to where Louisa was setting up trophies with some guy who'd just shown up. He'd managed to keep her in his sights all morning, and her comment about his busy night out had gotten under his skin more than he would've liked. What did she mean by that?

As he faced Warren, he noticed the man had the same bright-blue eyes Louisa had. He spotted JoEllen chatting with a group of ladies, all of them dressed up and half of them wearing big sun hats and sunglasses.

"Good to see you again, son," Warren said, his hand firmly wrapped around Cody's. "Looks like you've done a good job of getting people to come out and support your cause."

"That was all your daughter," Cody said. "She's pretty amazing with people."

"She is." Warren eyed him. Could he see the admiration Cody felt? Could he see more than the admiration he felt? "She's pretty amazing in general."

Cody nodded. "She is."

"Are you settling in out there at Brant Point?"

They made small talk for a few minutes, something Cody had prepared for that morning on his drive over. He generally despised small talk, but now that it was part of his job, he'd decided to at least make an effort.

It came so naturally to Louisa, chatting with people she didn't even know. He supposed that was because Louisa was genuinely interested in everyone and everything. Everyone had a story, and she wanted to know what it was.

"I hear you've been teaching Louisa how to sail?"

"She's catching on, sir," Cody said. "Mostly."

That was a lie. Louisa would never make it in the Coast Guard; that much was clear. After the week they'd had, he wasn't sure she'd even make it as a passenger, but he had given her two easy jobs, and he planned to do the rest. They wouldn't win, but he'd get to be near her—that was worth more than some trophy and bragging rights anyway.

"Is that . . . ?"

Cody followed Warren's eyes across the yard and saw a tall man with silver hair, wearing a lightweight tan suit, a crisp white button-down, and what was certainly a very expensive watch on his left wrist.

"Sir?"

Warren turned fidgety as the other man waved a hello. "What is he doing here?" He muttered the words under his breath. And then, all at once, his entire demeanor changed. "Ted, didn't expect to see you here today."

Ted? Ted Kauffmann?

The man extended a hand in greeting, which Warren shook vigorously. Was he sweating?

"You've got your daughter to thank for that," Ted said. "She sent me a personal invitation. She's a smart cookie gathering all this money in one place." Ted flashed them what appeared to be a well-practiced smile.

Warren glanced toward the tent where Louisa still worked. "Louisa invited you?"

Ted was looking at Cody now, which Warren noticed belatedly. He fumbled over his introduction so badly it became clear something was wrong. "Sorry; where are my manners? Ted, this is Cody Boggs. Cody, my old friend and colleague Ted Kauffmann."

Cody shook the stranger's hand as Warren pulled a handkerchief from his pocket and dabbed his forehead.

"Boggs?" Ted squinted at Cody. "Daniel's son?"

"That's correct, sir," Cody said. "You knew my father?"

Ted finally let go of his hand. "Good man."

"The best," Warren said. "The very best."

In the distance, JoEllen waved at her husband.

"I'm sorry, gentlemen," Warren said. "I think I'm being summoned."

Ted nodded. "You best answer the call."

Warren rushed off, leaving Cody standing awkwardly with a man he didn't know, but who had known his father. A man who, according to Louisa, had replaced Warren as Maggie's financial adviser. Maybe there was no connection, but what if there was?

He glanced at Louisa and found her looking in his direction. Had she set this up for his sake? Was this his only chance to ask Ted Kauffmann if he knew anything about any of this?

"So you're in the Coast Guard?" Ted asked. "Your dad would be proud of that. He was such a stand-up guy. Better than Warren and me, that's for sure."

Cody frowned. "What do you mean?"

"Daniel was such a Boy Scout." Ted slid a hand into his pocket. "Tried to corrupt him more than once, but he always resisted, no matter how appealing the payoff." Ted took a drink from the glass he was holding with his unpocketed hand, the ice cubes clinking against the edges. "Warren always said your dad was too smart, and he really was."

Cody looked over at Louisa's dad, who stood with his wife under one of the red beach umbrellas Louisa had attached to the tall tables to help shade people from the sun. Warren looked back at them nervously.

What was going on?

"Warren, on the other hand, now I could always count on him to overplay his hand."

"I'm not sure I follow, sir."

"Poker," Ted said. "The high-stakes kind. That guy is fearless. Not always smart, though—I took more money off Warren Chambers than anyone who ever played the game." His laugh cracked through the air. "He got in pretty deep, I think. Stopped playing not long after your dad passed—God rest his soul. I think that really shook him up. Shook us all up. Made no sense God took the good one and left the rest of us here."

Cody's stomach turned. He didn't follow any of this, but the mere mention of his father had left the taste of bile in his throat.

Before he could ask Ted a single question, Warren was back. "Should we get a drink?"

Ted held up his glass. "I've got a drink."

"Well, I don't." Warren glanced at Cody. "Good luck in the race."

Cody stood there dumbly as the two men walked off.

Ted hadn't said anything incriminating, so why did it feel like Warren was hiding something? So he played poker. High-stakes poker was big among rich guys, wasn't it? Cody spotted Louisa walking toward him. She'd changed out of her white dress and now wore shorts and a tank top over her bathing suit—a navy-blue-and-white polka-dot thing that he never minded seeing her in.

Should he tell her about his conversation with Ted Kauffmann? After all, she was the reason the man was here.

She reached him, but her face remained expressionless. "Let's get this over with."

And off she went in the direction of the sailboats, where the rest of the men were gathering with their partners.

He sighed. Whatever he'd done to tick her off, he'd done a good job of it.

~

Louisa sat near the back of the boat, waiting for the guardsmen to stop razzing each other so they could get the race under way. She truly hoped Cody wasn't counting on winning because with her on the jib, it was unlikely.

Manning the small sail toward the front of the boat and keeping an eye on the compass were the only two jobs she had.

She was unsure of both.

Cody shook hands with two of the guys standing on the deck, then moved into place. As he passed by her, she inhaled his familiar scent, and it frustrated her that in spite of her irritation with him, she still found him terribly appealing.

"You doing okay?" He faced her, and the full weight of his attention sent her nerves dancing.

"I'm fine."

"You seem upset."

From the boat next to them, McKenzie Palmer let out a loud, joyous shout. "Hey, XPO Boggs, you sure you don't want to trade partners? I promise I know what I'm doing."

Louisa glared at McKenzie from behind her dark sunglasses, but she noticed Cody didn't respond. If he wanted to trade her in, Louisa would happily bow out. . . .

The announcer called for everyone's attention. This was it. They were starting.

He walked over and stood directly in front of her. "Is there something you need to say to me?"

She silently reminded herself of her vow to stop all this nonsense. She searched her mind for something—anything—other than the truth. "I saw you talking to my dad."

"This isn't about your dad," he said.

"Did you tell him we're still digging around?"

"Of course not."

"Promise?" She held up her pinkie like they were ten again. She caught herself and put her hand down. "Sorry. I think I'm just nervous." What was *wrong* with her?

He reached over and tugged the buckle on her life vest.

"It's secure."

He raised a brow. "Just making sure."

"I'm good. I'm ready." She really needed to get control of her emotions. It was as if they had a mind of their own. She turned away and started singing softly. "'Dancing queen, feel the beat from the tangerine . . .'"

"It's *tambourine*," he said as he moved into place.

She glanced at him. "Tangerine."

He shook his head and turned away, but not before she caught it—the undeniable smile he was trying to hide. That was enough to fill her up to her toes and put her straight back to where she'd been before—certain she could win him over, make him forgive her, and maybe even convince him he should ditch McKenzie Palmer and run off into the sunset with her.

She willed herself to stop behaving so badly, in spite of the fact that McKenzie was now one boat over wearing a very skimpy red bikini. She tossed a glance toward Cody as Charlie sidled up next to the blonde bombshell blogger, but Cody's eyes were fixed straight ahead.

"Don't slack on your job, Chambers," he called out.

For some unknown reason, she wanted to make him proud. "You got it, skipper!" she called out.

For a brief moment, he tossed a glance at her over his shoulder. She couldn't help it; she smiled in spite of herself. In spite of her certainty that he and McKenzie were more than friends. In spite of her worry that he would never forgive her. In spite of her inability to stop fantasizing that he might actually feel the same way about her that she felt about him.

To her utter delight, Cody Boggs smiled back.

CHAPTER THIRTY-THREE

TO SAY CODY BOGGS HAD A COMPETITIVE STREAK would be a gross understatement. And to say it didn't completely turn Louisa on would be a lie.

She tried to keep up with him, with the trash-talking between the Coasties, with the wind velocity and the changes in direction. Cody would call instructions out to her, and she'd do as he said, remembering their practice sessions, which had apparently sunk in more than she realized.

They were connected, as if by some strange invisible cord, as if she knew what he was thinking for the first time since he'd returned to the island. This was the kind of link she'd been hoping for, but that had up until this point always remained just out of reach.

They sped out in front of the competition and she glanced back long enough to admire the way he looked right now. His hat hid that curly dark hair, and a pair of sunglasses concealed her favorite brown eyes— but his bronze skin glowed under the light of the sun, and his muscles rippled underneath his gray Coast Guard T-shirt.

"Everything okay?" he called out.

She waved in response—words failed her.

"We're changing direction. You ready?"

She gave him a thumbs-up and braced herself, determined not to be the space case that cost him this race.

As they took the second half, only one other boat even stood a chance—Charlie Pope and McKenzie Palmer. Of course.

Blondie let out a loud cheer as they pulled ahead, and Cody's face turned serious. They raced neck and neck, the cheers of the crowd propelling them forward. The wind kicked up and Cody adjusted the sails, shooting a nose in front of the other boat. Louisa stood and cheered as the boat sped out in front, but her movement created enough of a disruption to Cody's perfectly calculated plan that the other boat passed them just in time to claim first place.

McKenzie and Charlie both whooped and hollered as they sailed swiftly in.

Louisa glanced back at Cody, who stood stone-faced and seemingly unaffected. She turned toward the victors, only to see McKenzie rush straight into Charlie's arms and plant a kiss square on his mouth.

The kiss turned decidedly PG-13, and Louisa looked away. "Does that bother you?"

Cody tossed a glance toward the make-out session, then shrugged, still maneuvering their boat. "Why would it?"

Louisa faced him now. "I mean, you and McKenzie have been getting close and everything."

"No, we haven't."

"The sunrise? The 'Still on for tonight?' Spending the evening at Queequeg's with her?"

He didn't stop in front of the yacht club. He sailed on past as if the other regatta attendees didn't even matter. To some, he might look like a sore loser, but Louisa knew it was something else. Had she upset him?

He didn't respond for a long time, just sailed them toward the shore, then hopped out and pulled the little boat up onto the beach.

She stayed still, feeling like a child about to get a stern talking-to, and she maintained the appropriate level of silence.

He took off his hat and messed up his hair, perfectly disheveled the way only his could be. "Louisa." He turned away from her.

She hopped out of the boat and walked toward him, the wind tugging strands of hair from her ponytail. "Sorry I said anything."

Was he upset about McKenzie? She didn't think it was possible for anyone to like the woman that much, but maybe she was wrong.

"I don't care about McKenzie," he said, answering the question she never asked aloud.

"You don't?"

"No." He faced her now, but the sunglasses made him hard to read.

"I just thought—"

"You thought wrong."

She stilled. "Sorry."

He removed his glasses and hung them on the collar of his shirt. "She wanted to interview me. Duncan thought it would be good publicity."

An interview . . . ?

"Besides, she's really not my type."

"Tiny blondes with perfect bodies aren't your type?"

His eyebrows shot up and she chewed the inside of her lip, wishing like crazy she hadn't just said that.

"Nope." He looked at her with such intensity Louisa had to wonder if he was purposely trying to knock her off-kilter. She searched his eyes for a clue—anything that would let her in on what was running through his mind—but nothing came.

Her guard went up and she told herself not to read into any of this, but oh, how she wanted to. She wanted this feeling to last—this bright-lighted sizzle of electricity, a stronger draw than any she'd ever felt in her life.

But this was Cody. She and Cody were just (barely) friends.

But this was Cody. And she couldn't ignore the power of that.

"So you have a type?" She dared the question because the silence overwhelmed her.

He took a step closer, eyes still fixed on hers, then reached out and tucked her hair behind her ear. His thumb traced the line of her jaw, and he held the hair safe from the wind.

"Not really a type," he said. "Just a person."

Her heart thumped against her rib cage so loudly he could probably hear it. If there had been a marching band nearby, it could've been the drum line. It pounded and crashed—an ocean of force—and everything else faded away.

"You don't mean . . . ?" *Me?* Her mind finished the sentence and followed it up with *Please mean me.*

"I do mean . . ."

And then he did something she would relive every single day until the day she died. He brought his free hand to her face, and for a brief moment she saw a flicker of indecision.

Kiss me. Kiss me. Kiss me. Her mind pleaded with him as she inched ever so slightly closer, not wanting to spook him but very much wanting to communicate her willingness to participate in whatever it was he was thinking of doing.

He wouldn't make grand proclamations, and that was fine by her, as long as she was able to feel the warmth of his skin underneath her fingertips.

Her hand wound up and around his wrist, and then, ever so gently, he brought his mouth to hers. His kiss was soft and gentle at first, and her mind shot off fireworks to mark the occasion.

Was this really happening? She opened her eyes slightly, just to be sure she wasn't dreaming, and there he was—in all his gorgeousness, kissing her in earnest. She quickly closed her eyes again and let herself get lost in him. She laced her hands around his neck and inhaled his scent as his kiss grew deeper and more intense.

"Louisa." The whisper of her name pulled her back years, back to simpler times when there was nothing between them but magic and light and all good things. Could they get back to that? Were they back to it now?

She drew in a breath as her tongue swept lightly along his bottom lip. He shivered, pulling her closer, kissing her so deeply it was as if he couldn't get enough—as if there wasn't enough of her to satisfy him. The sun shone brighter as she drank him in, and she was sure if she didn't pull away, her entire body would light on fire. She was not sure, however, that she would even care.

When he finally broke away from her, they were both breathless and she wanted to start that entire scene from the beginning just for the chance to do it all over again.

"You're really good at that," he said.

"So are you." She smiled at him as his face turned serious, and a feeling of dread washed over her. Was this when he told her that kiss was a huge mistake?

"McKenzie Palmer, really?"

She laughed and gave him a shove, certain that no day would ever be as perfect as today had turned out to be. And also certain she wouldn't survive if she didn't get to kiss him again this very moment.

"I thought you still hated me," she said quietly, unsure how to process this sudden change in their relationship.

"I never hated you, Lou," he said.

She let out a slow breath. "You maybe did a little."

He kept his gaze fixed on hers. "Yeah, maybe a little."

She looked down, but he hooked one finger underneath her chin and raised her face back toward him. "That was a joke."

"Does that mean you forgive me?" She heard the desperation in her own voice, but she didn't care about pretenses. She needed him to forgive her like she needed oxygen.

He pulled her in and held her close to his chest. She didn't squirm or move, and for a long time she didn't even breathe. She simply let herself be held.

"I'm so sorry." Her voice broke and he leaned back, meeting her gaze.

"It wasn't your fault, Louisa," he said.

"That's not what I asked you," she said.

His stare was so deep, so intense, she thought it might buckle her knees.

"I forgive you." He brushed her hair away from her face.

"You do?"

"You're forgiven."

She let out an exhale so emotionally charged it might've crackled the air between them. "Thank you."

He kissed her again with the urgency of a man who was feeling the same thing she felt. When they parted and made their way back to the regatta, the only complaint Louisa had was that they couldn't stay on that beach for the rest of the day.

She loved him. He at least liked her. His kisses turned her entire body to molten lava.

And he forgave her.

All was right with the world.

CHAPTER THIRTY-FOUR

WHEN CODY AND LOUISA RETURNED TO THE YACHT CLUB, they exited the
boat hand in hand. He couldn't help it—he didn't want to let her go.

Maybe it was foolish, but he didn't care. He couldn't shake the
idea that he had to at least give it a try with her. She was so different,
so full of life. How could he not?

"So you and McKenzie were never a thing?" she asked as they
spotted the winners of the race celebrating under a tent.

"Nope."

"But she obviously liked you."

"Well, who doesn't?" He grinned at her, and she rolled her eyes.
"I spent some time with her, but it didn't take. Turns out, it's hard
to convince yourself to fall for someone when you've already given
your heart away."

She stopped then and looked at him. "Cody, is this crazy?"

He shrugged. "I hope so."

She gave his arm a shove. "I'm serious."

"I don't have any answers here, but I'm pretty sure 'crazy' would
be ignoring the way I feel about you."

Her cheeks turned pink, and he resisted the urge to kiss her again. It wasn't easy. Now that he'd tasted her, it was all he could think of.

"Miss Chambers?"

They turned and found Jackson's parents standing behind them. Louisa straightened and smoothed her hair back. "Hello, Mr. and Mrs. Wirth."

"Please, call me Deborah," she said.

"Deborah."

The older woman glanced at Cody and managed a polite smile. "We just wanted to thank you. The work you've done to make this event happen—it's astounding."

Louisa's face brightened. "It was our pleasure, really." She reached over and touched Deborah's arm, squeezed it gently, and it amazed Cody how comfortable she was connecting with people. How did that come so easily to her?

He half listened as Louisa chatted—something about asking Deborah if she or Manny would like to say a few words before awards were handed out—but mostly he was focused on her. Her eyes flickered so brightly as she seemed to forget everyone else around them and paid attention only to the two people standing in front of her.

When they walked away, Louisa glanced at him, brow quirked in confusion. "What's wrong?"

He shook his head. "You have no idea how good you are at this."

Her laugh sounded nervous. "At what?"

"At your job," he said. "It's more than just work for you, isn't it?"

"Well, yeah. That was the whole reason I started this business. I wanted to make a difference in people's lives. To create experiences for them. I never expected to be planning a fundraiser like this, but it suits me, I think."

"Yeah, it really does."

Her eyes scanned the crowd, then landed on her parents, across the lawn. "I wonder if they'll ever think so."

He moved to block her view of Warren and JoEllen. "It doesn't matter, Louisa. You're doing exactly what you're supposed to be doing in exactly the right place to do it. Of course you struck out on your own—you wanted to do work that mattered." He paused until he was sure he had her full attention. "And I believe in you. Maybe that can be enough for a while?"

Her lower lip trembled and her eyes filled with tears. She wrapped her arms around him and hugged him tightly. "Thank you."

He inhaled the smell of sunshine in her hair and vowed to find ways to show her how special she was.

~

Letter in Louisa's mailbox the day after the regatta:

Louisa,

Thanks for sailing with me. Turns out we still make a pretty great team. Enclosed is a check for half of what you paid at the Coastie auction. I know you won't want to take it, but I want to contribute to Jackson's fundraiser. Let me, okay?

PS—I'm on the way to the station, but I hardly slept last night. Couldn't stop thinking about that kiss. When can we do it again?

Love,
Cody

~

Jackson Wirth died on Tuesday night. His parents made the hardest decision of their lives and took him off life support. His body lasted twenty-two minutes on its own, and then the boy was gone.

The funeral was two days later, and Louisa accompanied nearly all of the Coast Guardsmen who were stationed at Brant Point. That night, the whole of Nantucket launched paper lanterns over the ocean in his honor, an idea spearheaded by Louisa Chambers.

And Cody fell even more in love with her.

CHAPTER THIRTY-FIVE

OVER THE NEXT TWO WEEKS, Cody spent as much time with Louisa as his schedule would allow. The awkwardness between them had dwindled, and while they'd settled into a rhythm, the air between them was still charged with the newness of their mutual attraction.

He liked that he had the right to reach over and take her hand. He liked being welcomed into her house. He loved that she kissed him good night and that she still seemed shy about it. He might've known Louisa his entire life, but it was as if they were becoming reacquainted.

It excited him.

His first year in the Coast Guard, it became pretty clear that his lifestyle didn't lend itself to a relationship, and frankly, he'd never met anyone who made him want to change that. Until now.

Cody happily helped her prepare for Maggie's party, awed, as usual, by watching her work. She was so good at her job—how could that jerk ex-boyfriend of hers make her think otherwise?

Perfect strangers hired her—a moonlight picnic on the beach or a personal tour of the island—and it didn't matter what they wanted her to do; she did it with her whole heart.

It inspired him. Had he ever cared about anyone that completely before? Maybe not until now.

Every single detail of Maggie's party mattered to Louisa. Food, decorations, party favors, location, guest list—she left nothing out. And while it mattered to her for all the right reasons, Cody feared there was a lot of weight on this party's success for other reasons too. As if it were the magical cure for healing a past so broken anyone else would've deemed it beyond repair.

One evening, when they were supposed to be on their way to dinner, he found her stressing about tablecloths, as if choosing the wrong ones would have tragic results. He gave her hand a tug and pulled her up from the chair behind her desk, where she'd likely been sitting since early that morning. She sighed as she looked at him, and he waited for her to give him her full attention.

"Hey," he said.

She smiled. "Hey."

"You're putting a lot of importance on these tablecloths."

"I just want everything to be perfect," she said.

He wrapped his arms around her waist, drawing her body closer to his and inhaling the scent of her. "Perfect is boring."

She shook her head.

"Lou, I just don't want you to be disappointed."

Her body stiffened underneath his fingers, and she inched back. "What do you mean?"

"Nothing, forget it."

"No, not nothing." She was fully out of his arms now. He shouldn't have brought it up. "You still think it's a bad idea."

"I think you've got the biggest heart of anyone I know," he said. "And I don't want to see it broken because our parents are stubborn." His mom could carry a grudge like a treasure chest. How could he prepare Louisa for that?

She frowned as if she hadn't considered her plan would go any other way than the way she'd played it out in her head.

"Have you told her about us?" she asked.

He sighed. "Not yet."

"You think she'll be upset?"

"Yes," he said simply. "But she'll have to deal with it." He grabbed her arm and gave her a tug toward him. "Because this is what I want." He leaned in and kissed her, softly at first because she seemed preoccupied, but after a beat, she finally kissed him back as if she didn't have a care in the world. And that was a beautiful thing.

He liked it better this way, in their little bubble where everything was new and exciting. As it was, that meant a lot of kissing—on the beach after a picnic packed with Bartlett's Farm sandwiches, on her couch while ignoring the movie they were supposed to be watching, even on Seaside's back deck, which had started to feel less like his old house and more like their special place. He would've invited her to his place, but it wasn't presentable. And he didn't want to waste time he could be spending with her to make it so. And he still had only one chair.

He loved that he was still discovering things about her. Like the fact that she regularly sang the wrong lyrics to well-known songs. And she talked to herself when she cooked. And she couldn't drive by a yard sale without stopping to at least *see* if there was anything worth buying.

He wouldn't deny his feelings for her—he couldn't. She made him want to get up in the morning and be a better person. He loved her. He'd almost told her twice now, but it felt too soon—too vulnerable. Once he said it, he couldn't take it back.

Last night after she met him at the station, they went for a walk, which led them to the memorial on the beach. It was surreal, standing there with her. His mind easily wandered back to the last time they were in that exact spot, twelve years ago. Somehow, as she reached down and took his hand, some of the pain of that night slipped silently away.

She leaned into him, and he felt the warmth from her body, noticed the way it filled him up, and he wondered if her love for him would be enough to calm the angry demons that still haunted him at times.

"Still no idea who put this here?" Her question was quiet, as if she didn't want to remind him. But he didn't need the reminder. He routinely spent sleepless nights trying to figure it out—a mystery worth solving.

What difference did it make, really? So someone wanted to remember his dad. That was great—he should be thankful. But the not knowing nagged him. He kept replaying the seemingly disconnected details he did know, rolling them over in his mind along with Ted's comments about Warren and his affinity for high-stakes poker. None of it seemed to fit together.

The mix of emotions was something he'd always been successful at ignoring—but not here on the island and certainly not standing in front of that cross.

"You're quiet," she said.

"Yeah."

She slipped her hand in his and let him be still.

"But no, still no idea." He squeezed her hand and turned to face her.

Louisa looked at him, and all his senses were on high alert. She saw the pain he kept hidden from everyone else—with her, he couldn't hide. The thought terrified and comforted him at the same time.

"We won't stop trying," she said.

He felt like a jerk for not telling her about the poker. But he didn't want to ruin the moment or think about anything other than the way she felt in his arms. Besides, he didn't know much. Only that Warren played. Maybe Daniel had jumped into a game or two himself, and maybe he'd lost big. Maybe that's why they had no money when he died. All speculation. No facts. It drove him nuts.

No, he didn't want to talk about any of that. He'd tell Louisa another day. When the mood was different. Now he simply wanted to take her hand and continue down the beach, away from the memorial—away from the memories.

~

Found on Cody's porch in the early hours of a Saturday morning: a chair he and Louisa had seen at a yard sale earlier in the week with a note pinned to it.

> *You're not "just one guy" anymore. I'm going to need a place to sit. —Louisa*

~

That night, Louisa was tied up with an especially difficult client, so Cody assured her he'd go check in on Maggie. When she finished her work, Louisa would meet him at the old woman's house.

He left the station just in time to see McKenzie Palmer ride off with Charlie Pope—a perfect match in his mind. He thought back to the night at the bar when it became glaringly clear to him that he was not meant to stay and hang out with McKenzie or her friend. It was nice of them to include him, but the second the music started, he found himself on the dance floor itching to go home. Around them, he felt old and boring. Or maybe they felt young and obnoxious?

In the end, he'd left early but put a bug in McKenzie's ear that Charlie might be more the kind of guy she was looking for. She'd done that annoying pout thing with her lips that young girls seemed to do, but it had zero effect on him. He wasn't interested.

"Well, I still need to interview you for my article," she'd said.

"Fine," he said. "That I can do."

"You're missing out." She shimmied off.

He silently agreed. He *was* missing out. But not with McKenzie. At that point, a relationship with Louisa was nothing but a fantasy.

Last week, McKenzie's three-part blog series on Nantucket's finest Coasties was published, and Louisa pointed out that Charlie's photo was the big one at the top. Cody could not have cared less—he was just thankful the regatta had been successful and they'd been able to present the Wirth family with a nice-size check, though they'd all hoped they were contributing to Jackson's recovery—not his funeral.

In the end, they'd fostered goodwill in the community and genuinely helped someone in need. That had seemed to appease the master chief, for now anyway. Maybe that meant Cody could get back to doing what he loved—training the guys, saving lives, leading a crew.

He walked up Maggie's front steps, knocked on the door, then let himself in, thinking it was nice that he'd begun to make peace with Nantucket.

"Hello?" he called out into the silence, but there was no response. He followed the blue light of the television into the living room. "Maggie?"

She sat in an armchair, avocado-green-and-yellow afghan on her lap, staring at the muted television. She was so still, for a second Cody thought she was dead.

Then she coughed. She reached for a glass of water on the table beside her, and he rushed over and picked it up, placing it in her outstretched hand. "Here you go."

She drank slowly, then handed the glass back to him. "You're a good boy, Daniel."

He sat down next to her. "It's Cody, Mags. Remember?"

Her eyes lit for a brief moment, like the flicker of a candle that quickly went out. "Cody. That's what I meant."

He hated to think it, but even in the short time he'd been back, he could tell her health was in rapid decline. What if she didn't make it to her birthday?

"Has Louisa been here tonight?"

"Ally stopped by earlier. No Louisa."

"She'll be here soon," he said.

Slowly she dragged her eyes to his. "You love her."

He was thankful for the dark so she couldn't see his reaction. He cleared his throat instead of responding.

"It's okay; she loves you too. You guys were made for each other."

"You think so?"

Maggie clapped a wrinkled hand over his much larger one and exhaled a long sigh. "Everyone thinks so."

His eyes fell to their two hands. "Not everyone."

He could practically feel her frowning.

"Not my mother."

"Have you told her about the two of you?" Another cough.

He shook his head. He knew he was a coward, but he was avoiding that conversation.

"Your mother is coming this weekend."

He groaned. "Don't remind me."

"Best tell her now."

He stilled.

"You forgave Louisa, then?"

"I did," he said without hesitation.

"Time to forgive yourself, too, kiddo," she said pointedly.

He straightened, lips parted as if to speak, but no words formed.

"You're not fooling me."

He leaned back in his chair, staring at the door. He could be out of here in four strides—but then he'd have to face her again tomorrow. *Stop running.*

"What do you mean?" he finally asked.

"I could see that burden you've strapped to your back the first day you showed up here. It's obvious you're looking for absolution. Just like Louisa. That girl isn't going to be happy until everything is as it was."

"And if that doesn't happen?"

"It can't happen. Louisa doesn't understand that tragedy changes people. I'm afraid she's in for a rough time round about my birthday party."

"I told her the same thing." He sat for a long time, unmoving and silent. "Am I in for a rough time?"

From behind her glasses, Maggie studied him thoughtfully. "Only if you don't learn to lay some of this down. Anyone can see it's killing you."

"Nobody's ever mentioned it before."

She scoffed. "Then they aren't looking hard enough."

"Or maybe you're looking too hard." But he knew the truth. Nobody mentioned it because there was nobody close enough to him to notice.

Her hand was back on top of his. It made him feel like her captive. He wasn't sure he liked it. "Tell me you don't blame yourself for what happened to your father. Tell me you don't think it was all your fault and that you haven't replayed that night over and over again wishing you'd done something differently."

He pulled his hand away and leaned back in the chair, frustrated that her words were burrowing into his soul.

"Well, I have something to say about that, kiddo."

He looked over at her, hungry for something—anything—that might release him from this prison of guilt.

"As many times as you wish you could change that night, that's as many times as your father would do the exact same thing for you."

His eyes clouded. "What?" The word came out a whisper.

"It's like Jesus. Do you think he wanted to die? He knelt in that garden begging God for a different way, but he knew his sacrifice meant the rest of us could live."

"But my dad didn't have to die, Maggie. He only died because of me."

"He did have to die in order for you to live. Don't you see?" She coughed, but when he leaned forward to offer help, she held up a hand to stop him. Finally she cleared her throat and met his eyes. "It was his choice—and he would do it all over again in a heartbeat if given the chance. Don't take away the power of the sacrifice he made by doubting it or wishing it away. The alternative means that you don't get the life your father died for you to have. You owe it to him to live it big and full. Not to stay stuck here in shame and guilt."

The words hung there between them, filling the dark house with the faint glow of light, of promise, of forgiveness.

Maggie leaned forward this time, taking both of his hands in her own. "Forgive yourself the same way you forgave Louisa. What happened was nobody's fault. Not hers. Not yours. The sooner you realize that, the sooner you can get on with your life."

He hadn't come here for this. Still, he mulled over her words for several seconds, unsure how to move on, how to get past this when he was still so sorry for all the pain he'd caused.

Had this shame been keeping him from moving forward? Was that the real reason he never got close to anyone—was he afraid of losing them, or was he afraid of being the reason they were lost?

The door opened and Louisa rushed in. "Sorry I'm late. I have dinner." She stopped in the doorway, and her face fell. "What's going on? Are you guys okay?"

Cody glanced at Maggie. "Yeah, we're good."

Maggie winked at him, then leaned back in her chair. "We're starving. What took you so long?"

Louisa glanced from Maggie to Cody and back again. "Sorry; I got held up with the Tacione family." She opened the brown paper bag and pulled out Centre Street Bistro to-go containers as she talked. "Mrs. Tacione brought her five sisters to the island for the first time, and you know they aren't super wealthy, but I promised her we would make them feel like they were." Louisa was beaming now. "You should've seen their faces when they walked into their rental cottage. I got them an amazing deal with my friend Leo and—" She stopped and met Cody's eyes. "What's wrong?"

He smiled. "Nothing," he said. "Just admiring how good you are at what you do."

Her mouth spread into a slow smile, her lips soft pink and utterly kissable. He tossed Maggie a glance and saw that the old woman had dozed off again, so he stood, wrapped his arms around Louisa, and kissed her right there in the middle of Maggie's living room.

Kissing her had become his favorite thing to do, but there was something different about it now, as if something inside him had shifted in the moments before she arrived.

A single word kept running through his mind—a word that carried more weight to it than he'd expected, a word that filled him up like an overflowing pool. A word that summed up everything he'd been searching for since the day his family left Nantucket all those years ago.

Forgiven.

He wanted that. He'd given it to Louisa—it was time to give it to himself. And to accept the forgiveness of a God who offered grace for mistakes like his.

As the kiss melted into a deep embrace, he prayed for the strength to follow through.

It's what his father would've wanted.

CHAPTER THIRTY-SIX

SOMEHOW, AFTER THAT NIGHT IN MAGGIE'S HOUSE, Louisa felt like she and Cody grew even closer, as if every barrier that had been keeping them apart had suddenly fallen away.

She'd spent her life wishing for his forgiveness, but she had no idea how freeing it would actually be to have it.

They spent less time talking about the memorial and their parents and everything that had been broken between them before and more time focusing on what was in front of them now. How much better it was to have something to look forward to, instead of always being focused on what had come before.

Some nights, he showed up just as she was finishing her work and stood in the doorway of her office, watching her. It made working impossible. He'd never been much of a talker, but he *was* an observer, and being the object of that observation turned her insides wobbly.

If he had the day off, she adjusted her schedule so she could spend it with him. They ate picnics at the beach and went hiking and swimming and strolling on the cobblestone streets of the island they had both grown to love.

Today, only two days before Maggie's party, she'd cleared the morning so they would have some time together before his next shift the following day. They ate breakfast on the patio at Island Kitchen and were now strolling hand in hand down Main Street, looking in shops and smiling at the tourists taking in the island, maybe for the first time. Louisa was almost jealous of them—to still have so much of Nantucket to explore and discover would be such a gift—and yet, knowing that she knew all the island's secrets quickly erased any feelings of envy. She vacillated between wanting to share everything she knew about the island and wanting to keep it to herself.

She resisted the urge to tell each person all the things she thought they should do—touristy things like eating ice cream at the Juice Bar or taking a stroll through the Whaling Museum and non-touristy things like renting a bike and exploring off the beaten path.

Cody let go of her hand to look at something in the window of Mitchell's Book Corner, her favorite bookstore, at the intersection of Main and Orange Streets. She reached in her bag for a bottle of water, uncapped it, and took a drink, but as she scanned the people across the street, she was struck by a woman, standing on the opposite corner, staring right at her.

It had been a dozen years, but she would've recognized Marissa Boggs anywhere. The woman was stunningly beautiful then, and she was stunningly beautiful now. It was a wonder her own mother had ever befriended Marissa. JoEllen liked to be the prettiest one in the room.

"Lou, we should go to this," Cody called from behind her. "The Boston Pops concert—remember we used to listen from down the beach?"

He stood directly behind her now, but she hadn't moved—couldn't move. Her eyes were glued to his mother, who was watching them with a broken expression on her face.

"You didn't tell her about us." Louisa exhaled the realization.

"What?" Cody followed her gaze across the street, and the second he spotted his mom, he sighed. "She's early." He lifted a hand in a wave, but Marissa turned, dragged her suitcase behind her, and walked off in the other direction.

He looked at Louisa, panic on his face, and she gave him a nod that released him to run after his mom.

She should've known this cocoon of happiness would soon be cracked open. She'd been living in a fantasy.

~

It was hours before she heard from Cody. In that time, Louisa tried to work, but she mostly aggravated Ally with her distractedness.

"What is going on with you today?" Ally asked, refiling paperwork Louisa had filed incorrectly. "Trouble in paradise?"

"I'm fine."

"You told Linda Paulson you'd run her errands next week."

"So?"

"You swore to me last time you would never work with that woman again. I think it was around the time she asked you to take her dog's stool sample to the vet?"

Louisa groaned. How had she let that one slip by? Linda was notoriously high-maintenance and about the last thing she needed right now.

"So spill it." Ally refilled Louisa's mug of coffee. "And I don't mean the coffee."

Louisa let out a heavy sigh. She missed Cody. She wanted to know what he said to his mom. She wanted the chance to win Marissa over—she just wasn't prepared to do it yet. She'd been so content to keep her relationship with Cody to herself, she'd fooled herself into believing it could stay that way. How stupid! Of course it couldn't. They had the party this weekend! What had she planned to do— ignore him the whole night?

Now, more than ever, she had to figure out a way to set his

313

family and hers back on good terms. She *had* to. Their relationship depended on it.

She told Ally about Cody's mom, careful to add in the appropriate amount of *woe is me*, but Alyssa still shrugged her off.

"I'm sure it'll be fine," she said. "Nobody holds a grudge this many years. Besides, you guys are adults."

But Ally hadn't seen the death glare Marissa had given her on the street that morning.

"What if it's not fine?" she lamented. "What if this second chance is really just another failed attempt?"

Ally went still. "You love him, right?"

Louisa rubbed her temples and let out a pathetic "Yes."

"Then it'll be fine."

But Louisa knew better. Love didn't always conquer all. If it did, Cody's dad would still be alive.

"Let's just get back to work," Louisa said. "I'm tired of myself right now."

Cody showed up late that night—she hadn't heard from him all day—and she could tell things hadn't gone well with his mom. Worse, she'd spent hours overthinking the situation, which had only left her conflicted and confused.

"Sorry for disappearing," he said. "It's been a long day."

He stood on the porch, and while she couldn't say for sure, it seemed like some of the distance that used to exist between them was back. She reached for him, and he stiffened at her touch.

Okay, now she could say for sure. The distance was definitely back.

"What did she say?"

"I told her not to come here."

Louisa's heart sank. If she hadn't sent that invitation, this wouldn't be happening right now. "I'm sorry," she said.

He gave a sigh. "It's not your fault. She's an adult. She's got to figure out how to move on."

He sounded so certain. Louisa felt anything but.

"Louisa?" Concern washed over his face.

"I can't." She took a step back.

"You can't what?"

"I saw the look on your mom's face," Louisa said.

"She just needs time," he said.

But he didn't know that—not really. It had been years, and his mother looked every bit as angry as she had been the day she left the island.

"Maybe *we* need some time," Louisa said.

He frowned. "What are you saying?"

"Just that I don't want to be the reason for any of this. My whole summer has been about trying to find a way to fix things, to put our families back together—this is the opposite of that."

He let out a sound that was part scoff, part sigh and drilled her with his eyes. "So that's it? You're ending it because you're worried my mom doesn't like you? That's ridiculous, Lou, and you know it."

"No," she said quickly. "I'm not ending anything. You know how I feel about you."

"Then what?"

"We pause. Let this blow over. Figure things out after the party."

"The party—" He practically groaned the words. "You've got so much riding on this party. If it doesn't go the way you want it to, what then?"

She swallowed the lump in her throat. "I don't know."

"We're not kids anymore, Louisa."

He reached over and placed a hand on her cheek. She pressed her hand over his, closed her eyes, and drew him in, inhaling a scent that had become familiar and reassuring. She wanted to remember it always, so she marked it in her mind. Just in case.

"I'm tired of things tearing us apart," he said quietly. "I don't want to take a break."

"We'll figure it out. There's a lot of history to wade through." She opened her eyes and found him watching her.

He leaned in and kissed her on the cheek (a sure sign their relationship was doomed), jogged back out to his Jeep, started the engine, and drove away.

And Louisa went upstairs and cried herself to sleep.

CHAPTER THIRTY-SEVEN

"YOU LOOK TERRIBLE."

Louisa glared at her mom, who stood on the porch wearing a pink top, white linen pants, and the unmistakable expression of disapproval.

"I thought you would've been up for hours." Her mom pushed her way inside the house, stopping in the living room.

Louisa plopped back down on the couch, where she'd been since the sun rose several hours ago. She pulled the blanket up and closed her eyes.

"What's wrong?" her mom asked.

Louisa covered her face with a pillow. Her mother was the last person in the world she wanted to talk to right now. Why was she here? She didn't even like Louisa.

Louisa couldn't be sure, but she thought Mom had just sat down, which meant she wasn't leaving.

"Why are you here?" she asked from underneath the pillow.

"I came to see if you needed any help with Maggie's party," her mom said.

Louisa sat up. "It's tomorrow, Mother. You're a little late."

Her mom looked wounded at Louisa's cross words, which had come out much harsher than Louisa had intended.

"What's gotten into you?"

Would it be appropriate to scream into the pillow? Louisa was dangerously close to finding out.

She whipped the blanket off and tossed the pillow aside. "Mother, I am in love with Cody Boggs. I'm in love with him, and I've been in love with him practically since the day I was born. And I know I screwed up, but there's more to it than my mistake. Teenage foolishness wouldn't have kept you and Marissa apart, especially not after Daniel died. So tell me the truth—what happened between the four of you? What happened with you and Marissa, with you and Daniel, with Dad and Daniel? With all of you? Because whatever it was—it's ruined my chances of being with the man I love, so don't I deserve to know why?"

Her mother's eyebrows appeared to be permanently raised, the unmistakable expression of shock on her face. "Well, I don't know what's going on with you, Louisa Elizabeth Chambers, but I—"

"Mom." Louisa let the word serve as an entire sentence.

Her mother perched on the chair, the innocent expression falling from her face. Louisa could almost see the pretense drift away.

"What is it? *Were* you and Daniel having an affair?"

"No, Louisa," she said. "But I'm not so sure Marissa and your father weren't."

Louisa frowned. "What?"

"Marissa is one of the most beautiful women I've ever known," Mom said. "But I was just cocky enough not to worry about her stealing the eye of a man I was so certain loved nobody else in the world but me." She laughed to herself. "Warren and I were so taken with each other in those early days, it never seemed like a risk to bring Daniel and Marissa into our lives, especially since they were equally as taken with each other."

Louisa didn't tell her mother she had trouble picturing her parents "taken with each other." But it was hard to imagine.

"Marissa doesn't seem like the cheating type, Mom," Louisa said.

Her mother shot her a pointed look. "Oh, but I do?"

"No, of course not."

"And yet you've accused me of that exact thing twice now."

Her words shamed Louisa. Had she really gotten it all wrong? Had Marissa felt so guilty for betraying Daniel that she let the guilt turn to anger and drove them all apart?

"After Daniel died, she came to see your father. Came right up to the house and asked to speak to Warren." Her mother's face fell. "They wouldn't let me in on their discussion. They said it had to do with business, but if it was really business, why couldn't they discuss it in front of me? That's when I started to get suspicious."

"Did you ask Dad?"

She shook her head. "No. I couldn't bear to hear the answer. It was easier to pretend that everything was fine, and the only way to do that was to remove myself from Marissa's life completely."

Louisa wasn't sure what to say. She'd never seen even a sliver of weakness in her mother. And now here she was, baring her soul, and Louisa felt ill-equipped to handle it.

"I always thought you blamed me," Louisa admitted quietly.

Her mother's shoulders sagged slightly as if she'd only just now decided to relax. "I was full of blame, but the person I blamed the most was myself. I wasn't a good wife. I was thoughtless and selfish and it made sense to me that your father would turn to someone else for comfort and love. I was lousy at both."

"But, Mom, you don't even know if something happened between them."

Her mother's expression turned weary. "Your father was more than happy to go along with my plan not to see Marissa and the kids. He seemed downright relieved when I suggested it. I think maybe Daniel's death finally knocked some sense into him. He was a different man after that."

Louisa's mind wandered back. It was true—her father had been changed by the death of his best friend. But wouldn't anyone be?

"Maybe there was another explanation?"

She shook her head sadly. "I don't think I have the courage to find out."

For the first time in her life Louisa actually felt sorry for her mother. To live with this kind of question hanging over her head for so many years must've been overwhelming. The not knowing. The assuming. The perceived betrayal. And then to be accused of being the one to do the exact thing she suspected her husband of doing—by her own daughter.

A wave of regret washed over her. It was followed by a wave of dread. "Mom, Marissa is coming to the party tomorrow. She's on the island now."

Her mother's face tightened. Her lips drew into a thin line. "You invited Marissa?"

"I didn't know," Louisa said. "I thought it would be good for everyone to be back together—for Maggie's sake." And for her own sake, if she was honest.

This whole party was simply a way to ease her own conscience. How selfish she'd been. How wrong.

But this was what Louisa did. She took care of people—it was her job. Surely they understood how important it was to take care of the people she loved most of all. Right?

She'd been so stupid—so arrogant—to assume she had that kind of power.

At the mention of Maggie's name, Mom shifted. "Of course. For Maggie." But she quickly stood, hugged her purse to her body, and gave Louisa a nod. "Do take a shower, dear. You look like a mess."

With that, she was gone.

CHAPTER THIRTY-EIGHT

"EVERYTHING IS PERFECT." Ally had been doling out extra compliments in light of Louisa's sour mood.

Everything was not perfect. In fact, nothing was perfect. But at least when Louisa made mistakes, she made them big: planning a party disguised as a reconciliation for people who didn't want to be reconciled, inviting Marissa, pushing Cody away. What would she do next—marry Eric, abandon her business, and live a boring, pathetic life?

She groaned.

"What is it?" Ally asked.

"Nothing," Louisa said. "I just need to get through this night."

"Get through?" Ally grimaced. "You always said we started The Good Life to stop 'getting through.' This party has been on your radar all summer—you don't *get through* it; you enjoy it. It might be the last time you get to do something wonderful for Maggie."

Louisa was embarrassed she needed this reminder.

But she did. She'd grown so selfish she needed to be reminded that one of her dearest friends was dying, and if she were honest, she'd watched Maggie's condition worsen over the last few weeks. How much longer did the old woman have?

"You're right," Louisa said. "You're so right."

Ally nodded as if to say, *Of course I am.* "Why are we standing here? We have guests to greet."

They'd set up tables and chairs out on Maggie's favorite beach just behind her house. In the distance, Louisa could see her father heating the oil for the fish fry, and her mom walked around with a tray of hors d'oeuvres.

They'd decided to keep the entire affair low-key. Simple and un-fussy, just like Maggie. The woman had made it clear she didn't want "fancy." She wanted comfortable. Louisa looked around at the family-style meal they were about to serve—all of Maggie's favorite foods, even though they didn't necessarily go together. Louisa had even or-dered single-serve containers of Lucky Charms, which were lined up on a table next to the cutest little milk bottles she'd ever seen, neatly arranged in a tub of ice. They'd hired a DJ who'd been instructed to only play the oldies, and while Louisa wasn't sure if that meant songs from the fifties or songs from the thirties, she decided to let him figure it out. Currently "I Can't Help Myself" was playing in the background, and the guests who'd already arrived seemed to approve.

They'd put up two large tents, and Louisa had created a spot for their guest of honor, a seat that almost resembled a throne. It was fitting. Maggie wasn't regal or elegant, but she was still a queen.

The beach began to fill with people—friends, neighbors, former coworkers. Everyone was happy to come out and celebrate this no-nonsense woman who'd spent her years speaking truth and life into all of them.

Maggie sat under the tent in a white Adirondack chair, sur-rounded by pillows and covered with her afghan from inside. She greeted everyone with her trademark down-home love as if they were the only person in the world who mattered—because of course, in that moment, they were.

"You ready for this?"

Louisa followed Ally's gaze to the yard, where Cody, his mom, and his sister had just appeared.

Her eyes locked on to his, and for a moment, she was paralyzed with desire. She missed him more than she should. He looked away and her heart sank. He was back to avoiding her. And it was all her fault.

She turned and found Maggie staring at her. The old woman held her gaze for several long seconds, and then she winked.

Louisa should warn her about all that had transpired lately. As Maggie's health had worsened, Louisa found there wasn't time for their usual heart-to-hearts. Maggie didn't know Louisa and Cody were on a break. Louisa couldn't have told her that even if she'd wanted to—she would've choked on the words.

She watched as Cody led his mom and sister down to where Maggie sat. Marley had certainly grown up and now looked a lot like an older version of Barbie's little sister, Skipper. Her hair was much lighter than Cody's, but she was as beautiful as he was handsome.

Louisa's eyes drifted over to her own father, who'd sat up straighter and focused on the three newcomers with great interest and was that worry knit across his brow?

She turned just in time to see her mother walking toward the house.

"I'm going to go help my mother," Louisa told Ally. She strode off toward the cottage, doing her best to avoid Cody, as if that were possible.

"Hey." He was at her side.

She stopped. It was painful to look at him. How had they gotten here, with the past burrowing its way between them once again? She hated it.

"I don't know how to do this," he said. "I'm not sure where we stand."

"I know." She rubbed her forehead. "I'm sorry." Her eyes wandered past him and saw that Marissa and Marley were both watching them with the same interest and worry as her father. The thought turned her stomach.

All she really wanted to do was drag Cody away from the rest of the party and kiss him until the sun came up. Had they been fooling themselves all along? Had they been doomed from the start?

"Did you talk to your mom any more—about us?" she asked, not really wanting to know the answer.

"A little."

"And?"

"She'll be fine," he said flippantly.

"She doesn't want us together."

"Lou, I told you she just needs some time."

"Maybe," Louisa said. "But our families despise each other. We may never fully understand why, but that's the truth of it."

"Well, they'll have to get over it. The last two days without you nearly killed me."

Louisa's eyes drifted back to Marissa. How arrogant she'd been to think she could put everything and everyone back together. As if they were puzzle pieces that simply needed sorting. "I don't think it's as easy as that."

"Can you let me make this decision? It's my family we're talking about." There was agony in his voice, and he gripped her arms with both hands. "I don't want to lose you again."

"I don't want to lose you either, but I know how important they are to you—and I really don't want to be the reason you lose anyone else you love." But she also *really* didn't want to lose him.

His sigh was heavy, pronounced.

"Let's just get through tonight and then figure things out."

He didn't respond.

She inched back. "Okay?"

His nod was barely detectable.

At that moment, her mother walked out of the house, carrying Maggie's birthday cake, lit up with candles.

Louisa slipped her arms from his grasp, but his hand slid to hers and squeezed. She forced herself to smile, though she was sure that smile was punctuated with sadness, and then she walked over to Maggie's seat of honor and joined the rest of them in singing "Happy Birthday."

Cody stood, unmoving, his eyes glassed over and focused on only one thing—Louisa. And the pain of that sliced straight through her like the knife through Maggie's last birthday cake.

CHAPTER THIRTY-NINE

CODY KNEW THIS WOULD HAPPEN.

His mother might be the only person in the world Louisa couldn't charm. And that would drive her crazy. Of course she'd balk. Of course she'd run away. Of course she'd say that horrible thing about not wanting to take more family members away from him. She was Louisa—fixer of all people.

He glanced at his mom, who quickly averted her gaze. Anger rose within him. These people were adults—why weren't they acting like it?

He watched as the crowd gathered around Maggie. Louisa sang heartily, doing an impressive job of acting like things were fine, but as the song came to a close, she looked his way, and he saw that sometimes, even she was good at pretending.

Maggie leaned forward and blew out her candles, and just as JoEllen whisked the cake away to be cut, the crowd dispersed and the old woman started coughing. Louisa was at her side with a bottle of water, which she opened and handed over, but Maggie seemed unable to stop long enough to take a drink.

He'd been around long enough to know now that these coughing fits could be brutal, and he imagined Maggie didn't want to have one in front of her guests, but at this point, moving her wasn't an option.

He made his way toward the beach where Maggie sat. Ally was trying to distract the crowd, but it was clear people were curious. How many of them knew about Maggie's condition?

Cody caught Louisa's eye just as the old woman drew in a difficult breath, and he saw the worry skitter across her face. He came in closer and took Maggie's hand, while Louisa did the same on the other side.

"What do you need, Mags?" Louisa asked.

Maggie's cough sputtered to a halt. "You two—" she clung to them both, struggling for breath—"together."

The cough had subsided, but Maggie clung to her chest as if she were in pain. Her breathing turned labored. Louisa's eyes flashed with fear. She raced off toward the house. Cody pulled out his phone and called 911. He gave the dispatcher their information and quickly hung up. By the time he'd finished the call, Louisa had returned with Maggie's home oxygen tank. Cody put the mask over the old woman's face. Behind them, the crowd had hushed.

"Just try to breathe," he said quietly. He wrapped his fingers around her wrist and took her pulse, noticing that Maggie's skin had gone pale. The siren in the distance gave him hope that they'd get her to the hospital in time, and the oxygen appeared to be helping, at least a little.

Ally had successfully moved the majority of the crowd away from them, but when he glanced up, he found Warren and JoEllen standing behind Louisa, and his mom and sister standing behind him.

Maggie's hands tensed and she reached up to remove the mask.

"Maggie, don't," Louisa said.

But the old woman wanted to speak, even in her weakened state. She choked out one word: "Enough." Slowly her gaze moved from Cody's family to Louisa's. "Forgive. Before it's too late."

Cody didn't look at the rest of them—he couldn't. He was too afraid all he would find on their faces was the same stubbornness that had always been there.

A cough silenced her just as two paramedics Cody knew from work rushed around the side of the house and down toward the beach. He stood, waving them over, then gave them her vitals and helped load her onto the stretcher.

"Is she going to be okay?" Louisa asked, her voice breaking mid-sentence.

"We're going to do everything we can for her," the paramedic said. They fastened the belt around Maggie, and Louisa let go of her hand as they wheeled her off.

"I'm going to the hospital," Louisa told Ally. "Can you handle things here?"

"Of course."

She ran off, her parents close behind, leaving him standing with his mom and sister.

"This is heavy," Marley said.

His mom's eyes had filled with tears. "I didn't get to say goodbye."

For a brief moment, he wondered if she was talking about Maggie or his father.

"Let's go to the hospital," he said. "We should be there."

His mother looked away. "I don't know if they want us there."

"Who cares?" Marley said. "Maggie is our friend too. We should be there."

"She's right," Cody said. "Maybe it's time we start listening to what Maggie said."

Anger flashed across his mother's face. "What do you mean?"

"Mom—" he placed a hand on her arm—"aren't you tired of being angry?"

Her jaw twitched.

"You loved them once. All of them."

A tear slid down his mother's cheek. "That was a long time ago."

"I'm going to the hospital. Are you coming?"

His mother didn't move for a long moment; then finally she nodded. "Let's go."

⁓

Louisa paced the waiting room of the Nantucket Cottage Hospital. Since they weren't family, none of them were allowed to go back while Maggie was being examined. It was an absurd rule—she was more of a family to Maggie than anyone related to her by blood. And vice versa, sadly.

Her parents sat in the corner, Mom watching an HGTV show that droned on from a television mounted to the wall and Dad flipping through an issue of *Forbes* magazine. They'd only been there about ten minutes when Cody and his mom and sister walked in. Time stopped. He looked concerned, a line of worry deeply etched in his forehead.

He met her eyes. "Any word?"

"Not yet. We can't go back because we aren't family."

His nod was followed by an unbearable beat of awkward silence.

"Do you mind if we wait with you?" he finally asked.

Louisa's eyes drifted from Cody to his mom (who wasn't looking at her) to Marley. "Of course not." She motioned toward an empty row of chairs. Marissa and Marley sat.

"Should I get us coffee?" Cody asked.

It was strange, having a stilted conversation in front of the rest of them. She hated this distance between them. Hated that he was right in front of her and just out of reach.

"Do you guys want coffee?" she asked her parents.

"I'm okay," they both said.

She turned back to Cody. "I guess we're okay."

"You're okay?" His question was so earnest, it nearly broke her heart. She wasn't okay. Not even close.

She nodded and sat down next to her mother, aware that her family was on one side of the room and his was on the other. Marissa whispered something to Marley, and JoEllen looked from the television to the pair of them. Never in her life had Louisa experienced this kind of tension. They sat in silence for what felt like hours but was, in reality, only minutes. She worked hard to avoid Cody's eyes, praying silently that Maggie would be okay. She wasn't ready to lose her yet.

Did anyone else in the room remember how it had felt to love each other? Did anyone else have memories of the good times? The laughter? The endless days and nights they'd spent together? Did anyone else want that back?

After about twenty minutes, Dr. Smithton Jeffries entered the room. A white coat covered his dress pants, shirt, and tie, and his face looked weary.

Louisa stood.

He met her eyes, and his face fell. "I'm sorry, Louisa."

"No." She heard the word in her own voice, but it sounded muffled and quiet, like she was underwater again.

"I think she was just ready to go home," the doctor said.

Then she *was* underwater again, the waves knocking her over, stealing her breath. She tumbled upside down as her knees buckled. Cody was at her side in a flash, catching her, righting her, saving her.

No. No. No. No. Not today. Not Maggie.

Her mind spun. Her heart broke. The old woman was her touchstone—God couldn't have needed her more than Louisa did.

Cody's face was buried in her hair as he pulled her to his chest. The rest of the room went silent as she struggled, once again, for air. The doctor was still talking, but his voice faded as if he were an image on the television with the volume turned down. And then he walked away.

Cody led her to a chair, away from the others. They'd all gone. They'd all had lives somewhere else. Louisa had Nantucket, and that meant she had Maggie. In all her loneliness, she'd always had Maggie.

And now she didn't. Now she had no one.

She covered her face with her hands and wiped her cheeks dry, aware that Cody's body was so close to hers she could sink into him if she let herself. Instead, she tensed. She dug down deep and forced herself to be strong, the way Maggie taught her to be.

"Will you listen to her now?" she asked out loud to the entire room. She scanned their faces and found confusion on every one. "She told us to forgive. It was the last thing she said to us. Are any of you willing to listen? Is anyone willing to admit they were wrong? Is anyone able to say they're sorry?"

Nobody spoke. Eyes collectively fell to the floor. Cody reached for her hand, but she tore it away.

"I'll go first," she said through tears. "I'm sorry for being stupid enough to think that if we were all together again, you would remember what it was like when we were family."

"It wasn't stupid, Lou," Cody said quietly.

"It was," she said sadly, her voice quivering. She looked at Marissa. "I'm sorry for what I did to Cody all those years ago. I'm sorry for everything that happened that night. If I could change it, I would— you don't know how many times I've wished for that. How many letters I've written and not sent. How many prayers I've prayed."

"Louisa." Cody's tone warned, but she couldn't stop. She knew she was likely ruining any chance at absolving herself, but she had to continue.

She looked at her mom. "I'm sorry I accused you of having an affair with Daniel."

Marissa's eyes shot to JoEllen.

"I know it wasn't true, and I shouldn't have said the things I said to you." She looked at Cody. "And I'm sorry for ever breaking your heart."

"Lou, it's fine. We're past this."

"But we aren't." She waved a hand around the room. "Look at us. Look how broken we still are." She choked on a sob. "I wanted us all back together because somehow I thought that meant I didn't have anything to be sorry for. Somehow if you would just be friends again, if we could all put things back to the way we were, that made all of my choices okay. Maggie wanted us put back together too, but she wanted it for the right reasons. See, she had a secret. She never held a grudge. She forgave quickly and completely. She said she didn't want bitterness taking up space in her heart when she had so much love to give." Louisa scoffed softly. "I was so naive."

There was a long pause—a heart-wrenching silence in which nobody said a word, nobody shifted in their seat, nobody even seemed to breathe.

Louisa wished she could take it all back. It was futile—every attempt she'd made so far to repair what was broken had ended in disaster. Why would Maggie's death change that?

She stood. "I need to get some air." She was walking toward the door, anxious to be alone with her thoughts, when she heard her father clear his throat from behind her.

"Louisa." His tone was commanding—always—but now it seemed filled with something other than control. It was filled with regret.

Was this when Warren Chambers finally came clean? Was this where he confessed to an affair with his best friend's wife, who also happened to be the former best friend of his own wife? Louisa froze in place.

"Wait a minute."

She turned and found her father standing. He wore a pair of khakis and a light-blue button-down, sleeves rolled to the elbows. He was tan and handsome, and she wanted to remember him in this moment, the moment before he broke everyone's hearts. Because she had a feeling that after what he was about to say, she'd never look at him the same way again.

"Warren?" JoEllen gave his hand a tug, and he turned to her, tears pooling in his eyes.

"I'm sorry, Joey," he said.

JoEllen's face fell as if she knew what was coming—as if he were about to speak aloud her greatest fear, humiliating her in one single sentence.

"Don't," she said, her voice pleading.

He shook his head, then looked at Marissa. "I knew the moment I saw you today that it was time to stop running."

Louisa's heart clenched as if it had been slipped inside a vise that tightened a little more with every second that ticked by.

"Warren, please." Louisa's mother was crying, a horrifying desperation clear in her voice.

Louisa dared a glance at Cody, who looked on with a mix of confusion and fear. Maybe she was wrong. Maybe the truth would only make things worse.

"Dad—"

He held up a hand to silence her. "I've been living with this for over a decade, kitten. It's time to get it out on the table."

What if she didn't want it on the table? What if she wanted to stuff it away in a cupboard? To make it disappear? Had she made yet another mistake with her outburst?

She scanned the room.

No. The truth was the only thing with the power to repair this brokenness. That was obvious to her now. It was also obvious that the truth was going to hurt.

She forced herself to look at her father, who'd paced the width of the waiting room twice and now stood in the empty space at the center of the chairs. HGTV hummed quietly in the background, and the sound of her mom's crying was the only other noise in the room. Louisa glanced at Marissa, who, she realized, seemed as confused by her father's behavior as everyone else.

"It was my fault," her father whispered.

Again, nobody spoke.

She wanted to rush to Cody, to shield him from whatever it was her father was about to say—but as quickly as the thought entered her mind, she wondered who was going to shield her. This could be painful for all of them.

"What was your fault?" Cody finally asked.

Her father wouldn't look at him. "Everything."

Louisa felt her forehead pull into a deep frown. "What do you mean?"

Slowly her dad dragged his gaze from the floor to Marissa. "It was my fault you lost everything."

What? It was his fault they had an affair? It was his fault he stole his best friend's wife? That's what he was supposed to say.

"When you came to me that day to ask me for money—"

"You said no," Marissa interrupted. "You said you wouldn't help."

"I said I *couldn't* help." Her father's eyes drew downward with the kind of regret that drained life from a person.

"I don't understand," Marissa said.

"Warren, what are you saying?" Even Louisa's mom seemed confused.

Her father raked his hands over his thinning hair, looking exhausted by the thought of continuing.

Cody stood. "The money was for you."

Her father spun toward him, panic-stricken.

"What do you mean?" Marissa stood now.

Louisa's father held out his hands. "Let me explain."

"Dad?"

"You lost the money playing poker." Cody sounded like a person solving a puzzle—a puzzle that Louisa did not have all the pieces for.

"What are you talking about?" She turned to her father. "Dad, what is he talking about?"

"Ted Kauffmann told me you liked to bet big. You took risks. He said he'd seen you lose it all more than once—apparently that's what made you so good at your job."

Louisa didn't understand. Ted Kauffmann? When had Cody spoken with Ted Kauffmann? And why hadn't he told her?

"I had a problem," her father said. "An addiction."

Now Louisa's mom was standing, and there was anger on her face. She'd braced herself—they both had—for the confession of an affair. This was something else entirely, something none of them had foreseen.

"I told myself, 'No risk, no reward.'" Her father sighed. "But then I made some really big mistakes."

Louisa tried to find sympathy for him, but none came.

"I convinced Maggie to give me a lot of money. I convinced her I was going to make her rich. She never cared about money, but she said she'd love to start a charity for kids or something someday, so she wrote me a check."

"And you gambled it away?" Louisa couldn't keep the disgust out of her voice.

Her father didn't look at her. "And then some."

"So you went to Dad for help," Cody said.

"He found out about it," her father said. "He said he'd bail me out under two conditions—that I got help for my problem and turned Maggie's accounts over to someone else."

Louisa looked at Cody, her mind spinning back to the paperwork they'd found among Maggie's things. Daniel had made sure the old woman was taken care of. He'd even made sure that Louisa's family was taken care of. Again, he'd made a huge sacrifice—one none of them deserved.

"You need to know, Daniel had a plan for recouping the investment," her father continued. "He would've had one lean month— maybe two—and I had a plan to pay him back."

"But you didn't pay him back," Marissa said. "And we had to start over from scratch."

Louisa watched as her father slowly shook his head. "When he died, I did turn my life around. But it took some time. And by the time I had the money, I don't know—I guess it was easier to pretend none of it ever happened."

Marissa scoffed. "So were you relieved when my husband died?"

He took a step toward her. "Danny was my closest friend. He saved my life. He sacrificed to save me, and I owe him everything. I don't know if I'll ever recover from his death. But I've been such a coward, Marissa." He looked at Cody. "I know I don't deserve it, but

I hope you can forgive me. Someday." He paused. "And of course, I'll pay back every cent."

Marissa methodically bent over and picked up her purse. She slung it over her shoulder, then walked right up to Louisa's dad and smacked him across the face.

"You are a terrible man," she said. "As long as I live, I will never forgive you for what you've done."

Louisa's heart dropped. This was not the way this was supposed to go.

"Marissa, please—" Louisa's mom took a step toward them, but Marissa's glare stopped her in her tracks.

"Did you know about this?"

"She didn't know anything," Louisa's dad said. "Nobody did, except Daniel. I asked him to keep it from all of you. I was so ashamed."

"So your secret died with him, and you let it," Marissa snapped, obvious disgust on her face. She looked at Cody. "Let's go."

Cody stood still for several seconds, as if being held in place by a magnetic force. Louisa knew that once he left, that would be it—they would be over.

She looked at the fallout of her father's confession. If they'd been broken before, they were shattered now. And Louisa could dream all she wanted to—but even she couldn't put the pieces back together.

~

Maggie Fisher was buried on a Wednesday.

All of Nantucket came out to pay their respects, yet somehow Louisa had never felt more alone in her entire life.

CHAPTER FORTY

THE WEEK AFTER MAGGIE DIED, Louisa finally went to the old woman's house. She assumed it was up to her to get the thing cleaned out and put on the market, though part of her wished she could keep the old cottage for herself. She could take up collecting the cottages of the people she loved.

The view of the water was unmatched, and she still felt Maggie inside these walls.

She hauled boxes down the stairs and tried not to think about Cody. Marissa and Marley had left the island the evening of the funeral, something Louisa only knew because she overheard someone sending them off at the funeral luncheon. Her own parents would also leave in just a few days, and while that was a blessing, without Maggie there, how would Louisa keep from feeling truly, utterly, and horribly alone?

The island itself used to feel like a friend, but with Cody still here and the wide divide between them, even it felt like a traitor.

That afternoon, Maggie's lawyer, Henry Holbrook, would come

by to read the will. As far as she knew, she would be the only person in attendance for the reading, but Louisa thought that was fitting. Until this summer, it had been her and Maggie for a long time. Sure, her own parents popped in and out every summer for a few weeks, sometimes a month or two, but their presence hadn't left an indelible mark on either of them.

Until now.

Her father's mistakes had cost them everything. It was hard not to be livid with him. It was hard not to want him to suffer now that his secret was out. Yet it hadn't been too long ago she was certain it was her own mistakes that had been what cost them everything. What she would've given for someone—anyone—to offer her grace.

A knock at the door pulled her from the boxes she was sorting. She was embarrassed that Mr. Holbrook would have to sit in the middle of this mess, but she imagined he would understand.

When she opened the door, however, she saw that the lawyer wasn't alone.

She hadn't seen Cody since the funeral, which felt like an eternity ago. He looked the same, mostly, though maybe a little more tired than usual. She resisted the urge to ask if he'd been sleeping, if he'd been eating, if he still loved her.

Sometimes when she got really lonely, she took out her phone and scrolled through photos they'd taken during their brief romantic reunion. Selfies, mostly, but probably her favorite photos ever. She'd zoom in on his face and, filled with the kind of longing that would only go away with time, touch her index finger to his smile.

Now Cody stood on Maggie's porch, avoiding her eyes and certainly setting her healing back days, maybe even weeks. She would love him until the day she died—she was sure of it.

She tried to hide every single thought that floated through her mind as she opened the door wider to allow both men to enter. "Sorry about the mess." She inhaled as Cody passed by her but noticed (sadly) that he barely acknowledged her. The realization stung.

"The old girl sure liked to hold on to things, didn't she?" Mr. Holbrook's laugh was jolly, as if remembering Maggie should only bring happiness. As if Louisa's world weren't lying in pieces like a cracked egg on the kitchen floor.

At the silence, the lawyer straightened. "Right. Let's get to it then, shall we?"

Louisa glanced at Cody. "I didn't realize anyone else would be here."

He met her eyes then, and she realized it sounded accusatory, like he didn't have the right to come, which was, of course, not how she meant it. Somehow, though, she didn't have the ability to explain.

"Just the two of you," he said, his tone jovial.

"Please." Louisa motioned to the sofa and both men sat, leaving her with the armchair across from them. Maggie's favorite chair sat horribly empty.

All at once, the room seemed dead without her in it.

If she listened close enough, would she be able to hear Maggie's unmistakable cackle echoing down the halls? How did a person simply disappear from the earth, from her life? She hadn't felt this way since Cody's dad passed away, and she'd nearly forgotten what it was like. It was different from when Cody had vanished—she'd known he was out there somewhere. She could make up stories about where he was and what he was doing, always careful to imagine him happy and full of life. She hadn't been able to do that with Daniel Boggs. And she couldn't do it with Maggie.

"Louisa?"

She could tell by Mr. Holbrook's tone that she'd missed a question. "I'm sorry—what?"

"I asked if Maggie had discussed any of this with you?"

Louisa folded her hands in her lap, feeling embarrassed by her inability to concentrate. "No, sir," she said. "She never did."

"Well, then, we *are* in for a surprise."

Louisa's frown matched Cody's as they waited for the man to continue. Before that could happen, he had to finish chuckling, sort through a stack of papers, and apparently sit back on the couch *just so*. Finally he looked up. "Are we ready?"

"Ready," Louisa said. *Hurry up.*

It was torture, this sitting in the same room with Cody, this wishing his arm was around her, this knowing that they'd come so close to happiness, only to have it ripped away—again—by their cruel, cruel past.

"Turns out our girl was quite wealthy."

She didn't bother to correct him in his use of the phrase "our girl," though she was absolutely certain Maggie would have.

"No, she wasn't." Louisa knew from sorting through some of her bank statements that Maggie was anything but poor—but she wouldn't say the old woman was wealthy.

"Oh, but she was." He chuckled again. "I'm not sure even she knew how wealthy. She never really cared much for the details."

"All she had in the world was this house, Mr. Holbrook. She inherited it, but she wasn't rich. She prided herself on it." Louisa straightened.

He winked at her. Odd. "Many years ago, Maggie invested a good sum of money—she's lived off of the money she made on that investment for years now."

"Her allowance," Louisa said.

"I'm sorry?"

"She called it her allowance. She never told me where it came from, only that each month, money was deposited in her account. She gave a lot of it away."

"Well, that was just the tip of the iceberg. She had another account." He handed over a sheet of paper with a bunch of numbers on it, and as Louisa scanned to the bottom, she saw *TK/dab* typed out, just like in the statements she and Cody had found.

"You said there was one investment?" Cody asked.

"Right. Someone very smart set her up." He grinned, his bushy white eyebrows reminding Louisa of Maggie's. Didn't anybody over the age of sixty own a pair of tweezers? He shuffled through more papers. "Oh, well, look here, son. Wasn't your father's name Daniel?"

Cody nodded.

"Then we have him to thank for this. He made sure Miss Fisher was well taken care of."

"What do you mean?"

"Now that Maggie is gone, I've been given access to her accounts. She dealt mostly with another man—" he scanned the paper in his hand—"Ted Kauffmann?"

"Right, he took over her investments from my father," Louisa said.

"True!" Mr. Holbrook said it as if she'd given the correct answer on a game show. "But he wasn't the one who invested her money for her."

"How do you know this? We scoured Maggie's accounts—we found nothing linking them to Cody's dad," Louisa said.

"I spoke with Mr. Kauffmann earlier this week," Mr. Holbrook said. "I congratulated him on this fine portfolio he put together for Maggie, but he said he couldn't take the credit." He looked at Cody. "Said it was your father who set the whole thing up. Apparently he wanted to remain anonymous, but he was a brilliant financial planner. A real shame he was taken so soon."

Finally Cody dared a look in Louisa's direction. It was as if the last piece of the puzzle had just been placed and they now had a complete picture. But how did that picture make Cody feel? Was he proud of his father for taking care of Maggie so well, or did it only remind him that his own family had been sacrificed in the process? She wished she could ask him. Did he at least feel her concern through the silence of the room?

"I understand you're standing in for your mother at this reading?" Mr. Holbrook was on to the next topic, though Louisa's heart was still lingering on Cody.

"That's right," Cody said.

"Well, she will hopefully be pleased with this." He handed over a business envelope.

"Should I open it now?" Cody asked.

The man's eyes glimmered with anticipation. "I wish you would."

Louisa watched as he tore open the envelope, withdrew what appeared to be a handwritten letter and a check. Cody looked at the papers in his hand, but his expression held steady. He would've been a worthy adversary at one of her father's poker games.

The old man smiled as if he were Santa Claus on Christmas Day. "Your mom can retire for certain."

Cody put the check back in the envelope with a nod. "Thank you, sir."

Mr. Holbrook seemed disappointed in Cody's grim reaction. He turned to Louisa. "And for you."

He handed over another envelope, which she opened. Her poker face was a lot easier to read, she was sure. The amount of the check enclosed was astounding. Maggie was rich? Behind the check was a folded sheet of lined paper—a letter. Louisa pulled it out, took one look at the old woman's handwriting, and decided to save this for later. She didn't want to cry in mixed company.

"I assume this will put you in a very good position as well," Mr. Holbrook said merrily.

Louisa stuttered a reply that even she knew made no sense. She was still trying to understand how it was that Maggie had all this money and nobody knew. With this check, Louisa could live life like the rest of the people on Nantucket. She couldn't wrap her mind around the amount of money he'd just handed her.

She tucked the envelope away in her purse and watched Mr. Holbrook as he sorted through the rest of the papers.

"Last but not least." He took out a folded document. "The house."

"I figured we'd put it on the market," Louisa said.

"If that's what the new owner wants to do with it." He handed the document to Cody.

"Me?"

"She said it was time for you to put down some roots. I guess she thought this would be a good place to do it."

"I live in government housing," he said lamely. "I don't have roots."

"Now you have a house." He patted the seat. "And furniture."

Louisa's eyes filled with tears. The thought of Cody moving into Maggie's house was so devastatingly perfect she could hardly contain her joy.

"Of course you can always sell it," Mr. Holbrook said. "If that's what you want to do."

Why did he have to suggest that? *Don't give him ideas!*

"Thank you, sir," Cody said formally. "I'll think it over."

"You both have options—wonderful options." Mr. Holbrook beamed. "Maggie was my favorite client. I always thought if we'd met sooner, we would've made a handsome couple." He grinned.

Their eyebrows alone might've kept them from being "handsome," but the thought of Maggie in love did make Louisa smile. "She would've been very happy to hear that."

"Oh, she heard it plenty," he said. "I asked her to go out with me every time I saw her. I think she thought I was kidding. Goes to show you should make your true intentions known." He winked at Louisa again, then looked at Cody. "That's a bit of free advice for you."

"Mr. Holbrook," Louisa said, "how was it that Maggie didn't seem to know how wealthy she was? I feel like if she knew she had this much money, she would've done something with it—something worthy. She talked about opening up a nonprofit to help people—she used to dream of it. But one day she just stopped talking about it."

"Well, first of all, she wasn't always this wealthy," he said. "Maybe that's why she was so down-to-earth. These investments took time to accrue, and it's only been in the last few years that we've seen this kind of growth."

"I see," Louisa said.

"Maggie came in not long after she learned the seriousness of her heart condition. We had a good cry, especially because that's when she found out how much money she really had." Mr. Holbrook turned thoughtful. "And this is only some of her fortune. She designated a large sum to charity upon her death as well, and the Ackerman Arts Center will be receiving a healthy donation. But she talked about your two families with so much love."

Louisa dared a glance at stone-faced Cody Boggs and saw the briefest flicker of emotion skitter across his face.

"She said she wanted to bless you both."

That sounded like Maggie. If she'd been able to pick them all up in their brokenness and put them back together, she would've, but Louisa knew not even Maggie could do that. They had to figure out a way to do it without her.

The lawyer cleared his throat. "All right, folks—" he packed up his papers as he spoke—"always love when I get to tell someone they're now very rich. I hope you both enjoy these gifts Maggie left for you." He stood. Louisa showed him to the door. "She was very proud of you. It made her happy when she learned how much money she was able to leave you. She said you'd know just what to do with it."

Louisa was unable to speak. Maggie had so much faith in her. She'd do everything she could to make the old woman proud.

She closed the door behind him and turned to find Cody awkwardly standing in the entryway.

"I suppose I should leave you my key," she said dumbly.

"No, it's fine. Take whatever you want first," he said.

"Do you think you'll sell it?"

He shrugged. "I won't be stationed here forever. Seems kind of silly to keep a house for just me."

I could move in. I could fix it up and get rid of the old magazines and turn it into a home for the two of us, and we could fill the place with babies and get a dog or two while we're at it. It'll be fun. . . . What d'ya say?

"Yeah."

He looked at her, that intense gaze that told her he was reading past whatever would be obvious to the rest of the world. She begged him to say something to her—something that mattered.

Instead, he slid his own set of house keys into his pocket and looked away. "I should go."

He started out the door, and she involuntarily reached for his arm. He tightened at her touch, and she wondered if he felt it too—the heat that passed between them. He brought his eyes to hers, and she could feel his utter despair—it mixed with her own and pooled at their feet.

"I'm sorry," she said. "For my father."

His eyes dipped to her lips, then back up. He slid his arm from her touch, and her fingers stung at the absence of his skin. "Me too."

"Our birthday is soon," she said without thinking. "Have you written out your wish?"

"Louisa—don't." He studied her. "It's hard enough as it is."

While she wished his words had served as a bucket of water to extinguish her desire for him, quite the opposite had happened, and she couldn't make sense of it. Would she ever stop loving him now that she'd tasted him? Would she ever be able to recover from a heart this broken?

"I have to go," he said. "I'll be in touch about the house."

And then he was gone.

~

Dear Louisa,

We both knew this day would come—the day I left you in favor of the pearly gates. I know you're probably thinking it'll be a miracle if they let me into heaven, but I've got a plan to bribe the big guy with my famous peach crumble.

Think it'll work?

I'm kidding, of course. You know I don't talk about it often, but I'm ready to meet my Maker. He and I have had some pretty great conversations over the years—many about you, if I'm honest. He loves when you talk to him, Lou. Do it more often, okay?

I always thought knowing my time on earth was coming to a close would be more of a curse than a blessing, but as I near the end, I have to say, I'm glad the doctor told me when he did. It gave me more time to really appreciate what I had this side of heaven. It gave me time to reflect on the things and people I love.

You are always at the top of that list.

I know I don't show it, and I'm a little hard to deal with at times, but I hope you never doubted my love for you. I didn't get to have my own kids, but if I had, I would have loved to have one as wonderful and kind and good-hearted as you.

I'm proud of you. I don't say it enough, but there it is.

The other day, I went in to discuss my will with Henry. He hit on me again. (Honestly! The man never tires of embarrassing me!) He told me how much money I would be able to leave you, and I nearly keeled over right there. The lesson here is to always open the mail your financial advisers send you—I could've done really good things if I'd realized how much money I had.

But now you get to do really good things with this money. And maybe that's how it was always supposed to be.

What can I say? I love ya. I hope all of your dreams come true. Live well. Love well. And someday tell your kids about their crazy aunt Maggie.

You were one of my favorite things about being alive.

Mags

CHAPTER FORTY-ONE

CODY LEFT NANTUCKET TWO DAYS AFTER MR. HOLBROOK gave him the check for his mother and the deed to Maggie's house. He'd made arrangements to take some leave to "clear his head," he told Duncan.

"You've been through a lot," Duncan said. "Take your time."

Cody turned to go, but something stopped him. "How hard would it be to put in for a transfer?"

Duncan frowned. "I thought you were liking it here."

Cody shrugged. "I don't think it's right for me."

"That's too bad," the master chief said. "They're talking about promoting you. Everyone's been really impressed with the job you've done here."

Cody thought about the job he'd done. He thought about how he'd begun to treat the guys the way Louisa treated everyone she met. It had made a difference, and he'd made an impact. Leaving would be difficult for a lot of unexpected reasons.

"If they promoted me, where would you go?"

"They want me back in San Diego." Duncan had family out there, and Cody knew it would be a good transfer for his friend.

Cody shook his head. "Nantucket is no good for me, Chief." He stood opposite Duncan's desk, unwilling to go into details but certain that the only way he'd ever move on—from Louisa, from her father's confession, from the ghost of his own father—was to get off the island once and for all.

"Take your two weeks' leave. Think it over." He studied Cody for a long moment. "I'll be hoping you reconsider."

Now, as he boarded a plane from Boston to Chicago, he checked and double-checked to be certain the envelope for his mother was tucked safely inside his carry-on.

Two weeks. That meant he'd be off island for their golden birthday.

The pain of that realization was matched only by the knowledge that it was time to let Louisa go.

~

Cody took an Uber to his mother's apartment in a small suburb outside of Chicago. Marley had moved out for college, and after graduation she found her own place downtown with friends. While he had two weeks off, he didn't plan to spend them with his mom. He was only here to give her the check.

And maybe also to gauge her anger level.

He knocked on the door and waited until she opened it. Her eyes lit up like she hadn't just seen him a week and a half ago, and she pulled him in for a hug, one it seemed she needed.

"Look at you," she said. "I made spaghetti and meatballs—your favorite."

The scent of garlic and oregano struck him as he walked through the door. He inhaled a deep breath. "It smells amazing."

She glided back into the kitchen, removed the lid from a pot on the stove, and stirred the contents with a wooden spoon. "Flight was good?"

Cody dropped his bag on the floor by the door and took out the white envelope. "Everything's good, Ma."

"Great." She looked up with a smile, which quickly faded when she met his eyes. "Then why are you here? You hardly ever get leave."

He slid the envelope across the counter.

"What's this?"

"Open it."

She covered the pot and did as he said, eyes widening as she saw what was inside. "What on earth?"

"It's what Maggie left us," Cody said. "That's what her lawyer wanted me to give you."

"I don't understand."

"She was rich," he said. "Because of Dad."

His mom frowned.

"After Warren lost Maggie's money, Dad repaid it—but he invested it, the way Warren was supposed to."

Her frown deepened.

"I know it's easy to think that Dad took care of everyone else but us, but I don't think that was it. I think he had a plan to take care of us, too—it just got interrupted the night he died."

His mother's body went rigid.

Cody had been thinking about it for days now— his father's choices and how they impacted their lives. It would be easy to be angry or bitter, but that wasn't what his father would've wanted. It wasn't how he'd lived his life.

"Dad loved Warren and JoEllen," Cody said. "And he loved Maggie."

His mother stood, unmoving, like a statue.

"He loved them enough to take care of them, to sacrifice for them. It's rare, that kind of love. Remember? He called it 'Jesus love.'"

The phrase had come to him on the plane, inside a fresh memory of his father leaving on Christmas Day to bring dinner to a single mom from their church. Cody remembered being so sad that his dad was leaving, but his father knelt down and explained, "This is how we show the world what real love looks like, Son. For some people, all they see is sadness and anger and negativity. If we can shine a little light in their lives, shouldn't we do that?"

Cody nodded.

"You know I'm coming home as soon as I can. Those kids can't say the same about their dad."

"I know." His father hugged him. When he stepped away, he tugged his coat off the hanger by the door and Cody stopped him.

"Dad? Can I come with you?"

His father glanced over at his mother, and something passed between them—something Cody didn't recognize.

"I think that's a great idea," Dad finally said.

They drove in silence to an old house on the other side of town. They pulled containers of food from the trunk and walked up to the woman's door, where they were met by four small children. The mom appeared in the back of the house, baby on her hip. She instantly burst into tears.

Cody could still smell the musty stench of the house. He could see the dust in the corners and the dirty dishes in the sink. The woman asked Cody and his father to join them for dinner, but they were careful not to eat too much of the food—they wanted the family to have leftovers. Cody felt awkward and out of place, even though one of the boys was right around the same age he was.

As they left, the woman thanked them through a stifled sob.

Cody ran to the car and grabbed the new remote-control truck he'd gotten for Christmas. It was the only thing he really cared about, and he hadn't been a bit surprised to find it under the tree. He'd never doubted that he would.

He rushed back to the house and knocked on the door. The little boy, the one who was about his age, pulled it open, and Cody handed him the truck. "Merry Christmas."

The boy's eyes widened. "I get to keep it?"

Cody nodded. "It's for you."

His face lit up. "Cool! Thanks!"

Cody turned and saw his dad standing by the car, waiting for him. While he knew his dad was proud of him, it wasn't his father's approval that warmed him from the inside that day—it was the way the other boy's happiness made him feel.

The memory had come, unwanted, on the flight, but it stuck with him. How long had it been since he'd shown anyone that same kind of love? How long had it been since he stopped wallowing in his own pain and started focusing on how he could make other people happy? Even Louisa—whom he loved more than anyone—hadn't received that from him. He'd withdrawn his love from her the moment it got hard.

It shamed him to think of it now.

"Love without condition," Cody said. "Dad taught me that. His sacrifice to save my life nearly killed me in a lot of ways, but I know he'd do it again if he had the choice. That was how he chose to live. We haven't been living that way. We've been living angry."

His mother stiffened again. "You know how hard this has been."

"I do," he said. "And I know that we made it. We're still okay."

She set the check on the counter. "This doesn't change anything. Maggie's generosity is appreciated, but it can't bring him back."

"I don't think she was hoping to replace Dad." Cody could feel his own frustration brewing. "She just wanted to help."

"Why didn't she help twelve years ago?" She was crying now, and he realized it was the first time he'd ever seen her cry over his father's death. Her stone-faced exterior was one of anger and bitterness, but it only masked a deeper pain, one she didn't allow herself to process.

Maybe he'd adopted some of her defense mechanisms. Maybe this was why he found it easier to push people away. Maybe the fear of feeling that pain was so overwhelming they'd both built walls around themselves to stay safe. Walls constructed out of bricks of anger.

His father wouldn't want them to live there another day.

"Mom?"

She met his eyes.

"This terrible thing happened. Our family was torn apart, completely shredded. And you still kept us together."

She scoffed. "I don't feel put together at all."

"But you are. You did it."

"Do you think that makes everything okay? Do you think what Warren did was okay?"

"Of course not, Mom," Cody said.

"I know you think you love Louisa, Cody."

"This is not about Louisa."

She held up a hand to silence him. "But you will never understand what I went through after your father died. He left us with almost nothing. And when I went to Warren—your father's closest friend—to ask for help, he said no."

"Dad had a plan—"

"Well, it didn't work. Life doesn't go the way we plan."

"Mom, do you regret what Dad did that night?" Cody's voice broke, but he quickly recovered. "Do you regret that he saved me?"

Her face went pale. "Of course not—I couldn't have lived a single day if something happened to you."

"Then maybe you should be grateful to him. Maybe we should be grateful instead of angry. Maybe we should be looking for ways to honor him with our lives, instead of letting the past hold us prisoner like it has."

She crossed her arms over her chest.

"We've got to let it go," he said. "We've got to move on."

She brought her eyes to his. "Let's talk about something else."

Cody felt like he was a tire and someone had just slashed him. She wasn't listening. He wasn't getting through to her. Did she know what it was doing to him to be apart from Louisa? Did she know that this wasn't the kind of sacrifice his father wanted them to make—at least not for these reasons?

He saw her body turn rigid as she returned to the pot on the stove. He saw her jaw tense as she reflected on their exchange. He saw what anger could do to a person once it turned bitter.

And he wanted no part of it.

CHAPTER FORTY-TWO

A FEW DAYS AFTER MR. HOLBROOK dropped his money bomb on Cody and Louisa, she finally found the courage to cash the check.

She'd been mulling over the lawyer's words to her—*"Maggie said you'd know just what to do with it."*

Louisa wondered how. How would she know what to do with it? Maggie had left no instruction in her letter, as if she trusted that Louisa would figure it out on her own. She'd spent hours thinking about it every day, and while most people would probably want to celebrate with a great trip somewhere, Louisa already lived in a vacation destination—she didn't need to escape Nantucket.

Unless it meant escaping the haunting ghost of a nonexistent Cody Boggs.

While she would never admit it, she'd tried to put herself in the places she knew he might go—Bartlett's Farm (he loved their sandwiches), the Handlebar Café (he loved their coffee), the beach by his father's memorial. Twice she'd even found legitimate reasons to visit the station at Brant Point.

She hadn't run into him once. She was beginning to think he'd vanished again. The thought of it made mincemeat of her already-broken heart.

When she finished cleaning out Maggie's house, she texted him to let him know. He never responded. The silence was worse the second time around. What would she do if she had to wait another decade to see him again?

Now, sitting in her office, she tried to focus on whatever Ally was talking about—a client wanted to add a few events to her family's vacation itinerary, and she needed help. On a normal day, Louisa would be excited by the challenge, but as she peered at her phone—and its taunting lack of new text messages or phone calls—she felt anything but excited.

"You're doing it again," Ally said dryly, closing her notebook and giving Louisa a pointed look.

Louisa glanced up from her phone.

"Why don't you just call him?"

"I can't," she said.

"I'm sure he would love to hear from you."

Ally didn't understand. After what Louisa's father had admitted, she was certain any chance of taking back her original request to "pause" their relationship was out of the question. If he wanted to see her, he would've seen her by now. The end of their relationship was as plain to her as the lighthouse at the edge of the island.

"Louisa, I need to ask you a question." Ally folded her hands in her lap.

Louisa stiffened. Her friend was often serious—it was what made her so good at her job—but she still found it unnerving. "Okay . . . ?"

"Are you going to give up the business now that you don't need the money?"

Louisa snapped back to reality. "No way."

"Don't say it like that," Ally said. "It wouldn't be unheard of. People who come into money don't need to work. You have money. You don't need to work."

"But I like this work," Louisa said.

"I was hoping you'd say that," she said. "Because I don't have money. And I like the work too."

Louisa tossed her an amused look. "But your part of this business is so boring."

"I've always been better with numbers than with people," Ally said. Then, after a pause, "So what are you going to do with the money?"

Louisa shrugged. "I can't decide. Maybe just leave it in the bank for a while?"

But she knew it was meant for more than that. She didn't care about being rich or wearing designer clothes. She didn't even care about having a big, fancy house or eating in the poshest restaurants on the island. She loved her work because she loved making other people happy.

"Ally?"

Her friend glanced up from her phone. "Hm?"

"I just got an idea."

~

If anyone had told Louisa a month ago that she'd be welcoming McKenzie Palmer into her office with open arms, she would've laughed. But McKenzie, like her or not, was an influencer—and right now Louisa needed an influencer.

She knew she couldn't change the past. She knew her mistakes had been forgiven. She even knew that the broken parts of her family would eventually heal. Her parents were in counseling, and her father was finally free of the shame of what he'd done, making arrangements to pay back the money he'd borrowed from Daniel. It was all behind her now, and dwelling on it wouldn't help anyone.

Instead, she'd decided to focus her attention on what she could do in the present. She asked herself hard questions about what she wanted the future to look like, and all of it—every single bit— revolved around what her life had always revolved around: making as much magic as possible for other people.

With that, she'd gotten the idea for her nonprofit, not unlike the one Maggie used to talk about starting. The Good Life would expand to include a branch that would grant wishes to families in need. Vacations for local heroes, cancer patients and survivors, single parents—people who could never afford the island on their own would be spoiled for days. She'd partner with local businesses to bring slivers of goodness to her clients, and those clients wouldn't have to pay a dime.

She contacted Make-A-Wish and organizations that specialized in helping abused women rebuild their lives. She reached out to other nonprofits and shared her plans with them. And now, sitting at her desk across from Ally and McKenzie, she laid the whole thing out for one of the island's most influential bloggers.

"I assume you're telling me all this so I'll write about it," she said when Louisa had finished her pitch.

Louisa forced a smile. "I was hoping you'd find it newsworthy."

"Nervy since you stole Cody Boggs away from me, but it's good karma, so I'll do a piece on it."

"I didn't steal anyone." Louisa ignored Ally's wide eyes that seemed to say, *Chill out—we need her.* "In case you haven't noticed, Cody and I aren't together."

"You're not doing long-distance?" McKenzie tossed her long, wavy locks over her shoulder, lips puckered in surprise.

"Long-distance?"

"I just assumed that you'd figure out a way to make his transfer work." She shrugged. "Charlie said the guys are all bummed about it. I guess your boyfriend is pretty good at his job."

Transfer?

McKenzie slipped her pink padfolio into her sleek black bag and met Louisa's eyes. She must've found confusion on Louisa's face because in an instant, the blonde's expression changed. "Oh. You didn't know."

Ally stood. "Of course she knew. She just doesn't like talking about it. Thanks so much, McKenzie. We've given you all the details, the printouts, the launch plan, but please let us know if you have any more questions."

Louisa sat, unable to move.

"I'll be in touch, girls." McKenzie strolled toward the door but turned before exiting. "For what it's worth, Louisa, I think he really did love you."

Louisa bit the inside of her cheek to keep from crying. It must be really bad if McKenzie Palmer was being nice to her.

"Thanks, McKenzie." Ally opened the door and practically pushed the other woman out. She turned back and faced Louisa, who couldn't keep the tears inside for another moment.

"Oh, Lou," Ally said. "I'm so, so sorry."

It was stupid. She knew it was stupid. Of course he'd requested a transfer—he never wanted to be there in the first place. But knowing he was already gone—it felt like he couldn't get away from her fast enough.

He'd left without a single word. *Just like last time.*

She wiped her cheeks dry, but the tears kept falling. Ally reached across the desk and took Louisa's hands. "Ice cream?"

Louisa took a deep breath. "I guess so. Tomorrow *is* my birthday, after all."

But the words only made everything worse.

Her golden birthday. *Their* golden birthday. She'd already written out her wish—only one this year—which was pointless. She couldn't go to Brant Point. She couldn't show up and find that he hadn't—it would destroy her.

She'd been holding on to that shred of hope, and even though it was foolish and wrong, a part of her still wanted to believe they lived in a world where they could be together. But clearly that had been a misguided wish, the kind she might've made as a teenage girl with no experience in matters of the heart.

She wasn't that girl anymore.

It was time to say goodbye—for real this time—to any notion that her life might ever coincide with the life of Cody Boggs.

CHAPTER FORTY-THREE

AFTER FOUR DAYS IN HIS MOM'S APARTMENT, Cody boarded a plane. Spending time with her had made it clear what he needed to do.

His flight was short, but it felt like an eternity, his mind racing with what to say and what not to say. His palms turned clammy the second the plane landed.

He grabbed his carry-on and made his way off the plane, out of the terminal, and onto the street, where he caught his Uber. As they drove, he replayed his planned-out speech for the thousandth time.

At his stop, he pulled his bag out of the car and slung it over his shoulder, looked at the house, and inhaled a deep breath. *Now or never.*

He'd spent the past week thinking about his dad, about the way he treated people and the way he taught Cody to treat people. And for the first time in his life, he realized he wanted to make his dad proud. He didn't want to atone for his death or make himself pay some sort of penance—he wanted to show the world that his father's influence was greater than anyone else's.

He rang the doorbell and waited, surveying the quiet street until the door opened.

JoEllen stared at him from the other side of the screen. "Cody?"

"Hi, Mrs. Chambers," he said.

She opened the door and motioned for him to come inside. "You know you're not allowed to call me that."

He willed away the tension that hung between them. "Hey, Mama Jo."

Her face melted into a sad smile, hope etched on its edges.

"Is Mr. Chambers here?"

"You mean Warren?"

He nodded.

"Follow me."

He did, straight through the wide entryway and into the house, noting the photos of Louisa that lined tables and walls.

JoEllen turned and caught him staring. She stilled. "Have you talked to her?"

He shook his head, wishing his answer were different.

"I understand it's hard," she said. "But my daughter loves you. I mean, Louisa loves everyone, but she *really* loves you."

He forced himself not to dwell on her words. He wasn't here for Louisa. He was here for himself. Besides, he didn't doubt that they loved each other—he only doubted that their circumstances would allow their love to exist.

JoEllen continued on toward the back of the house. She led him to the living room, where the Red Sox game played on a huge television. He wouldn't think about the quality of their life compared to the quality of his mother's. He wouldn't think about it because if he did, he'd have to leave. And he'd come for a reason.

"Warren, you have a visitor," JoEllen said.

Louisa's dad turned, and when he saw Cody, his face fell. The regret and shame he'd displayed that night in the hospital waiting room had returned. Cody wanted him to feel those things. It was an ugly desire, and he tried to force it aside.

"Cody?" Warren stood. "Is everything all right? Your mother—?"

"She's fine, sir," Cody said.

JoEllen turned toward him. "Would you like something to drink, Cody?"

"Water would be great."

She raced off toward the kitchen, which was three times the size of his mother's, he'd noticed on the way in.

Stop it.

"Have a seat, son," Warren said.

Cody obeyed, sitting on the love seat next to the sofa where Warren sat. A tense weight of silence and knowing formed in the space between them, and Cody searched for the words he'd been practicing on the flight to Boston from Chicago. They were nowhere to be found.

"You a baseball fan?"

The Red Sox were playing the Yankees. Cody watched the games when he was off, but he wouldn't call himself a fan. He gave Warren a shrug.

JoEllen returned with a bottle of cold water and handed it to Cody.

"Thank you." He uncapped the bottle and took a swig. He hadn't realized until that moment that his mouth was dry, like he was chewing on sandpaper.

JoEllen stood there, seemingly unsure as to whether or not she was invited to this conversation. "How are things?" she finally asked.

Cody set the bottle on the coffee table and leaned toward Warren, elbows on his knees. "You put up the memorial on the beach, right?"

Warren paused the television, a surprised expression on his face. He pressed his lips into a tight line and nodded.

"And the letter on the back of it?"

"My sad attempt at alleviating my guilt."

"Did it work?"

He sighed. "No. I knew telling the truth was the only way to do that."

"So you feel better now that it's out?" Cody kept his tone neutral, like a journalist looking for facts.

Warren shook his head. "I feel—" he searched for the word, eyes scanning the ceiling—"unburdened, I guess. But I know it's only the beginning. I know I don't deserve your forgiveness or your mother's, but I've got to learn to forgive myself and find some peace. I'm going to have a check sent to your mother—"

"She won't cash it."

"She has to."

There was a pause then, and Cody willed himself to continue. "You and my dad were close."

"The closest."

"You meant a lot to him."

Warren went still. "I know."

"I understand why he gave you the money. I'd do the same for a friend, especially one I loved. But what I don't understand is how you could keep it all a secret, even after my mom came to you."

Warren let out a sad sigh. "It's the single biggest regret of my life. I should've taken care of you all. I should've made sure your mom lived the way Daniel wanted her to. I was a coward. I was a fool. I see that now, and I understand if you hate me." His plea seemed genuine.

"I don't hate you," Cody said after a moment of silence. "I don't hate you, because my father loved you. And love means—" he shrugged—"second chances. In spite of our mistakes."

Warren broke—a sob escaped seemingly against his will. It was uncomfortable, seeing this man break down in front of him.

Then, slowly, Cody found the words he'd been practicing all morning. "I forgive you. I'm still angry, and I'm going to work through that, but if I ever have it in my power to offer forgiveness, I'm going to. I want my dad's sacrifice to mean something."

Warren pressed the heels of his hands into his eyes.

JoEllen reached across the sofa and put her hand over Cody's. "Your father would be so, so proud of you."

Cody wouldn't go into details with them, but he was starting to learn that even though he might have a *right* to be angry, he had a choice not to give in to that feeling. He would offer forgiveness to someone who didn't deserve it, the way his father had offered his life to save Cody's. Though Cody's sacrifice wasn't nearly as great, it still meant laying down a piece of himself. It still meant setting aside his offenses in order to bring about peace.

He hoped JoEllen was right—he hoped his choice would've made his father proud.

"That's all I came to say, sir." Cody got to his feet.

Warren stood and faced him, extending a hand in Cody's direction.

Cody looked at it, then clasped his hand around it. Louisa's dad pulled him into a bear hug. "Thank you."

Cody took a step back, but Warren still held on to his hand.

"I mean it, son," he said, tears in his eyes. "Thank you."

JoEllen was at his side. "I've got tuna salad in the fridge. You could stay for lunch?"

"Thanks, but I can't."

"Will you see Louisa tomorrow?" JoEllen asked as she walked him to the door. "It's a big day."

He looked away. He didn't think Louisa would welcome him at Brant Point, pact or no pact.

"Oh," JoEllen said sadly. "Well, we wish you a very happy birthday anyway."

~

Louisa Elizabeth Chambers was born at 2:52 p.m. on July 30.

Cody Daniel Boggs was born at 5:27 p.m. on July 30.

And thirty years later, on July 30, from 2:52 p.m. until 5:27 p.m., the pact said they would find a way to reunite at Brant Point lighthouse for a picnic lunch and the exchanging of birthday wishes.

But as the clock neared 2:52 p.m., the beach around the lighthouse was horribly, eerily empty.

~

Hey Dad,

I did it. I forgave Warren. I didn't want to, but I did it because I think it's what you would've wanted me to do. It's weird, but somehow I feel lighter now. Like I felt the day I decided to forgive myself.

It's true that being forgiven changes a person. To know the depth of my own humanity, the ugly side of my sin—and to know that I'm still loved and forgiven. That's powerful.

I think my words were powerful for Warren, too.

I'm on the ferry back to the island. I have business to take care of. I have a choice to make about the master chief position—they've officially offered it to me, even though I never told Duncan I'd consider it. It's a good opportunity.

But it's Nantucket.

Staying would be hard. How could I live on that island and not have Louisa in my life? But then how could I leave and know she won't be in my future?

I wish you were here to tell me what to do. I wish you knew her—the person she became. I have a feeling you'd love her. She's just so easy to love.

And she seems to be a lot like you—the way she loves people, the way she'd do anything for anyone. I didn't realize how important that was until recently, but it's like Louisa has always known it, from the beginning.

Thanks for living a life that taught me so much. Thanks for saving me, for giving me another chance.

I promise not to waste another day.

Cody

CHAPTER FORTY-FOUR

THE FERRY WOULD ARRIVE ON THE ISLAND AT 5:15. Cody had purposely taken this boat so he wouldn't feel anxious about being on Brant Point. If he'd arrived any earlier, he would've been tempted to check and see if Louisa was there.

He leaned back in his seat and stared out the window. He watched the boat glide through the water, and he itched to get back out there with his guys. He wondered if they'd had any rescues while he'd been away. He wondered if they'd been keeping up maintenance on the cutter. He wondered when he started thinking of Nantucket as home.

He shook the thought aside as his phone buzzed in his hand. He turned it over and saw a text from McKenzie Palmer:

My new blog post. Thought you might be interested.

He clicked on the link and read the headline: *Local Business Owner Starts Nonprofit.*

Louisa Chambers is in the business of making magic . . . and if she has her way, that magic will be sprinkled on some very worthy recipients—at no cost to them.

He read the article and learned about Louisa's plans to develop a nonprofit arm of The Good Life—free vacations fully funded and planned by her and her team.

He stopped scrolling as the image of Louisa's beautiful face appeared on his phone. Her smile, her eyes, her pale skin and red hair—it all stared back at him, accompanied by the years-old memories that mingled with more recent ones. Memories he'd revisited more times than he cared to admit.

He missed her.

When Chambers came into an unexpected sum of money, she knew she had a choice. She could pocket the cash and retire, or she could continue to share her love of this island with people who otherwise would have no chance of experiencing it.

Plans are already under way for three deserving single moms to visit the island next month, with local businesses happily donating goods and services to make their vacation one to remember.

"I just love Nantucket so much," Chambers said. "It's been a part of me for as long as I can remember. And sharing it with everyone—brightening someone's day with a whale-watching tour or a fishing expedition or even a simple stroll through the historic district—that's when I'm happiest. When I see the way the island makes other people feel, when I get to play a small role in that—there's nothing better."

All at once Cody realized this separation between them was ludicrous. It wasn't what either of them wanted. He couldn't put his life on hold waiting to see if his mom would ever come around, and he couldn't let her anger—or his own—dictate his life.

Louisa was good and kind and real. There wasn't a mean bone in her body. He could spend the whole day thinking of things he loved about her, and it wouldn't be enough time. Nothing her father had done ages ago changed that.

Why had he ever agreed to this break she'd put them on in the first place? He needed to make her see they were meant to be together. No matter what they had to sacrifice in the process.

He pulled out his phone to check the time. They'd be on the island in just a few minutes. Brant Point appeared up ahead, and Cody went out onto the deck of the ship, eyes straining, searching the space around the lighthouse for any sign of Louisa, for any sign of anyone—but he was still too far out to tell if she was there.

If he got straight off the ferry and ran over to Brant Point, he could hopefully get there before their 5:27 deadline. What if she'd already gone? What if he missed her? Or worse, what if she'd never shown up at all?

He shoved the thoughts aside and tapped his thumb against the railing of the ferry while it sailed into the harbor. He could win an award for his impatience at this point—what was taking so long?

Finally they were at the dock, but he got stuck behind three old ladies on the exit. After what felt like six years, he got around them but was quickly caught up in a crowd with suitcases and strollers and even one couple with a dog, pouring out onto the street.

He found his way out of the fray and down Straight Wharf. He turned on Beach Street and picked up his pace, anxious to get to Brant Point, anxious to get to her. He had to tell her he hadn't forgotten their pact. It meant as much to him as it did to her—he'd just gotten lost for a little while. Could he convince her?

Had she made a wish—written it out on paper the way they did all those years ago? Was it foolish that he had? Even when he believed they had no future, he'd still kept up their tradition. He needed to show her. He needed to at least try.

He hurried past the bike rental place and Children's Beach, and once Brant Point was in view, he broke into an all-out run, scanning every passing pedestrian, carefully watching for her fiery hair.

He ran toward the lighthouse, toward their spot, memories of her kisses still fresh in his mind. How had he been stupid enough to let her go? He'd lost her once, he knew the emptiness of life without Louisa—what made him think he could survive that again?

He raced ahead until the ground turned to sand underneath his feet. He pressed on, winded, until he reached the lighthouse, guided by the oversize American flag affixed to its side.

He looked around, trying to catch his breath. But Louisa wasn't there. He took out his phone. 5:25 p.m. Their golden birthday.

And she wasn't there.

He walked toward the lighthouse, toward the deck that led straight to its door, but veered around to the right, taking in the quiet of the evening and wishing things were different.

He'd been so careless about letting her go. Why hadn't he fought for her? Why had he simply accepted her reasoning for breaking them apart? He'd ruined everything, and now he feared it was too late.

The pact was important to her. If she'd given up on it, then she'd given up on him.

And he had no idea how to fix it.

CHAPTER FORTY-FIVE

IT HAD BEEN AGES SINCE LOUISA HAD HOSTED A PARTY, but it was her birthday, and Ally had insisted on it.

"It'll take your mind off that silly pact," she'd said.

Louisa didn't bother correcting her because the pact did seem silly. Everything about her relationship with Cody made her feel silly. She'd behaved badly. She'd foolishly believed love could overcome all the odds stacked against them. It was embarrassing to think about now.

Whoever said all you need is love was an idiot.

And for the record, the party was doing a terrible job of keeping her mind off the pact. She was thirty years old, and in her pocket was a slip of paper with her birthday wish on it. A wish that made her seem a lot like a teenager. Talk about embarrassing.

People filtered in and out of her house, but the majority of them were gathered on the back deck. Louisa put on her best hostess smile, trying not to look at the time but hopelessly aware that the pact had ended and soon the sun would set on her—their—golden birthday. And Cody Boggs was horribly absent.

A cake emerged from the kitchen after dinner, and Louisa blew out the candles as her friends cheered and sang for her. She scanned the crowd as she balanced a glass of iced tea and a small plate with a slice of cake—everyone seemed to be having fun. Even McKenzie Palmer seemed to be enjoying herself—and Charlie seemed to be enjoying her. It should warm her heart to see it, but instead, it made her feel empty.

She missed Maggie. She missed Cody. She missed having the sliver of hope she'd worn like a charm around her neck. It was gone now, and the emptiness of that realization tormented her.

The sun had begun to set, and she'd started to wonder when people might leave, dreadfully aware that some people were just arriving. Everyone seemed content to hang out. They were there for the duration.

"Louisa," Ally called out from the kitchen. "Can you come in here a minute?"

Only if I can crawl into bed and you make all these people go home.

It was ugly of her to think such a thing when everyone was there to celebrate her, but her heart hurt.

She made her way across the deck and inside the house, where Ally stood, wide-eyed.

"What's up?" Louisa asked.

"You have a visitor," Ally said.

Louisa laughed. "I have a lot of visitors." But she followed Ally's gaze into the living room, where she found Marissa Boggs, clutching a large handbag and wearing a worried expression.

"Mrs. Boggs?" Louisa heard the gasp in her own voice.

"Happy birthday, Louisa," the woman said.

"What are you doing here?"

"Can we go somewhere to talk?" Marissa slowly looked around the space. "It's hard for me to be here."

"Of course. Let's go out front." Louisa rushed past her, head spinning, Marissa following close behind. In the yard, she turned back to Marissa. "Would you like to walk?"

She nodded. "That would be nice."

They started off down the road, the noise from the party slowly beginning to fade.

"I'll get right to it, Louisa," she said. "I'm worried about my son."

"Is he okay?" Louisa's heart raced. "Did something happen?"

"Oh no, physically he's fine."

They turned the corner and walked toward the water. Louisa noticed the sun had begun to dip lower in the sky. Her mind wandered across the island to the lighthouse. It pained her to think that after all this time, after all this buildup, after their almost second chance, neither of them was there at this precise moment.

"I had forgotten about your birthday wishes," Marissa said, nostalgia coming through in her voice. She started rummaging through her bag. "Then I found this. He left it behind when he stayed with me this week." She handed over a sheet of folded paper.

Louisa slowly opened it. On it, in Cody's familiar scrawl, was written:

Birthday wish for my thirtieth year:
  I wish my mom would learn to forgive And I wish Louisa and I could be together.

Louisa's heart caught in her throat. She glanced at Marissa, who was staring straight ahead.

"I was cleaning after he left, and it caught me off guard. I didn't realize I was one of the reasons the two of you weren't together."

"I didn't want to be the reason he lost his family," Louisa said sadly.

Marissa shifted. "Obviously I have a reason to be angry."

"Of course," Louisa said quietly.

"But not enough of a reason to ruin the rest of my son's life." Marissa faced her. "You make him happy. You always have."

Tears sprang to Louisa's eyes, but she didn't even bother to blink them away. "I love him, Mrs. Boggs."

Marissa reached over and took Louisa by the arms. "I know you do. And I think your love has taught me a lot about what I need to work on." She stilled. "I called your mom."

Louisa stared at her with wide eyes. "You did?"

"We're going to have coffee."

Louisa couldn't keep a laugh from escaping. "You have no idea how happy that makes me."

"Forgiveness is a powerful thing, I'm starting to see. Daniel was so good at it, I think I almost resented him for it." Her face turned sad. "It came so easy to him, just like everything else."

Louisa understood, at least partly. The day Cody forgave her, she felt like she'd been set free. She studied the older woman for a moment, then dared the question she'd been turning over in her mind. "Mrs. Boggs, do you forgive me?"

Marissa reached out and put a hand on Louisa's face. "I forgive you, LuLu."

Tears streamed down Louisa's face. "Thank you," she whispered.

"Thank *you*," Marissa said, "for loving my son."

Louisa wiped her eyes. "I do love him, but I pushed him away. I always find ways to lose him, don't I?"

Marissa squeezed her arm. "I don't think you've lost him, dear. Your birthday isn't over yet."

Louisa smiled sadly. "If only that mattered. I don't even know where he is."

"He's here somewhere," Marissa said.

She frowned. "Here on the island?"

"He arrived this evening. He has a lot of decisions to make. But maybe we should start by making his birthday wish come true?"

Louisa looked down at the paper in her hands. She nodded, unable to contain her joy at learning Cody was here—in Nantucket.

Now she just had to convince him to stay.

CHAPTER FORTY-SIX

MARISSA TOLD LOUISA SHE WANTED TO SPEND SOME TIME at Daniel's memorial—alone—and Louisa agreed. She hugged Cody's mom, thanked her profusely, then rushed back home. The party was still going strong.

Ally raced over to her. "What was that about?"

Louisa found her keys in a small bowl on the table in the entryway. "I'll explain later," she said. "Can you hold down the fort here?"

"You're leaving?"

Louisa smiled, feeling hopeful for the first time in days. "We already did cake. Nobody will even notice I'm not here."

"It's your party."

She took Ally's hands. "I promise I'll be back. There's just something I have to do." She leveled her friend's gaze. "You know I wouldn't leave if it wasn't important."

After a beat, Ally's eyes lit up. "Cody?"

"I'll be back!" Louisa rushed out, maneuvered her Vespa around the other vehicles parked in her driveway and in front of Seaside, then

375

sped off toward Cody's house. The place appeared to be empty, but Louisa knocked on the door just in case. As she suspected, there was no answer. If he was back on the island, he wasn't here.

She heaved a sigh, then hopped back on her scooter and motored back to her own house. After parking, she headed next door to Maggie's, which, at first glance, also seemed to be deserted. She walked up the steps and onto the porch, fishing her key from her purse. She pushed open the door and called out into the darkness, but there was no answer.

He wasn't here either.

She was starting to feel discouraged—maybe she should check the party one more time? Or maybe Cody wasn't on the island like Marissa thought. Maybe he'd planned to come, then realized it would be better not to. Maybe he'd put her behind him once and for all.

There was only one other place she could think to look without launching an all-out search in every restaurant and bar downtown.

Odds were, if he wasn't home, he was at the station. But that meant driving out to Brant Point and being faced with the realization that their pact was now part of their past—and nothing had come of it. All it was now was a broken promise.

She tried not to think about it as she drove through town, down Beach Street, past Children's Beach. She arrived at the station, parked, and went inside. She found a few of the guys in the common area.

"Louisa!" Carlos Delgado, one of the guys from the auction, grinned at her.

"Hey, Carlos." She looked around the station, growing sadder by the minute. "You haven't seen Cody, have you?"

Carlos frowned. "Oh. He's gone. Didn't you know?"

The other guys were staring at her now, and she wondered if she appeared as frantic and frazzled as she felt. "I heard he might be back."

They exchanged glances and shrugs across the room.

"Sorry; we haven't seen him," Carlos said. "If he shows up, do you want me to tell him you stopped by?"

Louisa felt like the air had been sucked straight out of her lungs.

Was she suffocating? Was she back underwater, just one wave away from certain death?

"Louisa?"

She shook the memory away, angry that it still haunted her at all. But losing him felt a lot like flailing around in that water. It felt a lot like drowning.

"Sorry," she said. "No, you don't have to tell him anything."

"Okay. Have a good night." They resumed their chatter, and the sound of laughter filled the space behind her as she walked toward the door.

It was almost like walking in slow motion through quicksand, knowing that her own choices were the reason she was here. She'd pushed him away—she'd given up her second chance. Did she really feel entitled to a third?

She stepped outside into the darkness, the moon casting a yellowish hue over the ocean, over the lighthouse. The memory of her own laughter mixing with Cody's echoed through her mind. They'd loved each other so wholly, yet they'd given up so easily.

She'd spent years wishing for—praying for—a second chance. How could she have discarded it with such ease? And why? Because there were challenges to overcome?

She walked in the shadows toward the lighthouse, as if it beckoned her over in spite of her sorrow. She'd been meant to spend her birthday right in that very spot, and now here she was—alone.

That cruel realization stung.

The night was warm, but there was a breeze coming off the ocean. The sound of the waves drew her in. Louisa loved this island. She'd loved and lost here on these shores. She found Cody's number in her phone. She opened a new text message and was instantly reminded her last three messages had gone unanswered. She almost clicked it off without texting, but something stopped her.

Quickly, before she changed her mind, she typed, Happy birthday! and hit Send.

Seconds later, she saw a light just a few yards away.

She followed it and discovered the light was coming from a phone, held by a person, sitting in the sand near the ocean. The light went out, and the person didn't move.

She opened her phone again and typed Cody? into a new text, then saw the phone light up again. She could barely make out his silhouette in the darkness, but she was certain that was him. He sat with his knees up, leaning on them, perfectly still.

Her heart leaped. He was here? He was at the lighthouse—at their spot? How long had he been here, and why hadn't she come?

She started walking toward him but stopped. He hadn't responded to her messages. His phone had gone black again, and now he sat in darkness. Was it possible he didn't want to hear from her at all? Were her fears founded—had he given up on them?

No sense holding back now, though, was there? She'd come this far—she'd never forgive herself if she left without talking to him.

She continued walking but stopped again when he clicked his phone on and started typing. Her phone buzzed in her hand.

Happy birthday, Lou. I hope all your wishes come true.

Her eyes clouded over, and she tucked the phone away. "I hope so too," she called out.

She couldn't see his face, but she saw him stand. "Louisa?"

"What are you doing out here?" she asked as she approached.

When she reached him, he tore his gaze from hers and fished his wallet out of his pocket. He opened it and pulled out a small, folded white napkin. "I made a promise."

In a flash, every detail of that day rushed back. It had been his idea. His way of giving them something to look forward to, of reassuring her that no matter what, they'd find their way back to each other on this exact day.

Her heart beat so loud and fast against her rib cage, she had to resist the urge not to clutch her chest in a sad attempt to quiet it down. She looked at him. "You came."

He reached for her hand, brought it to his lips, and pressed a tender kiss to the inside of her palm. "Of course I did."

She smiled. "I'm sorry I'm late."

He shrugged lightly. "You're here now—that's all that matters."

"I'm sorry for a lot of things," she said.

"Can you tell me about them later?" He took her face in his hands. "Right now, all I really want to do is kiss you."

"Okay. Kissing now, talking later."

He kissed her tentatively at first, as if he were remembering how—but it didn't take long for the memories to kick in, for the kiss to turn hurried, like their absence had made them both hungry for each other, for the love they shared, for the promise of a future.

She pulled away, her breath ragged, and let her forehead fall to his. "I missed you."

He wrapped his arms around her the way she'd dreamed he would.

"I can't believe you're here." She couldn't hold him close enough.

"I screwed up, leaving like I did," he said.

"I screwed up, pushing you away."

He shook his head. "I understand why you did it, but I just realized our families are going to have to figure it out."

She took a step back. "I think they are figuring it out. Your mom came to see me. She's the reason I'm here." She reached into her pocket and pulled out the folded piece of paper Marissa had given her. "She gave me this."

Cody opened and read it, then met Louisa's eyes.

"She said she wanted us to be together," Louisa said. "She said I make you happy."

His lips tugged into a gentle smile. "You do make me happy."

"Can I keep making you happy for the rest of my life?"

"Did you just propose to me?" He closed the gap between them. Her eyes widened. "No!"

He grinned. "Bummer."

She smiled back. "Happy birthday, Cody Boggs."

He answered with a kiss so deep she felt it in every part of her body, making it a very happy birthday indeed.

Journey back to Nantucket

in this charming love story by Courtney Walsh

Available in stores and online now

JOIN THE CONVERSATION AT

CP1620

PROLOGUE

Dear Emily,

As I write this, you are approximately six days, three hours, and thirty-two minutes old. We've been home from the hospital for four days, and I haven't been able to stop looking at you the entire time. You sleep in a bassinet next to my bed, and I lie awake at night, listening to you breathe.

To be honest, listening to you breathe is all I do. I feel like it's my sole responsibility to make sure that continues. It's a little scary, if I'm honest. And I'm always honest. You see, you came as a bit of a surprise to me, and I guess that's why I've been so nervous lately, in the days leading up to your birth. Because I don't want to mess anything up.

I don't want to mess you up.

People always talk about how wonderful it is to have a baby, but no one ever talks about how terrifying it is too. You see, I'm a little bit terrified, and I'm not sure who else to tell. I'm pretty sure my mother would use that fear against me somehow, so I'll only share it with you, my little girl.

I'll share it because I want you to know that sometimes we have to do things that are scary in order to get to something good. Sometimes the hardest things we're faced with bring us the best results. It's strange how that works, but it's true.

You're probably wondering why I'm writing you a letter when I could just pick you up and tell you this in person.

Well, I've always wondered about my own childhood. I remember once sitting on the floor of my friend Samantha's bedroom, looking at her baby book. It was a scrapbook, I guess, and her mom had written all kinds of funny stories about Samantha from the time she was a baby and stuck them down next to photos of her at every stage of life. My mom isn't the sentimental type, so I never had a book of stories. I don't know what she was thinking about anything, and I wish I did. Maybe then I wouldn't feel so alone.

I'm not the crafty type, so I decided letters were more the way to go. Lessons I've learned along the way and want to pass on to you. Love letters to my little girl. I'll put them all together in a book and keep it for you. And if for any reason I can't tell you these important lessons in person, you'll still have my words, so you'll never have to wonder what I would say.

I won't waste time on silly or frivolous lessons, only the ones that mean the most to me, so if this book falls into your hands, I hope you'll give it the attention it deserves.

I'm not a wise woman. Most people wouldn't call me a woman at all, not yet anyway . . . but I'm learning so many things about myself, and bringing another person into the world has made me grow up fast. I want to be the best mom I can for you, Emily. It's you and me against the world.

And you know what? I'm terrified. But I'm going to do the very best job I can. I know I'll make mistakes, but hopefully you'll forgive me. I never knew how much love I had to give until I held you in my arms.

And PS—I'll do my best to keep Alan and Eliza off your back . . . mostly I'm guessing they'll want to stay on mine!

Love you so much,
Mom (It's so weird to write that!)

CHAPTER 1

~~~

EMILY ACKERMAN HUMMED WHEN SHE WAS NERVOUS. No particular song, just whatever melody popped into her head. At that moment, it was the Harry Connick Jr. version of "It Had to Be You," the one in the old movie *When Harry Met Sally*. Her mom's favorite.

The bouncy melody danced around her mind as she closed her eyes and pretended she was anywhere but on the ferry from Hyannis to Nantucket. She made her living pretending, and she'd traveled the globe for the last ten years—why was this so hard?

She leaned her head back, thinking only of the song—of Harry's smooth, sultry voice—but instead of going blank, her mind wrapped itself around a memory. Her mother, dancing on "their" beach, singing "It Had to Be You" at the top of her lungs while Emily dug her feet in the cool sand and giggled at her silliness.

Emily opened her eyes and found a little boy with dark hair and big brown eyes staring at her.

"You're loud," he said.

"Andrew, that's not polite." The boy's mother wrapped an arm around him and pulled him closer. "I'm so sorry. We're working on manners."

Emily smiled at him. "Sorry. Sometimes I get lost in my own world."

"Me too," Andrew said. "I have an imaginary friend named Kenton."

Emily widened her eyes. "I had an imaginary friend when I was little!" She tried to sound more excited than she felt. She was an actress. It wasn't that hard.

And yet, for some reason, it left her feeling hollow.

"Mom says people will think I'm out of my mind if I keep talking to myself."

Andrew's mother gave him a squeeze. "Andrew, let's leave the nice lady alone."

Lady? Emily knew the other side of thirty was a downhill slope, but when people started calling you "lady," you might as well sign up for AARP.

"I'm Andrew," the boy said. Then he looked at his mother and blinked. "See? That's manners." Then back to Emily. "Now you tell me your name."

"I'm Emily."

"Mom says I'm not supposed to call grown-ups by their first name."

"Oh." Emily glanced at the boy's mother, whose expression was a cross between amused and apologetic. "I guess you can call me Miss Ackerman."

"Miss Ackerman," Andrew said. "Nice to meet you."

Emily decided she liked this boy. She hoped he didn't lose his charm as he got older, and she hoped even more that he remained genuine. So many men she'd known were the exact opposite. Not a single one worth holding on to.

Especially not Max, who, she was convinced, had never told her one honest thing the entire time they were together. Not that it mattered really. Emily's rules were set up to protect her from getting too attached. She'd never stick around long enough to find out if a man's motives were impure— three months and she was off. Max had taken their breakup harder than she'd expected. He'd actually cried.

Ugh. The memory of it made her feel like such a jerk.

Emily exhaled. She'd been doing so well. Why did she have to go and think about Max?

The regret wound its way back in, and she could feel her cheeks flush at the memory of him. Maybe he'd actually loved her? Maybe she should've given him more of a chance?

But no. She'd taken Mom's advice to heart, as she did in all things, but especially about this. Her mother knew something about heartache, after all.

Be passionate in other areas, but in matters of the heart, be mindful to use caution. Your heart isn't something to give freely and without thought. It should be protected at all costs so you can ensure your whole world doesn't come crashing down around you. Hear me on this, Emily. I know what I'm talking about.

Without thinking, Emily slid her hand inside her bag until it found the soft, worn cover of the book of letters. In all her travels, it was the one thing she always made sure to keep close.

While Emily didn't know all the details, she knew that Isabelle Ackerman had suffered a great heartache. She only wished her mother had gotten a bit of closure before she died.

The letters were unspecific about so many things, but this was not one of them. This was not an area where she had to wonder what her mom would say—Isabelle had found a way to get her message to her only daughter, and Emily had fully embraced it.

She'd kept her heart safe. When someone got too close—and they did sometimes—she knew it was time to run. Also time to run when she could feel herself liking someone too much, which was what had happened with Max. He was charming and handsome and wealthy, and Emily knew if she hadn't been careful, she could've convinced herself he was worth a little rule breaking.

Thank goodness she wised up before there was permanent damage to her heart.

She had enough damage to deal with, and sadly, none of that could be blamed on Max or anyone else. It had been her own stupid mistakes that had landed her here—penniless and reeling. She hated the way this felt.

An utter failure. That's what she was.

When she'd finished writing her play, she'd been so confident in it. She'd seen so much potential, and nothing could've dissuaded her—not even the rejections from several big-name directors who wanted nothing to do with the project. They'd left her no choice but to produce and direct it on her own.

She should've listened. She should've started small. She didn't. Instead, she sank everything she had into the show.

She'd given all her blood, sweat, and tears to her work—and yes, most of what was left of her trust fund. So when the play opened to terrible reviews (*"A meandering disaster that doesn't know what it's trying to be"*) and folded in two weeks' time, she was left with nothing but people to pay and a humiliating professional failure.

She'd bet on the wrong horse, so to speak. The show had so much promise—she'd been so sure it would be a huge hit. She'd been so wrong.

Worse, everyone in the theatre world now knew that she was a failure—there was a huge article about it in *Backstage* magazine. A cautionary tale of sorts.

"Former Child Star's Directorial Debut Is This Year's Worst."

At least she could take comfort in the fact that her grandparents didn't read *Backstage*.

She supposed it was the one blessing in GrandPop's dying when he did. He never found out she'd lost everything with her poor business decisions or her short-lived creative endeavors. He'd never known just how incompetent his granddaughter was, even after years of watching him make millions with his savvy business sense.

But that was over now. Now, sitting on the ferry next to her new best friend, Andrew, Emily screwed her eyes shut and willed herself to stop thinking about Max, her failures, her grandparents, and her empty bank account.

She wasn't sure which of those things would be most difficult to put out of her head. All of them seemed to have her attention at any given point of the day. She supposed that's what happened when you hit rock bottom. You wasted a lot of time replaying your mistakes, trying to figure out if there was any way to undo them in order to right your own ship.

So far, she'd found no indication such a solution existed. She only knew that when you found yourself at rock bottom, it would be nice to see a hand offering to pull you up.

For her, there was no hand, and that was maybe the worst part of all.

"You're humming again." It was Andrew. Earnest Andrew and his big brown eyes.

"Don't grow up to be a jerk, okay, Andrew?" Emily said absently. Andrew's mother frowned.

"Sorry," Emily said. "Sometimes I say inappropriate things."

"Kenton does that too. One time he spent the whole day talking about poo." Andrew's face was so serious Emily couldn't help but laugh.

He smiled at her. "What's your imaginary friend's name?"

"I don't see much of her anymore," Emily said. "But her name was Kellen."

"Kellen," Andrew said. "Kellen and Kenton. I bet they're friends."

"You ask him the next time you see him, okay?" Emily smiled. She'd been having such a lovely time with Andrew she didn't even notice the ferry had slowed and was now docking in Nantucket.

If she closed her eyes tightly enough, Emily could almost imagine she was just another Nantucket tourist. If she stopped her mind from wandering, she could almost believe it was her first time on the island, her first time seeing in real life what she'd only seen in photos—the cobblestone streets, the gray Shaker homes with big bushes of purplish-blue hydrangeas out front, the rows of brightly colored Vespas for rent, the lighthouses that beckoned weary travelers to come and rest here.

Nantucket made promises, but in her experience, the island didn't make good on them.

What she wouldn't give for this to be her first time.

But it wasn't, was it?

She glanced into her big, floppy bag, the one where she'd stuffed all the necessities, including the haphazardly assembled book of letters, worn with years of handling. Sometimes just touching it was enough to make her mother feel close, almost like she had a magic lamp she could rub and see her wishes come true.

But as she placed her hand on the tattered, hand-decorated cover, even her mom felt far away.

It was as if her presence had been pulled out of the book the second the island came into view. As if even her mother's memory wanted to forget.

All around her, other passengers were gathering their things, anxious to get the season started on the island. But Emily stayed in her seat, dazed and maybe kind of motion sick. Or perhaps the nausea had nothing to do with the boat ride at all.

If she were smart, she would've approached Nantucket the way she would a two-day-old Band-Aid.

One quick rip and it would all be over.

If only . . .

"You're getting off, aren't you?" Andrew stood in front of her now, his red-and-yellow tiny-person backpack wrapped around both of his shoulders, a red baseball cap doing its best to tame his unruly chocolate-colored hair.

"I'm thinking about it," Emily said with a smile.

"You like it here, don't you?"

Ooh. A trick question. What was she going to tell the kid? That this island had stolen everything from her and she was only back here because she had absolutely no other option? His mother would probably call the police.

"Yes, it's very lovely," she finally said. It wasn't a lie, not really. Nantucket *was* lovely. At least it was for other people.

"I love this place," Andrew said. "Here." He held out his fist and gave it a shake.

She held her hand out underneath his and he dropped a smooth white rock into it.

"I found this on the beach last summer." Andrew grinned and she could tell his front tooth was about to fall out. "You can have it."

Before she could protest, Andrew's mom gave his hand a tug.

He looked back at her and waved, and for the briefest second Emily's heart ached.

His mom was, quite possibly, younger than Emily. And she had that beautiful little boy and probably a devoted husband waiting for her somewhere. That life had never appealed to Emily, but in that moment—and it was a fleeting one—something tugged at her insides.

But Emily didn't have time for heartache when she was about to get off the ferry. She grabbed her suitcase, her purse, and the large bag she'd stuffed with toiletries, Kind bars (to keep from eating junk), dark chocolate–covered blueberries (because sometimes it was okay to eat junk), two books, and anything else that hadn't fit in her suitcase.

She made her way to the door of the ferry and drew in a deep, deep breath.

I can do hard things.

She'd tossed the mantra around in her head for so many months, the words were meaningless by now. Well, they were pretty much already meaningless because once a phrase caught on and became popular, it lost its value. Every fitness expert in America probably shouted those words out as they reached the fourteenth rep of a particularly challenging exercise.

But she *could* do hard things. She'd been doing hard things since she was eleven years old.

Emily stood at the edge of the island and took another salt-tinged breath, the faint smell of fish reminding her that not everything near the ocean was lovely. Certainly not.

She pinched the bridge of her nose and willed herself to press onward. She hadn't come this far to chicken out now, and besides, what other choice did she have?

Sometimes she wished Nantucket hadn't been ruined for her. Just another complaint to add to the pile, she supposed. If she wasn't careful, she'd rack up so many she'd become one of those cranky old women whose mouths were permanently frowning, like that cartoon character, Maxine, on the Hallmark cards.

Or her own grandmother.

But no, that would never be her. Not Emily Ackerman. Not the girl who looked for fun wherever she went (and usually found it). Not the free-spirited wanderer who'd worked acting jobs all over the world, had more friends than she could keep track of, and knew exactly how to turn every trip into an adventure.

This was just another trip, right? Never mind that this trip had a purpose other than fun. This trip was her second chance—and she could not screw it up.

That certainly put a damper on any plans for a good time.

She dragged her single suitcase behind her, aware how pathetic it was that at the age of thirty-one, she could fit nearly everything important to her in one suitcase—and it wasn't even the largest one in the set her grandmother had sent when she graduated from college nine years ago.

She heaved a sigh and moved with the flow of foot traffic as tourists flooded off the ferry and onto the street. When she was a girl, this was the moment she looked forward to all year long—the moment her flip-flops hit the cobblestones, the moment she and her mom arrived in Nantucket.

So much had changed.

As she watched Andrew's red-and-yellow backpack disappear into the crowd, she said a quick prayer that his days in Nantucket were filled with nothing but good things—lobster boils and fish fries, giant ice cream cones from the Juice Bar and long, sun-kissed days at Jetties Beach.

She wished for him all the things she would've held on to if Nantucket hadn't been ruined for her all those years ago.

And suddenly, she wasn't so sure she actually could do hard things. But she was about to find out.

MORE GREAT ROMANCES BY

COURTNEY WALSH

JOIN THE CONVERSATION AT

CP1518

A NOTE FROM THE AUTHOR

DEAR READER,

Thank you. From the bottom of my heart, I want you to know how much you mean to me. Knowing how many books there are for you to choose from, it humbles and amazes me that you would choose to spend time reading one of mine. It means the absolute world to me.

I think one of the best things about being an author has been getting to know many of you—I've met some of you in real life, and many are simply "online friends," but you all make my days brighter, and I'm grateful to you for that.

As seems to be a theme in many of my stories, forgiveness plays a large part in this one. Maybe it's because it's something I'm constantly striving to get right, or it's an area of my life that needs regular care and attention. Either way, it's a lesson worth keeping at the forefront of my mind, and I hope that maybe you can relate as Cody and Louisa grapple with their past mistakes, the guilt and shame they still feel over what they've done.

And I especially hope the unconditional love and sacrifice Cody in particular experienced resonates with you and that you know in your soul that you are equally as loved.

I sincerely hope you enjoyed this Nantucket love story, and I would *love* to know what you thought of it. I truly love to hear from my readers, especially when I get to know you a little better! I invite you to stay in touch by signing up for my newsletter on my website—courtneywalshwrites.com—or by dropping me a line via email: courtney@courtneywalshwrites.com.

With love and gratitude to you,
Courtney

ACKNOWLEDGMENTS

TO ADAM. Always and forever. Me + You. Thank you for never letting me quit on myself. Life is so much better with you on my side. You're my favorite.

My kids—Sophia, Ethan, and Sam. There is a lot about my life that I love, but nothing as much as I love you guys. I'm your biggest fan.

My Studio family. You've been one of my life's greatest blessings. I am so, so thankful for each and every one of you.

To Matt and Elizabeth Fine. Thank you for answering all of my Coast Guard questions with such kindness. I'm *so* grateful you set me straight and helped me understand such a fascinating world.

My parents, Bob and Cindy Fassler. Thank you for praying for me, for believing in me, and for cheering me on. I sure did luck out in the parent department!

Stephanie Broene. Thank you for pushing me, for believing in me, for making me better. I will forever be grateful to you.

Danika King. What can I say? You are simply the best. Thank you for being such an important part of this process.

Carrie Erikson. My sister, my friend, and sometimes my therapist. You are a gift.

To Katie Ganshert, Becky Wade, and Melissa Tagg. At the beginning of this writing journey, I never would've predicted that one of the very best by-products would be your sweet friendships. I am so thankful to each of you.

To Natasha Kern, my agent. Thank you for challenging me to be better and write stronger. I am so thankful for your wisdom on this journey.

To Deb Raney. Always my mentor and always my friend. For all you've done to help me understand story—I am grateful.

To the entire team at Tyndale. I know how very blessed I am to work with the best of the best. Thank you for allowing me to be a part of your family.

And especially to you, my readers. I count it among my greatest honors that I get to share my stories with you. Thank you for every comment, every post, every email, and every review. You bless my life more than you will ever know.

DISCUSSION QUESTIONS

1. Louisa is weighed down by shame and guilt over choices from her past. How much of this guilt is appropriate conviction, and how much is misplaced? By the end of the story, how has Louisa learned to work through this shame and guilt? What could that process look like in your own life?

2. When Cody is assigned to the Nantucket Coast Guard station, he must return to a place that holds painful memories. How does he respond? Have you ever been forced to go somewhere that was difficult for you to face? What was that experience like?

3. In a memory from Louisa's childhood, a thunderstorm catches Daniel Boggs off guard as he's grilling outside. As the rain pours down, he tells Louisa, "That's God making everything new. No matter what, he can always make things new." In this story, how do Louisa and Cody see God giving them second chances and making old things new? How have you seen this in your own life?

4. Cody keeps track of the people he failed to save by adding hash marks to his tattoo. What danger is there in having a tangible reminder like that always in front of you? What benefits are there to remembering the past—and learning from it?

5. Throughout the story, several characters struggle to forgive themselves and others. How does this struggle play out in the experiences of Cody, Louisa, Marissa, Warren, and JoEllen? Think of a time you had to work hard to forgive yourself or someone else. How did that process impact you?

6. One of the main reasons Louisa and Eric's relationship ended was because he didn't believe in her. Why was that a deal breaker for Louisa? What factors are most important to you in a healthy relationship?

7. Manny Wirth has a difficult time knowing how to relate to God after the accident that put his son, Jackson, in a coma. He writes, "Believing it was human error and not something God allowed to happen to our son is easier. Because if God simply turned his face in Jackson's hour of need, where does that leave us?" How can you maintain your faith in God when you or someone you love is suffering? Where have you seen God at work in the difficult circumstances of your life, even if you don't understand them?

8. Why does Louisa fight so hard to bring her family and Cody's back together? What does she hope that will accomplish, and what is the outcome of her efforts?

9. What is Maggie's role in Louisa's and Cody's lives? How does she influence them and their families to move forward in spite of tragedy and past hurts? Do you have an older mentor like this in your life—or could you pursue this kind of relationship with someone younger than you?

10. Toward the end of the story, Cody "was starting to learn that even though he might have a *right* to be angry, he had a choice not to give in to that feeling." What brings him to this place of growth and maturity? Can you think of a time when you chose to do what was right even though you didn't feel like it?

11. Louisa decided to take a risk after working at a hotel for several years—she started her own business, The Good Life. If you could start a business of any kind, what would it be? Why?

12. At the end of the story, the rift between the Boggs and Chambers family isn't completely mended, but things are heading in the right direction. What do you imagine the future years will hold for these two families and their relationship?

ABOUT THE AUTHOR

COURTNEY WALSH is the author of *If for Any Reason, Just Look Up, Just Let Go, Paper Hearts, Change of Heart,* and the Sweethaven series. Her debut novel, *A Sweethaven Summer,* was a *New York Times* and *USA Today* e-book bestseller and a Carol Award finalist in the debut author category. In addition, she has written two craft books and several full-length musicals. Courtney lives with her husband and three children in Illinois, where she is also an artist, theatre director, and playwright.

Visit her online at courtneywalshwrites.com.

TYNDALE HOUSE PUBLISHERS IS CRAZY4FICTION!

Fiction that entertains and inspires

Get to know us! Become a member of the Crazy4Fiction community. Whether you read our blog, like us on Facebook, follow us on Twitter, or receive our e-newsletter, you're sure to get the latest news on the best in Christian fiction. You might even win something along the way!

JOIN IN THE FUN TODAY.

 crazy4fiction.com

 Crazy4Fiction

 @Crazy4Fiction

FOR MORE GREAT TYNDALE DIGITAL PROMOTIONS, GO TO TYNDALE.COM/EBOOKS

CP0021